War M…

Mike Marqus… and cricket fanatic. H… Turn, *Defeat From the Jaws… Inside Kinnock's Labour Party* and *Anyone But England: Cricket and the National Malaise* (short-listed for the 1994 William Hill Sports Book of the Year).

Also by Mike Marqusee

Slow Turn (a novel)

Defeat from the Jaws of Victory:
Inside Kinnock's Labour Party
(co-author)

Anyone But England:
Cricket and the National Malaise

MIKE MARQUSEE

WAR

MINUS THE SHOOTING

A journey through south Asia
during cricket's World Cup

Mandarin

A Mandarin Paperback
WAR MINUS THE SHOOTING

First published in Great Britain 1996
by William Heinemann
This edition published 1997
by Mandarin Paperbacks
an imprint of Reed International Books Ltd
Michelin House, 81 Fulham Road, London SW3 6RB
and Auckland, Melbourne, Singapore and Toronto

A CIP catalogue record for this title
is available from the British Library
ISBN 0 7493 2333 7

Phototypeset in 10.5 on 13 Ehrhardt
by Intype London Ltd
Printed and bound in Great Britain
by Cox & Wyman Ltd, Reading, Berkshire

Contents

Acknowledgements

This book is dedicated to Achin Vanaik, Pamela Philipose and their sons, Anish and Samar. They were not only my patient hosts in Delhi, where I cluttered their flat with newspaper clippings and cricket books, but a constant source of support and stimulation in my efforts to make sense of the World Cup and the south Asian society in which it was being played.

Travelling as a stranger for three months in the sub-continent, I was the beneficiary of countless acts of kindness – from cricket officials, hotel workers, journalists and academics, political and social activists and ordinary fans. I am grateful to them all.

I wish to thank my colleagues in the Indian and Pakistani press, who made me feel welcome everywhere, and who shared their knowledge and contacts generously. Special thanks to my friend Pradeep Magazine for his constant encouragement and his quiet outrage at iniquity, whether in the cricket world or elsewhere. Sharda Ugra, one of the best young cricket writers in India, was helpful in detailing the historical background of cricket in Bombay. I am also indebted to Kamila Hyatt, whose knowledge and judgement helped me find my way through the labyrinth of Pakistani cricket politics. My account of Palwantar Baloo and the early years of the Bombay Pentangular is drawn from the original research of Ramachandra Guha.

Thanks also to Mushirul Hassan, N. Ram, Neelan Thiruchelvan, Jayadev Uyangoda, Mohammed Tehseen, Arun Daur, Emma Levine, Ian McDonald, Suresh Menon, G. Rajaraman, Clayton Murzello (whose Azhar imitation was the best I heard in India), A. Sivanandan, Huw Richards (for invaluable pedantry and sound advice), Colin Robinson, and Liz Davies.

1

Poetic justice

It had rained overnight and the pathways to Gaddafi Stadium were choked with mud. I felt giddy with nervousness as I hurried past the giant billboards erected by the ruling Pakistan People's Party, past the police armed with automatic rifles and long bamboo lathis, past the well-guarded entrance to the International Management Group's 'hospitality village', towards the inevitable rendezvous of dreams and realities. Not since I was a child, investing my untrammelled hopes in the New York Yankees, had I wanted a team to win a sporting contest so badly. All morning my fragile but persistent faith in a Sri Lankan victory warred with the dour knowledge that, by any rational calculation, the Australians would emerge as winners in this thirty-seventh and final match of the 1996 World Cup.

There was an improbable symmetry in these two teams meeting in the final. The World Cup had begun, and very nearly ended, with Australia's refusal to play in Colombo following the Tamil Tiger bombing there. For this and other reasons the encounter was pregnant with poetic justice. It was also demanded by the cold logic of cricket. During the course of the World Cup Australia and Sri Lanka had shown themselves the two most consistent, enterprising and unflappable sides in the tournament, led by the two shrewdest captains. Both had recovered from early setbacks to win their semi-finals in dramatic fashion. Both boasted depth in batting and variety in bowling. Both were playing away from home, but one enjoyed the near unanimous support of the local crowd.

The queue for the general stand snaked halfway around the stadium. These were the cheapest seats, now reduced by the ever-expanding executive, patrons' and club stands, VIP and media enclosures to a mere one third of the ground. The police were body-searching every ticket holder at the narrow entranceways, so the queue made slow progress. Sri Lankan flags and placards were being distributed by a Colombo businessman and snatched eagerly by Pakistani fans. Some had brought with them banners stitched together from Pakistani and Sri Lankan flags. As I took a photo of the queue, a young man asked, 'From which country?' I replied, 'From England'. He eyed me suspiciously, 'Which side?' 'Sri Lanka'. He broke into a grin and shook my hand.

For this day only, the Pakistani fans had metamorphosed into Sri Lankan fans. Many said this was because the Sri Lankans had vanquished the Indians in the semi-final, and thus exacted revenge for Pakistan's defeat at India's hands in the quarter-final. But there was more to it than that. The Australian refusal to play in Colombo at the outset of the Cup had offended Pakistanis almost as much as Sri Lankans and had aggravated the lingering resentment in Pakistan over the bribery allegations made against Salim Malik by Shane Warne and other Australian players. Sub-continental solidarity had been fractured by recent events in the World Cup, but here, at the tournament's end, it made a welcome return.

Sri Lanka was not, however, a true proxy for Pakistan. Although the fans in the queue would be delighted by a Sri Lankan victory, they would not be crushed by a defeat. The mood was infinitely more relaxed than it would have been had Pakistan been a finalist. And had this been an India–Pakistan final, Lahore would have been turned into a military camp. As it was, apart from the astronomical prices being charged by the hotels, the city was at its best – easy-paced and civilised – for those who can afford to make it so.

Gaddafi Stadium is a legacy of the reign of Zulfikar Ali Bhutto in the early seventies, and bears witness to Bhutto's brief alliance with the Libyan regime. Bhutto's daughter, Benazir, was now prime minister and last year had laid the foundation stone for the extensive refurbishment completed only days before the inauguration of the World Cup. The stadium boasted a new neatly pointed pink brick exterior, evocative of the Mughal architecture of the old city. Inside, a series of cusped arches surmounted the top tier, providing a decorative fringe to the covered stands. New hospitality boxes commanding the central position looking down the wicket had split the press box into two wings. In one sat the Australian and English journalists. In the other, the Indians and Pakistanis. No one had enforced this apartheid and there were perfectly good professional reasons for journalists from the same country to stick together, but it struck me as sad confirmation that this World Cup, which had been born amid such rancour at Lord's three years before, had done little to bring together the cricket cultures of the first and third worlds.

The prime minister and her entourage occupied the field-level VIP box. One of the patrons' stands was filled with 800 opposition party loyalists. Days before the match, the chief minister of Punjab province, Sardar Mohammed Arif Nakai, had physically seized the tickets for the entire block from the offices of the Pakistan Cricket Board. In addition, his secretariat had issued its own special passes to the final, and scuffles had broken out when ticket holders found themselves displaced by the chief minister's cronies. Politicians, judges, generals, industrialists, senior bureaucrats, film stars, fashion designers and former cricket greats – most of whom had secured their tickets without payment – occupied the bulk of the best seats. The final was the most prestigious social gathering Lahore had witnessed in years, an unmissable opportunity to see and be seen.

The English had never wanted this World Cup to be held in south Asia, but nowhere else would it have generated such drama, not least that of the last act, which I had come to Lahore to witness. Disfigured as it was by commerce and nationalism, the World Cup had nonetheless proved a showcase for cricket in all its gaudy variety, balancing the collective and the individual, power and guile and, as ever, the delightful boons and cruelties of fortune. It was a tournament that proved repeatedly that, in one-day cricket, fifty overs could be a very long time indeed.

The final at Lahore was the culmination of my personal romance with sub-continental cricket. For three years I had schemed to attend this event, and it had already proved more enthralling, more painful, more contradictory than I had dreamed. I was convinced that an Australian victory today would make a mockery of the World Cup. Justice was on the side of the Sri Lankans, not only because of their treatment by the Australians but because of the kind of cricket they played, and the way that cricket had transcended the political and ethnic strife that had turned the balmy Sri Lankan reverie into a nightmare. Besides, the Sri Lankans were the underdogs; in keeping with the principle that those least likely to win most need support, I would have backed them in any case.

I needed a Sri Lankan victory to make this exhausting, gripping, confusing World Cup experience cohere into a whole. It was a bizarrely metaphysical notion, and an example of the kind of sociopathic cricket mania that I had been dispassionately analysing as I crisscrossed the sub-continent. Back in England, I had predicted in print and on the air that Sri Lanka would win the Cup. I had noted that they had beaten Pakistan in Pakistan, something no other side had managed for fifteen years. They had won at Sharjah, chasing enormous totals with reckless flair. Still, they were no more than an outside bet, an intriguing long-shot.

I backed them more out of perversity than perspicacity. Now, to my amazement, they were in the final. In my years as a political activist, I hadn't had the good fortune to pick many winners, and in recent days I had found myself dreaming what it would be like to come out on top, for once. To be vindicated. I was asking a lot of Arjuna Ranatunga's team.

Unfortunately, an Australian victory remained the most likely outcome. The bookmakers made them favourites, as they had throughout the tournament, and you couldn't blame them. Australia had won twenty-three of their thirty-three one-day meetings with Sri Lanka. Their depth of bowling and batting, their well-drilled fielding, their pugnacity made them awesome opponents. Certainly, they were more resilient than any of the teams Sri Lanka had beaten on the way to the final: Zimbabwe, Kenya, England and India. And the Australians had trounced Sri Lanka in December in the course of a tour that had been acrimonious even by the standards of contemporary cricket. What's more, no host nation had ever won the World Cup; although this was Pakistan, Sri Lanka was one of the three co-hosts of the tournament and qualified for the jinx. So even as I kept telling everyone else that Sri Lanka would win the Cup, I never really believed it.

Of course, my feelings were a drop in the ocean of emotion churned during the World Cup. So extreme had been the reactions to victory and defeat that observers had dubbed the cricket craziness of the sub-continent a psychosis. Here was a global television spectacle which all three host nations hoped would boost their standing in the eyes of the world and especially the eyes of the world's financiers and investors. But the deep crises in all three societies kept erupting from under the glamour and hype. All three countries were opening their economies and following the well-worn IMF-charted path of privatisation, deregulation, cuts in public spending and encouragement of foreign investors. All three were building consumer sub-cultures in the midst of mass poverty. All three were racked with ethnic intolerance, and in all three the question of national identity was hotly contested. Not surprisingly the World Cup raised yet again C.L.R. James's ever-pertinent question: What do they know of cricket who only cricket know?

For the Sri Lankans the stakes at Lahore were high, but Ranatunga wisely disowned any motives of revenge. Pressed by journalists about his attitude towards this 'grudge' final, the Sri Lankan captain insisted it was just a cricket match: 'Some of these things are not easy to forget, but we see them as history.' Asked how he planned to deal with the threat of Shane Warne, Ranatunga observed with a sweet smile that the Australian leg-spinner was 'over-rated'. Sitting in the press box, I was told that the Sri Lankan cricketers were so relaxed that they had spent the morning visiting a carpet exhibition in their hotel. This was good news.

The teams lined up on the field for the national anthems, the Australians in canary yellow with green lettering and the Sri Lankans in deep blue with yellow lettering. I had become accustomed to the garish pyjamas but the music was an unwelcome innovation, another sop to the jingoists. The Australian anthem was played first, followed by another tune which nearly everyone at the ground assumed belonged to the Sri Lankans. It took me a moment to realise why the theme sounded so familiar. It was 'Nkosi Sikelele Afrika', the song of the liberation movement and now of the new, democratic nation of South Africa. I turned to the lone South African in our wing of the press box. We shared a bewildered look. When 'Nkosi' finished, the Australians trooped off casually, but the Sri Lankans remained in place, waiting for their anthem. After an embarrassing silence the loudspeakers crackled with 'Namo Namo Matha' (Hail Motherland), and the opening rites were concluded. As this bungled celebration of national identity was enacted, I surveyed the stadium. The boundaries and the stands were festooned with the insignia of multinational corporations: Coke, Shell, Visa, Philips, Fuji,

National Panasonic, ICI. Whatever happened in the field today, *they* had already walked off with the true spoils of the World Cup.

Sri Lanka's itinerant cheerleaders, the veteran Percy Abeysekere and his young apprentice, Lionel, had made the journey from Colombo, thanks to corporate benefactors. Throughout the match, they ran ceaselessly to and fro with their giant Sri Lankan flags, cheered by the Pakistani fans. There were small islands of Australian support, but they were engulfed in a sea of Sri Lankan enthusiasm. The afternoon was overcast and breezy and the brilliant colours of the lion flag, gold and crimson and orange and green, fluttered in luminous streams. Because of the rain, the verges of the outfield were sodden and the boundary rope had been drawn in. It was as if the organisers had dropped a school playing field into the middle of a vast modern arena. The short boundaries, I reasoned, would benefit Sri Lanka, with their penchant for hitting over the top in the first fifteen overs.

Ranatunga won the toss and invited the Australians to bat. This had been his policy throughout the World Cup, and he persisted with it at Lahore, despite the fact that no team batting second had ever won the World Cup. He had been under pressure to play an extra bowler, but he kept faith with all seven of his batsmen. The Sri Lankan brains trust, guided off the field by manager Dav Whatmore, born in Colombo but raised in Australia, remained confident that they could outscore any other team. The match began on schedule at 2:30 p.m. The general stand was half empty; the long queue was still working its way through the gates.

This was the fourth time I had seen the Sri Lankans play in this World Cup and I had grown more attached to the side and its diverse personalities with each exposure. In the field, they were a charming *mélange* of willowy youth and portly experience. The two Sri Lankan pace bowlers, Vaas and Wickremasinghe, tried to harry the Australian openers, but on this flat pitch anything short stood up and asked to be hit. With a meaty bat,

Taylor despatched the quick bowlers square on both sides of the wicket. Although Mark Waugh, thus far Australia's outstanding World Cup performer, was out early, clipping Vaas into the hands of Jayasuriya at square leg, the Australians seemed unperturbed. Ponting, helmetless, slashed Vaas to cover off the front foot. Then, with a sweet flick of the wrist, he deposited a short ball from Wickremasinghe high over mid wicket. Taylor continued to cut and drive crisply, and when spin replaced pace in the fourteenth over the score had already reached 79 for 1. My heart sank. The Australians looked like a well-oiled tank rolling to victory. What foolishness to think that the odds would be overturned, yet again, in this World Cup.

Luckily, Ranatunga and his men did not suffer such dark thoughts. Although Taylor and Ponting continued to take runs freely off the spinners, the Sri Lankans remained vigilant in the field, and Muralitharan and Dharmasena kept their nerve while searching for the right length on a pitch just beginning to turn. The Australians passed their hundred in the nineteenth over. In the press box old hands predicted a total of not less than 330. This first innings had begun to seem like an academic exercise. The real drama would come later, watching the Lankans do what they do better than anyone in one-day cricket history: chase outlandishly large totals.

The stadium was full at last. One of the fascinations of cricket in the sub-continent is deciphering the banners and placards on which fans paint a bewildering variety of messages. The artists and slogan composers aim to amuse fellow spectators, and with luck to catch the roving eye of the television cameras. They are the vanguard in the broader process through which a cricket match acquires shared meanings. 'THE HEART BEAT OF PAKISTAN – SRI LANKA' seemed to sum up the feelings of many. 'GOOD LUCK SRI LANKA FROM LA SALLIANS PAKISTAN' proved that the public school ethic was alive and well somewhere in Lahore. Support for the Sri Lankans was spiced with venom towards the Australians: 'TAYLOR-MADE FOR DEFEAT' and 'WANNA FORFEIT

NOW AUSSIES?'. There was a jibe at the arch-rivals, 'I HATE INDIAN CROWD'. And a soupçon of domestic politics – a Pakistani flag with the word 'IMRAN' stitched across it.

Ranatunga juggled his spinners. Jayasuriya replaced Murali and De Silva came on for Dharmasena. The boundaries dried up, though Taylor and Ponting kept the score moving by pushing for singles and posted a 100 partnership off only 110 balls. At the halfway stage, after twenty-five overs, they had reached 134 for 1, a strong position. Shortly after, De Silva induced the first and only false stroke of Mark Taylor's innings: the ball flew off the top edge to deep square leg where Jayasuriya, running around at full tilt, took a difficult catch. The day before the final, he had been named 'Player of the World Cup' and presented with a new Audi (breathlessly described by Tony Greig as 'state of the art German automotive technology'). It was a popular choice. Batting, bowling, fielding – the man had seemed irrepressible, injecting the spirit of the playground into the overwrought arena of global cricket. Now he popped up again, and the crowd was delighted. Sri Lankan flags fluttered.

Ponting, frustrated by his slow progress to 45 off 73 balls, tried to make room to run the ball down to third man but was deceived by De Silva's gentle turn. He lost his balance, missed and was clean bowled. In an attempt to knock the spinners off their line, Taylor sent in Shane Warne. At Madras, in the quarter-final against New Zealand, the ploy had worked. Warne's big hitting had stolen the momentum. But this time Taylor and Warne were out-thought by Ranatunga and Murali. As Warne went on to the front foot to turn the off spinner to the leg side, Murali pushed a faster ball through to the keeper, Kaluwitherana, who whipped off the bails even as the batsman completed his forward lunge. A huge cheer greeted Warne's dismissal. Steve Waugh was the next victim of spin strangulation. Shaping to flick Dharmasena to the leg side, he sent the ball flying off the leading edge high and deep over the bowler's head. De Silva, running from mid on, judged the catch perfectly and leapt in delight;

only three years before, he had been omitted from the Sri Lankan side after failing a fitness test. At the end of the thirty-fifth over the score was 170 for 5.

Stuart Law and Michael Bevan now faced the Lankan spinners. Bevan was listed on the scoreboard simply as 'Michael', a Pakistani payback for the countless times their names had been muddled by commentators abroad. These two had saved Australia from ignominy in the semi-final. Both were powerful and determined players, and expert at the one-day art of controlled acceleration. But their opponents were inspired by the clatter of Australian wickets. Earlier the Sri Lankans had been watchful, as if waiting for the prey to enter the trap. Now they scurried around, clapped and called to each other, responding with alacrity to Ranatunga's constant adjustments. In his second spell, Murali gave the ball more air and it turned and bounced disconcertingly. Suddenly it was impossible to pierce the field. The crowd emitted a continuous happy roar, which rose and fell every time a ball was bowled and every time a fielder intercepted a shot. I could not have been more wrong about the short boundaries. In their first five overs at the crease together, Bevan and Law managed to score only 8 runs. When Law pulled Dharmasena for six in the forty-third over, it was the first Australian boundary in seventeen overs. Soon after, he tried to slash a wide ball from Jayasuriya and only succeeded in spooning to De Silva in the gully. Bristling with belligerence, Ian Healy, the most experienced wicket keeper in the Cup, joined Bevan at the crease. De Silva tossed the ball in the air like an expert angler dangling a fly in front of a trout's nose. Going for a big hit off the front foot, Healy played around the ball and lost his off stump. At the end of the forty-fifth over the score was 205 for 7.

Dharmasena and Muralitharan, the front-line spinners, had completed their quota of overs, but Ranatunga decided not to bring back his seam bowlers, Vaas and Wickremasinghe. Throughout the Cup, he had relied on his part-time slow bowlers to frustrate the opposition, and he did so now, calling on Jayasuriya and De Silva to finish off the innings. Thanks to Bevan's improvising, the Australians put on 33 runs for the last five overs without losing any more wickets. Jayasuriya beat him through the air, but Kaluwitherana fumbled the stumping. In the field, the Sri Lankans maintained the pressure. Even the rotund Ranatunga threw himself full-length to cut off a single, and Wickremasinghe redeemed his patchy bowling by steaming across the turf to stop Bevan's reverse sweep reaching the rope. Murali, fast on his feet, with a swift pick up and hard, accurate throw, performed wonders in the deep. In the forty-ninth over Bevan made room to strike a leg side delivery high over extra cover. It was a strange inside-out shot which he repeated off Jayasuriya in the final over; these were the only two boundaries in his innings of 36 not out off 49 balls.

To have restricted the Australians to 241 for 7 after their brilliant early dash for runs was an achievement. But was 241 still too many? A run rate of 4.84 per over would not normally be a daunting target for this Sri Lankan side, but the Australians had successfully defended a smaller total against the West Indies at Chandigarh. The consensus in the press box was that the Sri Lankans would fall short. On a turning wicket, the Australians could call not only on Shane Warne but on Mark Waugh and Michael Bevan. All three turned the ball away from the left-hander, and the Sri Lankan side was packed with left-handers. Everything, it was said, would depend on Jayasuriya and Kaluwitherana, the opening batsmen. An early onslaught of the type they had made famous in the course of the Cup would enable Sri Lanka to mount a challenge. An Indian friend shook his head sadly and sceptically: 'They won't get it. Not on this pitch. Not under floodlights. Not against Australia. Not in a World Cup final.' And no team batting second had ever won the World Cup.

2

Preparations

'If the American abroad is puzzled by the English attachment to cricket, he is dumbfounded by the Indian passion for it.' Thus begins the entry on India in Barclay's *World of Cricket*, edited by those two panjandrums of the English cricket establishment, E. W. Swanton and John Woodcock. Like much else in the book, this sentence tells us more about the authors than the subject. In this respect, it is similar to the piquant aphorism with which Ashis Nandy begins *The Tao of Cricket*: 'Cricket is an Indian game accidentally discovered by the English.' Everywhere, it seems, people want to harness cricket to nation.

I had first journeyed to India as a hippie tourist, drawn by the mountains and the monuments. I quickly discovered, wherever I went, that there was one thing I could talk about with almost everyone. Cricket was a gateway into what initially seemed an alien but inviting culture. It was an enthusiasm that could be shared across borders and across languages. I cannot count the number of conversations I have had in India and Pakistan that consisted exclusively of the names of cricketers. In the course of that first visit, I acquired an insatiable curiosity about the sub-continent, and have never tired of trying to disentangle its mixture of ugliness and beauty, stasis and dynamism, generosity and cruelty. Every time I return, I discover how little I know about these societies and how complex they are. Cricket (and politics) took me off the tourist trail and into modern south Asia. For me, every day there is a school day; I am always learning. And my World Cup trip proved a course of study in itself. My relationship with sub-continental cricket was a romance in the medieval sense – a quest for a higher knowledge.

In the sub-continent I discovered that the English game which had seduced me was not English at all. Here the fabric of the game seemed at the same time familiar and strange. Familiar, because not only were the laws of cricket the same as in England, so were its skills, challenges and dilemmas, its mix of excitement and tedium; strange, because all of these carried foreign resonances. Even the longueurs, a feature of cricket worldwide, were filled with speculations of a different nature than the ones that arose at Lord's or the Oval. Coming to cricket at the advanced age of twenty-three from an American childhood and a love of baseball, I had been entranced at first by the game's placid rituals and mossy mysteries. When, soon after, I encountered Indian cricket, with its spin bowlers, raucous crowds and labyrinthine politics, it seemed an exotic variation on an exotic theme, an eccentricity within an eccentricity. But as I came to know both cricket and the sub-continent better, I realised that sub-continental cricket was not a quaint legacy of the Raj but something new and vital in world sports. In the last twenty years, it has spread far beyond its old metropolitan enclaves and is now unrivalled as the national sport in all three countries. To a foreign traveller the game seems ubiquitous. In narrow slum streets, village *maidans*, posh suburbs and cluttered middle-class housing blocks, boys and young men (and increasingly girls) play in all kinds of awkward spaces with whatever implements come to hand.

Much has been written about how and why cricket took hold in the sub-continent but little of it is convincing. The trickle-down theory – that the game percolated from the colonial elite to the princes to the Parsi merchants to the middle classes and thence to the masses – may reflect little more than the social assumptions of those who have written cricket's history. In all probability, the game was introduced by English soldiers and sailors, and it can safely be assumed that they played it without the hierarchical etiquette which some have claimed made it especially appealing to Indians. Calcutta and Bombay, urban and cosmopolitan, were the game's first homes in south Asia, and ever since cricket has been at the cutting edge of modernisation in the region. In India, Pakistan and Sri Lanka, cricket is trendy, even sexy, which is the last thing that could be said about it in England.

Today, at least 90 per cent of the world's cricket followers live in the sub-continent. And for better or for worse, cricket is taken more seriously there than anywhere else. As Tony Greig observed, 'Nowhere else in the world is a cricketer made to feel so important.' In England, taking a keen interest in cricket is considered mildly eccentric and cricket fans view themselves as a breed apart. In the sub-continent, *not* taking an interest in cricket is considered eccentric, and to be a cricket fan is to be in the mainstream of public discourse. With the gradual demise of hockey, cricket stands unchallenged in public interest and affection, whereas it competes with – and for the most part lags behind – football, rugby and other games in England, South Africa and Australia.

A caveat must be applied to this last generalisation. It is *international* cricket which commands public interest in the sub-continent. Local football clubs in India enjoy a larger and more devoted parochial following than Ranji Trophy sides, not to mention the corporate and departmental teams which compete in club cricket. But cricket nationalism – the assertion of national identity through cricket – has no parallel in other sports.

With a US passport, and long disillusioned with cricket in my adopted homeland, I could claim to be the only true neutral covering the World Cup. Free of partisan loyalties, I was able to chart my own odyssey across the sub-continent. Being neutral doesn't mean you don't care who wins, though it may mean you don't care *that much* who wins. It means that you can pick and choose the sides you wish to support from match to match. You can even change sides in the course of a match. When it comes to a tournament like the World Cup, you can switch horses at any stage. My abiding loyalty throughout was to Sri Lanka, but at various times I supported India, Holland, Pakistan, the West Indies, New Zealand, South Africa and Kenya. Cricket without the edge of partisanship is abstract and cold, but the World Cup was to demonstrate that partisanship could turn cricket into a knife that wounds.

It is in the sub-continent that the one-day game – an attempt to squeeze cricket's amorphous pre-industrial sprawl into its designated niche in the modern marketplace – has been most ruthlessly exploited by nationalist and commercial forces. I knew from experience that a one-day international in the sub-continent could be many things at once: a popular festival, a global media event, an elite social occasion, a political platform, a gladiatorial contest, an aesthetic delight and a nationalist jamboree. The 1996 World Cup was bound to bring out the best and the worst in south Asian cricket. I had to be there.

I assembled the most motley set of press credentials ever submitted to the Test and County Cricket Board. I don't know what they made at Lord's of the letters from the *New Statesman* (in its pre-Blairite days), *The Caribbean Times*, *Race and Class*, and the fanzine *Johnny Miller 96**, but I was accredited for all the matches I wished to attend. In planning my itinerary I had followed a few elementary guidelines: I wanted to see cricket in all three host countries; I wanted to see as many of the twelve teams as possible, including all three of the qualifiers, Holland, United Arab Emirates and Kenya; I wanted to see matches at Bombay, Bangalore, Madras and Calcutta (my favourite grounds in India); I wanted to see India play Pakistan; I wanted to see the final in Lahore, whoever played in it; and I wanted to avoid the

English. Amazingly, I succeeded in all these aims. For me, it was a lucky World Cup.

The World Cup is a newcomer among cricket's traditions. First staged in England in 1975, it was an instant success. Pundits scoffed, but fans worldwide welcomed the chance to see the world's great cricketers competing together. With each successive World Cup the event grew in importance – for the fans, for the players, for the cricket boards, and above all for the commercial interests which dominate sport everywhere.

Which is why, at Lord's, on 2 February 1993, Alan Smith, chief executive of the TCCB, and a notoriously tight-lipped devotee of cricket's cult of official secrecy, blew his cool. Seething after a record-breaking fourteen-hour meeting of the International Cricket Council, he called an unprecedented press conference to lambaste what he described as 'by a long way the worst meeting I have ever attended . . . fractious and unpleasant . . . beset by procedural wrangling'.

The English cricket establishment had fought a bitter battle to stop the 1996 World Cup being held in the sub-continent, and it had lost. In the *Daily Telegraph*, Christopher Martin-Jenkins argued that England was 'the ideal venue' whose 'advantages cannot be matched by the rival bidders from a vast and frequently unruly sub-continent'. He decried the ICC decision as a triumph for 'money and politics' over cricket. In so doing, he rewrote two hundred years of cricket history, dominated as they had been by *English* money and politics. When national pride is pricked, facts and logic are quickly superseded by myth and emotion.

Colin Cowdrey had chaired the meeting in his capacity as president of the MCC, which had run the ICC from a filing cabinet at Lord's since its inception in 1909. This was to be the last meeting held under the *ancien regime*, soon to be replaced by officers elected from among all the Test-playing nations. Cowdrey, though technically the neutral chairman of an international body, 'batted for England', in the words of one of the Indian delegation.

He started the meeting by asking all present to introduce themselves by their 'Christian names'. A member of the Indian delegation, I.S. Bindra, introduced himself simply as Bindra, which is how he was known in the sub-continent. Cowdrey asked him if that was his Christian name. 'I am Bindra' was the reply. This perturbed the MCC secretary, former Lieutenant-Colonel John Stephenson, acting *ex-officio* as the ICC secretary. 'There were some funnies at the meeting,' he recalled.

Paranoia about the sub-continental plot to steal the Cup from England was rampant, but the English never began to understand whom they were dealing with. Bindra was a senior civil servant, a former secretary to the president of India. Madhavrao Scindia, president of the Indian Cricket Board, was a Congress MP and member of the cabinet. Jagmohan Dalmiya, Cricket Board secretary, was a millionaire construction and real estate tycoon from Calcutta. The English accused the south Asian boards of 'bribing' the associate members, i.e., offering them a greater slice of the World Cup pie than the English were prepared to, which was a strange accusation since this was an auction, under the rules of which the highest bidder is usually the winner. The English stood on their dignity and made fools of themselves.

I caught up with Bindra in October 1994 at the Delhi Golf Club, a sprawling colonial remnant, now one of the Indian capital's elite watering holes. As waiters in livery hovered and fussed, we helped ourselves from the Chinese buffet, then sat down under the enormous chandelier to discuss preparations for the World Cup. Bindra had succeeded Scindia as president of the Indian Cricket Board. Soft-spoken but firm, the dapper, bearded Punjabi began our interview by accusing the English of sour grapes.

'The reality was that the majority of ICC members opposed the English bid and supported ours. They did so because we offered a better financial package. The TCCB has not got over the Raj hangover. They seem not to like their erstwhile colonial subjects coming to London and beating them at what they still consider their own game.' Bindra reminded me that India and Pakistan had jointly hosted the 1987 World Cup. 'Everyone agreed it was a great success. Not one flight was cancelled, not one piece of baggage was lost.'

Soon after the fractious meeting at Lord's, the sub-continental cricket boards had established Pilcom (the Pakistan-India-Lanka Committee) to oversee this improbably gigantic undertaking. I asked Bindra how it was possible for two countries locked in an unofficial state of war to stage a cricket tournament together. After all, they hadn't been able to play each other on home soil since 1989. 'Before the 1987 World Cup, the problem seemed intractable,' he said. 'Our armies were eyeball to eyeball on the border. But in the end it went off without a hitch. Our slogan was "cricket for peace" and cricket does bring peace. We do not feel that we represent different countries. The World Cup is a single enterprise. Remember that the total population of the sub-continent is involved in the World Cup. It is too big for small politicians on either side to disrupt.'

Throughout our conversation we were gingerly interrupted by deferential suitors seeking favours from Bindra, who was polite and modest with all-comers but clearly a man in command. After all, Inderjit Singh Bindra was the finest flower of the Indian Administrative Service, currently secretary for the Departments of Industry, Youth and Sport in Punjab. He was accustomed to weaving his way around politicians, adept at soothing journalists and dispensing patronage. Bindra was confident that the World Cup would boost India's status as the new epicentre of a global game, commanding a huge internal market now linked by satellite and cable television to the vast Indian diaspora in Europe, North America, the Middle East and south-east Asia. He believed the World Cup would unlock new markets for cricket, especially in the United States. It might even spark a craze for cricket in Japan or China.

Bindra was beaming over news of the £8 million title sponsorship deal struck with ITC, the Indian tobacco giant – twice the sum named by a top British agency as the most the Indians could hope for, and the biggest single investment in a sporting event in sub-continental history. The competition was to be dubbed the 'Wills World Cup', after ITC's leading cigarette brand. Bindra was confident that this was the first of many deals, and that the sub-continent would demonstrate how to market the game in a professional manner: 'Already we expect our television revenues to be four times what the Australians brought in for the last World Cup.'

Back in the early eighties, Scyld Berry had predicted that, whatever happened elsewhere, Test cricket would always retain its popularity in India. But since the country's World Cup victory at Lord's in 1983, the one-day game had superseded Test matches. Indeed, in the four years between the 1992 and 1996 World Cups, the Indian side had played more than 60 one-day internationals and only 21 Tests. 'India has more aspirant international cricket venues than the rest of the world combined,' Bindra explained. 'We cannot possibly stage enough Test matches to please all those who want to host international cricket. So the one-day game has allowed us to take cricket to new parts of the country and to expand the base of the game.'

I asked Bindra how he answered critics who claimed that the cricket authorities' only god was money. He insisted that 'the vigorous approach to commercial opportunities' was a means to an end. He cited increases in match fees for first-class cricketers and heavy subsidies for domestic and junior cricket. 'This is the sole purpose of all our marketing activities, to promote and develop the game. Nothing else. The number of people now playing cricket in India is testimony to the Board's hard work in taking cricket to places which had never seen it before. It is no longer an elitist sport. It is for the common man. Most of our Test cricketers now come from lower-middle-class backgrounds. The whole country is now represented by the Test side. Because of this, cricket plays an important role in building national unity.'

This is the major cliché about cricket in the sub-continent. It trips lightly off the tongues of cricket officials and politicians alike. It is true that in recent decades, in Pakistan and Sri Lanka as well as India, cricketers from provincial cities, lower-middle-class backgrounds and minority groups have secured places in the national sides, which have therefore become more representative of the population as a whole. India's World Cup squad was captained by a Muslim (Azharuddin), had a Sikh opening batsman (Navjot Singh Sidhu), and its young stars Tendulkar and Kambli were, respectively, a Brahmin and a Dalit, a member of one of the castes formerly designated untouchable. So the cricket team did indeed seem to embody national unity, but at a time when national unity was under stress as never before. Even as cricket's base had become more democratic and inclusive, ethnic and communal divisions had grown more acute, and ethnic and communal politics more aggressive. These politics intervened repeatedly in cricket, and that was why India and Pakistan had been unable to meet on sub-continental soil for seven years.

'You say the game builds national unity,' I said to Bindra, 'but everywhere I have gone, people talk about the cricket team in terms of religion, region, politics or caste and everyone complains that Test selection is biased.'

'Of course, you cannot please everyone,' he replied. 'The biggest pastime in the country is talking about cricket. We have several hundred million armchair selectors out there. It only shows the depth of public involvement in our cricket.'

Bindra's vision of the future of Indian cricket was in keeping with India's current policy of economic globalisation. *Swadeshi* (self-sufficiency) had been one of the battle-cries of the independence movement, and for decades the declared aim of Indian policy-makers. Now the target was integration into the world economy. The doors were flung open. The Nehruvian rhetoric of public service and social development was replaced by Thatcherite devotion to private enterprise and conspicuous consumption. And the World Cup was organised in that spirit.

Not since Thomas Lord began charging admission to cricket matches at his West End ground had cricket and commerce revelled so shamelessly together. Every sponsorship deal, television tie-in, merchandising scheme was announced with the fanfare usually reserved for victory in the field. For the first time in the sub-continent, a Pilcom official revealed portentously, it would be possible to purchase tickets by credit card. And for the first time, hospitality tents would appear on south Asian grounds (Bindra had been impressed on a visit to Wimbledon). Everything was sponsored (drinks trolleys, sight-screens, umpires) or contracted out (ticket printing, catering, media facilities). Some wag calculated that each ball bowled would be worth two lakh rupees (£4,000). There would be World Cup software packages and web sites; the opening ceremony in Calcutta would rival the Olympics or the football World Cup.

'We in the sub-continent want to prove to the rest of the world that whatever they can do, we can do better,' Bindra declared. So confident were the Pilcom bosses that they could do it better that they fired Saatchi and Saatchi as marketing agents on the grounds that they were not doing justice to the World Cup.

But the Grand Trunk Road of globalisation wound its way through obscure detours and had to negotiate unexpected obstacles. The sixteen matches allotted to India were not enough to satisfy demand. When Guwahati was denied a fixture, the Assam Cricket Association took Pilcom to court. The chairman of the Madhya Pradesh Cricket Association resigned when Gwalior (Scindia's base) was preferred to Indore, the state's traditional cricket capital. Cuttack and Delhi were granted matches only on condition that organisational responsibility be removed from local cricket associations. In November 1995, twelve people died when a stadium wall at Nagpur collapsed during a one-day international between India and New Zealand. The wall had been part of a new stand hastily constructed for the World Cup. Investigations were promised and prosecutions threatened. 'The country's honour is at stake,' said Bindra. Pilcom announced a cash award to the families of the dead. Meanwhile, work on extension and renovation, in many cases months behind schedule, continued frenetically at other World Cup venues. Media, players and visiting dignitaries were promised the best of everything, but there were doubts about how much notice was being taken of the comfort or safety of ordinary ticket holders.

When clashes between government forces and local militants in Kashmir prompted an exchange of venom between the Pakistani and Indian governments, the President of the Pakistan Cricket Board reassured cricket fans (and sponsors) that 'political problems will have no effect on the World Cup. Problems have always existed but they will not affect the game.' In India, Jagmohan Dalmiya urged the Election Commission to avoid any clash between the World Cup and the forthcoming general election. As the World Cup schedule was already agreed, it was clear that the election was expected to cede precedence.

The contradictions of globalisation were neatly illustrated by the imbroglio over the right to telecast the World Cup matches in India. Pilcom had sold global television rights to WorldTel, an American-based outfit run by an expatriate Indian. WorldTel, in turn, sold exclusive Indian rights to Doordarshan, the state television network, for US$4.75 million, the highest price Doordarshan had ever paid for a sporting event. Like the BBC, Doordarshan was under pressure to prove itself a market-worthy entity; unlike the BBC, it broadcast commercials, and World Cup coverage promised a bonanza. For Doordarshan, the World Cup was a vital political and financial acquisition. Consternation therefore followed WorldTel's announcement in December 1995 that Doordarshan had defaulted on its payments and that its contract for the World Cup was to be cancelled forthwith. Forty-eight hours later WorldTel sold the Indian rights to Star TV, Rupert Murdoch's Hong Kong based satellite network, for a fee of US$5 million. Doordarshan was outraged. The government threatened to deny WorldTel the use of the state-owned satellite uplink facility. With weeks to go to the opening ceremony, it suddenly seemed possible that no World Cup matches would be screened in India; the issue was sent to the courts.

This was only the latest episode in a long-running battle for the right to exploit televised cricket in India. Star TV's footprint covers south-east Asia, the sub-continent and the Gulf. Cricket has always been at the core of its marketing strategy; there was no better way to target south Asia's consumers. But at most, Star TV reached only 10 per cent of the Indian population. Doordarshan claimed to reach 60 per cent. What mattered, however, was not the size of the audience but the weight of its collective bank balance. Star's viewers commanded the bulk of the country's disposable income. In television's global marketplace, these few counted for more than Doordarshan's hundreds of millions. Star's claims rested on the compulsions of the market; Doordarshan's on the dictates of democracy.

'A solution must be found,' Bindra declared. 'The country's pride is involved.' But Pilcom's interests in this controversy were complex. For years, Doordarshan had broadcast cricket without paying any fee to the Indian Board. But television rights to international matches were now the Board's single most lucrative asset and it wanted the freedom to sell them to the highest bidder, even if that bidder was a foreign-owned satellite channel. On the other hand, Doordarshan was needed to take cricket to the people. Indeed, without Doordarshan, cricket would never have become big business in India. Bindra and his colleagues wanted to ensure the grass roots were watered, but were not prepared to sacrifice a drop from their own swimming pools.

The WorldTel–Doordarshan conflict left government ministers in a hopeless bind. Like politicians nearly everywhere, they were eager to placate Rupert Murdoch and prove to the IMF that they knew business was business, even if it meant bending the rules to the disadvantage of a state-owned corporation. On the other hand, they knew that any politician held responsible for keeping the World Cup off Doordarshan, and therefore inaccessible to the majority, would pay for it at the polls. Only days before the opening ceremony, and to no one's surprise, the courts brokered a compromise. Doordarshan was awarded sole uplinking rights to matches played in India. In its capacity as 'host broadcaster' it would relay these to all international subscribers. In return, Doordarshan was ordered to pay its outstanding debt to WorldTel, and to allow Star TV to telecast the matches and commercially exploit the 'Indian footprint' of the satellite transmission. Editorial and technical control were assigned exclusively to Grand Slam, the multinational company hired by WorldTel to produce the World Cup coverage. In addition, Doordarshan was enjoined from accepting advertising during World Cup matches from any competing entity of ITC, the tournament sponsors.

So every World Cup match was broadcast on both Doordarshan and Star. The judges made it clear that they intended to set no legal precedent; in making their ruling, they had been mindful of 'the international importance of the event'. In other words, they were suspending the normal course of the law because of the World Cup.

I arrived in India two weeks before the opening ceremony to set up a base of operations at the home of my friends, Achin and Pam, who lived in south Delhi with their sons, Anish and Samar. I first met Achin when I edited *The Painful Transition*, his groundbreaking book on Indian democracy. Over the years we found we had much in common, not only political passions but a boyhood fascination with the Yankees (Achin had lived in New York in the late fifties and early sixties). He was now completing a study of the politics of religion, and was much preoccupied with the need to strengthen the principles of secularism against the Hindutva menace. Pam edited the *Indian Express*'s lively weekend magazine, and despite her personal indifference to cricket was drawn into the World Cup controversies by professional diligence. The Pilcom publicity machine was in high gear. Every day brought forth another boast: this World Cup would be the first, the biggest, the most, the best, the newest. The superlatives seemed inexhaustible. And wherever one looked, on billboards or newspapers or television, people were trying to cash in on cricket. Banks, builders, publishers, travel agents and television repair shops, soft drink and tobacco giants, hotels and restaurants – all vied for a slice of World Cup action. 'It is a big challenge for the marketing strategists,' observed an advertising agency executive, 'the sub-continent has never seen anything like this. There may not be another event like this for twelve years here.'

Amid the World Cup hype, the *hawala* affair unfolded. *Hawala* ('reference' in Hindi) is basically a money-laundering scheme. In mid January, charge sheets were filed against a score of nationally known politicians, including three cabinet ministers (among them Madhavrao Scindia, president of Pilcom) and leading figures in the right-wing Hindu nationalist opposition, the Bharatiya Janata Party. Only the left-wing parties remained untainted by the biggest bribery scandal in Indian political history. Secret diaries kept by the Jain family, ambitious industrialists based in Madhya Pradesh, had been seized by the Central Bureau of Investigation in 1991. It had long been rumoured that the diaries contained details of payments made to eminent personages, but it took a citizens' petition and an admonishment from the courts to force the Bureau to act. The pay-offs enumerated in the Jain diaries amounted to a total of Rs65.47 crore (more than £13 million), and the beneficiaries comprised a roster of India's ruling elite. Among them was the late prime minister, Rajiv Gandhi, listed as receiving Rs2 crore (£500,000). Cabinet members, governors, leaders of the opposition, chief ministers and civil servants were all recipients of the Jains' largesse, 80 per cent of it deriving from foreign companies (French, Swedish, Russian) seeking government contracts or favourable terms of investment in India; the Jains were conduits in a transnational network of illicit currency transactions. According to a special report in the indispensable fortnightly news magazine, *Frontline*, 'Hawala has evolved into a vibrant international racket with credibility among the salaried expatriates in the Gulf and the middle class at home.'

Hawala, then, was the bastard child of globalisation. Scindia, accused of taking Rs75 lakh from the Jains, addressed a huge rally of supporters in Gwalior, his family's ancestral fiefdom. 'I am going to fight back. I don't need any hawala money nor do I need any agency's or constable's certificate of my honesty. The certificate I want is from the people.'

There was, in my mind, one redeeming feature of the drive to 'globalise' south Asian cricket. It would compel India and Pakistan to meet on the cricket field. Only when the global spotlight was on both countries, and their prestige in the world market at stake, would they bury the hatchet long enough to play a cricket match.

My friends were aghast at the prospect. Ardent advocates of India–Pakistan friendship, a cause that can make you very unpopular on either side of the border, they viewed an Indo–Pak cricket match as nothing more than an excuse for mischief. Was I not aware of how the BJP and Shiv Sena exploited these matches to whip up anti-Muslim sentiment? Of how communalist forces in both countries turned cricket contests into religious crusades, into grand battles between sworn enemies? Yes, I was. 'It will bring out the worst elements in both countries,' Achin warned. 'Politically it is vital that neither India nor Pakistan win the World Cup, and indeed that they do not meet at all during the World Cup, for the simple reason that one side would have to lose to the other.' Yes, I understood. The consequences of defeat in an India–Pakistan match were not the same as the consequences of defeat in any other sporting encounter.

George Orwell disparaged international sport as 'war minus the shooting'. At Eton, the games ethic had been shoved down his throat, and as an adult he reviled its hypocrisy. Behind the injunctions to 'play up, play up, and play the game' lay the realities of violence and jingoism. But I was not convinced that cricket had to be war minus the shooting or any other kind of war. I wanted to see the two countries play each other. What was the point of having a World Cup in the sub-continent if it did not feature the fiercest rivalry in one-day cricket? And surely avoiding the match, and continuing to export the rivalry off-shore to Sharjah or Singapore, was conceding the struggle to the forces of bigotry and reaction. Why should the malign champions of Hindutva – self-proclaimed defenders of the 'Hinduness' of the Indian nation – dictate who plays cricket in the sub-continent? It was necessary to overcome these anxieties, to see an India–Pakistan match as an affirmation of what the two countries had in common rather than a wedge to drive them apart.

Throughout the media-magnified countdown to the World Cup, Indian and Pakistani troops continued to exchange small arms and rocket fire on the disputed Kashmir border. Pakistan was seeking new weapons from the USA and India was testing its Prithvi missiles, whose only conceivable target was Pakistan. At a government-declared Kashmir Solidarity Day Benazir Bhutto promised to support the Kashmiri cause 'to our last breath'. She warned, 'India knows Pakistan's strength. India knows that Pakistan is capable of matching India in every field if the situation arises. We will never accept Indian hegemony.' Farookh Ahmed Leghari, president of Pakistan (and patron of the Pakistan Cricket Board), warned that Pakistan would have to build its own nuclear missiles if India continued with its programme. The Indian foreign minister shot back, 'There is no question of abandoning the Prithvi programme. India cannot compromise its security requirements.'

As a football fan and committed Brazil supporter, Achin took only a half-hearted interest in cricket, unlike his young sons, who were true students of the game. In Delhi we set up a pool on the World Cup winner, and Achin backed the Australians, even though he disliked them. When I insisted on backing Sri Lanka, he was scornful of my sentimentality. Profoundly committed to the socialist transformation of society, he had been prone to despondency of late as he contemplated the apparent triumph of global capitalism. It was in keeping with this mood that he advised me, 'Always bet on your fears, rather than your hopes. That way you win whatever happens.'

3

First rites

Arriving in Calcutta for the opening ceremony, I found that cricket had displaced hawala as the front-page lead. The West Bengal state government had promised to refurbish the city 'as per world standards'. Welcome arches (designed to reflect 'the intrinsic culture of West Bengal') were being haphazardly installed and main road junctions frantically tidied up. Sign-painters put finishing touches on billboards and adverts: 'HIT A SIXER WITH UCO BANK', 'TAKE EXTRA COVER AGAINST ACCIDENTS' (New India Assurance), 'BIJOLI GRILL SINGS THE GLORY OF CRICKET', 'A PERFECT VIEW OF WORLD CRICKET . . . AND AN EXTRA COVER ABSOLUTELY FREE' (GKB Optical), 'GET BOWLED BY THE SHEER MAGIC OF HYDERABADI PEARL' (Noor Jewellery), 'STUMP CAMERA, WIDE ANGLE VIEW' (*The Statesman*). The Peerless Hotel hosted a 'Criquette 1996' food festival, featuring Sunny's Flick, Tendu's Straight Grill, and Malik's Fishy Bribe. As part of their effort to bring Calcutta up to world standards, city authorities cleared unsightly street hawkers from the Esplanade leading to Eden Gardens. The hawkers' union accused the police of 'torturing' their members, and organised a one-thousand-strong sit-in protest outside the Metro cinema on the eve of the opening ceremony.

Pilcom had booked India, Pakistan and Sri Lanka into the Taj Bengal, and England, Australia, New Zealand and South Africa into the Oberoi Grand. These were the two top hotels in the city, and if there was a hint of apartheid here at least it was a case of separate but equal. Holland, Kenya, UAE and Zimbabwe had been billeted in the Park Hotel, a star or two downmarket in the luxury accommodation hierarchy. 'There is certainly some sort of discrimination in the set-up,' observed a Kenyan official.

Calcutta was the homebase of Jagmohan Dalmiya, secretary of the Indian Cricket Board and effectively Pilcom's chief executive officer. By birth Dalmiya was not a Bengali, but a member of the Marwari business community which had replaced the British as the city's chief money-makers. In his construction and real estate enterprises, he had proved equally adept at dealing with foreign investors and local politicians, enjoying friendly relations with the communist-dominated West Bengal state government, which had just awarded Dalmiya Construction a massive Rs200 crore (£40 million) contract for a new model town in the suburbs. Over the years, Dalmiya's personal wealth had enabled him to forge a powerbase in the Cricket Association of Bengal, gradually marginalising the old clubs and affiliates which had dominated it for generations. Using his business skills and political contacts, he had channelled funds into the development of Eden Gardens, and under his aegis the stadium hosted a series of spectacular floodlit one-day internationals and became the capital of India's brash new cricket culture.

The opening ceremony was to be Dalmiya's gift to Calcutta. Famous artists were booked to sing and dance. The parade of the World Cup teams was to be led by top Indian models, wearing saris specially designed by the country's leading couturier. Sushmita Sen, India's Miss Universe, would descend from a helicopter inside a laser-generated cricket ball. The whole spectacle was to be orchestrated by Gianfranco Lunetta, who had staged the opening ceremonies at the football World Cup in Italy in 1990 and the Barcelona Olympics in 1992. The star of the show would be a thirteen-minute laser presentation, dubbed 'Wills Batsman', depicting the rise of a young cricketer from the *galli* (urban alleyway) to the Test arena. 'It will be the most dazzling laser show the country has ever witnessed,' promised its British technical director, 'even the dust and smoke particles floating in the air will act as a reflecting medium to produce three-dimensional images and a wave of colours washing across the stadium.' This would be followed by an eighteen-minute fireworks display designed by a French specialist (the 3.5 tonnes of gunpowder were being supplied by a Bombay firm). 'It will be like a bomb blast,' Lunetta boasted, choosing his words with abandon, 'something never seen in the sub-continent before'.

A week before the ceremony, newspapers reported that Sushmita Sen would be taking off her clothes at Eden Gardens. Pilcom was inundated with calls. 'Even ministers want to know whether Sushmita is actually going to take her clothes off,' said an official, delighted with the publicity. Lunetta later admitted to starting the rumour, which was quickly scotched by Sen, who said she would not 'do anything which is disgraceful for my country'. For Dalmiya and the Pilcom top brass, the excitement over Sushmita was a trivial distraction as they wrestled with the biggest international cricket contretemps since the conclusion of the South Africa saga in the early 1990s.

On 31 January, five LTTE suicide bombers drove a truckload of explosives into the seven-storey Central Bank building in Colombo's Fort area, the financial hub of Sri Lanka. Days later, police were still clearing debris and pulling mangled bodies from the ruin. At least eighty died in the blast and one thousand were injured. Whatever the LTTE had expected to achieve by renewing terrorist action in the south of the island, it seems unlikely that they had considered its impact on world cricket and, in particular, on Sri Lankan–Australian relations.

In November, the Sri Lankan cricketers had arrived in Australia buoyed up by victories in Pakistan and Sharjah. There they endured one of the sternest trials undergone by a touring cricket side in recent years. First, they were accused of ball-tampering. Deeply offended, the Sri Lankan Board demanded clearance from the ICC, which quickly quashed the charge. Then Australian umpire Darryl Hair repeatedly no-balled off spinner Muttiah Muralitharan. The Sri Lankan players and officials rallied around Murali, the only Tamil in the team, and a bitter war of words was waged in Sri Lankan and Australian newspapers. As a result, the World Cup match between Australia and Sri Lanka, scheduled for 17 February in Colombo, promised to be more than just another easy-going first-round tie.

Long before the bomb went off in Colombo, the Australians had been muttering about not playing in Sri Lanka. Officials and players spoke of a security threat from partisan crowds. It was no surprise then that within hours of the blast Australian Board 'sources' were telling reporters that the team would not play in Colombo (and that they 'expected to enlist the support of England and possibly South Africa in this matter'). Graham Halbish, ACB chief executive, said the Board was consulting the government and would come to a decision later in the week. Ian Healy told the press, 'The bomb blast is no real surprise to me. It is why we were concerned in the first place.' On television, Michael Slater and Craig McDermott indicated that they would prefer not to play in Sri Lanka.

The Sri Lankan Board acted quickly to reassure the cricket world. 'There is still more time for the World Cup and we are sure things will settle down by then.' It pointed out that bombs had exploded before Test series in the past but that no cricket match had ever been disrupted. Nonetheless, in London, David Richards, the ICC Chief Executive, told the *Times* that he could not guarantee the players' safety in Colombo. The Sri Lankans received support from Zimbabwe and Kenya, both scheduled to play World Cup matches on the island. 'We've come from a war-torn country,' said Dennis Streak, the Zimbabwe manager, 'we're not going to get too concerned over it. You could get run over by a bus in the street – it's just one of those things.'

Australian papers reported that the players had already decided to boycott the match in Colombo 'regardless of what the ICC or Pilcom decide'. In public, Pilcom declared that it would be guided by whatever advice it received from Sri Lanka. 'They are in the best position to determine the security situation,' insisted Dalmiya. At the same time, the Indian papers reported that Pilcom and the ICC were putting pressure on Sri Lanka 'to give up the matches in the larger interests of the event'. And local cricket associations in Hyderabad, Bombay and Bangalore all sought to profit from the Sri Lankan's discomfort by offering to stage the displaced ties.

Presiding over independence day celebrations in Colombo, President Chandrika Kumaratunga restated her commitment to finding a political solution to the island's ethnic conflict, despite the bomb blast and the continuing war in the north. She also offered her government's guarantee of maximum security for the Australian cricketers. Ian Chappell warned that the Australians were about to make 'a decision that could be shown in a poor light a few years on, especially if teams such as Zimbabwe and Kenya agree to play in Sri Lanka and don't experience any trouble'. Like other observers, he wondered if the Australians had ever had any intention of playing in Colombo: 'I would feel much better about the situation if I knew that the ACB, along with the Foreign Affairs department, were exploring every contingency plan to ensure the Australians could fulfil their playing obligations.'

Australian trepidation was exacerbated by a hoax bomb threat telephoned to Craig McDermott's house. Shane Warne told Channel 9 that he was one of six players who had informed the ACB that they would not play in Sri Lanka. Mark Taylor, the Waugh brothers, McDermott and Healy, the experienced core of the team, were said to be the others. Healy and Mark Waugh denied the story. 'I don't know why Shane would make these big comments,' said Waugh. 'I haven't said either way.' In *The Hindu*, a columnist observed, 'This over-cautious attitude doesn't quite fit the typical Aussie image of a beer-guzzling, tough-fighting sportsman.'

On 6 February, the lead story on every front page in the subcontinent was the Australians' formal request to Pilcom to shift their match against Sri Lanka to India. 'The ACB is not prepared to play in Sri Lanka,' Halbish explained, 'because of serious concerns about the safety and security of the players.' Taylor insisted that his players had not pressed the ACB into the decision. 'I don't like to give in to anything but I don't want to see us being used as pawns.' Because of the format of the tournament, the Australians only had to beat Zimbabwe and Kenya in the league round to pass into the knock-out stage of the Cup. Under a different format, would they have been prepared to risk forfeiting the tie in Colombo?

The West Indies joined Australia in requesting a change of venue. Dalmiya remained hopeful. 'We still believe there could be a change of mind. After all, there is a legal contract between the participating countries and Pilcom.' The ICC was silent. According to the Indian press, Richards was pressing Pilcom to accede to Australia.

Throughout the controversy, Shane Warne was the most voluble of the Australian cricketers. 'What happens if I'm shopping downtown and there's a drive-by bombing?' he asked. 'I don't want to waste my life.' Sri Lankan Foreign Minister Lakshman Kadirgarmar was quick to respond: 'Who has time for shopping during a one-day game?' he asked, adding spitefully, 'Shopping is for sissies'. Kadirgamar warned Gareth Evans, his Australian counterpart, that any attempt by the ACB to persuade others to join its boycott of Sri Lanka would be considered 'a hostile act'. Unimpressed, Evans backed the ACB's stand, but tried to temper the mounting animosity. 'It would be nice to change the venue because we have no grudge against Sri Lankan cricket or the Sri Lankan cricket team. We would like to play against them in the World Cup.'

Some were surprised at the aggressive tone adopted by Kadirgamar, a member of the Tamil elite, former international civil servant and eminent barrister. But he was driven by the need to send out an unequivocal message to his two audiences: the global business community, who had to be convinced that Sri Lanka was a safe place to invest, and his electorate in Sri Lanka, who had to be convinced that their leaders were standing up for the country in the eyes of the world. The Colombo *Daily News* reported with satisfaction that an Australian television interviewer who had tried to embarrass Kadirgamar had been deftly outwitted. 'The interviewer may not have been aware that he was contending with a former President of the Oxford Union, a distinguished President's Counsel and one who hails from a country with a cherished history and culture of over 2000 years.'

From the Sri Lankan perspective, the refusal of the Australians even to reconsider their position, despite the daily offers of enhanced security and despite President Kumaratunga's personal assurances, was insulting. Their intransigence seemed to confirm suspicions that the LTTE bomb was merely an excuse. 'To even the deaf and the blind and the rabid Aussie supporter, it is obvious that they have chickened out because of their dirty tactics against Sri Lanka in the recently concluded series on their home turf,' wrote Elmo Rodrigopalle, one of the country's leading cricket commentators. 'They are aware that if they played here they would have been fairly and squarely beaten.' Meanwhile, in Brisbane, bodyguards hired by the ACB watched over the Australian team training session. Was it thought that the long arm of the LTTE would reach out to them even in the Gabba?

Amid rumours that the entire World Cup would be cancelled and that the ICC would split, Pilcom was reported to be working behind the scenes to get both Australia and Sri Lanka 'to relent'. 'We will leave no stone unturned to see that all the matches are held as scheduled,' promised an official, who added that Australia and West Indies might be sued for lost income. Pilcom was contractually obliged to sponsors, advertisers and television networks to provide a total of thirty-seven World Cup matches. If any were cancelled, it could be financially penalised. In London, ICC chairman Clyde Walcott confirmed that a major effort was underway behind the scenes to resolve 'the present difficulties'. Bindra, however, expressed scepticism. He was not aware of any compromise formula. Kadirgarmar kept the phone lines to Delhi and Islamabad busy, pressing the Indian and Pakistani governments to make sure that their respective cricket boards stood firm. As a gesture of reconciliation, he sent Gareth Evans a bouquet of flowers, noting that 'sending flowers is not a sissie thing to do'.

In a final effort to resolve the deadlock, Pilcom announced that it was convening an emergency meeting of ICC officials and Cricket Board representatives on the Saturday before the opening ceremony. 'A lot of moves are being made at various levels to salvage the World Cup,' Dalmiya told reporters, 'but we are unable to give any good news at this stage.' He called on the UN to appoint an independent observer to report on security in Sri Lanka. Gavaskar urged the Australians to change their minds and play in Sri Lanka, 'or are their minds as unfathomable as Warne's flippers?' he wondered, neatly reversing a trite metaphor favoured by generations of white cricket writers. A *Times of India* editorial headlined 'NOT CRICKET' condemned the Australians for 'unfair play'. It seemed that the more cricket was engulfed in political chicanery, the more people sought to cling to public school mythology.

The argument took a new turn with the explosion in London's Canary Wharf which ended the seventeen-month IRA ceasefire. Would the Australians now refuse to play in England? The Sri Lankan high commissioner in London was quick to make the connection. 'In several ways the bomb in London is similar to the one in Sri Lanka. Both were placed in the financial district. Both were about 500 pounds. There is the same shattered glass.

Even the pictures look similar. However, not a single sports event has been cancelled in London this weekend.'

In an extraordinary statement, an LTTE spokesperson in Europe assured West Indies and Australia that cricketers would not be harmed. 'We have nothing against any foreigner and they have nothing to fear from us. Our targets are the Sri Lankan government and its military.' He denied that the Australian boycott had anything to do with fear of the LTTE. 'Sinhalese reactions to the chucking allegations have created a bitter climate and that is the main consideration behind the Australian decision'. Clearly, the LTTE did not wish to be blamed for the boycott. The reality which it could not acknowledge – given its separatist ideology and commitment to armed struggle – was that both Sinhalese and Tamils were angry at the Australian treatment of Sri Lanka and that the World Cup enterprise enjoyed support in all ethnic communities. An India Abroad news service report noted that 'without proclaiming it loudly, overseas Tamil groups seem far from happy at the international embarrassment the Sri Lankan government has faced over cricket dislocations.'

Nonetheless, the ACB remained adamant, despatching its leading hard-liner, Malcolm Gray, to the Calcutta conclave. Pilcom insisted that there were no grounds for switching the Colombo matches to another venue, but proclaimed that all options were being discussed. Calling for cool heads, Ali Bacher reminded his colleagues that 'what we must all work for – and the effort is on – is that once the World Cup is launched, the show rolls on. This tournament is a big advertisement for the sport and we can't allow controversies to dominate.'

The meeting on Saturday proved a prolonged and bitter stand-off. Pilcom offered to reschedule the India *v* Kenya match to Colombo as a goodwill gesture. In this way the Indians would prove to the Australians and West Indians that their fears were groundless. Premadasa Stadium would be sealed off for seventy-two hours before the matches. Every spectator would be individually searched two hours before play commenced. If necessary, matches would be played before an empty stadium with aerial surveillance and all approach roads sealed. The Australians and West Indians could lodge in Madras and fly in army helicopters directly to the ground in Colombo on the morning of the match and leave immediately after the close of play. The Australians, relying on a 'confidential security report', refused to budge. They would not permit their cricketers to play in Colombo under any circumstances.

The World Cup playing conditions contained no provision for forfeitures. The Pilcom Technical Committee, comprising the eminent band of Sunil Gavaskar, Zaheer Abbas, Kapil Dev, Hanif Muhammed and Michael Tissera, had urged the ICC to penalise any forfeit by the West Indies and Australia with the loss of additional first-round points. The recommendation was lost at the ICC conclave by 8–6, with Clyde Walcott, representing the ICC itself, strongly opposing the idea. Pilcom's position was backed by Zimbabwe, Kenya, South Africa and the UAE. New Zealand and Holland were said to be non-committal. The TCCB spokesperson said that while the English had no fears about playing in Colombo, they could understand the fears of others.

On the eve of the opening ceremony, I attended a World Cup 'chat show' in Calcutta. Only in the sub-continent could a public meeting on cricket (which was what the chat show amounted to) on a Saturday night attract 500 people. Circumnavigating the security guards, I entered the hall early and fell into conversation with three grey-headed Calcutta *badroloks* (gentle people), one of whom had been an official with the West Bengal Tennis Federation. He told me that the French Davis Cup team had once threatened to pull out of a rubber in Calcutta because of a bomb incident. West Bengal's communist chief minister, Jyoti Basu, had intervened, and the French team played in the city, but their manners had been atrocious. 'Tennis and cricket are no longer gentlemen's games,' he mourned.

It was an elegant, middle-class crowd, one third of whom

were women. Five slightly pissed Englishmen sat behind me commenting lasciviously on the silk saris. Intermittently they discussed cricket. 'Wassisname? Suneet Gavashur?' barked one. 'Whos'ee? Frankie Vaughan?' they chortled when Ali Bacher joined the panel on stage. Zaheer Abbas, Clive Lloyd, Ian Chappell, Omar Kureishi, and Sidath Wettimuny were already in their places. The veteran Indian cricket commentator Kishore Bhimani took the chair. 'Who will win the World Cup?' was supposed to be the topic of the evening, but a verdict on the Australia–West Indies boycott was what the audience wanted to hear, and they did not have to wait long.

'Before the bomb blast in Colombo Australia were favourite,' said Ian Chappell, 'but now their mental state must be fragile.' Then, his voice firm and clear as it is when people want their audience to know that they mean what they are saying, he added, 'I want to state that I hope very much Australians do not become the first international team to forfeit a match.' The remark won fervent applause. Here was the man who had virtually invented the modern Australian cricketer, the original 'ugly Australian', renouncing his country's policy. (Sitting next to me, Gulu Ezekiel, who had just published a book on the history of the World Cup, whispered that Chappell was wrong; Sri Lanka itself had forfeited a match to Israel, for political reasons, in the 1979 ICC Trophy.) Clive Lloyd also called on the Australians and West Indians to play in Sri Lanka. 'It would be a tragedy if they do not.' The mood of the assembly was unequivocal, and Bhimani, in the chair, could not help but interject, 'Cricket-loving people bring peace. If the Australians play in Sri Lanka, they will be welcomed.'

Ali Bacher explained why he was confident that South Africa would win the Cup. 'Our twelfth man is Nelson Mandela. The team will go out of their way not to let him down.' This too won applause. Omar Kureishi, doyen of Pakistani cricket commentators, ruminated on the spectacle that was about to unfold. 'I thought the main business of the World Cup was cricket but

I am now discovering that the main business of the World Cup is business. One-day cricket is no longer a sideshow. It is the main event.' Turning to the ostensible topic of debate, he declared, 'Australia are the best prepared. South Africa the most committed. Pakistan have got their act together. Wasim is the best player in the World Cup. His performance may prove decisive. What we are seeing now is the element of science coming into one-day cricket. The game is evolving and it is now being played in the mind as much as on the field.' I had read Kureishi many times but this was my first encounter with him in the flesh. I admired his droll eloquence, and the note of critical realism he struck so easily, a note often lacking in English cricket commentary, which sometimes veers wildly between sentimentality and cynicism.

Chappell observed that the Indians had included three spinners in their World Cup squad. 'This tells you something about what the pitches will be like,' he noted with a conspiratorial smile. Dry and deliberate, Kureishi replied, 'Nothing has a greater hold on the human mind than nonsense fortified by technicalities. What are the Indians up to in picking three spinners? There is no end of theories. But the reason is simple. That is their strength. They just don't have the pace bowlers.' The consensus among the panel was that Australia were the favourites, followed by Pakistan and South Africa. No one tipped Sri Lanka.

A cheeky boy asked with a grin if Pakistan would play the final if it were held on a Friday (it was scheduled for a Sunday). Disturbingly, the anti-Muslim jibe elicited a vigorous round of applause. Communal sentiments had become increasingly respectable among the middle class. Unfazed, Kureishi responded, 'If you are a true believer, all seven days will be lucky.'

Pilcom, ICC officials and representatives of the various parties met throughout that night. When I arrived the next morning at the Taj Bengal for the scheduled Pilcom press conference, the word was that no agreement had been reached. In the coffee shop (where place mats, serviettes, tumblers and menus all sported the World Cup logos), Ali Bacher sat alone, glum and irritated. The WorldTel team breakfasted with cellphones glued to their ears. Outside the conference room where the captains and managers of the World Cup sides were gathered together (for the first and only time in the tournament) affluent Indians jostled for glimpses of the stars. The room was guarded by troopers in flak jackets with scarves tied round their heads like bandits, but they seemed flummoxed by the elite crowd. Should they clear them out of the way or ignore their antics? In this situation, snub-nose automatics were useless. When the cricketers emerged, they were engulfed in a mêlée of autograph hunters.

The press conference was Jagmohan Dalmiya's show. Flanked on the one side by Sir Clyde Walcott, chairman of the ICC, and David Richards, its chief executive, and on the other by Arif Ali Abassi, chief executive of the Pakistan Cricket Board, and Ana Punchihewa, president of the Sri Lankan Board, Dalmiya read out a hard-hitting statement:

> Pilcom has decided not to change the schedule for the Wills World Cup 1996. The Australian Cricket Board and the West Indies Cricket Board of Control on the other hand are not prepared to change their decision not to play their matches in Sri Lanka . . . Several alternative suggestions and offers were made to the ACB and the WICBC . . . but the ACB and WICBC were adamant. To demonstrate complete confidence in the Board of Control for Cricket in Sri Lanka and as a gesture of solidarity, a team comprising cricketers from India and Pakistan (called the Wills XI) will play a goodwill match against Sri Lanka on 13 February 1996.

There followed the team list, a list which included Azhar and Tendulkar, Wasim and Waqar, a sub-continental dream team. A historic team. A symbolic team. It set my mind racing. I've always been a sucker for the word 'solidarity'. It's not one that crops up frequently in cricket (the only time I've ever noted it used in English cricket was in reference to the sanctions-busting teams that visited South Africa in the 1980s – when it referred to solidarity with the beleaguered, white-dominated cricket body backed by the apartheid regime). I knew that this was a match I would have to see.

'Rescheduling the matches is out of the question because Pilcom is not convinced of the security risk,' Dalmiya thundered. 'We even offered to hold the matches in an empty ground, with no crowd at all! We were prepared to take the teams by helicopter from India and return them the day of the match. What more could we offer? It is still not too late. Our gates are open.' Then, in a note of warning, he added, 'We will deal with the question of penalties and compensation after the tournament. One learns from mistakes. Next time, contracts will stipulate that teams must play all their matches.'

The Indian press gobbled it up. Questions were fired at Walcott. Why hadn't the ICC intervened to compel the Australians and West Indians to play in Colombo? Why hadn't cricket's premier world body made its voice heard? Was it irrevocably divided? 'ICC is not divided,' Walcott insisted, 'ICC delegated authority to Pilcom. It's no good complaining about ICC. ICC can only do certain things. It needs more clout.' An Indian colleague sitting next to me observed, *sotto voce*, that if it had more clout it would have used it to over-ride Pilcom. Walcott was asked if he would have played in Sri Lanka. 'That's not a fair question. Australia and West Indies had information from reliable sources.' This statement only inflamed the journalists. What were these sources? Why had they been given precedence over official sources? What evidence did they have that cricketers were in danger? 'I'm not a security expert,' said Walcott, taken aback by the barrage. 'The information Australia and West Indies have is confidential. How can confidential information be shared?'

Dalmiya intervened. 'Australia and West Indies have refused to show their security reports to Pilcom, ICC or Sri Lanka. If the situation warrants it, then we would move the matches, but not on the basis of private sources that cannot be confirmed. We were faced with closed minds. We offered to play the first match there, to show we were not asking anyone to take any risk we ourselves wouldn't take. This situation is not unprecedented. We have been to London when it was suffering from IRA bombs. We went to South Africa when the violence there was at its height. We offered to take the risk first.' Dalmiya knew he had the press behind him, and was growing bolder by the minute. Abassi joined in. 'The most civilised thing for them to have done was agree to go to Colombo after all the assurances Pilcom and the Sri Lankan government had provided. But how can you talk to someone who has already made up his mind?'

Punchihewa said little. His Indian and Pakistani counterparts seemed more than happy fighting Sri Lanka's battles. Asked how he felt about the Australian–West Indian snub, he demurred in a soft voice. 'Unhappy, yes. Sad? Very sad. Angry? Maybe. But we in Sri Lanka have to take it in our stride.' His dignified bearing heightened the journalists' scorn for the absent Australians. Walcott was peppered with hostile questions. Why had the ICC not taken Pilcom's view as authoritative? 'I'm here to moderate the meeting and give guidance.' In that case had he failed as ICC chairman? 'What do you expect the ICC chairman to do?' It was a poor performance by Walcott, left to twist in the breeze by his chief executive, Richards, who said not a word throughout the grilling. I was reminded that over thirty years ago C.L.R. James had written wryly that Walcott was 'no cricket Bolshevik'. The first non-English chairman of cricket's international governing body had proved supine before the old white powers. He was asked if there was a first world–third world split in the ICC. 'West Indies is third world,' he replied. 'And in hock to the Australians,' said my increasingly irritated colleague. He leapt up to ask if India or Pakistan would consider boycotting Britain this summer in light of the IRA bomb. Dalmiya, delighted with the question, responded in a flash: 'India believes terrorism should not be given any heed. India will play under any circumstances.' Was he speaking for the cricket board, the players, the government, the Indian people? The press didn't care. This was hot copy. Abassi chipped in, 'Pakistan had similar experiences in 1974 in London when they had to vacate their hotel. So we will be going to England this summer in spite of the bomb.'

The nationalist card is always an easy one to play in front of a home crowd, but in this case it was also a regionalist card, which made it that much more powerful. The Australians had succeeded where countless appeals to higher ideals had failed: they had made south Asian solidarity a fleeting reality.

Why did the Australians persevere with their boycott in the face of all the entreaties and threats? Perhaps it had something to do with the impending general election at home. But if the Labour government thought it would benefit from taking a hard line with the Sri Lankans, it proved mistaken. Within weeks it was swept from office by its right-wing opponents. Sydney newspapers reported that while 89 per cent of Australians backed the boycott, 55 per cent believed the Sri Lankans had been unfairly treated during their tour of Australia. Was the intransigence to do with player paranoia, which seemed to have replaced the player power Ian Chappell had fought for in the seventies? Taylor told the press that the decision had been the Board's. The Board insisted it had to respect the players' concerns.

The West Indians were exempt from the opprobrium heaped on the Australians. It suited many to see the conflict as one between white and black, first and third world, and in that context the Australians became the preferred target. There was also a realistic awareness that the West Indies had succumbed to Australian pressure; the regular exchange of tours with Australia provided vital revenue for the always penurious West Indies' board. What's more, among the old men running the board was a contingent of Anglophiles, loyal to the game's ancient ruling axis.

In both Australia and England, the ambitions of the Pilcom alliance (first forged during the long argument over ICC policy towards apartheid) were perceived as a threat to the good governance of the game. These *arrivistes* had been throwing their financial weight around but they had to be taught that certain standards would be insisted upon by the older Test-playing nations. In south Asia, the Australian decision smacked of first world arrogance and hypocrisy. The IMF had dictated their economic policies and the US was trying to dictate their nuclear weapons policies. The south Asians had hoped that they could call the shots when cricket was played on their home territory. And they were convinced they were the victims of the old Anglo–Australian double-standard. As Omar Kureishi wrote, 'I doubt if the Australians would have reacted the way they have had there been a bomb blast in a white country.'

The ICC's handling of the Colombo controversy confirmed what had been clear from the way it had dealt with recent bribery and chucking allegations: cricket was now a global game without a global authority, and without a global consensus over what constituted 'fair play', either on the pitch or off. Dalmiya and others have argued that the remedy is to create a powerful, modernised ICC, but surely the last thing cricket needs is a FIFA or IOC type of politburo or a dictator in the Havelange or Samaranch mould. What the game does need is an accountable and transparent system of governance, in which the interests of those who play and watch it (at all levels) are represented, and upheld against sponsors, media and governments. In its absence, cricket fans will be buffeted by the continuing strife between elite factions claiming to represent national (or regional) interests.

After the hype in the press, and the drama following the LTTE bomb, the opening ceremony could be politely dubbed an anti-climax. The vast crowd had entered Eden Gardens in an orderly manner, filing neatly through a maze of wooden fenced corrals. Half an hour before showtime the stadium was packed. As the smog settled in, the floodlights came on and the festivities began. While one thousand schoolgirls in colour-coordinated outfits created abstract patterns on the outfield, recorded music (mainly

Alisha Chenoy's execrably catchy Ind-pop hit, 'Made in India') echoed cacophonously around the stands. A refugee from Disney-world dressed up as 'Googlee', the World Cup's official mascot, with a red ball for a body and a Be Happy! grin flashing from under an outsize helmet, pranced around the podium. Compère Saeed Jaffrey introduced himself (at great length) as one of the stars of John Huston's 'classic film' *The Man Who Would Be King*, presumably for the benefit of the global television audience which would be unaware of his scores of Indian film and television credits. Jaffrey appeared to be unrehearsed. He introduced Zimbabwe as South Africa and UAE as Zimbabwe. He called 'Jyoti Basu!' to the stage as if the chief minister were a film star, but incorrectly identified him as 'the governor of West Bengal'. Basu was mercifully brief. Perhaps he was embarrassed by the sheer tackiness of the event. Sushmita Sen did not descend from a helicopter, but ambled around the central podium handing out flags to the twelve bewildered-looking captains, who had been escorted on to the field by models in tee-shirts (the saris were held up in traffic somewhere in the city). A helicopter scattered jasmine petals, obscuring the endless choreography on the out-field and leaving the distant cricketers looking like tiny stick figures in a snow blizzard. Asha Bosle, one of Bollywood's great playback singers, sang a haunting Sanskrit hymn and Tanushree Shankar danced an original, hypnotic creation, but they were minute figures in the giant bowl of the stadium, lost amid the undulating parade of schoolgirls, the flashing lights and the chaotic presentation, which meant that no one was sure what they were supposed to be looking at.

The crowd applauded all the teams, including the Australians, though the biggest hand was reserved for the Indians. Significantly, the second biggest greeted the entry of the Pakistanis. This was their first appearance on Indian soil in seven years. And the applause was the first indication of just how this war minus the shooting would be conducted in the 1996 World Cup. I wondered if my friends had been wrong. Perhaps an India–

Pakistan match could bring out the best in both countries. The biggest flop of the evening was the laser show. Gusty winds swirling around the ground played havoc with the enormous gauze sheets hanging like giant mosquito nets from the four-sided central stage. The imagery disintegrated and the 'Wills batsman' narrative was incomprehensible. The crowd was left trying to interpret a random array of flickering coloured lines and blobs. Patient throughout, though frequently bored, they were utterly baffled at the end. The technical hitches just made a sloppy *mélange* look sloppier. The whole enterprise was an unhappy stylistic mixture of the traditional and indigenous with the modern and global, and in the end was neither one thing nor the other. It exposed, for the first but not the last time in the World Cup, the tensions between Pilcom's globalising ambitions and the incompetence, muddle and corruption that beset its workings.

As I walked down Chowringhee on my way back to my hotel after the opening ceremony, I was joined by a young student who had somehow secured a ticket to Dalmiya's extravaganza. He thought it was poor stuff, but took his disappointment philosophically. The conversation shifted to the behaviour of the Australians. We agreed that it was most unfair. 'What is the point of worrying about bomb?' he said. 'All must die one day. If I am killed by bomb playing for my country, I am proud.' It was a statement that left me feeling uneasy.

I spent the next morning frantically searching for a flight to Sri Lanka. Thanks to the Australians, my carefully designed itinerary had to be thrown away at the very outset of the World Cup. A friendly young Bengali woman at a travel agency tried everything she could think of but Air Lanka insisted all tickets were booked and the waiting list was closed. As she flipped through flight schedules and dialled one contact after another, we chatted about the opening ceremony, which she had attended. 'It was an embarrassment to all of us. Why didn't they have traditional Indian performers like Ravi Shankar?' When I mentioned that I was hoping to see India meet Pakistan on the cricket field at some point during the tournament, she was appalled. 'I hate it when we play Pakistan. It is too much tension. I cannot stand it. It is like a war.' In the end, she advised me to fly to Madras, where I was to insist on boarding the plane to Sri Lanka. 'You are a journalist. You are covering the World Cup. Tell them it is absolutely essential.' I followed her advice, and with the help of a last-minute phone call from the omnipotent Bindra, found my name on the passenger list for the late-night flight to Colombo.

4

Solidarity

We were searched three times in Madras before being allowed on to the Air Lanka flight. Once aboard, there was an interminable delay on the tarmac. With a third of the plane empty, I wondered what all the fuss had been about. Then on marched the players – Sri Lankan, Indian and Pakistani – with accompanying officials, and it became clear what we had been waiting for. As Azhar snoozed behind me, I chatted with Hemant Malik, ITC's Wills World Cup manager and the key link man between Pilcom and the sponsors.

Hemant was a lean, moustachioed whiz kid in his thirties, with a lively sense of humour and an unflinching focus on his employers' interests. I asked him if ITC's record-breaking title sponsorship deal (supplemented by a £5 million promotional blitz) was proving value for money. 'With the exposure on television, we've already recouped our investment many times over. By the time we get to the final, who knows what it will have been worth?' Like everyone else, he was both angered and mystified by the Australians. He told me how he and his colleagues ('You'll note there are three ITC officials going to Colombo and none from Pilcom') had dashed around Madras between flights to purchase a trophy, the Wills Solidarity Cup, to be presented to the winner of the match.

Over the previous year ITC had been embroiled in a widely publicised battle with the multinational BAT, which owns 31 per cent of the Indian company. The Indian chairman of the Board fought off attempts by BAT to remove him by playing the nationalist card. The papers were full of a dramatic boardroom battle between an immovable indigenous capitalist and an irresistible western-based multinational. For the moment, Hemant explained, the struggle had gone quiet, but he was annoyed that BAT should try to dictate ITC's behaviour in a market of which it knew little: 'We are a successful Indian company. We know what we're doing.'

I asked him about the criticisms of the Wills World Cup sponsorship made by the anti-smoking lobby (who had been reminding people that 2200 Indians die each day from smoking-related illnesses). 'We are not converting anyone to smoking,' Hemant said. But then why was ITC sponsoring the World Cup? 'Our market is expanding all the time – because people are being converted from *bidis* to cigarettes.' *Bidis*, strands of tobacco rolled in a coarse leaf, are smoked primarily by the poor, who were thus being enticed to climb the ladder of consumerism, spending more money on smoking more tobacco (and, incidentally, casting out of work millions of mainly lower-caste women employed in the bidi industry). With their markets in the West under pressure from legislation and changing mores, the tobacco giants now look to the third world for growth, and in south Asia that means hitching their wagon to cricket. Research undertaken by the Goa Cancer Society showed that within two months of the 1995 India–New Zealand series, during which several cigarette brand names were prominently displayed, there was a substantial increase in the number of teenagers prepared to try smoking, even though they knew that cigarettes were bad for their health. It seemed likely that the Wills World Cup would exacerbate India's health double whammy in which the afflictions of underdevelopment (cholera, tuberculosis, gastro-enteritis) are combined with those of the advanced industrial countries (cancer, heart disease). Indian legislation stipulates clearly that all cigarette advertisements must carry a health warning but the Wills logo, unadorned by warnings, was conspicuous at cricket grounds (and on television) throughout the World Cup. Rejecting a petition lodged by anti-tobacco activists against the sponsorship, the courts ruled (as they had in the Doordarshan–WorldTel case) that because of 'the international importance of the World Cup' the law of the land would be suspended.

Hemant knew all the arguments about tobacco inside out; it was late and he was not in the mood for them. What he really wanted to talk about was the morrow's match in Colombo. 'I hope the international media make something of this event,' he said, 'it is historic.' Recently he had visited Pakistan, for the first time, to liaise with his opposite number in PTC (a separate company which leases the Wills brand name from ITC). As a Punjabi, he felt at home in Lahore – 'more than in Calcutta', where he lives. The food, clothes, language, manners were all familiar, as was the love of cricket. 'These two countries should be friends. You know, this match could be the start of a new era.'

We arrived at a deserted Negombo airport (twenty kilometres north of Colombo) in the dead of night. Hemant and the visiting Indo–Pak stars were met by ministers and whisked off in limousines. I stood by the conveyor belt, leaning on my trolley, exhausted, waiting for my bags, wondering how I would keep my eyes open for the match that was due to start in only a few hours. Next to me stood the left-arm fast bowler Chaminda Vaas, and scattered around the hall were the other Sri Lankan players, collecting their own luggage (including their cricket equipment) from the belt, and wheeling it to the exits. I wondered how long it had been since Wasim or Azhar had done that.

The World Cup was supposed to be a showcase for Sri Lanka. The sports minister, S. B. Dissanayake, had explained, 'The game of cricket is an effective medium to create a good reputation among the global community on Sri Lanka.' But cricket could also be, as Sri Lankans knew too well, an effective medium for ruining that reputation, a showcase for a society in turmoil. They did not want a return to the evil days which followed the 1987 bomb blast during a New Zealand tour. For five years war in the north and bloody insurgency and counter-insurgency in the south had isolated the country and no international cricket had been played on the island. Sri Lankans felt that they had made progress since then and they wanted that progress acknowledged.

But how much progress had been made? The August 1994 general elections had brought an end to seventeen years of United National Party rule and led to the formation of a new, left-of-centre government by the People's Alliance. Three months later, the Alliance's presidential candidate, Chandrika Bandaranaike Kumaratunga, was swept into office with a mandate for peace from a war-weary public. The new government declared its intention of seeking a political solution to the war, and opened negotiations with the LTTE, which agreed a ceasefire, only to abrogate it within weeks. In August 1995, in an attempt to appeal over the heads of the LTTE to the Tamil community, the government published its devolution package. For all its faults, it was the most far-reaching attempt ever made by a Sri Lankan government to grapple with the grievances underlying the war. For most Tamils, however, the proposals were too modest, and for many Sinhalese they were too extreme. Kumaratunga's initiative stalled.

Meanwhile, the military campaign continued, and in late 1995 the Sri Lankan forces took Jaffna from the LTTE. The Lion flag was raised in the Tamil capital for the first time in eight years, but the army had 'liberated' a city that emptied as it approached. The LTTE made an orderly withdrawal and preserved most of its fighting capacity. Nonetheless, the fall of Jaffna was celebrated as a great Sinhala triumph. Suddenly the hard-line chauvinists, both inside and outside the government's ranks, were revitalised.

'We can still win it militarily,' they argued, 'we have the LTTE on the run. Why make concessions now?' The LTTE's answer was the bombing of the Central Bank.

The bombing was not only a blow to Kumaratunga's peace plan, but a severe embarrassment to the country's economic elite, who liked to talk about Colombo becoming 'a second Singapore'. The Australian boycott was keenly resented because it seemed to undermine the country's IMF-inspired efforts to assume its rightful place in the world market. What was at stake here was not so much Sri Lanka's national pride as its global image. It had to be seen as a player, not just in cricket tournaments but in a competitive international economy. The journal *Pravada* wondered whether the country had its priorities right: 'Are we come to a situation where the successful hosting of cricket matches is as much a matter of national prestige as finding solutions to a devastating war?'

After four hours' sleep, I boarded a three-wheeler to the Premadasa Stadium at Khetterama, in Colombo's north-eastern suburbs. Above the broad avenue leading to the ground, the government had hung banners declaring: 'LONG LIVE INDIA–PAKISTAN–SRI LANKA FRIENDSHIP', 'WE SALUTE YOUR MAGNIFICENT GESTURE OF SOLIDARITY', 'WE SALUTE THE BRAVE SONS OF INDIA AND PAKISTAN', 'GREETINGS TO SAARC SOLIDARITY'. Neat rows of schoolchildren in starched white uniforms lined the route, waiting to welcome the visiting cricketers.

Outside the pavilion, I joined the little knot of local journalists covering the historic event. Eventually, Azhar and Wasim and the rest appeared, escorted by dancers and musicians in traditional costumes and a gaudily decorated elephant. The milling throng of heavily armed soldiers joined in the applause for the northern neighbours, as did most of the journalists. At the press conference inside the clubhouse, Azhar, Wasim and Intikhab made all the right noises. 'This proves to the world we're all together. There's nothing wrong as far as sport is concerned,' Azhar mumbled earnestly. 'This is history,' a jubilant Intikhab insisted, 'it's the first time Indians and Pakistanis have played together on the same side. It's a tremendous sight – everybody's mixing like old friends. Let's hope it's a turning point in relations.' Wasim agreed. 'We are all very comfortable together. This is something for all our countries. I look forward to future joint teams, including Sri Lanka.' Asked if he was worried about playing in the UK after the bomb blast there, the Pakistan captain laughed, 'Ask other teams who are worried about bombs.' When a reporter from the BBC tried to get their response to reports that explosives had been found near the ground, all three dismissed the question out of hand.

Neither Azhar nor Wasim was to look as relaxed again until long after the World Cup was over. In India, Azhar's marital problems had been front-page news (he had left his wife and children in Hyderabad to move in with a Bombay-based television model named Sangeeta Bijlani), and his leadership was under attack from retired players. In Pakistan, Wasim was caught in the crossfire between Cricket Board factions. Their respective home supporters expected nothing less of both captains than World Cup victory. For the moment, however, the two men could bask in the Sri Lankans' gratitude. And their pleasure in playing together was genuine. After all, the Indian and Pakistani cricketers inhabit the same world, share many of the same experiences, not least the burden of national expectation placed on them every time they play each other. What a relief it must have been to be welcomed simply for turning up, and not to have to worry about winning or losing, especially on the eve of a tournament where winning and losing was to mean so much to so many.

Outside, the high commissioners of India and Pakistan joined Kadirgamar for the flag-raising ceremony. The Sri Lankan foreign minister was ready with his sound-bite: 'The world will note that south Asia can get its act together.' For all the pomp and ceremony and the heavy security, the atmosphere was relaxed. The cricketers were dressed in whites, a reversion to tradition foist upon the organisers by the undesirability of having the visiting side take the field in their clashing World Cup uniforms – Pakistan in dark green and India in pale blue. A red ball was to be used. The black sightscreens, prepared for the day–night match against Australia, had to be painted white early in the morning. The stadium, built in 1986 on reclaimed marshland and apparently unusable after the rainy season, sports a spongy outfield and a green pitch, the like of which I was not to see again until my return to England three months later. How the West Indies would have relished it! The Wills XI won the toss and invited Sri Lanka to bat.

Despite the last-minute announcement of the match (held on a working day), and despite the non-competitive nature of the occasion, 10,000 spectators were on hand as play got underway. And what was salient from the first was that all the banners and speeches, all the politicians' exhortations, were nothing compared to the warmth and passion of the crowd. They gave the visitors, and their own Sri Lankan heroes, an unofficial welcome far more stirring than anything the officials could cook up. Instead of scattering across the circle of empty seats, the spectators were packed together into the two tiers of the main large stand, which they had decorated with scores of home-made banners and placards: '3 MUSKETEERS – ARJUNA, AZHAR, AKRAM'; 'THANKS INDIA–PAKISTAN – JOIN WITH SRI LANKA – KEEP SOUTH ASIAN DIGNITY'; 'NEIGHBOURS IN NEED ARE NEIGHBOURS INDEED'; WILLS WORLD CUP BELONGS TO ASIA – INDIA, PAKISTAN, SRI LANKA, UAE'. The crowd were here not only to see something but to say something. As Wasim walked back to his mark to begin the first over, a man carrying a giant banner made of the flags of the three nations stitched together dashed up and down the boundary edge, and the crowd roared, 'Sri Lanka zindabad! India zindabad! Pakistan zindabad!' Briefly I imagined the chant becoming the slogan of the 1996 World Cup, carried by a million voices across the cricket grounds of Asia.

To expectant applause, the wicket keeper Romesh Kaluwitherana took strike. It was his first appearance in Colombo since his scorching performances as a newly promoted opener in Australia. He clipped Wasim's first ball off his legs through mid wicket for four, and a *baila* band in the upper tier of the big stand struck up a joyful noise. Baila, Sri Lanka's popular dance music, evolved from a Sinhala folk idiom under the influence of the Portuguese. For the rest of the day, the band kept us company, its brass ensemble tootling melodically over the light-hearted rhythms of drums and cymbals. At times the music recalled samba or calypso, and at its roughest and slurriest it sounded like township jazz.

The band paused briefly when Kalu, as he is called in Sri Lanka (the word means black in Sinhalese), was caught at short extra cover for six, resulting in the piquant scoreline, 'Kaluwitherana caught Tendulkar bowled Wasim Akram'. As bowler and fielder ran to embrace each other, it was hard to believe that not twenty-four hours before Indian and Pakistani troops were exchanging fire across the disputed Kashmir border. Not for the only time that day, I felt a lump in my throat. I'm usually fairly resistant to cricket sentimentality, but I had no defence against this spectacle of sub-continental amity.

Gurusinha and Ranatunga mounted the only extended partnership of the Sri Lankan innings. On his five foot eight-inch skeleton Ranatunga's ninety kilograms of flesh looked abundant indeed. He chipped and chivvied and accumulated his runs without strain. The unsmiling Gurusinha was nearly as hefty, but taller, and today his aggressive big hitting contrasted with Ranatunga's lethargic nibbling. Dashing back and forth in front of the main stand with a huge Sri Lankan flag, Percy and Lionel egged on the crowd, which cheered anything and everything of merit on either side:

> 'AUSSIE PRIME MINISTER IS KEATING
> AUSTRALIANS ARE CHEATING'

Spectators danced around the boundary, waving Pakistani and Indian flags, and periodically darted on to the field to embrace Wasim or Azhar, who reciprocated with smiles and laughter. Once Ranatunga and Gurusinha were out, Anil Kumble mesmerised the remaining Sri Lankan batsmen with his accuracy and unnerved them with his bounce, bowling his quota of eight overs for 12 runs and 4 wickets. The Sri Lankans finished with a score of 168.

At the lunch interval I left the stifling press box and bought a cold lager from the vendors behind the stands. Beer, such an integral component of the cricket culture in England, Australia and the West Indies, is barred from the cricket grounds of India and Pakistan, but ever-present in Sri Lanka, along with the music. While the baila band rested, local chart-toppers blared over the tannoy. The crowd, mostly middle-class Colombo youth in jeans (despite the heat) and baseball caps, looked happy and healthy. Poor kids with no shoes and scrawny legs threaded their way among these well-fed giants, hawking single cigarettes and sticks of gum. Beyond the entry gates, visible from the vendors' patch, there were green glimpses of dense tropical foliage.

Climbing to the upper tier, I joined the merry throng clustered around the trumpets, trombones, drums and cymbals. The flags of the three nations fluttered everywhere. Vaas opened the bowling and Tendulkar drove his first ball for four through cover. With the brass riffing and blowing over the non-stop dance rhythms, Tendulkar set about cutting and driving anything a fraction under- or over-pitched. In no time, his score raced to 38 (thanks to seven clean, crunching fours). Ranatunga now handed the ball to Muralitharan. This would be the off spinner's first bowl in front of a home crowd since being called for chucking in Australia. As he loped in, the members of the baila band rose to their feet and the massed brass blew a fanfare. Then came one of those dramatic moments that only sport can provide. Had it appeared in a novel or a film, it would have seemed hopelessly contrived. Murali flighted his first delivery, Tendulkar mistimed a drive and Dharmasena, reaching over his head at mid on, took the catch.

The brass fanfare splintered into a million improvised, ecstatic notes, the percussion rose to a thunderous din and the crowd danced with glee. The man next to me grabbed and shook my hand. 'MURALI, YOU ARE NOT GUILTY – YOU WERE ONLY CONVICTED BY A GRANDSON OF AN EX-CONVICT'; 'A NEW WORD FOR THE AUSSIES' DICTIONARY – MURALIPHOBIA'; 'LONDON BOMBED – WHERE WILL SISSY WARNE GO SHOPPING?'

Soon Murali had a sleepy-looking Aamir Sohail caught at deep extra cover. No bowler's action in modern times has been subject to as much high-tech scrutiny as Murali's, and all the evidence (from multi-angle super slow-mo video recordings to goniometric calibrations) has been in the bowler's favour. Today, no one questioned his action. The umpires, Cyril Mitchley and Mehboob Shah, had been scheduled to preside over the cancelled game against Australia. For Sri Lankan fans, by not no-balling Murali they had effectively given him an all-clear for the World Cup. The next day's *Island* headline summed up the events at Khetterama from a Sri Lankan perspective: 'SOLIDARITY MATCH: MURALI SURVIVES SCRUTINY AS SRI LANKA LOSE'. Thanks to contributions from Azhar, Jadeja and Latif, the visitors achieved an easy victory, with six overs and four wickets to spare.

The result may have been of no consequence, but this match was far from meaningless. What mattered was the fact that it had taken place, and the spectators celebrated that fact and articulated its significance. For once the cliché about cricket being a unifier of peoples and nations came alive. All of us who were present had witnessed a practical demonstration of the arbitrariness of the Indo–Pak border and the absurdity of Indo–Pak enmity. International cricket, it seemed, did not have to be war minus the shooting. After the match, the cricketers were whisked off to a tea party hosted by President Kumaratunga at Temple Trees, her family home. On the sprawling lawns, cricketers, ministers and diplomats (including the Australian High Commissioner) mingled. 'India and Pakistan have displayed tremendous solidarity with us,' Kumaratunga said. 'This is the first time these two countries have come together and I am glad that it happened in Sri Lanka. Sri Lanka may have lost the game but cricket won the day.' For the moment, at least, it seemed that regionalism had transcended nationalism.

The night after the solidarity match I was surrounded by waiters as I ate alone in my hotel. This was my first taste of robustly spiced Sri Lankan seafood. Trying a new cuisine is always a moment of revelation, a door into a new world, but I found it hard to concentrate on the squid and prawns as I was bombarded with cricket talk. Ignoring the other diners, the waiters analysed the day's play (they had all watched it on television), praised Azhar and Wasim, and gloated over Murali's wicket, repeating (the new mantra of the country) 'Aussies fear Muttiah – not bomb'. I asked about Vaas and Pushpakumara, Sri Lanka's young quick bowlers. The waiters considered them highly promising and likened the former to Wasim and the latter to Waqar. How cricket fans love archetypes!

I was told that in the fifties the bar here had been a favourite haunt of the legendary batsman Mahadev Sathasivam. Because there was no systematic first-class cricket on the island until the 1980s, the prehistory of Sri Lankan cricket (before Test status was achieved in 1981) relies mainly on oral sources and sporadic newspaper clippings. The former captain of India, Ghulam Ahmed, confided to Indian journalist Rajan Bala that Satha was the best batsman he had ever bowled to. Frank Worrell is reported to have said that Satha was 'the greatest batsman he had ever seen'. Over a twenty-year period Satha made forty-four centuries in top club cricket (playing home matches for Tamil Union at the Colombo Oval, the club's private ground and for decades the country's premier international cricket venue) and in a variety of representative matches, including an appearance for the Rest (under the captaincy of the great all-rounder V.S. Hazare, a

Christian) against the Hindus in the Bombay Pentangular in 1944. Satha was himself a Tamil Hindu, but he played for the Rest because that was the team that the other cricketers from Ceylon (all Sinhalese Buddhists or Christians) had played for. He captained Ceylon in 1948 against Bradman's Australians, who were stopping over en route to a triumphant tour of England. Satha's selection as captain was resented by a number of senior players from the Sinhalese Sports Club who boycotted the following match and were suspended by the Ceylon Cricket Association.

For several years Satha was wrongly incarcerated for the murder of his wife. During his time in prison he was visited by the three W's (Worrell, Weekes and Walcott), visiting the island on their way to Australia. Ultimately, Satha was cleared of the charge and returned to the game with his talent undimmed. In 1955, at the age of thirty-nine, he scored a double ton in a major club match. It seems he was no powerhouse stroke-maker but a master of footwork, timing and the minimalist flick of the wrist. In the field, he let others do the leg work and never, it is said, ran a single, preferring to saunter up and down the wicket with his bat tucked casually under his arm. He was a type – the party-going, hard-drinking, upper-class Tamil. With his cap for ever tilted at a rakish angle, he was (said one of his contemporaries) 'a quite impossible and irrepressible genius'. A flamboyant and sociable character, he excelled at tennis and golf, gambled with glee and smoked incessantly. Some say his tipple was whisky, some say arrack. No matter. All are agreed that, though he would drink all night before matches, he never seemed the worse for wear in the morning. When Gary Sobers stopped in Colombo on his way to play for South Australia in 1961, Satha took him on what is said to have been an epic pub crawl.

A Tamil friend had told me, 'The Sinhalese are hedonists. Even Tamils when they come down from the north give up their dourness.' Drinking my Lion beer in the company of the cricket-crazy waiters, and thinking of the legacy of Sathasivam, I began to draw together the threads that make up Sri Lankan cricket. Elitist amateurism, cavalier batsmanship, relaxed sociability. And hedonism.

The next day, the World Cup proper finally got underway. After the long hyperbolic build-up, the England *v* New Zealand tie at Ahmedabad seemed a damp squib. England made their first error in the third over, when Thorpe missed Astle in the slips because he was standing too far back. 'This isn't Australia or South Africa,' chided an appalled Tony Greig, 'this is India.' Astle went on to make a century, New Zealand won the match, and England never came to terms with the realities of the sub-continent.

5

Modern idols

The World Cup got off to a slow start in Pakistan. Some blamed it on Ramazan, some on the weather, and many on the Pakistan Cricket Board and the government.

I flew to Lahore via Karachi and took a taxi across the flat, densely cultivated Punjab plain to Faisalabad, where South Africa were scheduled to play New Zealand. A faint haze hung over the fields of cotton and sugarcane punctuated with teetering brick kilns. The highway was lined with textile mills and jammed with overflowing buses and lorries covered in the baroque graffiti beloved of Pakistan's sign-painters. The flat-roofed, brick-and-mud-built villages reminded me of the adobe settlements in the south western United States. 'Made in India' blared from the driver's cassette player. Irritating as this ditty was, it was comforting to hear the Pakistani driver hum along to its inane refrain. There had been much *angst* in the Pakistani press about alleged Indian cultural infiltration via satellite television, video cassettes and recorded music, but popular culture knows no boundaries, and like the American politicians who tried to stop white kids listening to black music in the 1950s, the autarchists would find themselves fighting a losing battle. As we entered the city, I caught sight of a man squatting on his haunches daubing 'COKE REFRESHES THE WORLD OF CRICKET' on a roadside wall.

Faisalabad is Pakistan's third largest and fastest growing city. Since independence it has expanded, without plan or controls, to become what Manchester was in the nineteenth century – a hive of mills and factories, home to a vast industrial proletariat. Despite its economic importance, it is on nobody's tourist itinerary and English cricketers derided it as a 'hole' even before it became notorious as the venue of Mike Gatting's confrontation with umpire Shakoor Rana in 1987. Faisalabad boasts the only cricket stadium in the world named after a poet, Muhammad Iqbal, born in 1877 in Sialkot (today the centre of Pakistan's sports goods industry, which thrives thanks to child labour, paying workers Rs20 per day (less than 50p) to stitch balls which will sell in London for £12). Although officially recognised as the national poet of Pakistan, Iqbal's legacy is a complex one for Pakistani nationalists. His early poems celebrated India's diverse heritage and called for unity against the British. He excoriated both brahmin and mullah for dividing and deceiving the people, but later turned against the Hindu-dominated Congress. Calling for devolved government within a federal India, he sought to forge a modern Muslim identity. He died in 1938, and though honoured as one of the fathers of Pakistan his attitude towards nationalism remained fiercely critical.

> Among modern idols the worst is the homeland
> Its robe is the shroud of religion

Iqbal stadium is owned by Faisalabad municipal authorities who were hard at work preparing the ground when I arrived the day before the match. Mr Rafi, groundsman for thirty-five years, showed me his marble-top grassless batting wicket with pride. Nearby, a scene unfolded which became for me a symbol of the World Cup. A member of the ground staff was squatting low and daubing the grass with green paint. Apparently the parched earth did not provide sufficient televisual contrast with the adjacent red-and-white Wills logo.

My reverie was interrupted. 'Where you from, mate?' The Yorkshire accent belonged to Rashid, on holiday from Huddersfield, where he worked as a council tax collector and played Quaid-I-Azam cricket on Sundays. He had family in Faisalabad and had timed his visit to coincide with the World Cup. We talked about the Gatting episode and the ball-tampering allegations. 'The English press are bloody useless and bloody racist,' he said, then, spotting a local minister inspecting the VIP facilities, added, 'and the Pakistan politicians are bloody useless and bloody corrupt. This could be a great country if it weren't for them.' He yearned for Imran to rise to the challenge and sweep them all away.

Back at my guesthouse on the outskirts of town, an *Iftar* (fast-breaking meal) was being held. Food was plentiful, but the hotel staff (from Pakistan's despised and poverty-stricken Christian minority) were perplexed. What did I eat? they asked with anxious looks. Pakistani food, of course, I replied, and they brightened instantly. I stuffed myself with butter chicken, biriyani, dal, chappatis and raita, while catching up on the televised highlights of the early World Cup matches. Thanks to Tendulkar's sizzling 127 not out, India had easily disposed of Kenya in Cuttack, where local journalists, denied press passes, picketed the ground; in Peshawar, England notched up a less than convincing victory over UAE before a sparse crowd.

Faisalabad was, I had been told, cricket-crazy, and international matches always attracted a full house, but the next day the police outnumbered spectators by at least three to one. Poor turn-outs in Rawalpindi and Peshawar had been blamed on the uncompetitive nature of the matches involving the 'minnows' (UAE and Holland), but today's contest promised to be anything but uncompetitive. So where were the crowds? Foreign journalists ascribed their absence to Ramazan, but locals assured me that matches had been held here during Ramazan in the past and had been packed to capacity.

The Iqbal Stadium press box had been renovated and freshly painted, but the South African and New Zealand correspondents were in a filthy mood because the bank of telephones and faxes worked only intermittently and the television was too small. The South African machine was soon in action. Kirsten threw out Astle, trying to scramble back to his crease, in the third over. Palframan, the second choice wicket keeper, dived low to snap up Spearman. Twose, slashing hard at Pollock, was brilliantly caught by McMillan at slip. Even in the slow motion replay, the speed of the big all-rounder's reaction seemed to defy human limitations. The field placings were specific to each batsman. The returns from the deep were fast, flat and unerring. The New Zealand batsmen hardly ran a two all morning. In respect for Ramazan, the players retreated inside to refresh themselves during the drinks interval. In the press box there were complaints that the Coca-Cola wasn't cold enough. The barefoot peons attending the journalists were clearly terrified of upsetting them but because of the language gap couldn't understand what the fuss was about. Finally, a South African journalist lost patience and shifted the small box containing the drinks to a position shaded from the sun. He won approval from Peter Baxter, the long-serving producer of BBC Radio's *Test Match Special.*

'I appreciate your efforts,' said Baxter, 'the British were here for three hundred years without making much of a dent.'

'Well, we had forty years of apartheid,' replied the South African.

Back on the field, McMillan bowled Fleming, the most stylish of the New Zealand batsmen, with a full-length delivery. Harris was run out by a stump-shattering throw from Kirsten. Parore followed, run out by Jonty Rhodes's instantaneous pick-up and flick from cover. Rhodes's exploits in the field have made him hugely popular across the sub-continent. Even in this derisory crowd there was a banner celebrating him as 'KING OF FIELDING'.

Every time he touched the ball, spectators cried 'Jawnteeee!' No wonder ITC had chosen him to serve as the company's World Cup icon. The Wills 'SHARE THE MAGIC' billboards, adorning every town and city in the sub-continent, showed Rhodes diving to take a catch at full stretch, suspended horizontally above the grass. He was global cricket's hyper-modern action man and, as a South African acceptable in both India and Pakistan, a symbol of cricket's future, a bridge between east and west, north and south.

Having limited the New Zealand batsmen to a score of 177 for 9 off fifty overs, the relentlessly efficient South African bowlers and fielders (who conceded only 7 extras) had effectively killed the match. In the absence of tension on the pitch, a small group of white South African fans, baking in the sun (only the press box and VIP enclosure are covered at Faisalabad), became the centre of attention. It was all good humoured until a squad of police officers decided to restore order by slapping around some of the more voluble Pakistani youths.

In the field the New Zealanders dropped both South African openers in the early overs. Captain Hansie Cronje arrived at the crease with the score 41 for 1 in the tenth over. For some reason, the usually sedate Cronje batted as if he had a plane to catch. Driving, pulling, pull driving, sweeping, he scored 78 off 64 balls (with 3 sixes and 11 fours) before he was out with the score on 146 in the twenty-eighth over. After that, the pace slowed, but the South Africans reached their target with 5 wickets and twelve overs to spare. It was a clinical demolition of an inferior side. After the match, Bob Woolmer, the English manager of the South African team, described it as 'the best fielding and bowling performance since I've been in charge. It was an awesome display.'

Asked if they were concerned about where they finished in their qualifying group (first and fourth place would remain in Pakistan for the quarter-finals, second and third would travel to India), Woolmer answered, 'We would like to stay in Pakistan if we can. We're used to the wickets – and we like it here.'

Through bitter experience, the South African cricket establishment had learned the value of diplomacy and multicultural sensitivity. During the Cup, they sent Eid felicitations to the people of Pakistan and brought a message from Mandela to President Leghari in Islamabad. Cronje had learned a few Urdu phrases, and his ability to exchange greetings with the crowd – 'Salaam aleikhum!' 'Valeikhum a salaam!' – won the team friends across the country. Many wondered why the English could not make a similar effort.

My taxi ferried me back to Lahore in record time. Thanks to the Eid holiday, the highway was empty. In the absence of the usual frantic flow of heavy goods vehicles, sections of the road had been colonised by cricket-playing youth. All over India and Pakistan, the paved road is the venue of choice for any informal game of cricket. Unlike the rocky and rutted surfaces of the unadorned earth, the flat, hard road yields even bounce. Lahore, the ancient city, seemed abandoned; with the streets and pavements denuded of human bustle, it was possible to appreciate the spaciousness for which the town had been noted in colonial times.

In the silence of Eid I settled down to watch the television. In Colombo, Murali and Vaas bowled well to restrict the Zimbabweans to 228. Then thanks to a sizzling partnership between De Silva and Gurusinha (173 runs off 164 balls) the Sri Lankans raced past the target with twelve overs to spare.

In Gwalior, Scindia's fiefdom, India met the West Indies under floodlights. On every seat was a glossy four-colour scorecard, compliments of Scindia, bearing his photo and a Hindi message from the local MP proclaiming the virtues of sportsmanship. Following the hawala charge, Narasimha Rao had forced Scindia off the official Congress ticket. For Scindia, campaigning to retain his seat as an independent, the Gwalior World Cup match was a welcome boost. Interviewed on television by Tony Greig, who credited the Scindia family with a multitude of good works for the people of Gwalior and the world of cricket, he played the modest, sports-loving servant of the people. 'The doubting Thomases have been shown up,' he said, pointing to the packed house and the happy spectators. 'We fought against the odds at Lord's and we stuck together in the face of the Australians' refusal to go to Colombo.' Neither Greig nor Scindia breathed the dreaded word hawala.

Like all the World Cup matches, the Gwalior contest was broadcast on both Star TV (for those with satellite or cable connections) and the state-run PTV (for the rest). On Star TV one had to grit one's teeth through the endlessly reiterated self-advertisements boasting 'cricket, CRICKET, *AND MORE CRICKET*!', and the babbling idiocy of Brian Langley (Star's answer to Sky's Charles Colville). But the cricket was broadcast without interruption, whereas PTV sometimes cut to adverts in the middle of an over, and even when the play was being telecast corporate logos were superimposed on the corner of the screen. PTV had paid WorldTel US$750,000 for World Cup rights and was intent on squeezing every drop of revenue it could from the event.

On one of the slow, flat wickets which were to determine the shape of all the World Cup matches until the semi-finals, Srinath performed wonders, making the ball seam and bounce and constantly threatening the West Indian batsmen. He was lucky, however, to have Lara given out caught behind off an edge discernible only to the umpire, who was, ironically, a Pakistani. Lara had been applauded all the way to the wicket. As a global cricket hero, he is revered by Indian fans, who have always warmly embraced West Indian cricketers. However, side by side with that hero worship exists brutal prejudice. '*Bhut*! *Bhut*!' bellowed the crowd (you could hear it on television). Bhut means ghost or spirit, and in India is a derogatory epithet applied to those with black skin (usually members of depressed castes). Racist chanting is not confined to Headingley.

The Indians looked aggressive in the field, Azhar excelling close in and Kambli entertaining the crowd with strong throws from the deep. Kumble was unplayable and those few West Indians who stayed at the crease for more than a few overs laboured. Their total of 177 looked indefensible, but Ambrose bowled his early overs as if he intended to eliminate the Indian side personally. He blasted out Jadeja and Sidhu but Tendulkar, aggressive from the start, leapt on to the front foot without fear and counter-punched brilliantly. He should have been caught out when on 22, in the tenth over, but wicket keeper Browne (one of three men used behind the stumps by the West Indians in the last eighteen months) fluffed a simple catch. It was probably the misfield of the World Cup. Mixing delicate drop shots with muscular boundaries, Tendulkar went on to score 70 before being run out in a mix-up with his former Shardashram school batting partner, Vinod Kambli, who compensated with a bold flurry of cuts and pulls. The Indians passed the West Indian total with 5 wickets and 62 balls to spare. Newspaper torches burned in the stands and firecrackers exploded. It had been a decisive victory that seemed to set India on course for the World Cup championship. A glowing Scindia presented Tendulkar with the man of the match cheque.

PTV's cricket telecasts had one redeeming feature, the music videos produced to celebrate the World Cup. Only in Pakistan could one find this blend of MTV and cricket. 'Hum jeetain Gae' (We Will Win) was jointly sponsored by Pepsi and PTV and dubbed its insistent, patriotic refrain over images of the Pakistan World Cup side practising at the Aitchison College grounds in Lahore. At its climax, Wasim and Waqar ran to each other and embraced in slow motion. Everyone in the country knew that the great fast-bowling pair, formerly best friends, had feuded bitterly in recent years. Their embrace was a symbol of national reconciliation (rendered somewhat less than convincing by the obvious unease with which the charade was acted out by the two). Then there was Saleem Javed's 'World Cup', invoking the 'cricket ke shehezad' (the princes of cricket) and predicting that the Pakistani players would stir up 'cricket mein toofani hai' (a storm in cricket). The song's refrain, 'Phir aaya ayaye, World Cup, World Cup' (It's come again, come again, World Cup, World Cup), was unconsciously echoed several months later in the 'football's coming home' chorus of Baddiel's and Skinner's hymn to Euro 96.

By far the best of the music videos was the soulful anthem, 'Jasbaan-e-Junoon' (very loosely translated, The Joy of Madness), created by the rock group Junoon. The lyrics made no mention of cricket. 'Those who don't lose strength, who don't give up, they touch the sky . . .' The video skilfully intertwined images of the Junoon stars performing the song (jeans, tee-shirts, long hair), of galli cricketers in ragged *salwar kameez* and of members of Pakistan's World Cup squad. With its repeated admonishment 'Pehchaan kabhina bhulo' (Never forget your identity) and its invocation of 'apne ghar, apne sarzamin' (our home, our native land) the song touched a nationalist chord less triumphalist than mournful. And its soaring chorus seemed intended to lift a nation that had lost its self-belief: 'Pakistan kabhina bhulo, Pakistan hai tumhara, Pakistan hai hamara . . .' (Never forget Pakistan, Pakistan is yours, Pakistan is ours . . .)

At the end, Wasim Akram emerged into the light, with round spectacles and white salwar kameez, giving the thumbs-up sign. The song and the video effectively evoked a populist yearning – but for what? For a World Cup victory? Was that the height of aspiration embodied in this song? I think not. Like Woody Guthrie's 'This Land is Your Land', 'Jasbaan-e-Junoon' was a song of reclamation. Its message was that the Pakistani people had to struggle to make the nation theirs, and that the basis of this struggle was unity and solidarity.

There were two common elements in all the World Cup videos and songs: the first was an invocation of the nation victorious, past and future, the second was the absence of Imran Khan, the man who had led Pakistan to its triumph in 1992.

To understand why the image and voice of Imran were banished from the airwaves during the World Cup you have to understand how deeply unpopular both the Bhutto government and the Muslim League opposition had become in recent years. Since the 1993 general elections, the thirty-nine million people living on incomes of less than Rs3500 per year (£70) had been hammered by massive price rises in essential items, a direct consequence of the IMF-dictated policies pursued by both Bhutto and her Muslim League predecessors. Pakistan is shamed by a literacy rate of 22 per cent (and falling) and only 50 per cent enrolment in primary schools. Yet it spends 1 per cent of its budget on education, and US$27 per capita per year on defence. Meanwhile, corruption, privatisation and a loose tax regime have led to a transfer of wealth to the top third of society. The resulting consumer boom in imported items – in a country where 50 per cent of people have no access to clean drinking water – precipitated a balance of payments crisis, which forced the government to devalue the rupee in November 1995. Another IMF loan was secured with the usual 'conditionalities' – more privatisation and fewer import restrictions.

Increasingly, Bhutto resorted to rule by executive decree. Opposition members were harassed and jailed on trumped-up charges. Like her father and the generals who overthrew him, Benazir Bhutto justified her high-handed acts in the name of 'national security', the same reason cited by the fundamentalists in their persecution of Christians, Ahmadis and Hindus. In Karachi, the government's war with the Mohajir Quami Movement had taken 2000 lives in the past year. 'There has never been so much despair and despondency felt in the country as at present,' reported *Economic and Political Weekly.*

Imran, touring the country to raise funds for his cancer hospital, inveighed against corruption and the misrule of the 'brown sahibs' – the selfish westernised elite. Organisationally backed by the cadre of the right-wing Jamaat-I-Islam, Imran drew enormous crowds and extensive media coverage. Scenting a threat, Bhutto banned appeals for the hospital from the airwaves on the grounds that they were a smokescreen for a political campaign. Subsequently Imran himself was banished from all state-controlled media, and did not appear on any of PTV's World Cup telecasts. Not since Stalin tried to airbrush Trotsky out of history had there been such a concerted attempt to deny a public figure's existence. All the World Cup videos included footage of the glorious triumph of 1992, but nowhere was Imran to be seen. The rap song chanting the names of the 'princes of Pakistan cricket' included everyone but Imran. Even PIA's calendar of World Cup captains omitted him. Bhutto's attempt to keep Imran off the air backfired. 'World Cup coverage without Imran is like celebrating Eid without wearing clothes,' complained a columnist in the *News.* The anti-Imran campaign was seen as petty and vindictive, a symptom of the administration's mounting paranoia. If anything, it legitimised Imran in the eyes of millions for whom the government can do no right, and gave him a political weight which he had previously lacked.

Imran, frustrated and furious, was driven to make explicit what many had suspected for some time. 'I have now decided to work openly for the replacement of the present system for which I am trying to raise a team.' In selecting players for his squad, he met with figures on both the left and right of Pakistani politics, from religious groups and secular non-governmental organisations (NGOs). Some welcomed him as a potential messiah, others feared him as a potential autocrat, a front man for the generals or the mullahs or both. Would he choose the constitutional road to power? Would he make his base among the fundamentalists or among the liberal intelligentsia? Salman Taseer, Pakistan Cricket Board treasurer and People's Party politician, derided Imran's ambitions. 'He does not understand the realities of politics. Politics in Pakistan is a nasty, slow, dangerous grind. I have been to jail fourteen times. Has Imran ever seen the back end of a jail?'

Determined to recapture the spotlight, Imran invited Princess Diana to Lahore to help raise funds for the hospital. The visit, timed to coincide with the World Cup, had been approved by neither the British Foreign Office nor the Pakistan government, both of which watched helplessly as the media descended upon this remarkable pairing of pariah aristocrats. Diana and Imran were playing parallel games, mutually boosting each other's legitimacy and public profile. They were games that could be played only because of the globalisation of the media. Imran, treated with contempt by his government, was shown on familiar terms with British royalty. 'Somebody forgot to tell the Brown Sahib that the British Raj has gone,' Salman Taseer sneered, but this was Imran's innings, and there was nothing the Pakistan People's Party could do about it.

The British press is baffled and annoyed by Imran. It cannot comprehend how such a worldly figure, an Oxford-educated sex symbol, could turn so bitterly nationalistic and 'anti-western'. From the *Guardian* to the *Express*, Imran's donning of salwar kameez was presented as damning evidence of his conversion to fundamentalist Islam, when in fact salwar kameez is worn by men and women of diverse political and religious convictions. Much has been made, not least by Imran himself, of his tribal Pathan ancestry, but his upbringing was Punjabi middle class and his father was an engineer. His success on the English social circuit had more to do with looks and bearing than any 'blue blood'. The real contradiction in his soul is not between east and west but between populism and elitism. He is pro-poor but not anti-capitalist, 'tolerant' but not 'secular', 'Islamic' but not 'fundamentalist'. He wants an end to arbitrary rule by law-breaking governments but is hazy about the details of democracy.

At the match between England and Holland in Peshawar, there were banners in Urdu reading simply 'PRIME MINISTER IMRAN KHAN'. The television cameras, operated by Urdu-bereft Westerners, highlighted them as they panned the crowd, unaware that such displays defied the prime minister's edict. There was nothing PTV could do. The amateur Dutch made fools of the professional English as they chased a target of 279 with gusto. Unable to adapt to the pitch, the English bowlers were whacked all over the ground by eighteen-year-old Bas Zuiderent, the youngest player in the competition, whose 54 drew more cheers from the sparse crowd than Hick's unbeaten 100 earlier in the day. The Dutch fell 50 runs short of their target, but once again the England performance was uninspired.

'I must tell you I am anti-cricket,' said Tehseen with slow deliberation. 'In fact I *hate* cricket. I hate the way it is used by politicians. Zia-ul-Haq was a master at this. Whenever there was a movement of some kind big cricket matches would be arranged and everyone would be diverted. Cricket breeds apathy.'

Tehseen hailed from a family of trouble-making communists and was a veteran of the bitter, eleven-year struggle against Zia's military rule. 'Once, we turned cricket against Zia. We smuggled a big banner into the ground during a Test match and unfurled it in front of the television cameras. It said "DOWN WITH MARTIAL LAW". We were on the screen in millions of homes before the police could get through the crowd to grab us.' I had been introduced to him through a mutual friend in the trade union movement. Tehseen is a Lahori born and bred and knows the city intimately. He is now the director of an NGO dedicated to fostering sustainable and just economic development, empowerment of the poor and a culture of tolerance and democratic discussion. He was appalled at the prospect of an India–Pakistan match. 'It would be a disaster. Oh yes. It would lead to violence in either or both countries. Please, I don't even want to think about it.'

He invited me to a meal at the home occupied by his extended family in Cavalry Colony. I was confronted by a remarkable gang of ageing leftist intellectuals who plied me with Scotch (freely available despite prohibition) and probed me on the state of cricket and the struggle for socialism. The patriarch, a tall man with long white hair, recalled bowling Denis Compton in a services match in Delhi during World War II. He was irritated when Tehseen and some of the younger men took themselves off to sing folk songs. 'This is parochialism,' he declared with a mournful shake of the head. 'Marx lit up the whole world. His song was for all humanity.'

In this family, Tehseen's brother, a businessman, was the black sheep. He had paid Rs10,000 to attend Imran's dinner for Princess Diana and was still star-struck by the experience. 'She was the most beautiful woman I have ever seen.' The elders rounded on him. 'You see now how even educated people can fall prey to reactionary mystifications.'

With the grotesque failure of either capitalism or Islam to provide a modicum of social justice in Pakistan, you would think the prospects for a left-wing opposition would be favourable. But here as elsewhere the left was in a shambles. The gentlemen I drank with at Cavalry Colony had been at the forefront of every struggle for democracy and dignity in Pakistan for forty years. They had lived through cycles of brutal repression, renewed democratic hopes and bitter disappointment. None of them had any faith in Imran, nor were they convinced the masses would follow where he led: 'Saints and mullahs and actors have stood for elections in the past and got nowhere. The people are desperate for an alternative, but it must be a meaningful alternative. What does Imran have to offer – this defender of feudalism? When has he spoken out on the issues that matter? On the IMF or the need for Indo–Pak friendship?'

According to Tehseen, Pakistani society was still racked by the aftereffects of the long trauma of martial rule. 'Zia's regime produced two social phenomena. The first is fundamentalism, which has only prospered in Pakistan when it has been nurtured by the state.' In the last election, he reminded me, the fundamentalist parties had won only 4 per cent of the vote. And I knew that mullahs here, like priests in Ireland and Italy, were the butt of countless popular jokes. 'But the fundamentalists can mobilise people and put pressure on the mainstream parties, who always cave in to them, because they do not want to be attacked as anti-Islamic.' The other product of Zia's rule, Tehseen explained, was a new generation of aspirant, individualist middle-class youth. 'They are complete philistines. They care only for consumer goods and they scoff at the very idea of social responsibility.' One of the older men explained that the secular tradition was strongest in the countryside, where the anti-mullah satires of the Sufi poets were still recited. 'Your rural man is secular. And where are your biggest concentrations of fundamentalists? In the engineering colleges in the cities. And,' he added, turning to me, 'these are your biggest cricket fanatics.' Another disagreed. 'Prose is the language of science and democracy – not Sufi poetry! The only antidote to religion remains the rationalist world view.' The spread of television and technology would inevitably curb religious irrationalism. 'Cricket also,' he added, 'this is a modernising and secularising force. It has brought the masses into contact with the wider world. It unites people by giving them a common experience, a common frame of reference.' But surely matches between India and Pakistan divided people? Were they not merely war minus the shooting? 'They are an excellent *substitute* for war.'

Dinner was served as the climax and culmination of the evening, a vast spread of fragrant biriyani, pungent mutton and lentil stew, fresh baked naan, and a cardamom-scented khir. Here more members of the family joined us and the conversation turned to Pakistan's prospects in the World Cup. No one gave them a chance. 'They spend too much time fighting each other,' observed a twelve-year-old boy. 'I think South Africa will win.'

Many Indian cricket journalists were making their first trip to Pakistan. Like the English, they had been fed a diet of horror stories about an intolerant and suspicious society and were pleasantly surprised to find instead a culture with which they were familiar and a people who were friendly. In Pakistan, the hostility towards India is mainly towards the Indian state, perceived as an arrogant superpower; anti-Hindu sentiment is confined largely to the right-wing fundamentalist lobby. And although Dalmiya's high-handedness was resented by some Pakistani officials, personal relations between Indians and Pakistanis who brushed shoulders during the World Cup were more often than not marked by real warmth. Not that this inhibited the ceaseless rivalry between the two nations in every sphere. Indians complained that they were making the deals and raising the revenue. They had the marketing expertise. 'We don't need the Pakistanis,' an Indian journalist said to me, 'next time we should go it alone.' In Pakistan there was the familiar *angst* about Indian superiority. The press complained that both the cricket authorities and the government had let the nation down. In marketing, stadium refurbishment, media facilities, merchandising, ticketing, the Pakistanis believed, often without reason, that they had been outstripped yet again by the Indians. 'We lose every race' was the lament. There was, of course, one exception. In cricket, the Pakistanis reigned supreme, and that made the game all the more important.

In Pakistan, the World Cup of 1987 was recalled as a well organised and modestly profitable event. But as the 1996 World Cup unfolded people stood aghast at the incessant churning of the money mill. Thanks to satellite television, projected income was much higher than in 1987 but so was the expenditure already accrued. The cost of renovations to the PCB's grounds in Karachi and Lahore exceeded £10 million. Work on the Gaddafi Stadium took twice as long and cost three times as much as originally estimated. Where did all the money go? No one will ever know. And if I were to list the names of all those said to have benefited from World Cup kickbacks I would spend the rest of my life in a libel court. In Pakistani cricket, the freedom with which people label each other crooks and scoundrels behind one another's backs is matched only by their cordiality face to face.

The PCB had contracted ticketing and promotions to the recently established Karachi subsidiary of IMG, which had concentrated on selling advertising space and hospitality packages to multinational corporations and for the most part ignored local businesses. 'I've never even been approached by Pilcom or anyone else,' a Lahori snack food manufacturer told me, 'they have not even sent me a rate card list for boundary boards. And we were the official snack food in 1987. They have priced themselves out of the local market – US$20,000 for one twenty-foot long boundary board! And you need at least four to make an impact. My company cannot afford it. I am only selling in Pakistan, not in the UK or Australia. Why should I pay extra for coverage that is useless to me?'

Running parallel to Pilcom and the PCB was the World Cup Committee appointed by the government and chaired by Asif Ali Zardari, PPP member of the national assembly and husband of the prime minister. It was given special 'gazetted' powers under executive decree. Stuffed with heavyweights from PTV, PIA, and the civil service, it was supposed to cut through red tape to ensure that the tournament unfolded smoothly. It was vital that no cock-ups embarrassed the nation. An editorial in the *News* admonished the administrators: 'The event is a showcase for the country and its people as a whole.' By government order all promotional activities on roads leading to World Cup venues were consigned for two months to the WCC, which auctioned off the billboard sites to ICI, Shell, Fuji and a host of banks and insurance companies. To clear the way for the WCC, the municipal corporation of Lahore announced it would remove 'unlawful encroachments' on the roads leading to Gadaffi Stadium. Overnight, the going rate for the bribes paid by the unlawful encroachers, who also happened to be the customary occupants of these public spaces, went up. Those who could not afford to pay, the owners of small stalls and carts, had their goods seized and auctioned off.

Bizarrely, *papier mâché* mushrooms sprouted on Lahore's grass verges and traffic circles. This was part of the WCC Cultural Committee's efforts to 'beautify' the city. The mushroom is neither cultivated nor eaten in Pakistan, and no one could explain the link with the World Cup, but this did not deter the designer elite of the Cultural Committee, who staged a series of concerts, plays and fashion shows which cost Rs30 million (£600,000) and sparked charges of nepotism and extravagance. Zardari was away in Australia leading a trade delegation during the first week of the World Cup. Muslim League politicians claimed he had been shunted out of the limelight because of the allegations of corruption that had dogged the WCC. A PPP spokesperson hit back, 'It is Arif Abassi, not Zardari, who is in it up to his neck. It is his friends in IMG who have benefited.'

The morning after my dinner with Tehseen and his family I attended the WCC Cultural Committee's *Basant Mela* (Spring Fair), organised under the patronage of a local PPP magnate. Basant is celebrated with kite-flying, an art at which the people of Pakistan excel. The traditional basant had, in fact, already come and gone, but the World Cup bigwigs decided to reproduce the folk festival as a garnish to the cricket. A 'people's event' was promised; the patrons would distribute 100,000 kites and 10,000 sets of bangles. Under a grey sky, the fair was held on the broad brick steps of the Old Fort. The steps formed a series of ascending terraces and each terrace represented a rung up the Lahori hierarchy. At the apex, VIPs lounged beneath a huge picture of Benazir Bhutto, while their children were entertained by men in Mickey Mouse and Ninja turtle costumes. Entry to the mela enclosure was by ticket only (though as a Westerner I was permitted free entry) and the tickets were strictly classified, admitting the holder only to a specified terrace. You had to have connections to get in here at all, but no one was satisfied with their allotted rung in the hierarchy. There was mayhem as families tried to talk, push or bribe their way into the higher terraces and cops with lathis and automatic rifles tried to maintain order. When the free kites and bangles came out, there was a frenzied rush, even though these objects could not be of much value to such a well-to-do crowd. I was struck by how agitated and discontent everyone looked and was reminded of a column I had read in *Dawn* on the perils of the pursuit of World Cup final tickets: 'We have a culture of favours and patronage in which people at both ends of the transaction consider themselves privileged. One's sense of self is immediately deflated when one does not belong to this category.'

A flotilla of armed cars escorted local politicians and their families to the enclosure. They mounted the steps to take their place at the top accompanied by henchmen shouting 'PPP zindabad!' The sky was full of kites, swirling in the wind like flocks of birds. The rain fell in thick droplets and the police plundered the vats of 'traditional desi food'. As dark clouds descended on this disturbing exhibition of elite-appropriated popular culture, I beat a retreat to my hotel and the comforts of Star TV.

Pakistani and Indian cricket share a common past, but since Partition they have pursued divergent paths. The Pakistanis, despite having a weaker domestic system (and sometimes no system at all) and even poorer facilities, have a better record overseas, and emerged as one of the superpowers of international cricket in the late seventies and early eighties. The historian Richard Cashman has suggested that one of the secrets of Pakistani success is the very anarchy of the country's domestic cricket. Natural ability flourishes, and thanks to individual patronage quality players can be blooded young. Whatever the cause, there can be little doubt that Pakistan produces cricket talent in abundance, and that it boasts a distinct cricket culture. The sheer rapidity of the evolution of separate cricket traditions in Pakistan and India suggests that the game is shaped not by ethnic identities but by politics and economics.

English perceptions of Pakistani cricket are profoundly coloured by the demonisation of Islam, the west's favourite post-cold war bogey. The perceived vices of Islam – corruption, hypocrisy, factionalism, fanaticism – are thought to be the vices of Pakistani cricket. Corruption, personality clashes and power struggles have indeed plagued cricket in Pakistan, as in other countries. In so far as they are more pronounced in Pakistan than elsewhere, the explanation is to be sought in the pattern of state intervention, in the fierce competition for power within the Pakistani elite and in the complete disenfranchisement of the cricket public rather than in the mysteries of an Islam about which there is little agreement in Pakistan.

The powers-that-be in Pakistani cricket were neatly illustrated by the occupations of the selectors who chose Pakistan's World Cup side: a top civil servant, a former army colonel and a PIA executive. Inevitably the political pressures on the Cricket Board are relentless. Success on the field is not always enough for survival, though failure almost always leads to demotion. During Nawaz Sharif's administration, the chairman of the Board was Chief Justice Nasim Hassan Shah – who had sat on the bench that hanged Zulfikar Ali Bhutto. When Sharif's government was removed, his appeal to the Supreme Court was upheld by Shah. After the general election of 1993, Farookh Leghari, the new president of Pakistan, and by rights patron of Pakistan cricket, dissolved the Cricket Board and appointed an ad hoc committee chaired by his official adviser on cricket affairs, Javed Burki, former Test batsman, cousin of Imran and Majid Khan, son of a former army officer and government minister. Burki brought in Arif Ali Abassi, recently sacked by Bhutto as managing director of PIA, to act as ad hoc committee secretary. After a fourteen-month interregnum, the general body of the PCB, composed of representatives of the leading corporations and government departments, was reconstituted by Leghari. The new president of the Board was Zulfikar Bukhari, scion of a feudal family in central Punjab and former ambassador to Spain. He had attended Aitchison College, the so-called Eton of Pakistan (Imran's alma mater) with Leghari. Salman Taseer became treasurer and Abassi was appointed the Board's first full-time chief executive.

It was said that Abassi had removed Majid as team manager because he was too well connected and therefore too independent. Intikhab, Majid's replacement, was more pliable. Abassi also sidelined Bukhari, about whom he whispered dreadful things to the press. Javed Burki was not pleased. Abassi had been accused of interfering in team selection and the preparation of pitches and of knowing little of cricket. The PCB elections had been postponed until after the World Cup, and Abassi was said to be doomed.

'Britain is a much more civilised place to hold a World Cup,' he purred urbanely when I telephoned to arrange an interview, 'I know it well. I went to Oxford.'

'Actually, I prefer it out here.' I explained that although I was based in Britain, I was all in favour of holding the World Cup in the sub-continent and thought the English criticisms of Pakistan were unfair. Instantly, Abassi changed his tune. With a rush of invective, he catalogued years of TCCB perfidy. 'It is the Raj hangover, you know. They cannot accept the colonials beating them at their own game.'

The next day we met in the newly refurbished dressing rooms at Gaddafi Stadium. He greeted me with a warm handshake and told me he had been 'in the business' for sixteen years. Initially, he had been a protégé of Air Marshal Nur Khan, who had headed the board during Zia's regime. In the last decade, he had probably passed through the revolving door of Pakistan cricket officialdom more frequently than any one else. 'I am also the treasurer of Pilcom,' he reminded me. 'We all wear many hats.' Like his Indian counterparts, he seemed more preoccupied with the global march of cricket than with the World Cup itself.

'The future of the game is shifting to the sub-continent. The geography of cricket is changing and the game will never be the same. The people with a bright future are the West Indies. Why? Because they can tie up with the US and hold the next World Cup there.'

That would upset the English, I observed. They believed the next World Cup had already been awarded to them. Abassi smiled wryly. 'Cricket has undergone a huge revolution, the second after Packer. After this World Cup, it will never readjust to a lower income. People will expect more and more. The English have to show us that they can deliver, that they will expand the game as we have done.' He reminded me that it was Pakistan which had persistently advocated the modernisation of the ICC in recent years, proposing a new constitution, a global format for one-day internationals, neutral umpires, and the allocation of increased funds to the development of the game in new regions.

'You must understand that the ICC is a company, registered in Monte Carlo. The shareholders are the boards of the cricket-playing countries. And every four years the ICC has a very valuable property to franchise. It is known as the World Cup. This time, the fees given to the participating countries have been record fees. And the fee taken by the ICC is also a record. Once you get used to a certain level of income you can't go back to a smaller one. No administrative measures can control an economic force and that is why the name of the game is going to be totally different, whatever the English think.

'This World Cup is going to generate something over US$60 million – biggest profits in the history of the game – and our share will be 50 per cent. That is how we will pay for all these constructions and improvements you see at our grounds. I've brought in money from abroad, converted it into rupees and given a big boost to local industry and jobs. The World Cup is self-financing, like a private company. I've made one logo deal that will make the players ten lakh rupees a year for three years. We are paying each player Rs25,000 for a one-day match and Rs100,000 for a Test match. We now have the best boxes anywhere in the world. Solid constructions with a capacity of fourteen. They've got an open balcony, a sliding-glass door, pantry, refrigerator, television, air conditioning. Even a separate ladies' and gents' right next door. There are thirty in Karachi and twenty-seven in Lahore.'

The boxes were being hired out for a four-year period for Rs11 lakh (£22,000). Abassi conceded that the price was high and that many boxes remained unsold, but he saw this as merely a tiny cloud on the bright horizon of Pakistani cricket.

'Why is all this happening? Because it will improve the image of the country. You're telling people there is nothing lacking here. And you've got to be a class act. We are trying to stage this World Cup differently from what is expected on the sub-continent. That's why we brought in IMG to help with event management. We are aiming for international standards.'

But where were the crowds? Abassi admitted there had been a cock-up about ticket sales. 'We are trying a more sophisticated system of ticketing, using computers and numbered tickets. There's been a delay in the supply. But the policy is being reviewed and tickets should be freely available soon. The public is important as it creates the atmosphere. But the sources of income have shifted. Gate money meets only a small part of our operating costs.'

'Why isn't the final being held in Karachi?' I asked, knowing Abassi was a Karachi man. 'The stadium's bigger.'

'You tell me!' he replied, his eyes opening wide at the injustice of it all. 'This was an arrangement made by my predecessors. In my own opinion it was a mistake, but we must live with it.'

Smirking, slouching, hands in pockets, Abassi affected a weird mixture of Oxford hauteur and American informality, like a man crashing a superior social occasion and trying hard to act as if he belonged. Every other day an article appeared in the press calling for his resignation and to many he seemed merely a figure of fun, a fantasist given to grandiose utterances. But I found him curiously likeable – for all his self-importance he had the sad air of a small-timer who knew his days at the top were numbered and intended to make the most of them.

Abassi claimed credit for having persuaded the ICC to use a single ball in each World Cup innings. 'In Australia we used two balls – one from each end. The new rule will be a big advantage for us because we have the best bowlers with the old ball.' But the Pakistani players had been at each other's throats for most of the last three years. Were they in the mood to retain the World Cup? 'Everything has been fine since my manager came back.

Intikhab is a father figure. Mike, the spirit in the dressing room is tremendous.'

In Gujranwala every building looked half-finished, and buffaloes, goats and donkeys huddled next to factories. It had rained heavily overnight and the roads leading to the Jinnah stadium were a muddy, pot-holed obstacle course. Along the route were huge painted portraits of Salim Malik, Javed Miandad and Ramiz Rajah. Above the pavilion entrance was a portrait of Jinnah, 'father of the nation', flanked by portraits of the captains of today's opposing teams, Wasim Akram of Pakistan and Sultan Zarawani of the United Arab Emirates.

It was Pakistan's first appearance in the 1996 World Cup. The four years since Imran had held the trophy aloft in Melbourne had been tumultuous. Their scintillating performances against England in the summer of 1992 were rewarded with allegations of ball-tampering and Paki-bashing from the British press. In the West Indies, their leading bowlers were accused of smoking dope and boozing. Miandad was dropped and Wasim became captain, only to face a rebellion led by his old friend and best man, Waqar Younis. It was said that Wasim was trying to act like Imran. 'He may look the part, tall and fair-skinned,' explained an Indian observer of the Pakistani cricket scene, 'but the players won't wear it if it isn't earned.' Wasim was replaced briefly by Waqar, then by Salim Malik, a compromise candidate who led Pakistan to an exciting Test series victory over Australia. Then in October 1994 came the disastrous tour of Zimbabwe and South Africa during which the gambling and bribery allegations first surfaced.

Gambling is illegal in Pakistan but widespread. In the past it was informal and small-scale, but the emergence of the Gulf as an off-shore entrepôt, and the development of telecommunications, has turned it into big business. It is said that during one-day internationals the volume of trade at the Karachi Stock Exchange dips as the brokers concentrate on laying wagers on the cricket, and bookies wander the floor shouting the changing odds on everything from the fall of the next wicket to the number of batsmen given out leg before wicket. Because gambling is an illegal activity, the government derives no tax revenue from it, though it is a rich source of kickbacks for the police.

That gambling interests have at times infiltrated the Pakistan dressing room is beyond doubt. That Salim Malik tried to bribe Australian players to throw a Test match, as alleged by Warne, Tim May and Mark Waugh, is as yet unproved. The Australian board refused to allow Warne, May and Waugh to travel to Pakistan to give evidence in support of their written statements and be cross-examined. The Pakistani judge who held the inquiry into the allegations was ridiculed in England and Australia for exonerating Salim, but what choice did he have given the refusal of the accusers to allow their evidence to be tested? The only body that could have ensured due process for all sides was the ICC, but Walcott and Richards claimed they were powerless and passed the buck back to the Pakistanis.

The gambling furore led to a year of chaos in Pakistan cricket. On their return from South Africa, Salim and Intikhab were sacked. Rashid Latif and Basit Ali quit. Majid Khan and Mushtaq Mohammed were placed in charge, and a number of hitherto unknown cricketers were drafted into the side. Under the captaincy of Moin Khan and Ramiz Rajah, Pakistan lost to Sri Lanka at home and then fared poorly in Sharjah. Majid and Mushtaq were sacrificed. Intikhab returned, as did Salim, Latif and the other exiles. In the late autumn of 1995 they toured Australia. Wasim was back in the captaincy as of right, and was accepted as such, even by Waqar. Under huge media pressure, a common front was preserved and a face-saving Test was well won at the end of the series. Despite everything, the Pakistani public had reason to look forward to a strong performance from their team in the World Cup. Bhutto called on the country to pray for divine intervention to help Wasim's men. Zardari announced an award of Rs50 lakh and a plot of land to every Pakistani player should the team retain the World Cup.

Imran denounced the award. 'The honour of playing for the country should be sufficient.' In truth, the money and plot of land were superfluous. For the cricketers, the World Cup was the chance of a lifetime. Most of them came from lower-middle-class backgrounds and had to support extended families. To retain the World Cup at home, against all precedent and after four years of insult and internal division, would place the cricketers among the gods. Their lives would be transformed. And people in Pakistan, disgusted though they were by the spectacle which their cricketers and cricket officials had made of themselves, were still largely convinced their team would win, simply because they believed, not without reason, that it exceeded all others in raw talent. The opening match against the UAE promised an easy entry to the competition.

When the UAE won the ICC qualifying tournament in Nairobi in 1994, there were protests from the defeated Kenyans, who complained that the team was almost entirely made up of foreigners. This was both harsh and naïve. After all, the majority of UAE residents are migrant workers, many from the subcontinent. They have made Sharjah the world's newest cricket capital and they comprise the game's base in the Gulf. Why shouldn't this migrant community be represented in world cricket? The ICC responded to the complaints by introducing a regulation requiring that a certain number of players in each side must be 'eligible' to hold the passport of the country they are representing on the cricket field. This amendment is unlikely to settle the issue. In an era of unprecedented population movement, torn by tensions between migrant and indigenous communities, the question of who is or is not eligible to hold a country's passport is a contentious one (not least in Britain). Seven of the side selected to play for UAE in Gujranwala were born in Pakistan and some had played under-19 cricket in Pakistani colours. Sultan Zarawani, the only UAE native in the side, and perforce its captain, had appealed to the Pakistani public in the name of Muslim brotherhood, but little support was forthcoming for this so-called Pakistan 2nd XI. There is a strong hostility in Pakistan to the UAE as a state, which is not surprising considering the harsh experiences of many Pakistanis who have worked there.

The Pakistani cricketers were eager to start the match, get those first two World Cup points under their belts, and return to Lahore, but play was delayed because the outfield was sodden. Barefoot ground staff tried to soak up the moisture with scraps of foam cushion. At the rate they were going, it seemed unlikely the ground would ever be fit. At 10:30 a.m. a Pakistan Air Force helicopter appeared. Abassi leapt in the cockpit and donned headphones. This seemed to be taking his boast of being a 'hands on' manager a flight too far. The helicopter wheeled around the ground, fanning the grass dry with its rotating propeller blades.

There had been mobs of people and heavy-handed security outside the ground but once inside all was calm. Too calm. This was Pakistan's first appearance in the World Cup, but there were hardly any spectators; it appeared that no tickets had been placed on public sale at the stadium. Embarrassed, the Gujranwala commissioner asked Abassi to open the gates. Abassi and the IMG representative demurred. When the Punjab chief minister, Arif Nakai, arrived, he was furious. 'Where's the bloody crowd?' he demanded. The gates were opened and the fans came flooding in. Soon one half of the ground – the general stand, blank rows of concrete steps – was full with banner-waving, slogan-chanting Pakistani fans. The citizens' stand, with numbered folding chairs, remained empty. These seats had been sold en bloc by the IMG to multinational corporations and government departments.

The match, reduced to thirty-three overs a side, finally started at 12:15. To everyone's disappointment, the UAE batted first, and were quickly exposed as out of their depth. After Mushtaq took three wickets in a spell of nine balls for four runs in the middle of the innings, they were lucky to crawl to the heights of 109 for 9.

Perhaps the most notable event of the day was the appearance in a Pakistani side, for the first time in two years, of the thirty-eight-year-old Javed Miandad. The great pressure player, the street scrapper, was back by public demand, or some said, Mohajir Quami Movement blackmail. Miandad was a Mohajir (as was the wicket keeper Rashid Latif) and a hero nonpareil in Karachi. It was whispered that Altaf Hussein, the MQM boss, had agreed to a suspension of violence in Karachi for the duration of the World Cup if Miandad was included in the squad. And, indeed, the levels of violence in Karachi did recede during the Cup. But was Miandad worth his place in the side? There were rumours that the captain did not think so. Tucked away in the deep throughout the UAE innings, Miandad saw little action in Gujranwala, but just by running out on to the field he set a record, becoming the only cricketer to appear in all six World Cups held so far. He took one catch at long on to remove Saleem Raza, the only UAE batsman who looked capable of standing up to the Pakistan attack, and basked in the wisecracks from the fans, whose other diversion was scheming to get themselves on television.

Aamir Sohail was out early but Saeed Anwar and Ijaz Ahmed stroked the ball with ease as the afternoon sunlight suffused the ground and picked out the minarets rising above the distant jumble of scaffolding, concrete pillars and television aerials. They put on 105 runs from 106 balls to win the match with nine wickets and thirteen overs to spare. Afterwards the players were piped out of the stadium by a Pakistan army band in tartan shawls and caps, looking like extras from a Hollywood epic awaiting a command from that one-time England captain and founder of the Hollywood Cricket Club, C. Aubrey Smith.

The UAE had performed without purpose or plan and were panned in the Pakistani press. As for the champions, this first outing revealed nothing. Wasim continued to project a quiet confidence. The press was preoccupied with the need for Pakistan to finish first in their group to ensure that they played their quarter-final in front of home supporters rather than before a hostile crowd in India. That night, after a thirteen-day lull (out of respect for Eid), fighting resumed on the Kashmir border. Pakistan claimed an Indian rocket attack had killed twenty civilians. New Delhi accused Islamabad of arming Kashmiri militants.

At Gujranwala, I had introduced myself to Omar Kureishi and asked if I could interview him. Courtly but casual, Kureishi invited me to join him the following day at his hotel, where we could watch England play South Africa on television. I had long admired his tart commentary on world cricket, and I knew that for more than three decades he had been at the heart of Pakistani cricket, as journalist, radio and television commentator, selector and tour manager. He was part of the establishment but also a critic of it. That evening, Lahore finally came to life after the long holidays. The shops opened late into the night, the neon signs flashed, families milled about in their finery. And cricket games sprouted like weeds on every empty patch of ground.

The next morning in Rawalpindi, England, in its fourth World Cup match and after a series of seven one-day internationals in South Africa, was still experimenting with its team selection. South Africa batted first and Cork dropped a skier off Palframan in the sixth over. Heads drooped and the thin crowd looked disenchanted. But without ever finding their rhythm the English bowlers restricted South Africa to a score of 230. For an English side brimming with one-day experience and expertise, this should have been a reachable target.

I joined Kureishi at lunch. In Calcutta he had said that the business of the World Cup was business. I said he had seemed a lone voice amid the din of triumphalist commercialism. 'I'm happy to be called a cricket reactionary,' he shrugged. 'The game should still represent certain values. What other justification does it have? Surely this commercialism must reach saturation point soon. It is part of a worldwide trend of privatisation of public services and I deplore it. Cricket becomes a sideshow. For me it's like seeing something you believed in all your life totally transformed.' Kureishi feared that in coming years private sector interests would organise their own mini-world cups and the ICC and the Boards would lose control of the players. 'The entrepreneurs will simply buy them up – because the game no longer has a binding ethic.'

The short, narrow-chested Kureishi cuts a gnomelike figure with bulging, parrotlike nose, fair skin and grey slicked-back hair. He smokes constantly and sprinkles his conversation liberally with four-letter words. Born and raised in Bombay, he attended the famous Cathedral School (and played cricket) with his contemporary, Zulfikar Ali Bhutto. Kureishi had maintained his friendship with Bhutto to the end, when the prime minister and founder of the People's Party of Pakistan was hanged by the military monster he had created, General Zia-ul-Haq. Kureishi was on good terms with the current prime minister, Bhutto's daughter Benazir, and served as vice-chair of Zardari's World Cup Committee. After leaving Bombay, he had studied at the University of Southern California (where Chet Huntley, the legendary American television news presenter, told him he had a talent for broadcasting), then worked in London, where he had married an Englishwoman. In the late fifties the couple moved to Karachi, where Kureishi's family had relocated after Partition.

Before Partition, there was no discernible difference between the cricket played in what became Pakistan and that played elsewhere in India. But since then, the two countries seemed to have evolved rapidly on independent courses. 'Yes, we are distinct from India in that we have a different temperament, a more aggressive temperament,' Kureishi observed. 'Cricket is important in India but it is even more important in Pakistan. Here it is a secular religion. Only two things really bind this country together. One is war and the other is cricket. Only during wartime or during an international cricket match do the people unite irrespective of ethnic or political differences.' Kureishi emphasised that the social base of the game had changed radically in Pakistan over the last generation, and that this was reflected in the composition of the national side. 'It is no longer drawn from a narrow elite or from just two cities. Cricket in this country provides one of the only avenues for upward mobility. A youth from the streets can become a Test cricketer and be accepted in the highest strata of society. People like Zaheer Abbas and Javed Miandad come from humble backgrounds but they became national heroes.'

Nowhere else, not even in India and Sri Lanka, had I seen so much cricket played so intensely by such a wide spectrum of the population. 'Absolutely,' said Kureishi, 'if you scaled K2 you would find people playing cricket. It is something of a mystery. If you looked at the cost of cricket equipment and at the GNP of this country and then fed the data into a computer, you would be told that this country should not be any good at cricket. It proves that cricket is not about money. God knows where these children get the cash to buy their bats and balls, but somehow they do.' He admired the 'wonderful spirit of adaptation' found in the informal cricket improvised in the streets and parks. 'One Pakistani cricketer said to me the other day, "What do you mean we haven't played night cricket before! We played night cricket all the time. We used the streetlights!" ' And Kureishi had noted another curious twist in the dynamic between galli cricket and big-time cricket. 'Watch the boys in the streets now, playing with their upturned crates as wickets, and you will see how they copy their behaviour from the big stars. From television. They shout their appeals, they give the high-fives. I've seen a street match with a little child doing commentary – imitating me!'

I told Kureishi I had seen boys playing cricket on the tarmac in Liberty Circle outside my hotel. Between balls, the batsman had marched down the pitch and carefully prodded the surface with the end of his bat, just like a big-time cricketer on a turf wicket. Kureishi chuckled. 'It is true that at domestic level our cricket is chaotic, but I have seen that as its strength. We have been able to discover natural cricketers who have not had the so-called benefit of coaches. This is the problem with English cricket. They must learn to burn the MCC manual. If we were better organised would we unearth more talent? I'm not so sure.' But didn't Pakistan need a structure to develop young cricketers, to ensure that talent was not wasted? Kureishi was unconvinced. 'A cricket academy can only be a finishing school for first-class cricketers. Talent has to flow from the bottom.' But surely the organisation of first-class cricket around companies and government departments was holding back the development of the game in Pakistan. Who would want to see Habib Bank *v* the Water and Power Development Authority? 'You have to weigh that against this: it solves the employment problem. We have no professional cricketers as in England. How do our cricketers eat? They need jobs. The only entities that can afford to give them a salaried job and allow them to spend most of their time playing cricket are banks and airlines and so forth.'

As we talked, we kept an eye on events in Rawalpindi, where the English were making a miserable hash of their reply to the South Africans. Atherton was out for a duck to Pollock. Stewart was jogging for an easy single with bat in the air when Pat Symcox hit the stumps from mid on. Hick had one of his mental blank outs and chipped to short mid wicket. The batsmen seemed to have lost all self-belief. 'What is wrong with Thorpe!' thundered Kureishi. The left-handed stroke-maker took eleven overs to strike a single boundary. When Fairbrother was caught behind attempting an awkward sweep, Kureishi could contain himself no longer. 'What a stupid shot! I cannot believe it!' He was somehow offended by the English performance, as if its rank incompetence devalued the tournament. When Defreitas was run out because he, like Stewart, failed to ground his bat, Kureishi seemed dumbfounded. 'These are the most experienced professionals in the world and they are playing like dunces.'

After another stinging appraisal of English ineptitude from Geoffrey Boycott, Kureishi nodded in appreciation. In south Asia, Boycott's no-bullshit realism, his willingness to scold the

English and to praise high quality performances by others has won him a popularity as a commentator he never enjoyed as a player. I mentioned to Kureishi that I was amazed at how Boycott's free-fire style of television commentary seemed so completely at odds with his turgid style of batsmanship. 'It's the same man, though,' Kureishi explained. 'What used to drive his team-mates crazy is what makes him such a good commentator: he has no allegiances.'

We discussed the disappointing attendance at the early matches and Kureishi suggested that the 'security overkill' may have played a part. 'This is a festival. The idea is to have fun. If you deny people the right to have fun, you don't have a festival. Security people all over the world are heavy-handed. It is their business to take no chances. But rowdyism is not terrorism. An orange is not a grenade. I am afraid the Australians have made everyone paranoid.'

How did he feel about the prospect of Pakistan playing India during the World Cup? He smiled broadly. 'I would very much like to see the two teams meet, preferably in the final.' The inveterate cricket connoisseur seemed almost to lick his lips in anticipation. 'It would be the most dramatic encounter in the history of cricket.'

But one fraught with danger?

'I would not foresee any serious problems. Not in Lahore. This issue of India–Pakistan cricket ties is the creation of communal politicians in India. It is basically an Indian domestic political problem. Emotions will run high, there is no doubt, and the most vulnerable people would be Muslims in India. But it would be an irresistible contest. The *raison d'être* of the World Cup.'

And an example of war minus the shooting?

'Sport *is* a substitute for war. It is because of the overall absence of war in the world today that international sport has assumed such huge importance. Where else but in sport do you see this level of jingoism?'

England sank to a 78-run defeat in Rawalpindi. The performance was so dispiriting that it prompted a rare outburst from Dennis Silk, the TCCB chairman. 'We are dropping further behind those we are competing against. I am told it is cyclical but frankly I do not believe it.' His proposed remedies were familiar. An academy, a 'more competitive' (i.e., smaller) county competition and the contracting of top players directly to the TCCB.

In keeping with his strategy of disowning his side's failures (and in defiance of World Cup playing conditions), Raymond Illingworth did not attend the post-match press conference at Rawalpindi. Atherton was left to face another ritual humiliation with only John Barclay, the assistant manager, at his side. When a local journalist pressed him repeatedly with a complicated question in halting English, Atherton muttered, 'Somebody remove this buffoon.' At the time, amid the hubbub of the press conference, the remark was hardly noticed. But when journalists played back their tape cassettes, there it was. Atherton had called a Pakistani journalist a buffoon. It was front-page news. Once again, the English were behaving like bad losers. The Pakistan Federal Union of Journalists demanded an apology. It seemed Atherton was disinclined to give them one. On the captain's behalf, Barclay issued a terse note of contrition, 'I am sorry if I caused offence to local journalists.' The 'apology' was accepted only grudgingly by the Pakistani press.

The English had already blotted their copy book. In contrast to the PR-minded South Africans, they had expressed disgruntlement at every turn, as if they still begrudged the decision to hold the World Cup in south Asia. At Peshawar, they wanted to practise on a pitch adjacent to the match strip. But as their opponents had already practised in the outfield and the ground staff had orders to keep the players away from the square, they were denied permission. An England player pulled out a thousand rupees and asked a senior official, in the presence of his subordinates, if this would make a difference. He was outraged. The newspapers reported that someone in the England camp had attempted to bribe the groundsmen. Barclay insisted that 'no money was offered in the sense described in the story'. According to the local press, at Rawalpindi, the day before the match against South Africa, the English had 'barged into the ground while the staff were drying it out' and then 'ignored the Deputy Commissioner's request not to use a ball'.

Of course, there was an element of revenge here. When the Pakistanis had last toured England in 1992, they had been vilified as 'cheats' by the British tabloids. But the irritation with the English spread to both sides of the border and had deeper roots. Every other team management in the World Cup briefed journalists of all countries together. Only the English insisted on briefing their 'own' journalists first. An elderly Indian cricket writer, a man who had studied in England and hero-worshipped Peter May and Ted Dexter, Fred Trueman and Jim Laker, singled me out to vent his disgust with the English cricket-writing fraternity. 'They want the best of everything when they come here, but they don't want to know us when we go there.' In Bombay's *Mid-Day*, Ayaz Menon observed that the English press lived a life of luxury in India and Pakistan, staying in the best hotels, dining in the most expensive restaurants, rarely exposed to the discomforts of life outside the air-con zones. 'Then they write about the hardship of touring the sub-continent.'

In India and Pakistan, many were mystified by Atherton's 'buffoon' remark. How could a well-spoken, Cambridge-educated chap commit such a blunder? It would appear that south Asians are as in thrall to stereotypes of the English as are the English to stereotypes of south Asians. Perhaps too much was made of Atherton's exhausted impatience, but the English, players and press alike, made things worse by dismissing every reaction to their casually offensive behaviour as 'oversensitive'. The England player who pulled out his thousand rupees had no intention of insulting. He would never have considered behaving in such a manner at home; indeed he would have been shocked had anyone else done so. Had someone somewhere told him that bribery was how business was conducted in the sub-continent? This received wisdom was in keeping with the traditional English view of the orient as a place of mystery where nothing and no one can be trusted – not the food, the officials, the pitches or the umpires – and everything and everyone could be bought. At the outset of the World Cup Atherton had observed that 'it's easy to get frustrated or negative when you come to the sub-continent'. Of course, the harsh inequalities in global economic development mean that life in the third world, even for the privileged, is rarely as smooth as it is in the first. But nowhere outside of south Asia are foreign cricketers made such a fuss of. Nowhere else would Atherton and his men receive such a warm welcome from ordinary people. The pity of the English perspective was that it prevented the players from enjoying either the sub-continent or the World Cup. Where other teams with limited resources played above themselves, the English consistently under-performed. I found myself in the unaccustomed position of explaining to friends in India and Pakistan that the English players were really much better than they appeared.

The siege mentality which the English adopted as soon as they set foot on sub-continental soil was, I suspect, their biggest handicap. Unable to establish a rapport with their environment, they lost faith in themselves. Sunil Gavaskar called them the *bakras* of the World Cup – its sacrificial goats.

A 'mob' was predicted for Pakistan's match with Holland, the first World Cup match at Lahore. The day before, police had staged a full-dress crowd control rehearsal. On the morning of the match, thousands of cops surrounded the stadium. Wearing chest protectors, knee and shin guards, and ancient metal helmets with rusting visors, they looked like batsmen going out to face a fast bowler on a green top. But there was no mob to police, just a desultory sprinkling of fans.

Half the Dutch side, including the captain, Steve Lubbers, had come down with diarrhoea after eating spaghetti at their hotel, but it didn't seem to dim their spirits. Before leaving for the World Cup, they had sought advice from Hans Jorritsma, the Dutch hockey star who had coached in Pakistan, who urged the team to relax and enjoy the trip. On the rain-softened grass Wasim and Waqar ran in gingerly, but were still too quick for the qualifiers. Nolan Clarke, at forty-seven the oldest man in the tournament, had once hit 160 against an MCC touring side in Barbados, but today, opening for Holland, he was out for a duck to Aqib. The highlight of the Dutch innings was the determined resistance of left-handed Flavian Aponso, who arrived at the crease with the score 29 for 3. Aponso was a Sri Lankan who had been barred from international cricket after joining the rebel Sri Lankan tour to South Africa in the mid eighties. He was now employed at the Sri Lankan embassy in the Hague, and at the age of forty-three was enjoying a last, unexpected appearance in big-time cricket. He struck Mushtaq for a six, but could not lay his bat on the fast bowlers. He worked the spinners for singles, played and missed, snicked and streaked, revelling in his luck. The pace remained funereal throughout and he had reached 58 from 106 balls when he was finally bowled by Waqar. The Dutch completed their fifty overs for 145 runs.

The crowd grew gradually during the day until it filled a quarter of the seats. 'DIL DIL JAAN JAAN PAKISTAN' (Heart, Life, Pakistan) read one banner. 'PAKI POWER' and 'PAKI TIGERS' declared others. Someone had superimposed a picture of Imran Khan on a Pakistani flag. Once again Sohail was out early to a rash stroke. Holland's two English county veterans, Bakker and Lefebvre, bowled their seamers with expertise to restrict the Pakistanis to 34 for 1 after fourteen overs. But as soon as the two front-line bowlers retired, Ijaz and Saeed cut and drove at will. The scattered spectators managed a Mexican wave. With rain threatening, the Pakistanis were under pressure to score quickly. They needed two points from this match to keep them on target for first place in their group, and a quarter-final fixture on Pakistani soil. Ijaz perished for 39, but Saeed finished the match with a six over long on, taking him to 83 off 93 balls. The rain came down and the crowd rushed from the stadium.

'Where are the crowds?' the editorials kept asking. It did not help that no one knew where or how to buy tickets. Even people who usually boasted of their connections seemed stymied. You could buy a corporate package from IMG for all the Lahore fixtures for Rs14,000 (£280), but where could you buy two ordinary seats for a single match? No tickets were on sale at any cricket grounds anywhere in the country. The National Bank of Pakistan was supposed to be the sales agent, but fans who besieged its branch offices were often told that tickets were sold out or not available. Bank officials claimed that Pilcom had given them all to sponsors or politicians. Others were being hoarded for sale later. If Pakistan played in the final, the tickets would be priceless.

Journalists of all nations united in their impatience with the first-round matches, and it was widely argued that the minnows had devalued the tournament. To me, one-sided first-round matches seem the necessary concomitant of any genuinely global tournament. No doubt the details of the format could be improved, but not at the expense of wider participation. As Hanif Mohammed said, 'Today's minnows are tomorrow's whales.' I suspect the intensity of the build-up left many people feeling deflated when the competition finally started and the initial results seemed so inconsequential. But it takes time for any sizeable tournament to gather steam, and I for one was thoroughly enjoying myself. I had not come here to ogle super-stars. I had come here to find out about cricket and what it meant to particular people in particular places. I decided that if Sri Lanka were eliminated, I wanted to see Pakistan retain the title, though not necessarily if they played India, in which case I had no idea whom I wanted to win.

6

Bombay *v* Mumbai

I arrived in Bombay sleepless after a night spent in Karachi airport writing an article for the Indian press about Atherton's 'buffoon' blunder and 'what's wrong with the English'. The drive to the centre of town took even longer than usual because of the dense morning traffic, augmented by spectators flocking to the Australia–India match at Wankhede Stadium. 'Catch a drop today!' the Pepsi adverts winked. 'It's the day of the Aussie attack. And cheering India on is gonna be thirsty work.' On a rickety old residence somewhere near Malabar Hill, a banner read, 'WORLD CUP ONLY BRIGHT SPOT ON INDIAN HORIZON'.

The poet Nissim Ezekiel, a member of Bombay's Bene-Israel community (his nephew Gulu, the cricket scholar, is compiling an exhaustive catalogue of the hidden links between cricket and Jews) called Bombay a 'barbaric city sick with slums'. That it is, but it is also a city of intoxicating intensity, a kaleidoscope of human variety. One of the reasons I have always liked Bombay is that it reminds me of New York. Not so much the New York of today, or even the New York of my youth, but the *noir* New York of the thirties and forties, the New York of movies and novels, glitter and slime. It is a city of strangers, a welter of neighbourhoods dense with economic activity, legal and illegal, luring provincials on to the road to riches, ruin, or both.

I checked into the cheapest hotel I could find within walking distance of the ground. The room was minute but clean, and there was a television. I showered and watched the New Zealand batsmen dismember the UAE attack in Faisalabad, then strolled out into the mid-day heat to fax my copy to the *Indian Express*.

Vast queues radiated outwards from every access to the stadium, spilling into adjacent roads and even over the Churchgate railway tracks. A local politician had sponsored a number of neatly painted banners hailing 'INDIAN–AUSTRALIAN FRIENDSHIP' in English and Hindi. A message on a rough-hewn banner carried by fans was more partisan: 'LET'S MAKE CHICKENS OUT OF KANGAROOS'. The queues moved at a snail's pace, supervised by an army of police and private security guards who confiscated 'unofficial' banners and placards, musical instruments, bottles, and newspapers, traditionally rolled up to use as flaming torches by Indian fans at day–night games. Even the journalists were searched on the way in, and attempts to relieve them of their newspapers, essential tools of their trade, provoked outraged protests.

At nearby University Stadium, the IMG had set up India's first corporate hospitality marquees. For US$500 per head, guests enjoyed air-conditioning, champagne, a buffet lunch and a supper. Coke, Star TV, Asian Paints and BPC had each booked an entire tent. If you wanted to, you could spend the whole day here, watching the cricket on television. The signal was sent from the ground to London, from London to Hong Kong and then back from Hong Kong to Bombay, so that you could hear the roar of the crowd seconds before your screen showed the wicket fall or the ball struck to the boundary.

Since my last visit, Wankhede had been spruced up at a cost of £2.4 million and a capacity reduced by 5000. New dressing rooms had been constructed. A state-of-the-art Megavision electronic scoreboard with giant replay screen had been installed over the west stand. Overhead, floodlights loomed like creatures from H.G. Wells's *War of the Worlds.* There was a new air-conditioned, glassed-in two-tier press box, with power points aplenty for laptops, and access to a media centre with all the high-tech trimmings. When I was last here, the press box was open to the air, separated from the crowd by only a wire fence. When Nana Patekar, Bollywood's reigning macho rebel, and a Shiv Sena supporter, entered the box, the fans in the adjacent seats pressed against the fence and cried out his name. He acknowledged the clamour with a cry of 'Jai Hind!' then sat himself down next to Sunil Gavaskar. Now we were hermetically sealed from the crowd. Their roar reached us as from a distance. I know this is the way it is at most top sports grounds, but I can't help but feel that it exacerbates the tunnel-vision to which journalists are prone. They see the same match as the spectators but they rarely share the same conditions. If they did, there might be more protest about the myriad inconveniences with which Indian cricket fans have to contend.

According to the *Times of India*, 'the scramble for tickets had reached unprecedented proportions.' On the tops of nearby buildings, spectators sat in chairs under temporary awnings. In this city of Mammon, many had paid exorbitantly for these unofficial vantage points. In contrast to Pakistan, where stadium advertising was largely restricted to multinationals, Wankhede was decked out with the insignia of indigenous industry: Roofit Cement Sheets, Sonora Wall Tiles, Vikram Premium Cements, Mahindra Armada, Bajaj. Symbolically, the two ends of the ground are named after Tata and Garware, two giant Indian industrial houses, and the stadium as a whole is named after a local politician (like New York's Shea Stadium, home of the Mets, but unlike any football or cricket ground in Britain).

As the crowd settled in their seats, unfurled their Indian flags and started to fan themselves with their 'official' Coca-Cola placards, the Megavision screen flickered to life for the first time, filled with the giant face of Manohar Joshi, chief minister of

Maharashtra, welcoming cricket lovers to Wankhede with his rigid politician's grin. The crowd were familiar with the face and ignored the message. Moments later, Joshi entered the VIP enclosure directly in front of the press box, and took a seat in one of the elaborately gilded, high-backed wooden chairs. A waiter in livery served tea and cold drinks, while the guests took turns paying homage to their chief minister, congratulating him on staging this wonderful World Cup spectacle.

The last time I had been in Bombay I had made a point of visiting Shivaji Park, named after Maharashtra's eighteenth-century martial hero. Today it is Indian cricket's field of dreams. Among the dozens of Test players it has nurtured are Gavaskar, Tendulkar and Vinod Kambli. On the afternoon I visited its coarse, stubbled acres, the park teemed with white-flannelled boys playing, practising and talking cricket. I tried to count the number of games underway, but they were so crammed together it was impossible to tell where one ended and another began. Parents and coaches cajoled their young charges, threatening punishment, promising the earth: the fame and wealth of a career in international cricket. As the sun sank into the Arabian Sea, Shivaji Park was animated with the same dream whose radiance lights up the basketball courts of Chicago housing projects and the football pitches of São Paulo slums: the dream that, with talent and luck, anyone can make it.

'Whatever I am in the game today', confessed Sunil Gavaskar, 'is due to the fact that I have been nursed in the cradle of cricket, that is Bombay.' Here, 150 years ago, Parsi merchants first set out to beat the English at their own game. By the end of the nineteenth century, cricket had spread to all religious communities in the city, and each community had its own club. In 1906, the Hindus played the Europeans for the first time, and the Hindus won, thanks to the extraordinary left-arm slow bowling of Palwankar Baloo. Baloo was not only the first great Indian spin bowler and perhaps the first great cricketer produced in

India, he was also the first untouchable to play for the Hindus, the Jackie Robinson of Indian cricket. Normally the brahmins who dominated the Hindu Gymkhana would not consider rubbing shoulders with a member of the *chamaar* (leather-working) caste, but their desire to defeat the English outweighed their prejudice. The Hindus' victory was hailed in the nationalist press, which saw in it a lesson for the emergent nation: India would be stronger if caste distinctions were overcome.

Joined by his three younger brothers, Baloo made the Hindus a force in the early years of the communal competition that became the country's pre-eminent annual cricket tournament. This was a fortnight-long festival of cricket, the high point of the city's social calendar, the original Indian cricket *tamasha* (popular spectacle). In 1907 it was launched as a Triangular contest, between Hindus, Parsis and Europeans. In 1912, when the Muslims joined, it became a Quadrangular. In 1937, a team comprised of the Rest (Christians, Jews, Buddhists, Eurasians) made it 'the Pentangular'. Because the teams were drawn from all over the country, it was highly competitive. If you wanted to make your mark on Indian cricket, you had to do so in Bombay.

Baloo was acknowledged by fans and fellow players as the leading Hindu cricketer of his day, but he never captained the Hindu team in the Triangular or Quadrangular, despite a campaign on his behalf in the press. For the lawyers and merchants who ran the gymkhana, it was one thing to have an untouchable in the team; quite another to appoint him its leader. At one point, Baloo's brothers boycotted the team in protest at the committee's 'unsportsmanlike' behaviour. In 1923, under the influence of Gandhi's campaign against untouchability, Baloo's brother Vithal was appointed captain, and the Hindus went on to win the championship for the first time in years. The nationalist press reported it as a victory for 'Hindus who forget caste prejudice'. (It is curious how elites in various societies fetishise cricket captaincy. Think of the long, rearguard resistance that had to be overcome before Len Hutton was appointed

England's first 'professional' captain, in 1952, and Frank Worrell the West Indies' first black captain, in 1960.) Baloo was a leader within his own community as well as on the cricket field. In 1932 he was one of three untouchables (along with the great Dr Ambedkar, who concluded that to break from caste it was necessary to break from Hinduism) who negotiated the compromise pact that ended Gandhi's fast against separate electorates for the depressed castes.

With the rise of the Muslim League and the growth of communal violence in the 1930s, a stream of nationalist opinion turned against the Quadrangular, which seemed to mirror the insidious 'two nation' theory. Newspapers attacked the competition as divisive and urged a public boycott. In 1934, the Ranji Trophy, India's first first-class competition, in which the teams were drawn up on a regional rather than communal basis, emerged as an alternative. In 1940, Gandhi himself came out against the 'unsportsmanlike divisions' of communal cricket. Despite Gandhi, despite the campaign waged on the streets by nationalists, the matches were packed that year, as always. However the tournament was perceived in the rest of India, in Bombay the crowds were said to be non-communal and generous to opponents. C.K. Nayudu, captain of the Hindus, said, 'It has brought the communities together, not divided them.' So even then there was the same conundrum I had been musing over since I arrived on the sub-continent: does competing in cricket bring people together or drive them apart?

The Pentangular was abandoned after World War II, a victim of the cascade of events that led to Partition. In the meantime Bombay had established itself as the premier force in the Ranji Trophy, which it has won thirty-three times, and a rich source of talent for the national side. Generation after generation, Bombay has produced great batsmen, noted for their powers of concentration, technical correctness, and reliability in a crisis: Vijay Merchant, Rusi Modi, Vijay Manjrekar, Polly Umrigar, Dilip Sardesai, Farookh Engineer, Ajit Wadekar, Eknath Solkar,

Sunil Gavaskar, Dillip Vengsarkar, Ravi Shastri. Indeed, Bombay's domination of Indian cricket, much resented by cricket lovers in other regions, gave rise to a classic cricket joke. Superman flies from Metropolis to offer his services to the Indian Test selectors, who are meeting in a secret room in an expensive hotel. They look at him suspiciously.

'Can you bat?' they ask.

'I guarantee that I will hit a six off every ball bowled to me and that I will never get out.'

'Can you bowl?'

'I guarantee to take a wicket with every ball I bowl and to bowl all day if need be.'

'Can you field?'

'I guarantee to stop the other team taking any runs off any ball they hit anywhere in the field.'

The selectors mutter among themselves.

'Ah,' they ask at last, 'but are you from Bombay?'

Over the years, the wealthy Parsis and Gujeratis who had dominated Bombay cricket were replaced by Marathi-speaking boys from Dadar and Shivaji Park. The first middle-class Maharashtrian to make it big in Bombay cricket was Vijay Manjrekar, and after him the floodgates opened. Among his successors are Gavaskar and Tendulkar and Vijay's son, Sanjay.

The changing balance of forces in Bombay cricket was symbolised by the transfer of Test matches from Brabourne Stadium to the new Wankhede in 1975. The Brabourne was the private property of a private club, the Cricket Club of India, just as Lord's is the property of the MCC. Indeed, the CCI had always relished the analogy. The Brabourne was India's first modern cricket stadium, built in 1937 by a consortium of merchants, industrialists and princes on land leased from the colonial government (Lord Brabourne was the governor). As the best appointed ground in the city, it hosted the Pentangular, the Ranji Trophy and the Tests. Although the CCI was only one of the three hundred clubs affiliated to the Bombay Cricket Association, which had responsibility for organising cricket in the city, it retained the bulk of the revenue from Test matches staged there. Meanwhile the burgeoning BCA demanded an increased ticket allowance for the big events at the Brabourne; under the chairmanship of Vijay Merchant, the former master opening batsman and one of the leading figures of the old elite, the CCI refused. The BCA decided to build its own stadium. Its president, S.K. Wankhede, a Congress politician, secured land from the state government (then under Congress control) only a mile from Brabourne and raised money from private corporations to build the stadium in less than a year. Since then, the Brabourne, still the home of the CCI – and still one of the most attractive big grounds in the country – has been denied Test cricket.

The takeover of Bombay cricket by the Maharashtrian middle class was mirrored by the rise of a political force that claimed to speak on its behalf. In 1966, Bal Thackeray harangued the first rally of the Shiv Sena in Shivaji Park. This army of Shivaji was to fight for jobs for Maharashtrians, which, Thackeray claimed, were being stolen by south Indians who had migrated to the city. Combining urban nativism and strong-arm tactics, Thackeray, described as 'part godman, part godfather', built Shiv Sena into a potent political force. He is the model for Raman Fielding in Salman Rushdie's *The Moor's Last Sigh*, a charismatic bully who divides his *goonda* (Party musclemen) into cricket-style 'elevens' before sending them out to bash up opponents.

Flamboyantly autocratic, Thackeray openly admires Hitler and detests leftists of all stripes. In alliance with local industrialists, his goonda helped break the year-long textile workers' strike of the early eighties, a struggle which played a role in recent Indian history analogous to the miners' strike in Britain in 1984–85. In the years that followed, in an attempt to spread its base outwards from Bombay, Shiv Sena boarded the Hindutva bandwagon. Its rhetoric became bombastically nationalistic, with Muslims increasingly singled out as the enemy within. 'It is the duty of Muslims to prove they are not Pakistani,' said Thackeray. He invented his own version of the Tebbit test, declaring that he wanted to see Indian Muslims 'with tears in their eyes' whenever India lost to Pakistan. That he predicated his test on the assumption of Indian defeat spoke volumes about the resentment and impotence he was trying to exploit. He also waged a campaign against Pakistan playing cricket in India. In the pages of *Saamna*, the Sena's venomously 'pro-Hindu' daily paper (with a circulation of 150,000), Thackeray argued that the very presence of the Pakistani team on Indian soil was an insult to the nation's integrity and a menace to its security. His threatening rhetoric became reality in October 1991, when a scheduled visit from the Pakistanis was cancelled after Shiv Sena activists poured oil on the Wankhede wicket. Thackeray had proved that he could exercise a veto on cricket in Bombay. It was a shock to cricket lovers, who fondly believed that Bombay, with its unparalleled devotion to the game, would remain out of the reach of politicians.

But Shiv Sena had made a beach-head in Bombay cricket even before the vandalism at Wankhede. In 1988, Manohar Joshi, the Shiv Sena member of the Legislative Assembly for the Dadar constituency, which includes Shivaji Park, was elected vice-president of the BCA. Joshi had no roots in cricket, but he sold himself as a cricket lover to the local clubs, which knew that in Bombay it was always useful to be on the Shiv Sena's good side. He was brought into the BCA by Ajit Wadekar, who hoped to exploit Joshi's political clout in his fight against the faction currently ruling the BCA, led by former Ranji player Madhav Mantri, who also happened to be Sunil Gavaskar's uncle. In the 1992 elections for BCA president, Mantri was defeated by Joshi, who had used Shiv Sena connections to mobilise the vote.

Shiv Sena had strongly backed the campaign to build a Ram temple on the site of the Babri Masjid in Ayodhya, and Thackeray exulted over the demolition of the mosque in December 1992. At last, the Hindus had struck back against 'Muslim arrogance'. In January 1993, Bombay was ripped asunder by the worst communal violence seen since Partition. Thirteen hundred were killed. The riot was, in fact, a pogrom against the Muslim community, organised by Shiv Sena goonda with the connivance of the local police. Muslims of all classes – including several who had played Ranji Trophy cricket for Bombay – were insulted and assaulted, their homes looted or burnt down. Police opened fire on two mosques and a Friday prayer congregation and slaughtered twelve Muslim workers in a bakery. Thackeray rejoiced: the Muslims had been taught 'a lesson'.

One of the heroes of that horror was Sunil Gavaskar, who intervened to stop some goonda from beating a Muslim family in the street near his home. It seems even the goonda were overawed at the matchless prestige which Gavaskar enjoys in Bombay. He had already clashed with the Shiv Sena earlier in the year. Once India had been eliminated from the 1992 World Cup, Gavaskar, commentating on television, said that he would now switch his allegiance to Pakistan, since they were India's neighbours. Grateful for the support, Imran Khan invited Gavaskar to attend the Pakistan victory celebration in Lahore. Thackeray warned Gavaskar not to go, and muttered darkly that he might not be welcome back in Bombay if he supped with Imran. Gavaskar shrugged off the threat. Bombay was more his city than Thackeray's.

Within months of the riots, Bombay's commercial heart was devastated by a massive, well-coordinated but mysterious series of explosions. The bomb blasts, assumed to be some kind of revenge for the anti-Muslim pogrom, gave rise to more conspiracy theories than JFK's assassination. A vast network of 'anti-national' forces was said to be behind the atrocity: Muslim Mafiosi, Bollywood actors, Gulf-based businessmen were all part of the plot, not to mention the Pakistani intelligence service. It was the same Bombay–Karachi–Dubai syndicate that was said to have corrupted Pakistani cricket.

In the March 1995 state elections, the Shiv Sena, in alliance with the BJP, swept to power in Maharashtra. Manohar Joshi was sworn in as chief minister in front of a huge, saffron-swathed crowd in Shivaji Park. In attendance was the sheriff of Bombay, Sunil Gavaskar, whose offer to resign the honorary post following the election result had been craftily rejected by Joshi. The new state government launched a crackdown on immigrants from Bangladesh and other parts of India ('We must start a permit system as in Russia,' said Thackeray), harassed Muslims by using the voters' lists to check for 'illegal immigrants', extended the ban on cow slaughter to bullocks, and changed the name of the city to Mumbai, invoking Mumbadevi, one of the area's resident Hindu deities.

'Bombay was central,' wrote Salman Rushdie, 'all rivers flowed into its human sea.' Over the years, however, ruthless commerce and political bigotry had transformed the temper of the city. The riots and bomb blasts had not deterred the entry of international capital, and there was talk of the city becoming a new Hong Kong. Land values multiplied and skyscrapers soared while one third of the population lived in cramped, makeshift hovels. The city that had been founded as a port of entry for British commerce, India's opening to the world and the world's access to India, was now the heartland of the most virulent and narrow-minded chauvinism. Delightfully cosmopolitan, chaotically multicultural Bombay was being refashioned into straitjacketed Mumbai. 'It was no longer my Bombay,' wrote Rushdie, 'no longer special, no longer the city of mixed-up mongrel joy.'

The transformation cost the city the right to stage a World Cup quarter- or semi-final. Joshi, now a vice-president of the Indian Cricket Board as well as president of the renamed Mumbai Cricket Association, appealed to the organisers to grant the city the kind of Cup fixture its status in Indian cricket demanded. But even as he did so he must have known that the authorities would not risk it, especially given Thackeray's latest outbursts. The ageing Shiv Sena boss warned that Pakistan intelligence would use the World Cup to infiltrate thousands of agents into India 'under the guise of being cricket fans'. Even the all-conquering multinationals were not beyond the range of

Thackeray's increasingly grandiose threats: 'If Pepsi or Coke sponsors Pakistan players, their bottles will be broken and their banners torn apart.'

The only way to guarantee that the Pakistanis would not play in Bombay was to deny the city a quarter- or semi-final. Accordingly it was assigned the commercially attractive but politically innocuous first-round league tie between India and Australia.

For all the nationalist rhetoric, Joshi's government proved itself eager to do business with foreign capital, and as chief minister he visited the boardrooms of Ford in Detroit and Hyundai in Korea. Over the years, Shiv Sena had gone upmarket. The original Maharashtrian base had been fragmented by economic development and the rise of caste-based politics. Now the Shiv Sena bosses were themselves part of the elite, and they used cricket to appeal to the sons and daughters of the elite. Thackeray's attempts to interfere in the World Cup were an embarrassment to many of his supporters, not least Manohar Joshi.

The day before the India–Australia tie large sections of the city were paralysed by a *band* (strike) called by Dalit, Muslim and left political groups. Although police arrested 1300 as a 'preventive measure', road and rail traffic was blocked, stones were thrown and cars set on fire. The demonstration was a protest against the Shiv Sena government's scrapping of the Minorities Commission and the Srikrishna Commission, which was inquiring into the riots of 1992–93, and the withdrawal of cases against Shiv Sena activists accused of atrocities against Dalits and Muslims. It was one of the most impressive displays of Dalit militancy, and of Dalit–Muslim unity, the city had seen in years.

Like Manohar Joshi, Gavaskar and Tendulkar are Brahmins. Vinod Kambli is a Dalit, one of a handful who have played for India since the days of Palwankar Baloo. It is said that these distinctions, like religious distinctions, mean nothing in the Bombay dressing room. Yet while the cricketers mix happily, as they do elsewhere, most of the Bombay players are casual supporters of Shiv Sena, whom they see as *apne log*, our people, i.e., Maharashtrians. They have little difficulty reconciling their loyalty to Shiv Sena with the impact of Shiv Sena on the lives of some of their team-mates. Non-Maharashtrian cricketers (Gujeratis, south Indians, Christians, Muslims) complain that they have been squeezed out of the side. 'I have to score 400 to every century a Maharashtrian player has to make,' said one. Maharashtrians reply that others are not willing to work at cricket as hard as they do.

Everyone at Wankhede was anticipating something special from two of the most ambitious teams in the tournament. If the Indians could win today, against the favourites, people would start to believe that they could go all the way to Lahore and take back the Cup. After their victory in Gwalior, they were confident, but questions remained. Had they prepared properly for this World Cup? Would their fielding let them down, as it had in the past? What would happen if Tendulkar was dismissed early? Above all, had they found the right mix of batsmen and bowlers? Kapil Dev's phenomenal career had left India with an addiction to all-rounders, and the side had looked unbalanced not merely since his retirement but since his powers had begun to wane several years earlier. Manoj Prabhakar had repeatedly proved himself a flinty competitor but was not in Kapil's class, either as bowler or batsman. And the decision to leave out Sidhu, and replace him with Manjrekar, did nothing to resolve this dilemma, though it succeeded in annoying Sidhu.

Having forfeited their tie in Colombo to the Sri Lankans, the Australians had played only one match so far, against Kenya. They had lost a couple of early wickets before the Waugh brothers had stroked them to a huge total. The Indians represented their first real challenge of the tournament and an indicator of their collective state of mind. Like other teams in the run-up to the World Cup, the Australians had been tinkering with their top order batting. At the beginning of the year, Mark Waugh had been promoted to open with Taylor, and had been scoring heavily. The surprise at Wankhede was that it was Taylor, and not Waugh, who assumed the aggressor's role in the early overs. In the past, the Australian captain had usually played the stonewaller, the stolid accumulator providing anchorage for the stroke-makers around him. Today, he took the charge to India, and in spite of challenging bowling from Srinath, and a succession of unsuccessful lbw appeals, he drove powerfully, often lofting the ball over the ring of fielders, while the phlegmatic Waugh took a backseat. In fifteen overs, they put on 74 runs, and psychologically nullified much of India's home advantage.

Nonetheless, the crowd refused to despair. They applauded Taylor's shots while encouraging the Indians in the field. And they were rewarded. Azhar's men kept their wits about them and refused to panic. Tight fielding and containing bowling from the spinners, Kumble and Raju, choked the flow of runs. With the score 117 for 1, in the twenty-first over, persistence paid off, when Taylor hoisted Raju to long on, where he was caught by Srinath for 59 off 73 balls. For the first time, the Indian flags waved. The duel between Waugh and Raju was a treat. Going around the wicket, Raju speared the ball into the batsman's legs. It was flat, defensive spin bowling, but it was defiant and mean. With delicate, deliberate steps, Waugh was always in position to play a controlled stroke. Even when pushing for singles he looked elegantly balanced. It was a tense passage of play in which minutiae counted for a great deal, and the crowd appreciated it. When Waugh reached his fifty by sweeping Raju for six, they applauded warmly.

With the score at 140 in the thirtieth over, the second wicket fell. Ponting miscued Raju to backward point, where Manjrekar, at full stretch, sneaked his fingertips between the ball and the grass. It was one of a series of catches taken in the World Cup that seemed to defy the laws of physics. That these laws are inexorable and blind to justice was, however, confirmed a few overers later when Raju deflected Mark Waugh's drive on to the stumps at the non-striker's end, running out Steve Waugh for 7. The Indians felt, for the first time, that the advantage might be swinging to them. Their bowlers and fielders maintained the pressure, but Mark Waugh's slowly maturing innings blossomed. Scoring freely, he was as precise in placing his singles as he was in driving to the boundary on either side of the wicket. With Law at the other end, Australia looked set to score 280 or more. As ever, when runs flowed, Azhar brought back Kumble. Throughout the tournament, Kumble darted in and out of the Indian attack, bowling abbreviated spells, and somehow maintained his concentration and perturbing length and bounce.

When Mark Waugh reached his 100 in 120 balls, the crowd rose to its feet. The new electronic scoreboard announced that this was the first time anyone had hit back-to-back centuries in the World Cup. But I think the spectators were acknowledging the memorable quality, not merely the record-breaking quantity, of Waugh's play. Australia's two hundred came up in the same over when Waugh smashed Srinath, hard, flat and low over mid wicket for six. In baseball, it would have been a perfect line drive double to left field. Together Waugh and Law put on 50 runs (and demolished Prabhakar) between the fortieth and forty-sixth overs, when Waugh was run out for 126, over half the Australian total. As he walked off, he received a prolonged standing ovation.

Thanks to India's best fielding display in the World Cup, Australia managed to add only 26 runs in the final five overs. Four wickets fell in the chaotic last over, off which no runs were scored. Warne was out for a duck, to the delight of the crowd, and a Mexican wave celebrated the strong Indian finish: 258 was an achievable target.

As darkness loomed, floodlights illuminated Wankhede for the first time. I am hooked on floodlit cricket; for me it combines grand opera, stadium rock, pantomime. In that pool of intense light, colours are garish, small gestures are exaggerated, drama is amplified. It is the ideal setting for the gladiatorial combat of one-day international cricket. At Wankhede, the grandeur of the scene penetrated even the glassed-in press box.

The electronic scoreboard told us that there were 41,000 spectators present. It was the flashiest cricket crowd I have ever seen in India, overwhelmingly upper middle class, with a fair number of young women in skirts and halters (a rare sight at Indian cricket grounds) and a sprinkling of celebrity glamour. During the interval, Bindra entered the VIP box in front of us. He paid his respects to Joshi, then left. The chief minister's smile remained fixed. Throughout the match, the Megavision scoreboard had flashed cues to the spectators: 'Top shot!', 'What a catch!', 'Come on India!' as if a Bombay crowd needed to be coached to do its part. In the United States, spectators at sports contests are spoonfed their entertainment, announcers read out statistics, recorded pop music sets the mood, appropriate chants are rehearsed on huge overhead monitors and professional cheerleaders act as mediators between the fans and the game. In other words, seeing sport live is made to seem as much as possible like seeing it on television. In the process the crowd is atomised and stripped of its collective creativity. It is a triumph for 'official' popular culture, at the expense of the spontaneity, irreverence, scepticism, and, yes, disorderliness of the 'unofficial' variety. Indian cricket has a long way to go before it reaches these depths, but the intrusion of the Megavision screen at Wankhede was a disturbing portent of things to come.

Like the Australians, but with less success, the Indians had been experimenting with their opening pair. As in Gwalior, they nominated Jadeja to join Tendulkar, but Jadeja (a member of the ex-royal family of Nawanagar, which also produced Ranjitsinhji and Duleepsinhji) looked edgy from the first. The Indians were trying to implement the fashionable 'pinch-hitter' theory, but like other teams which kept juggling their orders looking for the right blend of defence and attack, they ended up merely swapping a middle-order for a top-order batsman. The Sri Lankans, the

Pakistanis and the Australians had shown that there was an art to exploiting the fielding restrictions in the first fifteen overs, but it was an art that Jadeja had yet to master. With a confused squint, he shuffled across the line and was given out lbw to Fleming for 1.

Kambli joined Tendulkar, two Bombay boys batting together for India before their home crowd, as they had once done for Shardashram school. With jet-black ponytail poking through his baseball cap, rakish sideboards, goatee, and dropped gold earrings, no one could match Kambli as the fashion plate of the tournament. At bat, with his red bandanna tied around his forehead and his ponytail protruding from under his helmet, he looked like a ninja turtle prepared for cartoon battle. The decision to send Kambli in at number three, especially after the fall of an early wicket, set off agitated mutterings among the Indian press. What India needed now was that other Bombay boy, Sanjay Manjrekar, and Kambli should have been saved for the slog at the end. Fleming slanted the ball across the left-hander's body. For some unfathomable reason, Kambli tried to turn it to leg, played across the line and was bowled for a duck. The jeremiahs in the press box took no joy in their prophecies being fulfilled so quickly and comprehensively; not for the first time, they wanted to know: just what was going on inside that handsome head?

McGrath had bowled four overs for 4 runs when Tendulkar launched his assault. Pulling the quick bowler over the infield, hooking him off his chin, driving through the air (safely but only just), lashing him through the covers, Tendulkar set off on what Ian Chappell was to call 'one of the finest counter-attacks I've ever seen on a cricket field'. He cut Fleming backward of point, then drove him off the front foot through long on. But he was living dangerously. McGrath knocked a hard drive into the air but couldn't grab the rebound. Tendulkar had arrived at the crease with a string of big scores behind him. As he unveiled his ever-growing repertoire of scoring strokes before the adoring multitude under the Wankhede floodlights, he was more than confident. He was ambition – middle-class, Bombay ambition – personified. He wanted to show the world what he could do. Despite his height, Tendulkar is no chirpy urchin. His frame and his game are muscular.

The stadium reverberated with the roar of 'Sachin! Sachin! Sachin!' Each stroke was like a shot of adrenalin, yet each was accompanied by fear and trembling. There would be one too many daring shots, and it would all end, suddenly and catastrophically. For the partisan, which is to say for several hundred million people in India, there is a special nail-biting, hair-tearing drama to a Tendulkar innings. Where Mark Waugh was serene, playing all the classical strokes, and never seemed in danger, Tendulkar was impudent and experimental, and never seemed out of danger. To the technical orthodoxy he had inherited from the Bombay school of batsmanship, he added a new dimension of improvised but clinical power-hitting, developed to meet the demands of the one-day game. Critics had long urged him to curb his attacking instincts. They told him that if he played fewer risky shots he could emulate Lara, occupy the crease for hours and make huge scores. They wanted a second Gavaskar, but Gavaskar himself was wise enough to urge Tendulkar to perfect his own style.

The crowd revelled in Tendulkar's aggression. This was clean-edged, angular, kinetic one-day batting, worthy to stand, as a contrast and complement, to Waugh's efforts. 'Tonight,' said my friend Pradeep, sitting next to me, 'he is capable of anything.' Somehow the volume of the crowd seemed louder in the night and the Mexican waves more frenzied. But as Taylor introduced Warne to the attack, there was a hush. This was the encounter which the fans had been waiting for. The contest between Raju and Waugh had been tense but discreet. That between Warne and Tendulkar was played out in melodramatic gestures.

With a horizontal bat, Tendulkar swatted Warne's first ball straight back over the bowler's head for a six. He drove the next hard through the air – Warne got his fingertips to it but couldn't hold on. He then sliced a leg break over the slips for a lucky four. Tendulkar had scored ten runs off the over and was living dangerously, but he subsequently reappraised his tactics. In the meantime Azhar, dragging the ball on to his stumps without moving his feet, was bowled by Fleming, snapping up his third key wicket of the match. The night was now black and the floodlights brilliant. Dew glistened on the field and the Australians slipped and skidded as they chased the ball. Manjrekar joined Tendulkar. Taylor set the field with care, making minute but purposeful adjustments, and posting four close fielders for Warne, who now put on a display of flight and turn that at one point left Manjrekar, unable yet again to lay willow on a leg break, flapping one hand in frustration, as if to say, 'How can anyone hit that?' Warne ended his first spell having conceded only 12 runs off his last six overs.

The Indian crowd is fascinated by Warne. It is a common belief that Indians know how to play spin. The English and West Indians might be befuddled by the likes of Warne, but surely not one of their own. So there is a desire to see Indian batsmen prove that Warne is nothing special. But there is also a fascination with the man, combining admiration for his amazing prestidigitation with a cricket ball, and bemusement at his personality – by turns buoyant, matey, whining and aggressive. This morning, the man who had refused to visit Colombo had been seen strolling barefoot in shorts around the Gateway to India (built by the British to welcome themselves to the sub-continent). In Lahore, later in the tournament, he wandered outside the Pearl Continental and hitched a ride with some youths on motor-scooters.

While treating Warne with respect, Tendulkar and Manjrekar kept the score moving by taking easy singles off the bowlers at the other end, for whom the field was spread deep. Tendulkar, on the prowl for boundaries, swung Bevan over mid wicket. In the next over, facing Mark Waugh, he advanced down the pitch, determined to play a shot. Waugh saw him coming, and slipped in a quick, flat wide. Tendulkar missed and Healy stumped him. It had been an extraordinary innings – 90 off 84 balls – but it had ended too soon, as the crowd feared it would, and Tendulkar knew it. Waugh could enjoy the applause as he left the field knowing he had completed the job. For Tendulkar, there was no similar satisfaction. With twenty overs to go, India needed to score 5.75 runs per over. There were 6 wickets in hand, but with Tendulkar out the Indian tail suddenly looked long.

Prabhakar was run out for three. 'Oh for a Kapil Dev!' cried Rajaraman of the *Pioneer*, echoing the thoughts of millions across the country. And briefly, with the entrance on the Wankhede stage of wicket keeper Nayan Mongia in aggressive mood, they may have thought they had one. He cut and drove McGrath, proving not for the first or last time in this World Cup that extra pace on these wickets could work against the bowler in the second half of the innings. As the crowd chanted, 'Mon-gia! Mon-gia!', he and Manjrekar put on 50 runs for the sixth wicket in nine overs. Warne returned in the forty-first over. Pounding their hands together, the spectators beat out an ever-accelerating rhythm, urging the Indian batsmen on in the face of the enemy.

Defying the defensive norms that usually apply at this stage of an innings, Taylor had posted himself at slip. Warne bowled a slower ball. Mongia swung freely and nicked it straight to Taylor. This typically astute piece of captaincy – showing confidence in the bowler and giving him an incentive to attack – probably settled the outcome of the match. In the next over Steve Waugh had Manjrekar caught behind off a thin edge. India needed 53 runs from eight overs with 3 wickets standing. At the wicket, Kumble and Srinath seemed to believe they could do it. When Srinath cut his first ball from Steve Waugh to third man, the crowd perked up. They remembered Srinath's innings against West Indies at this very ground in November 1994, during the Test which saw him finally emerge out of the shadow of Kapil Dev. But Warne was now unplayable. Toying with the tail-enders, almost mocking their plight, he offered them nothing to hit.

Only two runs were scored off his final over, the forty-third of the Indian innings, and he ended with figures of ten overs for 28 runs and 1 wicket. Suddenly 37 runs were needed off 36 balls. The crowd had all but conceded the match, but the tail-enders persisted, chipping away at the total. All perished going for big hits. When Kumble was last out, bowled trying to sweep Fleming, the Indians still needed 16 runs off two overs.

Manohar Joshi joined Ian Chappell for the post-match presentations, and beamed as he handed the man of the match cheque to Mark Waugh. Azhar muttered something about his side playing well but not winning. Kumble looked ready to cry. Warne and Tendulkar engaged in earnest, unsmiling conversation. I wished I was a lip-reader. Slowly, the stadium decanted. A small troop of Australian fans in shorts posed with their national flag next to the wicket. Packed into the exit lanes surrounding the arena, the crowd made its way patiently, a little sadly, into the streets, almost satisfied with the evening's entertainment.

The tie had been advertised as a preview of the World Cup final, and the contest had proved worthy of a final. It provided what turned out to be the second closest finish of the tournament, and was vigorously contested throughout. It was one-day cricket at its dynamic, complex best, and proof that it can rival the pleasures of the extended game. Both sides put on a show of high quality seam and spin bowling, attacking and defensive batting, and athleticism in the field. Each new phase of the game opened new possibilities as varying skills entered the equation and the advantage swung back and forth. For me it confirmed Omar Kureishi's dictum. The element of mind had come to the fore in the one-day game.

The Australians emerged looking invincible. They had depth and variety of talent and a captain adept at marshalling it. In defending a catchable total, they showed efficiency, toughness and flexibility. The Indians had thrown everything they had at them, but it was not enough. In retrospect, Bombay witnessed India's best performance in the Cup, even though the result was disappointing. And despite the city's recent history, despite Manohar Joshi and the Shiv Sena, the Bombay crowd had shown that its first loyalty was still to cricket, and accepted the defeat with decorum and realism.

Late that night I adjourned with some Indian colleagues to Perry's on Veer Nariman Road to drink beer and eat chicken tikka and butter naan. After such an excellent match, the cricket conversation flowed. Azhar, they told me, was not the meek and inoffensive character he seemed, a point they illustrated by recounting labyrinthine tales of faction-fighting and off-the-record press briefings that reminded me of nothing so much as the British Labour Party. Eventually we turned to English cricket, and I was asked, why weren't Ramprakash and Hussain given the same number of chances as Hick? Before I could answer I was told, 'It's about this'. My colleague was touching the brown skin on his forearm.

Picking my way carefully around the street sleepers as I walked back to my hotel, I thought, this is still Bombay. That was the lesson I drew from the match at Wankhede, the best spectacle of pure cricket the World Cup had to offer. Despite Joshi and Thackeray and Shiv Sena, despite Doordarshan and the *Times of India* and Star TV and Pilcom – all of whom insist on calling the city Mumbai – it is still Bombay. A cacophonous *swapna nagar*, city of dreams, where the stuff of dreams is cricket.

7

Serendipity

The big match that day was in Karachi, where Pakistan faced South Africa in what promised to be the major clash of Group B. It was also the only serious test the Cup holders would face before the quarter-finals, and they would face it in front of one of the most fervent cricket crowds on earth.

But I was in Pune to watch Kenya take on the West Indies, and I felt a pang of regret. Maybe my itinerary hadn't been so cleverly designed after all. I had enjoyed the five-hour ride from Bombay the day before. The taxi shuddered and clanked its way up and over the dry, thorny Western Ghats, glove compartment flapping open, bonnet bouncing up and down. Periodically the driver doused the engine with buckets of cold water. Because I had forgotten to reserve a room in Pune, I found myself stuck in a grotty hotel room infested by menacing amber-coloured beetles. I was used to that, but when I realised that the television set didn't work, and that my umbilical link to Star Sports might be severed for forty-eight hours, I complained. A young man in a soiled hotel uniform came to fix it, and while rewiring the elaborate aerial connection, he looked up and asked, 'Osho or cricket?' Pune is home of the Osho Commune International, a plush ashram-cum-resort, a sort of New Age Disneyland founded by the self-styled Bhagwan Rajneesh, and a magnet for credit-card-carrying Western tourists who seek the mystical experience of the east without its discomforts. I explained firmly that I was a devotee of that more benign cult, cricket, and that my Bhagwan was Sunil Gavaskar (who owned a sports shop in the hotel foyer).

The atmosphere outside the Jawaharlal Nehru Stadium was relaxed. There was the usual supernumerary police presence, but with so few spectators the agents of law and order lolled about chatting to each other. Inside, it was apparent that the Rs1.25 crore (£250,000) renovation was incomplete. While the players' dressing rooms had been refurbished (though in Spartan style), the construction of the new tier above the existing seating had hardly begun. Sheltered by temporary canvas awnings, the stands (and the manual scoreboard) seemed to have been overgrown with a jungle of bamboo scaffolding lashed to rusting iron girders. Around the boundary, a string of identical banners advertised BRIHANS QUALITY PRODUCTS.

The press had been assigned a long, low-ceilinged room in the old Maharashtra Cricket Association clubhouse. Opposite was the newer Professor D.B. Deodhar clubhouse, where the local politicians and the sponsors were ensconced, and in the distance, under the grey sky, temple *sikhara* (towers) and satellite dishes were visible through the pollution (as well as a surfeit of educational, scientific and religious institutions, Pune boasts a booming chemical industry). From the kitchen downstairs, cooking smells wafted into the makeshift press box. I was greeted by Michael Henderson, the man from the *Times*, who immediately took issue with my *Indian Express* article about the English cricketers' poor behaviour in the sub-continent. Two years ago, Hendo had interrupted his report of the 'village cricket' championship at Lord's to denounce my book, *Anyone but England*, as the work of 'an American wowser' (I had to look it up). We met some time later at a county championship match in Uxbridge and struck up a rapport. We talked about novels, music and travel and shared our impatience with a variety of media fashions.

I think he was surprised to find I wasn't Dave Spart. For my part, I was surprised to find that he wasn't nearly as blimpish as he likes to pretend. In Pune he told me he felt my article 'had a point' but was unfair to the English: 'There are prejudices on both sides.' We bandied the issue back and forth for several minutes, but decided, in the end, that some gaps were just too great to bridge. Together we settled down to watch another of those one-sided league matches that were said to have devalued the World Cup.

Most of the senior cricket correspondents were in Karachi, leaving the Pune match to the younger second-stringers. Cricket journalism is an even less glamorous career in the sub-continent than it is here, and for most of these willing, able but underpaid hacks, covering the World Cup meant staying in cheap hotels or with friends or family, and hammering away endlessly at their keyboards in an attempt to satisfy their editors' insatiable craving for more and more cricket copy. We all turned up to these mismatches hoping to see something surprising, some exciting display by a hitherto unheralded star, hoping in our wildest, unspoken fantasies to see an upset, but more than happy to settle for some unexpected drama or simply a single outstanding performance. A Lara hundred; a burst by Ambrose; a spectacular catch. At the Nehru Stadium today we were all merely fulfilling our duties. In the World Cup, every match must be reported, even if its result is a foregone conclusion.

The Kenyans had been by far the most impressive of the minnows so far, showing panache with the bat and vigour in the field even while the likes of Tendulkar and the Waugh brothers plundered their bowlers at will. 'They look quite promising,' said Michael Holding, 'and with more experience they can be a real threat.' Until 1981 the Kenyans had formed part of the East African side, and indeed their manager in India was Harilal Shah, who had captained East Africa in the first World Cup in 1975. That was an all-Asian side. In the 1980s, Kenneth Odumbe became the first African to play for Kenya. His brothers Edward and Maurice, the most talented of all and now Kenya's captain, followed him. Next to the government estate where the Odumbes grew up was a ground where Asians played cricket. 'We cut wood into the shape of a bat and used maize corn to make a ball,' Maurice recalled. The brothers' prowess came to the notice of the Aga Khan Gymkhana and they moved to Nairobi. 'Cricket has given us a better life,' said Maurice. 'We can go and eat in restaurants.'

Most of the Kenyans are amateur cricketers and all of them play for one of the handful of well-established Nairobi clubs. During the season they meet to practise in the nets at 5:30 p.m., after work or study, and play fifty-over matches on the weekends before minuscule crowds. Interest in the game is still confined to a tiny segment of the population (and massively overshadowed by athletics). But like cricket administrators everywhere, the Kenyan officials are ambitious. Shah told anyone who would listen that Kenya would be ready for Test status in ten years. With the help of sympathisers in the Asian and African cricket boards, the Kenyan squad already had more experience of international cricket than many capped county players in England, having in the last twelve months toured Bangladesh and South Africa and played host to an India A squad (captained by Jadeja). The Kenyans also hosted the 1994 ICC trophy from which the three minnows had qualified, and were frustrated to have lost the final to a UAE side made up of immigrants, when they had made such an effort to integrate their side. The Kenyan World Cup squad was made up of equal numbers of Asians and Africans, but tensions remained. Prior to leaving Nairobi, Maurice Odumbe had led a brief rebellion against Shah and the Association; he demanded an increased daily allowance for the World Cup and alleged favouritism to players of Asian origin. Once in India, he aired his grievances to reporters.

'I'm in my mid-twenties but I actually feel as though I've played too much cricket already. I shouldn't be feeling like that. But the cricket we play back home is rubbish. We're playing against the same old people every week. I've got to the point on a Saturday when I sometimes bat at number 11 and don't bowl. I don't think it's going to improve in the near future. There is no one coming through. I love a challenge but the only challenge for good Kenyan players now, apart from the World Cup which is a dream come true, is to go abroad.' From the moment he landed in Bombay, Odumbe had talked about the match against the West Indies as the one the Kenyans most wanted to do well in. 'These West Indians have been my idols for years. I have watched them and based my cricket on them.' Now in Pune he told the press, 'It's great to be playing against men whom you only saw in magazines and videos. Imagine being on the same field as Brian Lara. You know I wanted to have my picture taken with him a few years ago in Swansea and he refused.'

The West Indies team which arrived in Pune bore little resemblance to the world-conquering idols who had fired Maurice Odumbe's imagination. They had forfeited to Sri Lanka, lost to India and defeated Zimbabwe, without playing as a unit or demonstrating any strategic nous. The past year had seen a string of poor results, personality clashes, and allegations of indiscipline. In the week before the Pune match, captain Richie Richardson had come under fire from Viv Richards. In the column he wrote for Sunil Gavaskar's Professional Management Group, syndicated throughout the sub-continent during the World Cup, Richards charged Richardson with 'lack of leadership' and chided him as the establishment's man. 'The board seems to be eager to be in control again. They want to put the players in their pockets, put them in a situation where maybe, they want the guys to run when they say run and jump when they say jump.'

For all the bickering that marred the last year, the West Indies board claimed one major success. United Breweries of India, makers of Kingfisher, India's top-selling beer, paid half a million dollars to sponsor the West Indies team. It was a modest sum by English or Indian standards, but the biggest single deal in West Indies cricket history. However, not everyone was pleased that a unique Caribbean institution had been auctioned off to a foreign company. Tempers rose when an over-jubilant UBI spokesperson announced that the team would from now on be known as 'the Kingfisher West Indies'. After complaints from the prime minister of Barbados, among others, the Cricket Board reassured the public that the team would still be known simply as 'the West Indies' – 'sponsored by Kingfisher'.

In recent years, UBI has made steady inroads into both the British and North American markets, and no doubt believed that sponsoring the West Indies would further that campaign. The company's principal market, however, remains at home, and sponsoring West Indies is above all a cheap way of selling Indian beer in India. For the West Indians, there was no alternative. No indigenous company could match UBI's offer. They remain the poorest of the Test-playing countries, and the only one (apart from Zimbabwe) without a mass middle-class audience. At the same time, their economies are increasingly dominated by US-based corporations, and a stream of immigrants has flowed to North America. It has often been claimed that cricket in the Caribbean is under threat from the Americanisation of the region. Whether that's true or not, there's no doubt that American mores have made an impact on the style of West Indian cricket. At the team photocall before the World Cup opening ceremony a number of the younger West Indian cricketers posed with their maroon caps reversed. A horrified Wes Hall intervened to ensure that West Indian dignity was upheld.

At Pune, West Indies won the toss and decided to field. In the press box, this decision was greeted as another mark against Richardson's captaincy. 'Surely they should bat first and make a big score,' it was argued, 'give their batsmen some time at the crease and set up something for the spectators to enjoy.' Several of the Bombay-based correspondents complained to me that the West Indies treated the Indian press with disdain and the ordinary fans with contempt. Even Keith Arthurton (who in two appearances at bat in the World Cup so far had scored a grand total of one run) was refusing interviews and autographs.

In the early overs, the pace of Ambrose, Walsh and Bishop, aided by morning dampness in the wicket, overwhelmed the top-order Kenyan batsmen, who were unflinching but unable to control their shots. In the tenth over they lost their third wicket for only 45 runs. Maurice Odumbe joined Steve Tikolo at the wicket. Despite the early collapse, the West Indies looked unhappy. Ambrose, whose first four overs cost only 13 runs, was in a filthy mood, muttering to himself and glaring impatiently at umpires and team-mates. Walsh and Bishop struggled with their run-ups, and sent down a hail of wides and no-balls.

Nonetheless, the steep bounce drove Tikolo and Odumbe, Kenya's two classiest batsmen, time and again on to the back foot. At one point, the West Indies were certain that Tikolo had trodden on his stumps, but after a long delay the third umpire ruled him not out. When he nudged the next ball, a loose leg side delivery, for an easy single, Bishop kicked the ground in annoyance. Odumbe soon perished, knocking off his own bails as he stepped back to turn Bishop to leg. His innings of four off thirty deliveries had been a painful effort. For Bishop, the Kenyan captain's wicket was small consolation for another erratic performance.

Harper was the only West Indian bowler to maintain a steady line and length. After a promising start, when he was mooted as a future West Indies captain, his career had foundered as his off spin was squeezed out by the domination of the great pace quartets. But at Pune his experience stood him in good stead when others in his side struggled. He had Tikolo (whose score of 29 runs was to prove the day's highest) caught behind attempting to sweep a ball off his middle stump and Martin Suji taken by Lara in the slips for a duck. The score was 81 for 6 in the twenty-third over. We looked at one another in the press box.

Uh oh, the jaded, knowing glances seemed to say, this match had the makings of a tedious embarrassment.

Odoyo and Modi kept their wickets intact but scored at funereal pace. They pushed past 100 in the thirtieth over, and added only 25 more runs over the next nine before Jimmy Adams stumped Odoyo off Harper, who finished with figures of 10–4–15–3. After bowling five wides and five no-balls in his first spell, Cameron Cuffy finally found the target to remove Edward Odumbe for 1. It was 126 for 8, but there was no rejoicing in the field; the West Indies players hardly exchanged a word. Richardson seemed an isolated, impotent figure at mid off, ignored by his bowlers and undermined by his star batsman, poised at first slip. Modi managed to accumulate 28 in 110 minutes off 75 balls, scoring only one boundary, before being caught by Adams, diving to his left, off Ambrose. In fact, Adams's performance was the one plus in the field for the West Indies. He had returned to the team in place of the hapless Courtney Browne, resuming the role of one-day wicket keeper-batsman he had last played during the first weeks of the West Indies tour of India in 1994. Not that Adams seemed to be enjoying himself any more than the rest of the side. Despite taking five catches (equalling Syed Kirmani's World Cup record) and a stumping, he looked tense, his teeth clenched and his high forehead creased in lava-like furrows.

The Kenyan total – all out for 166 – seemed modest; what's more, it had been achieved with much pain and little flair. After their previous batting performances against India and the Australians, it was a disappointment. But somehow, the Kenyans had managed to add 81 runs for the last four wickets. At the time, this statistic seemed nothing more than an indictment of West Indian lassitude in the field. It turned out, however, to be highly significant, as did another set of figures. The West Indies had conceded 35 extras – 8 leg byes, 14 wides and 13 no-balls.

Everyone in the press box relaxed. This was turning into an easy day, with little to report except a bad-tempered West Indian side and a Kenyan team who really hadn't the class to stand the pace. We gathered around the TV set in the corner. After a strong start, thanks to a century from Aamir Sohail, the Pakistani innings had stuttered, reaching only 242 for 6 in fifty overs. Miandad did not play. Some newspapers reported he was suffering a stiff back, others an upset stomach. There were rumours that he had argued with Wasim over his place in the batting order.

After lunch the gates at Pune were opened and more spectators drifted in. The crowd grew to 7000, including a group of 300 Kenyan students, many from a local college called the Symbiosis Institute. Pune was the only venue in the sub-continent where Kenyans in any numbers were able to attend the match. Yet it seemed they were to be treated to the team's worst performance.

Turning away from the crowd and the TV, I tried to examine the tattered old volumes locked away in the club's bookcases. The MCA had been founded by the great D.B. Deodhar, professor of Sanskrit and middle-order batsman whose mastery of difficult wickets was displayed during more than forty years of first-class cricket. Deodhar lived and died in Pune (in 1993 at the age of 101) and spurned many offers from princes to join their payrolls. In his late forties he led Maharashtra to their only Ranji Trophy championship. Impatient with the anglophilia of much of the cricket elite, and sceptical about the English conventions associated with the game, he became India's first independent middle-class cricketer, a modest forebear of Sunil Gavaskar and Sachin Tendulkar. I wondered what relics of the professor's career, what clues to the evolution of Indian cricket, might be mouldering behind the dusty glass. Here was something the Indian Board could spend its World Cup riches on. Certainly if someone doesn't set about assembling a national archive of Indian cricket, all the documentary evidence will wither away. I left the bookcases and returned to the match, which was to become a demonstration of what happens when a cricketing heritage is forgotten.

The Kenyan opening bowlers Rajib Ali and Martin Suji hit

their stride immediately and showed far more control than the West Indian speedsters. In the fourth over, Ali clean bowled Richardson for four. The Kenyans slapped each other on the back, laughed and clapped. Every West Indian wicket they took now would be a bonus, proof of what they could do against their heroes. From their point of view, they could not lose.

Lara entered to huge cheers, as he does every time he walks to the wicket in south Asia. People travel miles and pay fortunes to see this man bat. I should know, I've done it often enough. We are all driven by the desire to be present at one of his great innings. In the sub-continent, as well as in England, even the most partisan spectator is torn between a patriotic keenness to see Lara dismissed as quickly as possible and a personal yearning to savour his magic. For most of us in Pune that day, Lara at the crease offered us our best hope of witnessing something memorable. He was quickly off the mark with a peremptory four through the covers.

In the next over Suji knocked back Campbell's leg stump. With the score 22 for 2 in the fifth over, Chanderpaul came in. Lara heaved extravagantly outside the off stump and missed a ball from Suji that kept low. Suji pitched the ball up again. Lara swung wildly. The ball just missed his outside edge. 'What is he playing at?' Hendo demanded indignantly. 'Doesn't he care?' Perhaps not. In the next over, facing Ali, Lara again slashed outside the off stump. This time the ball caught a thin edge and was heading to the wicket keeper, the bulky, immobile, bewildered-looking Tariq Iqbal. I think at that moment every Kenyan in the field held his breath. Kennedy Otieno had shown himself an able keeper in the earlier matches, but had been replaced behind the stumps for this match by Iqbal – solely because Iqbal (the oldest man in the side at thirty-four) was such a cumbersome fielder that the only place the Kenyans could afford him was behind the stumps. On other days and against lesser players, Iqbal will fluff easier catches; but not today. Lara was out caught behind for 8 runs. It was 33 for 3 in the eighth over.

Lara sauntered back to the pavilion as if none of it was his fault, and (for the first time in India, I believe) was greeted with derisive chants of 'Lara – hai! hai!'. The people who had cheered him to the wicket, who had come with their home-made placards singing his praises, who waved the 'LARA KYAA MARA!' banners distributed by a local business outside the ground, were furious with their idol, and it was not hard to see why. He didn't seem bothered, one way or another, about either his team or his fans. 'Disgraceful!' huffed Hendo.

With Lara's departure a new prospect came into view for the first time, something more memorable even than a Lara hundred. Was an upset in the making? Surely not. The West Indies had plenty of batting to come. And the target, we reminded each other, was so modest. The required run rate was only 3.1 per over. Surely the experienced West Indian middle order would have no trouble with that. But Maurice Odumbe knew better. 'When we got Lara I thought we were in with a chance,' he recalled. 'That put them under pressure and I know these guys like to go for their shots when they're under pressure. That's why we had the fielders in the circle. We made them go for it.' In the stands the Indian fans scrawled new placards urging on the Kenyans. Keith Arthurton swanned to the wicket with his usual mixture of arrogance and abstractedness. After failing to score off six deliveries, he tried to scramble a quick single and was run out by a calm, accurate throw from Hitesh Modi. The third umpire was asked to adjudicate but the replay was unambiguous. On came the red light and off crept Arthurton, with yet another failure to sulk over. With the score 35 for 4 in the tenth over, the impossible seemed to have become merely improbable. 'The West Indies will still win it,' said Hendo, 'but they don't deserve to.' 'Kenya zindabad!' shouted the crowd, and the press box murmured assent.

Jimmy Adams joined the cautious Chanderpaul, whose grave, youthful features made him look like a boy lost in a grown-up world. The power faltered, as it so often does in India, and the lights and the television and the laptops flickered. But hardly a complaint was voiced (it usually takes very little to set off kvetching in the press box). We were all concentrating on the drama unfolding before us. Suji and Ali hammered away, remorseless in their pursuit of line and length. The Kenyan fielders stretched every fibre to cut off singles and squeeze down the runs. Unlike the previous West Indies batsmen, Chanderpaul and Adams at least looked like they knew they had a job to do. It was time to rest Suji (7–2–16–1) and Ali (7–2–17–2).

The entire Kenyan side gathered in the middle of the field. An animated discussion followed. The problem for the Kenyans was clear. Would their second-line bowlers be able to sustain the pressure? Could they defend a total of 166? Karim and Odumbe began bowling off spin from either end. Odumbe, bowling with a slip and a silly mid off, started with a maiden. Karim was soon replaced by Odoyo, the eighteen-year-old medium pacer. He was pulled for four over mid wicket by Chanderpaul, bringing up the West Indies fifty in the seventeenth over. Undaunted, Odoyo stuck to his middle and off stump line and forced Chanderpaul to treat him with respect. Meanwhile, Adams began to fidget impatiently. Against a stronger attack he would have been content to take his time. After all, he is one of the great accumulators of our time. But today, against the Kenyans, he didn't seem to know what kind of innings to play. His self-doubt must have soared when his partner chipped Odumbe to point where he was caught by Tikolo. With the score 55 for 5, Harper came in, and immediately called Adams for a quick single. The Kenyan fielder shied at the stumps and barely missed, but the ball ran for four precious byes. Then Odumbe's off break turned off Adams's pad, brushed his glove and was caught by Modi close in. He had made 9 in 56 minutes at the crease. The West Indies had 4 wickets left – and the asking rate had crept up to 5.68 per over.

In the space of an hour, a remote possibility had become a near-certainty. The West Indies have come back from brittle batting performances often enough over the last few years to stave off defeat, as England know. But the Kenyans refused to let them off the hook. As the wickets tumbled, the crowd danced, every voice bellowing 'Kenya! Kenya!' The Kenyan students huddled together in the incomplete stand next to the Deodhar pavilion were delirious. Their ranks seemed to swell as they were joined by locals gripped by the Kenya fever that swept through Pune that afternoon.

Bishop tried to blast his way out of the hole but the Kenyan spinners pinned him down. After twenty-five overs, with the score 78 for 6, Harper tickled Odumbe down the leg side and Iqbal lunged to take the catch with a speed of which he was thought incapable. 'We just did not want to let Harper get any boundaries,' Odumbe recalled. 'We'll make him do something crazy, we thought, and it worked. When he got out I knew it was just a matter of time. Seven wickets were down and I said to the lads, okay guys, relax. It's not over but be calm. Let's strangle them. Let's choke them. We just kept calm.'

Ambrose came to the wicket looking as if he resented even being there. He glanced around with dull, irritated eyes. Once again, his team-mates had let him down. Was he expected to win the match with bat as well as ball? Five overs later, he was run out (Modi again) for 3. In the press box, we could see the TV replay was a close one, but the roar from the stand was unambiguous. 'OUT! OUT! OUT!' It seemed a bigger noise for being made by such a small crowd. The press box was glowing. The second stringers were savouring their moment of reflected glory. To hell with Karachi, today the action was in Pune.

Odumbe finished off his ten overs with a maiden. He had conceded 15 runs and taken 3 wickets. This was truly a 'spell'. And it was not only the batsmen but Odumbe himself who seemed under it. As he trotted in briskly over after over, he welded pinprick focus to muscular relaxation. He had sensed the tension among the West Indian batsmen. He had seen the opening, and he knew if he persevered with his job quietly, he could pass through to the other side. His confidence infused the side. They did not falter as their prize came within reach. It was at this stage, in the final overs of the match, that I was most impressed by the Kenyans. Having done the hard work, and come so much further than they had expected, the sheer scale of what they were about to achieve might have overwhelmed them. Instead, they kept their nerve, concentrated fiercely and did the basic things cleanly and correctly. Their fielding grew sharper and more athletic. The crowd was beside itself with excitement, but the players seemed determined to carry out their remaining tasks.

Walsh stretched forward to fend off Karim's off break. The ball popped off the upper part of the bat, was knocked up by Modi's reflex reaction and then caught by Chudasama. Cameron Cuffy was the last man in. Rajib Ali returned. Cuffy leaned into an optimistic drive and played the ball on to his off stump. The West Indies were all out for 93, their lowest-ever score in a World Cup match.

The Kenyans leapt into one another's arms. They grabbed the stumps and ran, spontaneously and as one, fired by the sheer gusto of victory and the urge to share it, to their fellow Kenyans in the stand, who surged forward to envelop them. A chorus of 'Kenya Wu' rang out. Brandishing the stumps like triumphal torches, the players set off on a lap of honour. As they passed the press box, the hacks all rose to their feet and applauded the miracle-workers, the men who had turned a routine cricket report into a page one lead. Hendo pronounced himself 'quite moved' – and rightly so. This was more than a spectacular upset. We had witnessed a triumph of commitment and enthusiasm over world-weary cynicism.

Watching Odumbe mobbed by the press, I knew suddenly what the expression 'grinning from ear to ear' meant. When reporters asked him what the Kenyans were going to do tonight, he answered without hesitation, 'We are going to get pissed!' His unaffected delight was irresistible, and there was no one there who begrudged him or the Kenyans their tears of joy.

'Yes, there were tears,' said Odumbe afterwards. 'It was so unbelievable to beat the West Indies. Shedding tears was the least we could do. To beat the West Indies first time, I could not ask for more. It was the confidence in us which did it. We wanted to show the world that we can play cricket. The belief in ourselves did it. We believed that we could take them on. I just kept telling them, let's not experiment. Don't give them room for shots. Let's bowl wicket to wicket.'

Hanumant Singh, the former India Test batsman who coached the Kenyans, sat in a chair in the front of the pavilion surrounded by reporters and beaming with self-satisfaction. 'I told the boys the West Indies are flesh and blood like you. I remember when I first came to play in Bombay, I was overawed by the famous names. I had to learn that they were no different from me.' On the dressing-room steps, Richie Richardson, drawn but dignified, congratulated the Kenyans. 'They played very well,' he said softly, 'I haven't really got any words at the moment.' Then he led the West Indian players on a visit to the jubilant Kenyan dressing room. Lara embraced Odumbe (who reminded his hero of the snub in Swansea and smilingly demanded, 'Now you must ask for a picture with me'). The beers were opened – and the reporters hustled out.

All but one, an Indian reporter who managed to pass unnoticed amid the hubbub. Lara too stayed behind and when the other West Indians had left he shared his thoughts with the Kenyans, and unwittingly, the world. 'It wasn't that bad losing to you guys. You are black. Know what I mean. Now a team like South Africa is a different matter altogether. You know, this white thing comes into the picture. We can't stand losing to them.' But what was wrong with the West Indies? the Kenyans wanted to know. Lara obliged them. 'There's problems in the team. Some of us don't even talk to some of the others. It's that bad.' He looked at Hitesh Modi. 'I saw you the most yesterday at the hotel. Our guys just stick in their rooms. Hooper had no malaria. It was just this team situation that made him pull out. I come from

Trinidad and Tobago. The management doesn't like someone coming from there and making it big. You know at the press conferences when the guys ask them about me they go around saying stuff like one person doesn't make the team. He doesn't obviously. But they never say encouraging stuff like, "yes, he's a great player, others should learn from him." '

Karim asked about his dismissal. 'You had a swashbuckling approach, like you wanted to finish it off quickly. They sent a message for you to stay.' Apparently, Chanderpaul had come in with instructions for Lara to remain at the wicket. 'I wasn't quite crazy about the message. When I'm playing well they don't send messages.'

Then Lara came to the nub of the matter. 'You know if you have a good team but a bad management you can maybe get along. But if you have a bad team and a bad management you really get fucked. After this defeat, I think they'll be forced to sort out some of this shit.' Sure enough, within days Richie Richardson announced his retirement from international cricket, and Wes Hall and Andy Roberts were replaced by Clive Lloyd and Tony Marshall. Lara's remarks about the 'white thing' landed him in hot water. As usual, any expression of black racism was pounced upon by the press, as if somehow it proves that 'they're just as bad as us'. A lot of people in India were shocked by Lara's statement, but I wasn't. He was seeking common ground with the Kenyans, and found it in the shared history of colonialism and racism. What I did find shocking was Lara's self-obsessed whinging. Of course, later, he recanted it all and apologised in a dignified statement to the media, as he always does. But no one doubted he had given an accurate picture of the atmosphere inside the West Indian team.

It was often said during the World Cup that the best place to watch the cricket was at home in front of the television. Certainly if you wanted to analyse the game in detail and without distractions, that was true. Often, even though I had seen every ball bowled in a match, I came to understand what had happened and why only after viewing the highlights the next day on Star TV. Nonetheless, there remain compelling reasons for preferring the holistic sprawl of cricket in the flesh to the fragmented but highly focused experience of cricket on television.

First, you can enjoy the full panorama of the field, select your own highlights, manufacture your own interpretation of events. Second, you can do this with others. You can share the match, not merely with friends at home but with the anonymous mass of the crowd, through which you interact with the cricket and help give it meaning. Third, and most important, as was proved at Pune, is the ontological pleasure of being a witness to history, that irreversible act unfolding in time that is a cricket match. For me (and for thousands in the West Indies) the word Pune will always be linked with one of the most extraordinary upsets in the annals of cricket, and I will carry the time and the place with me wherever I go – *because I was there.*

When did it become apparent that Kenya would win? When did the last West Indian chance disappear? In a way, the pattern was there from the first overs bowled in the morning. The West Indies played as if they wanted to be somewhere else, doing something else. They seemed to have caught the English disease. In *Beyond a Boundary*, James wrote, 'West Indians crowding to Tests bring with them the whole past history and future hopes of the islands.' But the bond that tied Richardson's side in Pune to that history and those hopes seemed in danger of snapping. The gap between what remains essentially a provincial society on the margins of the world economy and the peripatetic five-star hotel existence led by the players is huge – and growing all the time. In these conditions the solidarity in diversity that made the West Indies one of the most successful touring sides in history had been eroded.

The next morning, I watched the Australia–Zimbabwe match in Nagpur (the Star TV link having been restored) and read the reports of Pakistan's defeat in Karachi. The South Africans had won with seven overs and 5 wickets to spare. Among the Pakistani bowlers, only the young off spinner Saqlain Mushtaq went for less than five an over. In addition, they had given up 26 extras and bowled 2.2 overs above their quota in wides and no-balls. In the *Indian Express* H. Natarajan reported from the scene of the débâcle:

> Pakistan look certain to cross the border to play their quarter-final on Indian soil. Not a bad prospect considering that the knives are already out, if the ordeal of fire that Akram had to endure at the media conference is any pointer. Not surprisingly, Akram said there would be less pressure on his team in India. Akram may have spent considerable time as a county pro in England but he was transparent in his honesty and eschewed the Englishman's trait to look for excuses where none exist. His opening line at the press conference was a surrender and acceptance of his team's collective failure, as he admitted that this team was 'outplayed'. But the subcontinental extremes were all too evident as the skipper, beaten on the field, left battered by the conference.

So even the massed ranks of the Shiv Sena had become preferable to the relentless demands of the home supporters. On television, the commentators remarked on the small size of the Nagpur crowd. Mark Nicholas was perplexed. How could the cricket-crazy people of India not rush to see the Australians, whatever they thought about the opposition? 'We had a packed match here a few months ago against New Zealand,' Ravi Shastri said. 'A lot of runs were scored. It was a great day for the crowd.' I waited. No, Shastri did not go on to add that it was a great day except for the twelve who died when the stadium wall collapsed. Clearly, the tragedy at Nagpur was to be consigned to oblivion, if the front-men of Indian cricket had their way.

I dashed across town in an autorick to the Blue Diamond Hotel where the West Indies and the Kenyans were staying. Over a drink by the pool I chatted to a West Indian friend who has followed the team closely for many years. 'Are you still recovering from the shock?' I asked.

'There was no shock. We looked like losers from the start. And we deserved it. West Indies and England have been the two most arrogant teams here. Our boys refuse autographs. They push the Indians around. And because of this we play badly. Yesterday's defeat was the greatest lesson we could learn. We must respond better to people. The English are cold. But the people here are warm and we should be able to reciprocate that. The players grumble about touring India. They have no education or knowledge of the people here, even those who come from Asian backgrounds.'

How were the players taking it?

'Team spirits are very low. The sponsors' function last night was a polite affair but very strange. The Kenyans were there and they have a spirit of camaraderie you won't feel with any other team. This whole World Cup has been a great adventure to them, not just another cricket tour. Our boys all went to bed early and now they're sulking in their rooms. No one wants to call home. The word coming back is that it's going to be bad. The newspapers are saying heads should roll. It's the same old nonsense we've had in West Indies cricket for generations. The success we enjoyed over the last twenty years obscured the divisions. But as soon as we lose the old insularity returns and people start questioning other people's patriotism.

'When we were winning we failed to exploit it. The board didn't recruit any sponsors, they didn't do anything to strengthen the game long term. They didn't expand it into the rural areas. It was as if they swallowed the old racist crap about West Indians being "natural" cricketers. For them the players were just pawns to make money. They sent them round and round the world. In the last eighteen months we went from India to New Zealand to Australia then played a series at home then went to England and to Sharjah and then back to Australia before coming here.

'There's a lot of reasons for the low morale. Part of the blame goes to this whole damn World Cup jamboree. The geographical spread of the venues and the constant travelling has prevented any sense of comradeship developing among the teams. There's no opportunity to form friendships. There's nothing like what you see in the Olympic village. The players only met together at the opening ceremony – which was meaningless and depressing because it was so badly organised. The World Cup's just big business now and you're nothing but a walking signboard for the sponsors. Yet the prize money is the same as in 1987. Do you know no member of Pilcom has even been introduced to the team? At Gwalior Scindia didn't bother to come to the dressing room. The whole thing has been made to feel impersonal.

'Still, the West Indies could host the next World Cup easily. I hadn't realised before. I thought we couldn't do it because we didn't have big enough stadiums. But all that matters is the television coverage. And a World Cup in the West Indies could be staged for prime-time exposure in North America.'

From the Blue Diamond my autorick took me to the Aga Khan's opulent nineteenth-century residence on the city outskirts. The same Aga Khan whose patronage founded the Odumbes' club in Nairobi. It was horse-racing that had brought him to Pune. But today his home is a memorial to the Indian freedom struggle. Here Gandhi and his entourage were imprisoned by the British during the Quit India movement of 1942. Kasturba Gandhi, the Mahatma's wife, died here and her *samadhi* (cremation marker) is in the garden. As I paid my respects, I realised my mind was elsewhere. I was still tingling with the aftereffects of yesterday's shock. There is something intoxicating about the triumph of the underdog. As you see the status quo upended so unexpectedly, as the odds are overturned and the experts confounded, you catch a fleeting glimpse of the limitlessness of human possibility. It's heady stuff.

The Kenyan victory vindicated not only the presence of the derided minnows in the World Cup but the competition as a whole. After all, one of the reasons we follow world sporting events is that they offer a stage for our David *v* Goliath fantasies. This was the greatest irony of the Kenyan victory: it came at the expense of the West Indies, who had so often inverted global hierarchies on the cricket field. With the inrush of warmth and gladness, the word serendipity came to mind. It derives from Serendip, the land of surprises, an old Arabic name for the island known today as Sri Lanka, and means the facility for making happy discoveries by accident, for unexpected but pleasurable windfalls.

I left Pune determined to bet on my hopes. Anything could happen in this World Cup.

8

Nest of VIPers

I knew the tie at the Feroz Shah Kotla would be a disaster when I met Sunil Dev, the Delhi and District Cricket Association secretary, in his office in south Delhi. Dev had played cricket for the elite St Stephen's College and for Delhi in the Ranji Trophy in the sixties as a wicket keeper-batsman. He was now running Agromet Exports ('We import fertilisers'), but seemed to spend most of his time playing cricket politics. On his walls were photos of himself with Kapil Dev, Rajiv Gandhi and Narasimha Rao. A Congress Party loyalist, he had assumed the helm of the DDCA for the third time in August 1995, and had taken charge of the preparations for the World Cup tie between India and Sri Lanka scheduled for 2 March.

'I know everyone in BCCI,' he told me, 'in and out and up and down.'

And from what I had heard, everyone in the BCCI knew Sunil Dev, and most of what they had to say about him was unprintable. The DDCA is reputed to be the most faction-ridden body in sub-continental cricket. Composed of a network of banks, businesses, government departments and exclusive social clubs, it had over the years become a honeypot for status-seekers and influence-peddlers. While the politicians and businessmen wrangled for control of the DDCA, the historic Feroz Shah Kotla ground, laid out in 1883, was left to go to seed. After India's World Cup victory in 1983, the BCCI staged a day–night contest between India and Pakistan at the Nehru Stadium, a modern athletics arena. The revenue from the match was put aside for development of the Kotla, but was then frozen for years because of factional disputes.

'When I was a player, the DDCA was ruled by the old Delhi wallas, from the mohallas in Chandi Chowk,' Dev recalled. 'They were not cricketers. After I stopped playing cricket, I came back as a grown-up citizen, and I realised it was not effective. I worked with Bishan Bedi to clean up the mess. We came into power by using our influence and some help from the media. Sanjay helped us, as did Kamal Nath.' Kamal Nath was one of the hawala charge-sheeted Congressmen, and Sanjay was Sanjay Gandhi, whose abuses of power during his mother's 'emergency' in the 1970s were notorious. Dev was proud of links not many in India would own to these days.

Dev first became DDCA secretary in 1984. 'I was too young and inexperienced and straightforward,' he sighed, 'I was still too much of a cricketer and too easy for politicians to get at.' Sitting opposite me in his suit and tie, with his round face and pencil moustache, and whining about his enemies, Sunil Dev looked and sounded like someone who might once have been young and inexperienced, but never straightforward. 'By 1986 I had liberalised DDCA up to a point. I had involved the cricketers. I had made the Ranji Trophy players members. I made Manmohan Sood the first Delhi player to become a Test selector.' But Sood had betrayed him and joined 'the opposition'. 'They took revenge. I had no allies. I went back to my business and Sood became secretary.'

Dev returned in 1988 with Rajiv Gandhi's backing. 'There was the same old conflict between the modernisers and the old guard. The Delhi seat is a hot seat. We have three governments here – the centre, the state and the municipal. So many politicians' sons want to play for Delhi and if you ignore them they say you will face tax and legal problems. But I have always insisted selection must be on merit.' He cited Delhi's recent victory in the Ranji Trophy North Zone as proof that his methods were working.

For seven years there were no DDCA elections. Every time one was scheduled, it would be halted by a court challenge from which ever faction expected to lose. Finally, the looming World Cup forced the Indian Board's hand. They awarded a tie to Delhi but only on condition that it was not directly managed by the DDCA. Instead, responsibility was assigned to a Special Committee of the good and the great, including former cricketers and the Delhi chief of police. The BCCI released the funds that had been frozen all these years and ambitious plans for the renovation of the Kotla were drawn up. Delhi, it was promised, would finally have an international cricket venue worthy of the nation's capital. Under instructions from the Indian Board, new DDCA elections were held. As before, all voting was by proxy. Rival factions set about collecting proxies from members and affiliated clubs, by any means necessary. This time, it was Dev's turn for revenge. Sood lost to him by 3–1.

'The biggest problem the day I came back was finance. In 1990 there were Rs70 lakhs in the kitty but in 1995 only Rs6 lakhs. Members were not paying their subscriptions or entry fees but were still using DDCA facilities to conduct their businesses and bribing our staff to get away with it. In the last four months I have brought in Rs50 lakh. I have quadrupled the paying membership. I have brought in Liberty to sponsor our Ranji team. Now the "company share" is of real value.' His self-satisfaction knew no bounds. But his attempt to assume the mantle of moderniser was unconvincing. Everyone in Indian cricket these days claims to be a moderniser, and everyone claims to have the interests of the game at heart; as often as not both claims are a cover for the pursuit of self-interest. Sunil Dev was an operator, his reflexes honed by years of political manoeuvring.

But as the World Cup tie drew near, he was under pressure, and his composure was beginning to fray.

Construction work at the Kotla had begun in November 1995. The Special Committee met rarely and somehow responsibility for the World Cup tie passed back to the DDCA. In December work was halted for three weeks by the municipal corporation of Delhi because the Association had failed to secure permissions from the appropriate authorities. Madan Lal Khurana, then the BJP chief minister of Delhi, intervened (two months later he was charge-sheeted in the hawala scandal). On 1 January 1996, the Delhi High Court ordered the work to resume 'without creating any precedent for any future case, and in the interest of justice and the public'. The municipal corporation still insisted that the DDCA secure the necessary authorisations, notably from the Delhi Fire Service, but the DDCA ignored the corporation and the work continued. When an Association member petitioned the High Court to stop it, the Court ruled that the DDCA had indeed initiated unauthorised construction but, 'considering the international importance of the fixture to be held on 2 March' allowed the work to continue. Then, in the first week of February, the Archaeological Survey of India asked police to halt construction because of its proximity to a protected monument – the Kotla Feroz Shah, a fourteenth-century ruin. The complaint was the result of a letter from Dr S. Sareen, a former DDCA secretary. The police declined to act, and the building work proceeded.

It was now at least a month behind schedule. The original plans had been drastically scaled down. 'The MCD only became involved because of Sood. It was his revenge. And this ASI business is just another attempt to discredit me. I went to the prime minister's office to deal with it.' Attacking factionalism in others, Dev revealed his own paranoia, the telltale sign of the arch-factionalist. I had tried for years to get people to tell me what this factionalism was all about. Was the DDCA racked by an ideological quarrel or a sociological divide? What were the issues at stake? People looked puzzled at the question. What was at stake was simply control of the DDCA and all that went with it: status and perquisites, trips to meetings and ceremonies, tickets to matches, dinners with celebrities, and above all a place on the Cricket Board, at the nerve centre of India's national game.

Dev conceded that the DDCA had overspent on the Kotla construction and was now financing the work on promises of future revenues. But he insisted over and over again that all would be ready for 2 March. 'If I had gone with the entire project – corporate boxes, more VIP seats, the third tier of the pavilion – we would never finish. I am cutting out two floors! I am aiming at better facilities for the players and the media! We will complete the rest after the World Cup. We will have spacious dressing rooms with direct entrance to the field, like in American football.' He leaned forward and tapped his finger on the desk. 'It is Sunil Dev who has made the hue and cry to get the construction done. But you know, in India, it is always hard. They will never let us get on with our work. There is always interference.'

I asked him about a newspaper article which claimed that the new construction at the Kotla was unsafe. 'They say there is this crack and that crack but I say, show them to me, I cannot oversee all the work myself.' One result of the construction carried out so far was to reduce the Kotla's 28,000 seating capacity by 2500. In this Delhi was not unique. Nearly all the grounds in India and Pakistan that underwent renovation for the World Cup ended up with fewer seats than before. Meanwhile, a greater proportion of the seats that remained were allocated directly to members, VIPs and sponsors. 'Nearly all our tickets have been allocated already,' Dev said with pride. 'Only a few hundred will go on sale to the public.'

I returned to Delhi from Pune the day before the match. The Supreme Court had removed responsibility for the CBI's hawala investigation from the prime minister's office, another blow to

Rao's credibility. At the same time, seven of the top politicians charge-sheeted in the affair, including Madhavrao Scindia, secured bail. The Ministry of Urban Affairs declared that the new buildings at the Kotla were unsafe. Recalling the disaster at Nagpur, it posted notices outside the DDCA office warning that the new constructions should not be used 'to avoid any mishappenings'. The DDCA refused to comment.

Through her brother, who works for ITC, Pam had secured three tickets to the match. Anish, the thirteen-year-old, had exams that morning, and it was decided that I would go to the Kotla with Samar, the ten-year-old, and Anish would meet us during the lunch interval. I wore my Aravinda De Silva tee-shirt (purchased in Colombo) but, as the morning was cool, covered it with a loose-fitting cotton open-necked shirt. As our taxi approached the ground, traffic ground to a halt. Every other car seemed to have a VIP or VVIP sticker on the windscreen. How many VIPs could there be in one city? In Delhi, that hotbed of politicking and networking, it seemed that anyone rich enough or well-connected enough to secure cricket tickets considered himself or herself a VIP, as often as not because he or she knew someone else who claimed to be a VIP.

Outside the Kotla chaos reigned. Streams of humanity flowed and counter-flowed and it was easy to get thrown off course by the currents. I gripped Samar's hand as we plodded forward in the press, side-stepping egg and bread vendors and steering clear of the menacing looking gangs of police in riot gear, their snub-nosed automatic rifles trained casually on passers-by. Throughout the World Cup, the security forces' supernumerary presence had different implications for different constituencies. For foreigners, they symbolised an event under threat from political terrorism. For the local elite, they were insurance against embarrassment on the world stage; for the local fans, they were at best an inconvenience and at worst a menace. For the troops themselves, World Cup duties represented not only a day at the cricket but an enhancement of their sense of self-importance, which not surprisingly led to abuses.

A dozen narrow gateways served as the only points of entrance for thousands of would-be spectators. Lengthy queues formed, and a running battle was fought between queue-jumpers and the queue-consolidators. A fat man with a Mickey Mouse tee-shirt walked up to me and announced, 'I am also a foreigner. I am from Singapore. You will let me into the queue.' 'Out of the question,' I snapped, much to the delight of the disciplined souls waiting their turn behind me.

Dozens of firms handed out cardboard and paper signs and sun shades. Scavenger children darted deftly through the throng, retrieving discarded materials, clutching their precious, life-sustaining hoard, looking small and ill-nourished amid the VIPs and VVIPs. Samar and I were moving slowly towards our assigned gateway when the queue in front of us was broken up by police on horseback. The animals shied and stumbled and bellowed as the crowd parted in front of them. I grabbed Samar by the shoulders and pulled him out of the horses' path. He was unflustered but I was terrified. Once the mounted troop had passed by, the queues re-formed, but in the meantime all kinds of people (presumably friends of the police) had found their way to the front. The horses and their riders now stood idly on the other side of the queue; there could have been only one purpose to the exercise. When we finally reached our gate, police body-searched some while letting others wander in freely. Large numbers of non-ticket holders gained admission. As so often in India, security managed to be heavy-handed yet ineffectual. The lower-ranking officers who are given these duties are badly paid and poorly instructed, and always under pressure from above to favour some and incommode others.

It had taken us more than one hour to enter the ground, and the first over was being bowled as we sought our seats. Unlike India's other major stadiums, all high-banked concrete arenas, the Kotla is a low sprawl of weed-infested brick and earth terraces with the pavilion at one end and not much else, more like an English county ground of thirty years ago than the premier international stadium of the capital city of a modern cricket superpower. When the Kotla is empty, it has a haunted charm. After all, a lot of history has been made on its batsmen's wickets. The pavilion is named after Lord Willingdon, the viceroy who suppressed Gandhi's civil disobedience movement and meddled to disastrous effect in India's nascent cricket politics (he was later president of the MCC). But today, overrun with agitated spectators, the ground looked a hazardous eyesore. The recent, incomplete improvements had left the Kotla shabbier than before. The scoreboard was still the worst in the country. The new pavilion was bigger but less attractive than the old, and it rose from the far end of the ground, unfinished, uncovered, like a concrete and steel claw. I was told by reporters who were stationed there they could feel the structure shiver in the wind.

The stands were nearly full, even though there were still thousands of people outside struggling to the head of the queues. It was clear that the DDCA, desperate to placate any and all influential persons, inside and outside the cricket world, had issued tickets and passes in excess of the ground's capacity. It was also clear that there were many people in the stadium without either tickets or passes. Naively, I had thought that our Rs500 ticket marked 'special enclosure' would admit us to some relatively luxurious part of the ground. But once inside the Kotla it became obvious that the DDCA had demarcated nearly the entire arena as special enclosure. There were no enclosures and no covered stands, just ragged rows of folding chairs. Numbered slips of paper had been attached to each chair back, but in most cases torn off as anxious spectators seized whatever vantage point they could get. I found three corpulent rayban-wearing middle-aged men parked in our seats and asked them to move. 'You sit there,' the one in the middle, clearly the ring-leader, barked at us, pointing to the empty chairs in front of them. 'You are lucky to have seats at all.' As I looked around and saw the last empty seats vanishing, and yet more people entering the ground from outside, I decided to take his advice, and Samar and I staked our claim to the empty seats. It was a decision I was to regret – and soon. The ring-leader pulled out a cellphone and loudly issued orders to an underling. Cellphone exhibitionists are the bane of English cricket grounds (and indeed of innumerable other public places). Clearly, they are a global caste. The man behind us made sure that everyone within earshot knew his business, or at least that he was in business. Worse yet, he passed the cellphone to his friends, who also called their offices and issued enigmatic but portentous commands. Could anything be more irritating than this private invasion of the public sphere? The cellphone is the definitive post-modern accessory, sported by stockbrokers, drug-dealers and political professionals, linking individuals without forming a community, indeed fragmenting existing communities, as at the Kotla.

At Delhi, the Sri Lankans met their first serious challenge of the World Cup, though thanks to the forfeitures by Australia and West Indies they were already top of Group A. They were sticking with the side that had beaten Zimbabwe. India, in an extreme over-reaction to the perfectly honourable defeat in Bombay, had dropped Raju, leaving Kumble as the only specialist spinner in the side. Sidhu was left out, for reasons that remained unclear. When reporters had asked Azhar if Sidhu was fit, they were told to ask Wadekar; when they did, they were told to ask Azhar. Kapil Dev had already condemned the selectors in the morning papers: India would need Sidhu's experience and determination. Kapil also noted how important it was for India to win this tie if it was 'to avoid Pakistan in the quarter-finals'. The decision to play four seamers defied the tested wisdom that India should always play spinners at home. It appeared that Azhar and Wadekar had decided that spinners would be unable to contain the Sri Lankan batsmen on such a small ground. The irony was that it had been rumoured that India had manipulated the first-round schedule to ensure the home team played at the smaller grounds to compensate for their somewhat static outfielding.

Samar was bitterly disappointed at Sidhu's omission. He is a Sidhu-ist (a rarity anywhere in India except Punjab), and cannot abide Tendulkar, whom his classmates idolise. Like his hero, Samar is a maverick and doggedly fights his corner; he may be the only ten-year-old male in India who hates Tendulkar. 'He is an idiot,' Samar opines at the least excuse. Why? I ask. 'He gets out in a silly way. The papers always say he's so great and he thinks he's the boss of everything. They can't take him out of the team even for one match. Sidhu has a higher one-day average but they take him out all the time.'

The batting line-up had been reshuffled as well. With Jadeja restored to the middle order, Prabhakar opened with Tendulkar. Both were cautious in the early overs as Vaas and Pushpakumara bowled with verve. It was a slow start, as batsmen and bowlers sought chinks in one another's armour, and the spectators took much of the morning to settle. Considering what many had to contend with just to gain admission, it was not surprising that they seemed continuously distracted and impatient with the defensive cricket. When, after a series of dot balls, two runs came from overthrows, people whistled and stamped their feet. Some even jumped up and danced. I like a celebration as much as anyone, but I was starting to get a bad feeling about this crowd. Even if the weather hadn't been cool, I would not have exposed my Aravinda De Silva tee-shirt.

In the middle, Prabhakar was struggling. The middle of his bat seemed to have disappeared. Some wags chanted, 'Prabhakar – hai! hai!' As captain of the Delhi Ranji Trophy side and the only Delhi player in the national squad, Prabhakar, I had assumed, would be the local hero. But Ranji Trophy cricket meant nothing to this crowd. In ten overs and fifty-five minutes he had scored 7 runs before he checked a drive and was caught at mid off. We didn't know it, but we had just witnessed Prabhakar's last international innings. In the stand across the ground a small cluster of Sri Lankan flags waved. In front of us a gang with a giant Indian flag ran back and forth. The morning's first cry of 'Pakistan – hai! hai!' rang out, emanating from the three businessmen behind us. Samar looked at me apprehensively; we both knew what we might be in for.

After his mad display in Bombay, Kambli had been demoted in the batting order and the sane and solid Manjrekar assigned the vexed number three spot. It was a dubious juggling act. The Indian management seemed unable to decide where and when defence should give way to aggression and vice versa. As Murali replaced Vaas, the three wise guys cried 'No ball!' and the crowd giggled.

For some unknown reason, a vacant grassy area just outside the high wire fence protecting the outfield was suddenly opened to spectators. Hundreds rushed forward, carrying their folding chairs with them. A mêlée ensued on the boundary. Police in the middle of it shouted and waved their lathis in the air – catching the odd spectator on the back or head – but only succeeded in adding to the chaos. After fifteen minutes of confusion, order was restored as some spectators retreated to their original positions and others settled down to enjoy their eye-level view from the boundary, close to the players but not a good place from which to follow the action.

Meanwhile, the cellphone exhibitionist had got himself involved in an exchange of Hindi insults with another loudmouth several rows behind. Three cops came over to tell him to calm down but his self-confidence was overweening and – much to the amusement of his friends – he treated the police as rudely as he had everyone else. Sensing that they were dealing with a man of means (and probably with contacts), the police backed away and left him and his friends free to shout whatever they liked. The fans around us busied themselves scrawling messages on pieces of cardboard.

'Brandy, whiskey, soda, pop
We want Indians on the top'

'India minus Kambli = India plus World Cup'

'CHEERS! IPKF!'

The Indian Peace Keeping Force, to which the placard referred, had been despatched by Rajiv Gandhi to Sri Lanka in the late eighties. It became hopelessly bogged down fighting an unwinnable war against the LTTE and was unceremoniously ejected from the country by President Premadasa. I wasn't at all sure what the placard meant, and how Sri Lankans watching on television would take it. Was this match too an instance of war minus the shooting?

Tendulkar batted as if he had finally decided to spare the nation the palpitations which accompanied his customary style. Perhaps he had also decided that he had to bat as long as possible if India were to win. His innings in Delhi was everything his spectacular effort in Bombay had not been: watchful, defensive, always in control. This was the mature Tendulkar, whom the critics had clamoured for, but this man with the weight of a nation on his shoulders was not necessarily what the crowd wanted. Having weathered the pace bowlers, Tendulkar found his run-scoring blocked by the spinners. In one over he tried to sweep Murali's off break and missed, then tried to turn him to leg only to find yet another sprightly Sri Lankan fielder. After twenty overs, the score was 74 for 1. Tendulkar had crawled to 29. Manjrekar, usually the slower scorer, had raced to 26. Early in his career, he was lauded for his faultless technique and seemed a worthy scion of the classical school of Bombay batsmanship. But one-day cricket and the insecurities of Indian selection had transformed him over the years into a pragmatic nibbler. In the twenty-fourth over, he attempted to sweep a short ball from Dharmasena, got a top edge, and was caught by the keeper diving in front of the wicket. With the score 93 for 2, Azhar joined Tendulkar at the crease.

At last the crowd calmed down. India's innings had reached a delicate phase. Azhar, without a helmet, used his wrists to turn the spinners square and behind, but Jayasuriya, Murali, Dharmasena and Ranatunga all kept their heads and their line. Suddenly, Sri Lanka's part-time bowling attack appeared formidably varied and disciplined. For a while the crowd seemed immersed in the tense battle between ball and bat. Ranatunga permutated his spinners and unobtrusively manipulated his field. Using mind rather than muscle to meet the challenge, the Indians pushed and prodded and occasionally swept, but rarely found the boundary.

The rain that had been threatening all morning came down just before noon. The players went off and the covers came on. Five minutes later the storm had passed, the sun came out and Jayasuriya resumed bowling. After forty overs the Indians were 172 for 2. The batsmen had tried the spectators' patience but had succeeded in laying a solid foundation for a final assault. 'We want SIXER! We want SIXER!' the crowd chanted. With the return to the attack of Pushpakumara and Vaas, their run-hunger was satiated. In the forty-fifth over, Tendulkar straight drove Pushpakumara for 4 to reach 99, then took a single to reach his 100, his second of the World Cup. Outside the ground, firecrackers exploded. With a cross bat, Azhar slapped Jayasuriya straight back for four. The forty-ninth over, bowled by Pushpakumara, went for 24 runs. Tendulkar pulled him for six over mid wicket, turned him to leg for four, then drove him for another six with a full, straight swing of the bat that sent the ball soaring over the long on boundary rope; finally, he swung him backward of square for four more. It was a spectacular display of on side power-hitting, reliant not on long arms but on swivelling, dipping shoulders. This was the pay-off for which Tendulkar had laboured through all those overs. And this was what the crowd had come to see. They were on their feet screaming for every shot. 'Sachin! Sachin!' they shouted, but also, for the first time, applauded good Sri Lankan returns from the boundary. With these runs in the bank, they felt they could afford to be generous.

Pushpakumara, Sri Lanka's answer to Waqar Younis, had panicked at the death, and was to be replaced for the rest of the World Cup by the more experienced Wickremasinghe. In the final over, Vaas, following up his own bowling, ran out Tendulkar for 137, made off 137 balls. With Azhar he had added 175, a record Indian World Cup partnership. Kambli came on but had no chance to make amends for Bombay. Azhar finished with 75 off 80 balls (with only four fours). Despite his still-hesitant footwork, the captain seemed to be coming into form at the right time. The Indian total of 271 for 3 seemed impressive. How naïve we all were.

At the time, Tendulkar appeared to have paced his innings to perfection. Having reached only 30 in the first twenty-five overs, he scored over 100 in the second twenty-five. The Indians had added 99 runs in the last ten overs. The patient build-up had been justified. What did Samar think of Tendulkar now? Though he was on his feet and cheering as excitedly as anyone, he still insisted, 'I think he's an idiot.' In sticking to his prejudice, Samar showed the makings of a true cricket fan.

All morning I had been worrying about how Anish would find us when he finished his exam. Given the mayhem outside the ground, the jostling inside it, and the difficulty of locating any one in these vast 'special enclosures', it seemed a long shot. It had been agreed that I would go to the gate and wait for him. I did not want to take Samar because I knew we would lose our seats, but I did not feel happy leaving him on his own in the crowd. But if Anish came to the gate and failed to find me, he too would be on his own in a huge crowd. Assuming the most authoritarian tone I could muster, I told Samar not to move from his chair until I got back, and wove my way through the mêlée towards the gate. What I saw there made it clear that the situation had deteriorated during the morning. People outside were still trying to get in and people inside were trying to get out. The police opened and closed the narrow gateway at whim and ignored the appeals for help from people trapped on one side or the other. I commandeered a chair to stand on so that I could see and be seen over the heads of the throng. Beyond the gateway, people pushed and shoved and shouted at each other. A policeman ordered me off the chair. I tried to explain that I was looking for a boy who might be lost, but when the copper raised his lathi I jumped down instantly, and soon, carried by the tide of humanity, found myself pushed outside the gate. Here anarchy ruled. I glimpsed a row of four policemen thrashing some spectators with lathis. I've seen police in that frenzied state in other countries, and experience has taught me to prefer flight to fight. But how could I get back into the ground? If I was kept out, what would happen to Samar? Had I managed to misplace both my young charges? What on earth would Achin and Pam say? But suddenly the human tide flowed back in and I was carried with it.

To my relief I found Samar where I had left him, kicking his heels and daydreaming, adrift in a world of his own far more pleasant than the Feroz Shah Kotla on a big match day. We unpacked the lunch Pam had prepared and began munching parathas and pickle and vegetable curry. I stood in my seat so that if Anish managed to get in he could see me (as the only white face in this section of the crowd I thought I would be readily visible). A warm surge of relief flooded through me when I heard him call out to us. He had come just in time; Samar and I had nearly finished all the food. Pam had collected Anish from school and driven him to the Kotla, but had to park outside the newspaper office where she works, a few minutes' walk from the ground. Here in a row of ghastly modern constructions are headquartered the *Indian Express*, the *Pioneer*, the *Times of India* and other journals. Outside their offices, disgruntled cricket fans had camped, holding signs saying 'We want our tickets refunded'. In his calm and methodical manner, Anish told me what happened next.

'As we went towards the entrance we saw mounted police not letting people in, even though they were waving their tickets. They're saying "it's already full, there's no place". So we went around to another area on the side where more people were trying to get in. Mama got through into the space between the outer wall and the ground but I was left outside. This policeman kept pulling up the rope on the pavement to keep me out. I couldn't see Mama inside. Then another journalist from Mama's office came and tried to help us, as he had a press card. He told the police, "His mother is inside, you've got to let him in." But the policeman wouldn't agree and when the man from Mama's office kept complaining the policeman slapped him. Meanwhile Mama had come out and when she tried to stop the fight the policeman grabbed her and pushed her aside. She said, "It's such a terrible crowd, let's leave." But eventually we found this gate marked Entrance for Foreigners. I didn't see any foreigners there but the police let me in.'

At the time, Anish seemed amazingly unperturbed by his experience, but he said something later that struck me as sad. He did not think he would ever again watch international cricket at the Kotla. So here was a knowledgeable young fan alienated from the game by the combined ambition and incompetence of the cricket authorities. Nonetheless, delighted that we had all found one another, against the odds, we turned our attention to the match.

It became commonplace during the World Cup to hear the phrase 'pinch-hitting' applied to aggressive opening batsmen who tried to loft the ball over the inner ring of fielders. The term was borrowed from baseball, but misapplied. In North America, a pinch-hitter is a substitute batter who comes on not at the beginning but at the end of the game, replacing a pitcher in the batting order when the team requires last-minute runs to stave off defeat. Pinch-hitters are not necessarily sloggers (or 'sluggers' in baseball parlance) but simply reliable batters adept at getting on base – though not sufficiently reliable to command a place in the starting line-up. If a term from another sport is to be adopted for this latest evolution in one-day cricket, perhaps 'pace maker' – the runner who sets a fast pace in the early laps of a middle- or long-distance race – would be more apposite.

At Delhi, the fury of the Indians' last ten overs at bat was mirrored by the Sri Lankans' first ten, as Jayasuriya and Kaluwitherana took turns striking the ball over or between the fielders. Prabhakar had no more luck opening the bowling than the batting. His first two overs cost 33 runs. Off his second, Jayasuriya lofted him over mid wicket for four, then over long off for six, then drove a four through long on, then cut backward of point for another. Each was in its own way an astonishing shot, daring in conception and uninhibited in execution, but none was applauded. As an Indian fan, Samar was despondent, but Anish, who took a more scientific interest in the game, knew just how extraordinary this performance was. After three overs the Sri Lankans had scored 42 for no wicket. Srinath managed to restore some sanity to the proceedings, conceding only 5 in the fourth over. Azhar then removed Prabhakar from the line of fire. The veteran all-rounder had met his Waterloo. He was to be dropped from the team for the remaining World Cup matches and, in a bitter farewell to the game and the authorities, announced his retirement after the final.

Was Prabhakar's bowling at the Kotla that bad? The Sri Lankan openers would have been severe on anyone that afternoon. But what signalled the end for Prabhakar was not so much waywardness in line or length as sheer lack of pace and menace. He had lost the edge which had enabled him to transcend the limits of his talent and compete successfully at the highest level. At Delhi, he looked a mere club cricketer, which is what his enemies in the game had said he was all along.

'Pakistan – hai! hai!'

'No, Prabhakar – hai! hai!'

Thanks to a tumbling, shoestring catch by Kumble at short cover, Prasad dismissed Kalu for a punchy 26 off 16 deliveries. The score was 53 for 1, but it was only the fifth over. Jayasuriya, undeterred, kept up the assault, striking the same bowler for a huge six over square leg. He reached his 50 in 36 balls, a World Cup record. The new batsman, Gurusinha, joined in, pivoting to lift Ankola high and deep over long leg. After twelve overs the score was an astonishing 96 for 1. At the start of the innings the asking rate had been 5.4 runs per over; suddenly it was down to 4.6. All the careful calculation of Tendulkar's innings, the maturity and gradualism, had been for nought. The Sri Lankans were playing a different game.

At the outset of the World Cup, absolutely no one predicted that Sanath Jayasuriya would outshine Lara, Tendulkar, Warne, Wasim, Jonty Rhodes *et al* to emerge as the star of the competition. Whether as opening bat, left arm spinner, or devilishly energetic deep fielder, he could not be kept out of the action. I was told in Colombo that in schools cricket Jayasuriya had been a renowned quick scorer and always an enthusiast for the game, but that he had taken a long time to settle at international level. Coming from a provincial, lower-middle-class background, he lacked clout in the higher circles of Sri Lankan cricket and as a result found himself bounced in and out of the squad and up and down the batting order. Now, at twenty-six, this quietly spoken man with a receding hairline, giant smile and flashing eyes, was reaching maturity at the right moment. But this was maturity without jadedness; this was still the schoolboy prodigy eager to score heaps of runs as quickly as possible. He pounced onto the front foot or the back, strode across the wicket or retreated from it, always with gusto, while the stroke itself was played with a free, fluent swing of the bat. The eyes did the work, not the arms. This was not slogging or 'pinch-hitting'. There were no bulging biceps on the master blaster of the World

Cup. Unassuming and unafraid, Jayasuriya at the crease seemed to live for the sheer joy of hitting a cricket ball.

For the first time, the cellphone man showed a flash of wit: 'Bring back the rain!' But the rest of the crowd had gone quiet, stunned by what the Sri Lankans had done to their bowlers, unable to assimilate this sudden reversal in the balance of power.

With Kumble's introduction to the attack, the batsmen began to think twice before aiming for the boundary. After a sequence of perfectly pitched balls, Jayasuriya acknowledged Kumble's mastery with an admiring nod of the head. Then came a collapse that nearly revived India's chances. Going for a second run, Gurusinha was run out by Prasad. A frustrated Jayasuriya tried to loft the unerring Kumble and was caught at deep mid on. His 79 was made off only 76 balls, with an astonishing total of nine fours and two sixes. Two overs later, Kumble saw De Silva coming down the track, pushed the ball through flat and fast, and had him stumped for 8. From 129 for 1 at the beginning of the nineteenth over, the Sri Lankans had tumbled to 141 for 4 at the end of the twenty-third. The Indian total looked a long way off.

The first Mexican wave of the day circled the ground, accompanied by cries of 'Bharat mata ki jai!' and 'Hindustan – zindabad!' Even Azhar perked up and posted two close fielders for Kumble. The crowd had grown by now beyond the capacity of the antiquated ground, which looked as if it would burst at the seams. Outside the ramshackle walls, people climbed trees, mounted rooftops and scrambled up building cranes to get a view of the play.

Kumble and Tendulkar tied down Ranatunga and Tillekeratne on a pitch that had dried out and turned dusty. In the absence of the off spinner Kapoor, Sachin, it seemed, was now expected to win the game with ball as well as bat. His bowling was economical, but he could not make the critical breakthrough; the batsmen could not be strangled out. There were already too many runs on the board. Ranatunga and Tillekeratne were free to play each ball on its merits. The genius of the opening assault was that it allowed the middle order to play percentage cricket. It also exposed the imbalance in the Indian attack. Azhar kept permutating his bowlers, but the arithmetic was against him. In the end, in the absence of Raju or Kapoor, he had to resummon Prabhakar – to bowl off spin. For Prabhakar, for India, it was the final humiliation of a humiliating day.

Impressive as the early onslaught was, the game was really won by the measured chase of the target that followed. The batsmen needed so many per over and that's what they set out to get, no more and no less. Ranatunga was single-minded in pursuit of victory, but showed no hint of the cold inhumanity that so often accompanies single-mindedness. Affable and self-effacing, he guided his team towards the target without fuss or fanfare, ably assisted (and ultimately outscored) by Tillekeratne, batting in traditional Test mode right through the 'slog overs'. Together their unbroken fifth-wicket partnership added 131 runs. As R. Mohan observed, they, as much as Jayasuriya and Kaluwitherana, 'defied all the canons of limited overs cricket. They did not play extravagant shots. They did not run the sharp single. In fact, they did the converse as they ambled from crease to crease, while also hitting every ball along the ground.' Ranatunga mistimed a drive to mid off where Ankola, running in from the boundary, skidded and dropped the catch. That was the end of any lingering Indian hopes. Later, Ankola was scapegoated for the defeat and dropped for the rest of the World Cup. But the Sri Lankans already had the game well under control.

As they marched to victory the crowd grew morose. The chants of 'Pakistan – hai! hai!' grew more frequent and more insistent, as if expressing hatred of the old enemy provided some emotional compensation for defeat at the hands of the new one. The businessmen behind us led the refrain, and when they grew bored with that, mocked the white cameramen, perched on their wooden platforms in baseball hats and shorts, who displayed the only legs on view during the whole World Cup.

Sri Lanka passed the Indian total in the forty-ninth over. Water bottles and Coke cans were hurled from the stands and small fires smouldered. The crowd, so agitated all day, now sulked as it left the ground, and the post-mortems began.

The next day, the Indian press pilloried Azhar and Wadekar. The selection of four seamers and the omission of an extra spinner were deemed symptomatic of an abject failure in strategic thinking. Azhar had not even bothered to inspect the wicket before the toss, it was said, and had stuck stubbornly to the original game plan despite the unpromising conditions. In the *Pioneer*, Rajaraman declared that India had lost 'the battle of wits'. He reminded Azhar, 'It is the pitch, more than the size of the ground, that determines team composition.' With two defeats in the first round, India was now likely to meet Pakistan in Bangalore. Wadekar insisted, 'We are not concerned who we'll meet in the quarter-finals,' but the pressure on his team was mounting. Before Delhi, the anxiety had been that India could not win if Tendulkar failed. Now the public had to face a new reality: India could lose even if Tendulkar succeeded.

Ranatunga was quietly pleased with his team's performance. 'It was a good toss to lose,' he conceded. Asked if Sri Lanka could win the Cup, he replied, 'It is still a long way to go.'

The press were even tougher on the police and the DDCA than on Azhar and Wadekar. Apparently, genuine VIPs – Clive Lloyd, Wes Hall, Scindia and Bindra himself – had been jostled outside the gates. That was bad news for Sunil Dev. The *Indian Express* accused 'an army of hostile, baton-wielding policemen' of making 'a farce of the arrangements'. The *Hindustan Times* reported that 'policemen in riot gear started systematically beating people up after 9 am'. A school student said, 'There were five of us. We reached the stadium at exactly 8 a.m. and found a huge queue. At about 8:45 we were told by the policemen that the gates have closed and we cannot enter. You have no idea how we managed the tickets. We had thronged the Syndicate

Bank branch at 6 a.m. And look at the outcome.' Ticket holders who persisted in trying to enter the ground were the worst treated of all. Describing a lathi charge by mounted police, an eyewitness said, 'People were running all over the place, driven by policemen who seemed to be playing polo with humans.'

There followed an exercise in buck-passing. 'Crowd control is the police's headache,' said Amrit Mathur, convener of the BCCI Special Committee.

'At 10:30 a.m. they told us that the stadium was packed and we stopped entry,' a police spokesperson replied. 'We were left to manage the chaotic situation and the thousands of people left outside. The organisers and the sponsors had grabbed all the VIP seats and hundreds of ticket holders had no seat.'

As for the lathi charge, the local constabulary blamed the specially assigned contingents of the Delhi armed police.

The *Hindustan Times* accused the DDCA of 'rank amateurishness'. An anonymous DDCA member informed the press that 'at least 25 per cent extra tickets were sold with the full knowledge that the stadium does not have such capacity'.

Sunil Dev was not available for comment.

As a cricket contest, the India–Sri Lanka tie was excellent, with much to admire and much food for thought. But the day had been marred not only by the police and the DDCA but by the crowd itself. In the *Hindu*, Mohan lamented the absence of a 'sporting ethos in the capital'. He criticised the crowd for its failure to enjoy sport 'as a universal activity in which one nation wins one day and another on any other day . . . sport is sport and politics is politics and never the twain should meet . . . Let us not forget to applaud the stylish and the elegant merely because nationalism seems to come in the way.'

One acquaintance who attended the Kotla told me that his view of play was constantly obstructed by children waving placards. When he asked their mother to restrain them, he was told, 'If you want to watch the cricket go home and watch it on television. We are here to make a noise.' The noise they wanted to make was one celebrating an Indian triumph. That was why the superb cricket from the Sri Lankans went largely unacknowledged. The Delhi crowd is disparaged in other Indian cricket centres and the chaos and unpleasantness at Feroz Shah Kotla was attributed to the capital's *arriviste* boorishness. 'Delhi has no culture,' the wags insist, 'only agriculture – and agree-culture.' Reading about the mess at Feroz Shah Kotla, the rest of the country gloated. What was curious was how many Delhiwallas seemed to join in; it is hard to get anyone to say a good word for the capital and hard to find anyone who lives there who does not hanker to live somewhere else.

Since it was re-founded by the British at the turn of the century, the capital has sprawled outwards, its innumerable medieval ruins scattered among sprawling residential colonies. With the worst public transport system in any major Indian city and a terrifying proliferation of private vehicles of all kinds, from gasping autoricks to sleek imported Rollers, it has become a city of throat-searing pollution and massive daily inconvenience. At the heart of political power and patronage, and of the vast north Indian plain, it is a magnet for the ambitious and the aspirant. And these consumer goods-buying, status-seeking climbers also tend to be casually communal (they are quick to assure you that Muslims are 'pandered to' by politicians and have no one to blame but themselves for their 'backwardness') and stridently nationalistic. The well-heeled hooligans who sat behind us and chanted 'Pakistan hai hai' with such relish were typical. These are the people who vote for the BJP, and who have made the capital city a stronghold of Hindutva. The section of the population most integrated into the new global marketplace is also the most chauvinist.

'Pakistan hai! hai!' is a chant I have heard at many Indian cricket grounds over the years, principally in the north, and everywhere it is engaged in by only a minority, but at Delhi it seemed particularly frequent and ferocious – a perverse compensation for India's misfortunes in the field. Liverpool and

Manchester United supporters are in the habit of abusing each other when playing a third party, and although some of this abuse can be tasteless ('Who's that lying on the runway, who's that dying in the snow . . .' – a reference to the Munich air crash), the rivalry between the two clubs remains just that – rivalry between two clubs. This cannot be said of the rivalry between India and Pakistan, in which nations and even religions pair off in mortal combat.

The root of the trouble in Delhi, inside as well as outside the ground, was the VIP culture, the curse of sub-continental cricket. In India the cricket ticket has become a status symbol, a currency of patronage, and the ambitious and the aspirant flock to one-day internationals to secure and celebrate their superiority. Liberalisation has intensified the scramble for scarce privileges, and few seem to care who gets trampled as they grab hold of the next rung of the ladder. But events at Delhi encapsulated the dilemma of liberalisation: not everyone can be a winner, not everyone can be a VIP. The system demands losers but offers them no accommodation, no place of honour. If the spirit of cricket is the spirit of winning, as the adverts for textile giant Vimal claimed, what is left of that spirit when your team is defeated? You turn on absent enemies. What does it say about the impoverished, mean-minded state of Indian nationalism today that it so often finds expression in empty verbal abuse of its principal neighbour, a country with which it shares so much, not least a common passion for cricket?

Sub-continental cricket's biggest problem is the emerging conflict between two cultures, between those who adore cricket for its own sake and those for whom it is primarily a means to an end, to either personal or national self-aggrandisement, or, increasingly, some venomous cocktail of the two. This is not a conflict of generations or between modernisers and traditionalists, or between a sophisticated elite and lumpen mass – all used to explain the events in Delhi and later in Calcutta. At Delhi it seemed to me the war was between the VIPs and the OCFs

(Ordinary Cricket Fans) and that if the VIPs were victorious, cricket would be reduced to a grotesque charade, a medium for the expression of insecurity, both national and individual.

Two days later, at Jaipur, the West Indies redeemed themselves by beating Australia. Ambrose and Walsh were scintillating in the early overs and for the first time in the World Cup the team looked alert in the field. Nonetheless, the Australians took 71 off the last ten overs, Ponting hit 102 off 111 balls and Bishop was still struggling. Browne, back in the side, opened with Campbell in an attempt to deepen the batting, but both were out early, Browne sacrificing himself to save Lara, who had issued a suicidal call for a quick single. But at last Lara and Richardson gelled. Lara's 60 was brisk. Richardson, in contrast, laboured and rode his luck to reach 93 not out, and neither mastered Warne, who conceded only 30 runs in his ten overs. Richardson dedicated West Indies' victory to 'all our friends around the world'.

But had the Australians thrown the tie? In the press there were stories that they had eased up to ensure the West Indies passage into the quarter-finals, where they would provide an obstacle in South Africa's path. Mark Taylor dismissed the notion, and offered a more realistic explanation for what had happened at Jaipur: 'They were really keen and enthusiastic to beat us. For us win or lose did not make any difference to our place in the group. So it was the intensity. The West Indians had it. We didn't.' Certainly the West Indians must have been powerfully motivated by a desire to stave off the reception that would await them at home if they failed to reach the quarter-finals.

Despite the pressure to win, Courtney Walsh declined to run out Stuart Law when the latter was backing up too far at the non-striker's end. Instead, he stopped in his run up, gave Law a warning glare, the eyes steady and pinprick-focused, and returned to his mark. Later, Taylor signalled that he had not caught Browne at slip, though Browne himself had started to walk.

In Karachi, Pakistan buried the notion that they would tank the remaining matches to secure a home quarter-final by beating England with ease before 32,000 of cricket's most vocal spectators. Miandad was promoted up the order so that he could make a farewell performance at his home ground. He managed only a scratchy, unconvincing 11, but the crowd cheered as if he had scored a century in the final. He was mobbed as he came off the pitch and his achievement of playing in all six World Cups was honoured with a cheque for Rs600,000 (£12,000). An article in the *Indian Express* asked, 'Will Lanka throw the tie to Kenya?' In Kandy, rumours circulated that Sri Lanka would let Kenya win in order to knock the West Indies out of the Cup and revenge the boycott of Colombo. 'Officials here are convinced that Australia threw their tie against West Indies to keep Kenya out of the competition,' the *Express* reported. And the anomaly in the calculation of run rates (which might have determined the final standings in Group A) created by the boycott finally came back to haunt the organisers. Kenyan officials asked Pilcom to rule that either West Indies should be judged to have scored zero runs from fifty overs against Sri Lanka or that the Kenyan team's worst defeat (against Australia) should be discounted. The request was logical. After all, why should they be penalised for fulfilling their commitments and playing all their matches? But Pilcom, guided by *realpolitik*, made no response.

Far from giving the Kenyans a passage to the quarter-finals, the Sri Lankan batsmen blasted their bowlers for a World Cup record 398, thanks not least to De Silva's stroke-filled 145 off 115 balls. Ranatunga proved that he could be as much a master of presto-tempo batting as his openers by making 75 in only 40 balls. The Kenyans had no hope of reaching the total, but did not disgrace themselves. With Steve Tikolo playing a Lankan-like innings of 96, they reached 254 before the overs ran out. Sri Lanka had topped their group, taking a maximum of ten points from five matches, as had South Africa, who did not enjoy the benefit of two forfeitures. The two leading sides of the first round would meet the fourth-placed qualifiers – England and West Indies, respectively – in the quarter-finals.

On the same day, the last of the first round, Pakistan beat New Zealand in Lahore and India beat Zimbabwe in Kanpur. The quarter-final confrontation between the two sub-continental powers was guaranteed. Pakistan batted well, with fifties from Sohail, Saeed and Malik, but the most consequential moment was when Wasim pulled a side muscle while batting. Foolishly, he refused to come off or even to have a runner, and later insisted on bowling, though physical distress was written all over his face. Undoubtedly, this was Wasim's idea of leading from the front. The crowd in Lahore (Wasim's home town) may have loved it, but the price was to be paid later in Bangalore. The Pakistani captain said he was looking forward to travelling to India. 'It's going to be a great game,' he assured everyone. 'It's going to be fun.'

In Kanpur, India lost Tendulkar, Manjrekar and Azharuddin early on, sinking to 32 for 3. But Sidhu, restored to the side, made 80, and Kambli, with the selector's axe hanging over him, 106 in 110 balls. Jadeja, with 44 not out in 27 balls, and 2 for 32 in seven overs, was man of the match. The nation's cricket equilibrium seemed to have been restored.

Before the match, Wadekar, usually cautious with the media and eager to placate all vested interests, publicly attacked Indian Airlines, the official carrier for the World Cup (at least in India; in Pakistan that honour seemed to belong to PIA). 'The airline has once again deprived us of a chance to have a proper session in the nets. Our flight was late as usual, and for the second time in a row our practice schedule has been upset. Same was the case in Delhi. Had we been allowed to use the services of other airlines, we would have been happier.'

So the Indian cricket team, like the Indian economy, was being held back from competing successfully on the world stage by an inefficient, monolithic public sector (Wadekar works for the nationalised State Bank of India). Indian Airlines is a favourite whipping boy for the Indian press, and Wadekar must have known he was on safe ground, despite the cowboys running the new private air services not having proved themselves markedly more efficient than the reviled civil servants who run Indian Airlines.

9

The last gentlemen

The Sri Lankans had long been patronised as the cuddly cubs of the cricket world, admired for their modesty and decorum on the pitch but consigned to the second rank of the international hierarchy, along with Zimbabwe and New Zealand. Now suddenly they seemed a team packed with classy cricketers, mixing flair and discipline, adventure and experience to maximum effect. Where had these guys come from? Who were they? And how had Sri Lankan cricket survived, and apparently flourished, amid war, racism and repression?

During my stay in Colombo, I had scrutinised the Sri Lankan newspapers with fascination. There was an advert for Janasakthi Life Insurance that filled most of a single page:

> Not for the sake of a ribboned coat,
> Or the selfish hope of a season's fame,
> But his captain's hand on his shoulder smote,
> Play up! play up! and play the game.
>
> We wish our boys all success in the Wills World Cup
> and look forward to seeing them flourish
> in their inimitable style and spirit.

On the page opposite, the Bank of Ceylon welcomed World Cup guests to the 'land of renowned sportsmanship' and the National Savings Bank wished everyone 'a glorious display of cricket, lovely cricket played like gentlemen and played with zest'. You wouldn't find adverts like these in India or Pakistan – or England. A passage in the *Daily News* schools cricket review caught my eye: 'Self-discipline, strength and clear-mindedness are vital for cricketers . . . Cricket is gentlemen's game. It teaches you discipline and character.' The island seemed haunted not only by the spectre of ethnic violence but by the ghosts of Hughes and Newbolt.

'An element of nineteenth-century colonial ideology survives here through cricket,' a Marxist acquaintance had told me. 'The public school ethos is more alive here than it is in England, and it saturates Sri Lankan education, whether it's private or state or whatever religion or language. If you want to understand Sri Lankan cricket, you must see schools cricket.' During my stay in Colombo, schools in Sri Lanka were closed on government orders, a response to the LTTE threat that some believed had undermined the assurances given to the Australians. But schools cricket went on as it always has – through war, peace, ethnic pogroms and election violence.

The distinctive ethos of Sri Lankan schools cricket can be traced back to the first meeting between Royal College and St Thomas's in 1879. The fixture was the brainchild of the Cambridge Blue turned Royal College master, Ashley Walker, but it is now an entirely Sri Lankan institution. The Royal Thomian remains one of the biggest events of the season, regularly attracting crowds of 15–20,000, and at times out-drawing Test matches. While the new boys compete at cricket, the old boys of both schools drink themselves silly. There is music and dancing and cheering and good-natured barracking, none of which you would see at the Eton–Harrow prototype. Schools cricket is the seedbed of Sri Lanka's international stars. All its World Cup players were developed through the school system as surely as

Bevan, Law and Ponting were developed by the Australian academy. The season runs from September to the end of March and is covered thoroughly in the local press. Successful players become household names. Coca-Cola sponsors the nationwide inter-schools league, with 160 teams in three divisions, in which all sides play at least a dozen two-day, two-innings games a year. Points are awarded for runs made and wickets taken as well as for wins and draws.

When I arrived at the Nalanda 'playground', the visitors, Dharmapala (named after the nineteenth-century progenitor of modern Sri Lankan Buddhist nationalism), were conducting a second innings rearguard action against the superior home team, who had bundled them out in their first innings for 133 and then declared at 288 for 5. At a glance, it became apparent that this was serious cricket. The eighteen-year-old all-rounder Maheli Jayawardene, who had hit 140 the day before and was now bowling off cutters (he took 2 for 13 in the end), had already played international cricket (for Sri Lanka Under-19s). The pitch was green and true. The boundaries were deep, and encircled by a stone wall on one side and the clubhouse and a small covered stand on the other. There was an outlandishly large old-fashioned scoreboard at the far end. The boys were decked out in crisp whites with floppy sunhats and spiked shoes. The umpires wore white coats. This was traditional, tactically complex two-innings cricket, with close fielders clustered around the bat and a mixture of bowling styles.

Strangely, there were no spectators. 'There will be plenty for our match against Ananda,' explained the Nalanda coach, who had played for Sri Lanka in the seventies, and so just missed out on Test glory. Oh yes, he was a Nalanda old boy himself, and his father had captained Nalanda in 1942–44. Three members of the World Cup side were Nalanda boys – Gurusinha, Mahanama and Dharmasena – as was Bandula Warnepura, Sri Lanka's first Test captain. Their arch-rivals Ananda, whom they would face at Khetterama Stadium the following week, could boast Arjuna

Ranatunga and Sidath Wettimuny. This would be the sixty-seventh annual 'battle of the Maroons', as this meeting between the country's two premier Buddhist schools was known, and old boys and families would flock to it, even though by tradition they are dour contests, three quarters having ended as draws.

The coach invited me to take a seat in the clubhouse, an inelegant gloss-painted concrete structure with a corrugated tin roof. A plaque listed the First XI cricket captains going back to 1924, the year the school was founded. The coach informed me that Nalanda was now a government school with 4200 pupils, and five cricket teams. He had worked here for ten years, without pay. In that time the school's First XI had never lost a two-innings match and had won the league title four times. I told him it was rare to find cricket played like this at schools in England these days. A large but quiet man, he acknowledged the praise with a small nod. 'They must all learn both batting and bowling and thinking about the game,' he explained, and then identified the specialities of each of his Nalanda protégés: right arm inswing, right arm outswing, off cutter, leg spin, left arm finger spin, left arm wrist spin, and classic off spin.

'Schools cricket has become much more competitive. Before 1987, all our matches were friendlies. But with the establishment of the league, rivalry has become more intense and there is a drive to win at any cost.' A Dharmapala wicket fell, and the batsman swiped angrily at the ground. The Nalanda players exchanged exuberant high fives. 'This they have learned from television,' the coach said. It saddened him, but there was nothing he could do about it.

We had lunch in the bare, dark refectory behind the clubhouse: fish curry, green beans, potatoes, a hard-boiled egg and slices of white bread. The boys sat around a long table conversing in low voices while I joined the coach, the cricket master, and the umpires at a smaller table. Everyone was kind but somewhat baffled by my curiosity. After all, Sri Lanka had not yet won the World Cup. People in Sri Lanka knew there was something special about their schools cricket, but they didn't think anyone else would be interested. The cricket master complained that the young were getting into bad habits, imitating the Test players. The umpires agreed. 'Everything is about winning nowadays,' said one. 'It starts too early,' said the coach, returning to his theme. 'Even under-13s play too hard and don't have enough fun.'

I stayed to watch Nalanda make further inroads in the Dharmapala batting; it was obvious they would win, and replace old rivals Ananda at the top of the 'Coca-Cola League'. Next week's Battle of the Maroons promised much. As I left, my hosts were kind enough to present me with a copy of the printed brochure commemorating last year's Ananda–Nalanda match. In it the Nalanda principal wrote:

> Cricket is universally recognised as a gentlemen's game. The respectability of this game and the finer characteristic features have added immense popularity to schools. It helps students to cultivate patience, love and obedience to their leaders. The Battle of the Maroons is not performed to find the winner but to appreciate the finer strokes of the game in a very fascinating manner which gives thrilling sensation to spectators.

The echoes of *Tom Brown's Schooldays* were deafening, but there remained something very un-English, very un-puritanical in that reference to the game giving 'thrilling sensation to spectators'. It was the Sri Lankan hedonism buried amid the waffle about the game's higher purpose. As Gary Sobers had observed, 'Sri Lankans seem to combine something of the Caribbean spirit of cricket coming from their own nature and at the same time are bound by a very traditional approach to the game.'

I had discovered that the rhetoric of the 'gentlemen's game' flourished in Sri Lanka, but was the rhetoric any closer to reality here than elsewhere? Just before the World Cup, *Sri Lankan Cricket*, the country's only English-language cricket magazine, hit the streets for the first time after a nine-year interregnum, a harbinger of better times to come. Its editorial spoke of cricket in terms even the most ancient MCC die-hard would blush to mouth.

> Cricket is basically a gentle English game, played by persons who would be described as 'Gentlemen' in the highest sense of the word. Cricket is a character building game, where a straight bat at the crease means dignity and integrity in the game of life. Let us keep it that way! Making mischievous, spreading rumours around, creating discontent and discrimination, making allegations against individuals is not a part of cricket. Booing and jeering players on the field, thereby causing indifferent performances, is not a part of cricket.

Even in Sri Lanka, it seemed, cricket had fallen from grace. The editorial was only one of many local protests against the incursion of bad manners and modern politics into the 'gentlemen's game'. But was the public school ethos the leader writers eulogised all it was cracked up to be? These institutions had produced not only Ranatunga and De Silva but generations of Sinhala chauvinist politicians, guilty of thuggery against the minority community and other behaviour far less acceptable than booing and jeering. And at school these men were cricketers, and later administrators of cricket; their vices were the vices of schools cricket. In Shyam Selvadurai's *Funny Boy*, an observant and touching novel set in Colombo during the tumultuous years leading to the great anti-Tamil pogrom of 1983, the gay Tamil hero's first act of rebellion is to refuse to play cricket with his older brother. Later, at a school modelled on St Thomas's, he is forced to memorise and recite 'Vitaï Lampada', the Newbolt poem that inspired Janasakthi Life Insurance. He finds it a bewildering experience:

> There were many expressions and words I wasn't familiar with and the precise meaning of the poems eluded me. They spoke of a reality I didn't understand. 'Vitaï Lampada' was about cricket, but not cricket the way I understood it. It said that through playing cricket one learned to be honest and brave and patriotic. This was not true at the Victoria Academy. Cricket, here, consisted of trying to make it on the first-eleven team by any means, often by cheating and fawning over the cricket master. Cricket was anything but honest.

Sri Lanka's cricketers may have emerged into the world's consciousness only in recent years, but Sri Lankan cricket has always been worldly, always aware and in touch with the game beyond its shores. In 1882, Ivo Bligh's MCC team stopped off in Colombo on their way to recapturing the Ashes. Thereafter, it was a regular and welcome port of call for shipboard touring teams. The Maharajah of Vizianagaram took a guest team to the island in 1930 that included Deodhar and Nayadu, as well as Hobbs and Sutcliffe. Dr Churchill Hector Gunasekara (the 'Father of Ceylon cricket') played for Middlesex; his MCC membership was proposed by no less a figure than Sir Pelham Warner.

The visit of the 1948 Australians was a major event in the island's history and everyone claims to have been there. The green wicket at the Oval was so fast and bouncy that Keith Miller said he wanted to roll it up and carry it with him in his pocket. Decades later, upper-class women still swooned over memories of Bradman's billowing white shirt. As for Bradman, he was most impressed by the Oval scoreboard, which, he said, 'gives more information than any board in the world – a tribute to local enthusiasm'. A few years later, Learie Constantine, who had been coaching in the island, wanted to take a Ceylon team to England. His plan was vetoed by F.C. De Saram, who many years before had made a century for Oxford against an Australian attack led by Clarrie Grimmett. De Saram said his players weren't ready yet. He was imprisoned in 1962 for his alleged involvement in a military coup, but was later awarded an OBE for services to cricket.

But this cosmopolitanism was restricted to the gentlemen hedonists of Colombo, whose legacy is a city with three Test venues and at least thirty-five other club or school grounds. In the rest of the country football and the indigenous game of *elle* remained dominant. In recent decades, that has changed. Radio commentary in Sinhala was introduced in the seventies. With the arrival of official Test cricket in the early eighties, the state-owned Rupavahini telecast the game across the island. 'What we have seen,' my Marxist acquaintance explained, 'is the vernacularisation of Sri Lankan cricket. It has been taken up in all regions and by all social classes. You'll see it now played by street urchins and in rural villages. The old aristocratic traditions are still there – but the game is now becoming a genuinely popular cultural force.'

In the early years of Test status, the squad was dominated by the English-speaking elite, graduates of Royal or St Thomas, for whom Sinhala was a second language. Now, the team was made up largely of members of the Sinhala-speaking lower-middle classes. Many hailed from the provinces (Jayasuriya and Wickremasinghe from Matara in the backward south, Muralitharan from Kandy in the central highlands, Pushpakumara from Panadura and Chandana from Galle down the coast). Yet all were products of top-flight cricket-playing schools and nearly all played for one of the prestigious Colombo clubs. Though no longer merely a pastime of the urban elite, the game was still in thrall to elite urban institutions. Rural and working-class cricketers have still to rely on being spotted by a famous school and subsequently introduced to a famous club if they wish to make headway in what has become an extremely competitive profession. 'Everything depends on the grapevine,' my acquaintance said. 'Cricket has been democratised – but you still need contacts.'

Visiting Sri Lanka in June 1983, one month before Colombo exploded in anti-Tamil carnage, the writer Shiva Naipul observed, 'Cricket is not played in Sri Lanka because of any post-imperial nostalgia. The clubs are only nominally oases of exclusivity. Many are shabby, fly-blown places battling to make ends meet. The young men who play cricket may, by the standard of the island, constitute an elite. But they are a peculiar and modest elite, an elite on the make.' Despite the rapid development of cricket in the island, professional cricketers must still secure an income outside the game. Ranatunga has pursued a career in insurance and De Silva, who owns a trading firm, has declared, 'After I retire, it's going to be imports, exports and handling cheque books.' Most cricketers still rely on corporate patronage secured through personal contact, and companies in search of reflected glory give them jobs because they are cricketers. However, more opportunities to earn money playing cricket are opening up all the time. Every year an increasing number of Sri Lankans seek employment as club professionals in the English leagues. Others work in Malaysia and the Gulf. The trade winds that once blew the game to the island, together with so many other exotic influences, now carry Sri Lankan cricketers far afield.

But has this democratised, globalised sport succeeded in bridging the ethnic chasm that runs through the country? I asked everyone I met, and all had trouble answering. Vaas, Kaluwitherana and manager Duleep Mendis were all Christians, and Australian coach Davenal Whatmore came from a Sri Lankan burgher family. But what about the country's principal minority, the Tamils? Upper-class, urban, English-speaking Tamils had played a major role in the game and the Tamil Union Oval was for decades the country's foremost cricket ground. However Murali is today the only Tamil in the Sri Lankan side. Indeed, he is the only Tamil in the Tamil Union side. Outside Sri Lanka, Murali has been hailed as a symbol of national unity. Inside, his presence seems less significant. For one thing, he is not one of the Sri Lankan or 'Jaffna' Tamils, based in the north and tracing their presence in the island back thousands of years, but what is known as an 'Indian', 'Kandy' or 'hill' Tamil, a descendant of plantation workers imported by the British in the nineteenth century. Though stripped of their citizenship and the franchise by the Sri Lankan government in the 1950s, the hill Tamils have stayed out of the ethnic conflict and feel they have little in common with the Tamils of the north. 'Most of the cricket fans here consider Murali an honorary Sinhalese,' said my informant. 'He's what some people like to call "an intelligent Tamil". When the cricketers visit the Buddhist shrines, Murali always goes with them.'

Do Sri Lankan Tamils fail the Tebbit test? Sinhala chauvinists will insist that, secretly, all Tamils support the nation's enemies. But despite the war and their many grievances against the majority community, Tamils have usually backed Sri Lankan cricket sides as passionately as other Sri Lankans. Trilingual commentaries of all Sri Lanka's matches are now broadcast nationwide, and in the war-ravaged regions people made extraordinary efforts to follow the World Cup. Even the LTTE indicated that it thought 'Sri Lanka will win the World Cup', which was as close to a declaration of support for the national side as could be made by an organisation dedicated to violent secession. Even veteran Tamil civil rights activists assured me there had been no discrimination in cricket: 'People are sceptical, I know, but when it comes to cricket, ethnic divisions have not yet intruded,' said one. 'If there is any sentiment of Sri Lankan nationhood left, it may be in cricket.' Father Harry Miller, a human rights advocate, reported that the Tamil boys at his college in war-scarred Batticaloa wanted Sri Lanka to win. 'Generally, people here have separated the cricket from the war.' An American sociologist working in the same city observed that whenever the threat of violence from the LTTE or the government ebbed, the cricket flowed. She had concluded that the presence of cricketers in the streets and parks was the best indicator of the fluctuating level of insecurity. My Marxist acquaintance agreed. 'I visited Jaffna during the peace negotiations last year. It was still under LTTE control. I stayed at St John's, a famous cricketing school, which was playing a big match against Hindu College. This is an old rivalry and people had revived it at the first opportunity. It was like a carnival. It was a major cultural event, and it didn't matter whether the LTTE or the government was running the show.'

The Sinhalese Sports Club lies in the heart of Colombo's Cinnamon Gardens, an old colonial quarter of shady verandas and ample lawns. The historic, palm-fringed ground is pert and well maintained. Like the MCC, the SSC is a private club and leases its premises to the Cricket Board for international matches. Unlike the MCC, the club boasts a top-class cricket side whose current members include Ranatunga, Wickremasinghe and Gurusinha. It has come a long way since the days when it was derided as 'Suddha SC' (white man's SC). The day I visited there were no cricketers to be seen, but the ground was a hive of activity. Workers were repairing cracks in the concrete stanchions, fitting new plastic moulded seats, hanging signboards, painting balconies and stairs, and scrupulously and generously watering every inch of outfield. Women weeded the wicket by hand while men trimmed the grass surrounds. A new electronic scoreboard was being installed and a new carpark cleared adjacent to the ground.

Inside the modern clubhouse, Ana Punchihewa, the president of the Board of Control for Cricket in Sri Lanka, stole a precious half hour from his hectic schedule to answer my questions; I was grateful. I knew he had a lot on his mind: the continuing fall-out from the Australian–West Indies boycott, the countless demands for tickets and other favours that shower down on cricket officials across the sub-continent, not to mention his full-time duties as managing director of Coca-Cola Sri Lanka. A young-looking forty-year-old with a smooth face, suave, soft-spoken and modest, Punchihewa patiently explained the power structure of Sri Lankan cricket. The thirty-two controlling clubs (pre-eminent among them old colonial establishments like the SSC) had two votes each, like the Test-playing members of the ICC. In addition, the seventeen affiliated clubs, district cricket associations and anomalous bodies like the Schools Cricket Association had one each. Together they elected the Board's officers and executive committee, who all served on a voluntary basis. The only paid staff were clerical workers. Punchihewa was keen to change that. He hoped to appoint a full-time chief executive next year, but that would require an amendment to the Board's constitution.

Punchihewa was palpably earnest about his mission: to

modernise Sri Lankan cricket. 'We have set ourselves the mission of being the best cricketing nation by the year 2000. We have drawn up a five-year plan and now need US$1.5 to US$2 million per year.' In order to raise the funds, Punchihewa had launched Cricket Fund 2000, an ambitious scheme which was very much his baby. 'I got the idea when we won our first overseas Test in New Zealand and we met all these expatriate Sri Lankans who were so proud of what we had done. Victories like that raise Sri Lanka's status in the world, not just in cricket. So we're appealing to Sri Lankans based overseas. There are 170,000 in the UK, and others in the Middle East, south-east Asia and Australia. They are a vital resource for us. Davenal Whatmore is a good example; he was born here but emigrated with his family when he was eight years old. Now he's come back and is a tremendous asset to our cricket.' I wondered how the Cricket 2000 Fund appeal would go down with the 400,000 Tamils in Europe and North America, many of them deeply hostile to the Sinhalese establishment. I asked Punchihewa the same question I had asked everyone else: how had the war which had driven them overseas affected Sri Lankan cricket? He gave me the same answer. 'International schedules were disrupted but domestic cricket and cricket development went on regardless.' And then reverted to his favourite topic. 'We're selling the Cricket Fund 2000 logo to local companies, but only to one company in each sector – one cellphone company, one soft drinks company, etc. We hope to open our new cricket academy in June, right here at the SSC. We'll have a full-time paid director and for the first year we'll have the twenty-two players just below Test level.'

Punchihewa was something new and different in the hierarchy of Sri Lankan cricket. As president of Galle Cricket Club (for which Kaluwitherana plays) he was, he noted with pride, the first out-station president of the Sri Lankan Board. 'We need to develop the out-stations,' he insisted. 'We've already designated three centres of excellence – Kandy, Kurunagela, and Galle. And we plan to develop these as Test centres.' He was also the first non-politician to head the Board since independence. He is a product of the public school tradition (he attended Millfield with David Graveney), and has represented Sri Lanka in that most exclusive of third-world pastimes, golf. But he belongs as much to the multinational corporate culture as to the old Sri Lankan elite. He is proud of his role in involving big business in the island's cricket. He recited the litany of current sponsors: Coke for schools and club cricket; Singer for the inter-district competition and the Test side; Unilever for the under-13s and under-15s.

Listening to Punchihewa's persuasive tones and glancing at the ageing wooden plaque bearing the names of his predecessors, I felt, as so often in cricket, the new struggle for birth within the musty womb of the old. Sri Lanka is by no means the only country where politicians have played a role in cricket, but what is exceptional here is that the role of the state in administering cricket is explicit (under Sri Lanka's constitution, the Sports Minister appoints the selectors and approves team selection). For decades the Cricket Board has been directly run by a succession of senior politicians. I read their names on the wall behind Punchihewa. There was J.R. Jayawardene who as Board president in the fifties had persuaded Learie Constantine to coach in the island and who still today serves as president of the SSC. There were other UNP stalwarts, including Robert Senanayake, son of the country's first prime minister, and Tyrone Fernando, a Royal College and Oxford man, a Catholic and a member of the Cabinet for over fifteen years. His political base is in Moratuwa, south of Colombo, and there he had constructed the Tyrone Fernando Stadium, the fifth and most recent of Sri Lanka's international cricket venues. There was also N.M. Perera, a one-time Trotskyist interned by the British, leader of the leftist LSSP, finance minister in Mrs Bandaranaike's 1970 SLFP-led coalition and president of the Non-Descripts Cricket Club (for which Aravinda De Silva plays).

Above all there was the late Gamini Dessanayake, a politician of charm, energy and limitless ambition, and perhaps the single most influential figure in Sri Lanka's recent cricket development. First elected president of the Board in 1981, he was instrumental in the last-minute ICC lobbying that secured Test status for Sri Lanka. 'Sri Lanka does not consider Test status to be a privilege,' he told the press waiting outside the committee room that day at Lord's. 'It is a burden to raise the standard and lay out an infrastructure.' Cricket, he believed, must be a career for young people, and through his Sri Lankan Cricket Foundation he brought the country's private sector into the business of cricket. He recognised that the development of the game was profoundly skewed by the domination of a handful of Colombo clubs, so he initiated district and provincial tournaments with three-day matches, giving Sri Lanka, for the first time, a competition akin to what was called first-class in other countries. He constructed new stadiums in Kandy and Matara in the south (Jayasuriya's home town), as well as indoor nets and the board office in which I met Punchihewa. He also served as president of the Asian Cricket Conference (the first Asia Cup in 1986 was his brainchild), and enlisted Gary Sobers to teach the island's players the realities of Test cricket. Like all Sri Lankan cricket officials, he spent much of his time soothing egos and manipulating factions. 'I find it easier to run two ministries and a trade union than the Cricket Board,' he confessed to Sobers.

During the 1981 election Dessanayake, already a cabinet minister and at that time the fastest rising star in the UNP, was campaigning in Jaffna when uniformed government security officers, abetted by plainclothes thugs, burnt the historic Jaffna Public Library to the ground. Ninety-five thousand books and priceless manuscripts – an irreplaceable cultural treasure and, most importantly, symbol of Tamil identity – were consumed in flames. No one doubted Dessanayake's complicity. Pandering to Sinhalese bigotry by attacking the Tamils has been the stock in trade of nearly all Sri Lanka's leading politicians since independence, both UNP and SLFP. Even the left parties have a shameful record. But Dessanayake also came under fire for his handling of the giant Mahaweli dam and irrigation project. Heavily subsidised by the World Bank and other foreign donors, the Mahaweli project was castigated by environmentalists (it stripped the island of much of what was left of its forest cover) and by local inhabitants who were moved from their homes and who saw the transplantation of Sinhalese colonists to the area as an attempt by the UNP to establish a new electoral base.

In 1991, Dessanayake tried to remove President Premadasa, whose increasing megalomania had led to discontent inside the UNP. He failed and was hounded out of the party. He took refuge with other dissidents in a new organisation, the Democratic United National Front. But after Premadasa was assassinated by the LTTE in 1993, he returned to the fold. When the UNP lost the parliamentary elections in August 1994 and fell from power for the first time in seventeen years, Dessanayake became leader of the opposition, and prepared to run against Chandrika Kumaratunga as candidate for president. The new People's Alliance government lost no time in indicting him for bribery. In Parliament, he mounted a lengthy and passionate defence. Indignant as he was to find his political and financial record under scrutiny, he was absolutely outraged at the suggestion that he had profited from his hard work for Sri Lankan cricket. 'Mr Speaker, you know the situation that prevailed before I took over as president of the Board. With all my other commitments, I devoted my time and energies to help our country achieve Test status, to build headquarters for the Cricket Board, to launch the Cricket Foundation in order to help out-station cricketers, and to get down international cricketers such as Sir Garfield Sobers. I was rewarded by having a Commission foisted on me.'

Shortly afterwards, in the middle of the presidential campaign, Dessanayake was killed (together with fifty-three others) by an LTTE suicide bomber. The RDX plastic explosive was the same that had blown apart Rajiv Gandhi and Premadasa. The Jaffna Library had been avenged.

Given the direct involvement in cricket of government ministers and opposition leaders, it is not surprising to find that the ups-and-downs of party politics have disrupted the game. In the years following the Sri Lankans' entry into Test cricket, the constant electioneering within the Board bred instability and insecurity within the Test side. The factionalism was in part to blame for the decision of a number of leading cricketers to join a rebel tour to South Africa, a development that set back the maturation of the Test side by several years. When Sidath Wettimuny retired not long after scoring 190 at Lord's in 1984, it was said that he had been pushed out. When Ranatunga was relieved of command after a tour of New Zealand in 1990–91, questions were raised in Parliament.

Punchihewa, Dessanayake's determinedly non-political successor, talked as if those days were dead and buried. His ambition, he said, was to imbue Sri Lankan cricket with a 'corporate strategy' and 'the culture of the private sector'. The Board had to professionalise its operations. 'When I was first elected, I couldn't believe how badly it was run, like a government department.' Punchihewa had his work cut out, but under Sri Lanka's Sports Law he was allowed to serve only two one-year terms in succession. His first year would expire after the World Cup and a single extra term would not be enough. He conceded the problem: 'A good manager is someone who grooms his successor.'

Without naming anyone, and in his gentlest tones, Punchihewa criticised his predecessors. 'Unfortunately, they did not agree any profit sharing in regard to the World Cup. We only get the revenue from television and perimeter advertising.' And because of the Australian and West Indies boycott, that revenue was likely to be cut by 80 per cent. The Board had sold about Rs5 million worth of tickets (£63,000) for the two cancelled matches, all of which would have to be returned, and had taken only half as much for the remaining matches against Kenya and Zimbabwe. 'But it's not just the money. It was a terrible blow to our prestige.' However, unlike many in Sri Lanka, Punchihewa wanted to put the Australian action in context. 'Australia have been good friends to us in the past. They came here in 1992 for three Tests when no one had been willing to play here for years.' The West Indies, in contrast, had done nothing to help Sri Lankan cricket. 'We've had only one Test against them so far – in nearly fourteen years of playing Test cricket' – a worse record even than the English, who have 'only promised us one Test in 1997 and two more in 2001'. Why didn't he demand more? I asked. Punchihewa laughed and winked at me, as if to say I should know better. 'If I had shouted for more I might have ended up with only one Test – in 3001.'

I mentioned anxieties people had expressed about the changing culture of Sri Lankan cricket. Punchihewa was sympathetic but firm: 'Changes were inevitable. You have television. You have the development of the economy. We need change, but we don't want everything to change. We wish to keep the enjoyment. We still want to play for fun.' He was proud of Raman Subba Row's declaration that he would travel a thousand miles to watch Sri Lanka play 'because you play the way we did in the old days'.

For Sri Lankan cricket the last two years had been eventful. After the team had been thrashed by the Indians in early 1994 the Board had imposed fitness tests on all the players. De Silva failed the test and was dropped for a series at Sharjah. In protest, Ranatunga and other leading players boycotted the tour. The Sri Lankans lost and the burly veterans returned. In February 1995, they beat New Zealand at Napier to record their first overseas Test victory. Ranatunga and De Silva had emerged stronger for their confrontation with the administration and saw eye to eye with the new management team of Dav Whatmore and Duleep Mendis. For the first time, there was a modicum of stability in the country's cricket regime. Later that year came the visit to Pakistan, where they came from behind to win both Test and one-day series, the Champions Cup in Sharjah, where they disposed of West Indies in the final, and the beleaguered tour of Australia, where their new opening pair, Kaluwitherana and Jayasuriya, first made a mark. Sri Lanka now had five batsmen in their late twenties or early thirties, all reaching maturity after years on the international circuit. It had six players boasting more than 100 one-day caps each and its total of 1114 caps in the squad was bettered only by the Pakistanis. I asked Punchihewa if he thought they could win the World Cup. 'It is not impossible,' he answered with a quiet smile.

10

Nothing official about it

The World Cup saw the climax of a remarkable battle for supremacy in sub-continental cricket: the battle between Pepsi and Coke.

Since their readmission to India, the two soft drink giants have been eager to use cricket as a vehicle to reach consumers. Pepsi squeezed its foot in the door first, sponsoring one-day international contests and even the largely unwatched (and sometimes unwatchable) Ranji Trophy, just as Britannic Assurance sponsored the County Championship in England. The difference between a soft drink and an insurance company spoke volumes about the difference in cricket's popular image in the two countries. But when it came to official sponsorship of the World Cup – the biggest prize sub-continental cricket had to offer – Pepsi found itself ill rewarded; loyalty was sacrificed to cash calculation. At the end of a fierce bidding war (which saw the initial offer quadrupled) Coca-Cola emerged victorious; for US$3.5 million it secured the right to dub itself the 'official drink of the World Cup', to supply soft drinks at the grounds and to stick its brand logo under spectators' noses at every opportunity.

Coke plastered lamp-posts and billboards across the country with highly stylised images of faceless batsmen and bowlers thrashing or hurling the ball. The caption read simply 'the official drink' ('of the World Cup' was apparently deemed superfluous). The campaign's visual evocation of power and place emphasised the muscular dynamism of the game. The company referred to the graphics as 'computer-generated'; certainly the minimalist, streamlined representations of physical action evoked a high-tech modernity in keeping with the profile projected by Pilcom. The multinational soft drink, the second most widely recognised word on the planet (the first is 'OK'), hoped to link itself not merely to a game enormously popular among its target audience, but specifically to what that game has come to represent for that audience: a vehicle for the triumph of individual performance on a global stage. The images were instantly recognisable but cold and anonymous. A marketing consultant observed, 'They kept on saying "Coke is the real thing". But a real thing should be for real people – which they did not show.'

Coke's rival did not make the same mistake. In one of the most effective counter-coups in the history of advertising, Pepsi turned defeat in the bidding war to its advantage. Its World Cup catch-phrase, 'Nothing official about it', was an instant hit. According to Ravesh Srivastava (Marketer of the Year gold award winner in 1995), the Pepsi adverts 'captured the heart and mind of the entire nation . . . "nothing official about it" has become part and parcel of our day-to-day vocabulary.'

Pepsi's marketing research had managed to uncover the obvious: for young people aged 14–25 (the target audience) the word 'official' was pejorative; the sheer cheek of broad-casting the soft drink's 'unofficial' status was conversely irresistible. One glance at the adverts and the audience knew that Pepsi had succeeded in cashing in on the World Cup without actually paying for it. You had to laugh. The knowing flippancy of the campaign (designed for Pepsi by the Hindustan Thompson agency) was testimony to the increasing self-awareness of sub-continental consumers.

In its television adverts, Pepsi cannily exploited cricket's contradictory cultures. While a complacent voice intoned, 'Officially cricket is played in white . . . at a leisurely pace . . . officially, the players are gentlemen . . . who have to drink the official drink . . .' the TV screen flickered with the helter-skelter of the one-day game, displaying Pepsi's colour-clad roster of super-stars in the grip of competitive fury, snarling, letting rip deafening appeals, celebrating triumph with extravagant gestures. Pepsi's strategists knew or guessed that cricket officialdom has always been perceived as hidebound and puritanical. The dichotomy between the establishment which guards the rituals and etiquette of the game and the fans who flock to the grounds seeking the thrills of physical action and the relentless pursuit of victory is both ancient and international. In the sub-continent, that dichotomy has been reinforced by an amused popular awareness that cricket as it is played and watched in India and Pakistan today has little to do with the traditional ethos of the game as celebrated in reams of English and Anglophile prose. The Pepsi ads played shamelessly to the gallery by hinting that 'our cricket' had superseded 'their cricket', that 'our game' was more modern and compelling than 'theirs'. Thus the fast, physical and remorselessly competitive new cricket loathed by Indian traditionalists was celebrated by a multinational corporation as the authentic game of the sub-continental masses.

Pepsi scored because it made sure its message was carried by names and faces familiar to potential consumers. Throughout the World Cup, every town and city had its quota of Pepsi billboards with Tendulkar, Azhar or Kambli in jeans and casual sports shirts. Giant painted cut-outs of Sachin looked down over busy intersections, the superhuman smile shaped like a bloated kidney, and stuffed with more white teeth than could fit into anyone's mouth. These were icons of youthful self-confidence, upward mobility and casual affluence. Azhar, Tendulkar and Kambli all featured in Pepsi's television campaign, as did Courtney Walsh and Ian Bishop. Revealingly, the only English cricketer signed up for Pepsi's World Cup campaign was Dominic Cork, whose aggressive expressiveness struck a chord with sub-continental fans. Bizarrely, they also signed up Dickie Bird ('the final arbiter of Cola Justice'), stuck him in a judge's wig and had him declaim with a nervous smirk, 'there's nothing official about it'. In one of the most popular Pepsi adverts, Tendulkar is seen playing cricket with some poorly dressed kids in a galli. 'Sachin Tendulkar is just plain greedy,' the voice-over tells us, 'when it comes to runs or . . .' Tendulkar accidentally hits the ball through a lorry windscreen and the Sikh driver chases him in anger – only to present him with a Pepsi. 'Nothing official about it,' chirps the Indian batsman, bottle in hand, before turning his baseball cap front to back with an impish grin.

Here was the super-star as street urchin. India's thoroughly modern cricket millionaire, out-earning even Shane Warne and Brian Lara, became a symbol of the informality and brashness of the new cricket culture. How curious to find the reversed baseball cap – a product of the rap and hip-hop culture of the North American ghettos, a badge of cocky, streetwise insouciance in a hostile, demeaning environment – transmuted to the sub-continental context and transformed into an emblem of cool-and-casual post-modernity.

Pepsi was not alone in seeking to associate itself with the uncompromising aggression of one-day international cricket. Vimal's adverts 'saluting the spirit of winning' lacked the wit and self-mockery of the Pepsi ads, but one suspects they were still more resonant than Onida's series of woeful parables invoking the 'spirit of cricket'. 'You were desperate for a big score just to stay in the team. Your senior partner makes a faulty call and is stranded in the middle. Again you think of the team. You run yourself out. THAT'S CRICKET.' Or, 'The non-striker is in his nineties. In his excitement he's strayed out of the crease. No, you don't break the wicket. You simply break stride in your run-up, and you smile. THAT'S CRICKET.' Onida was trying to persuade people to buy its television to watch the World Cup, but the adverts lacked credibility. The gap between the altruistic cricket they praised and the anything but altruistic game being shown on TV screens was too great. Some commentators tried to ignore this gap; Pepsi revelled in it.

Talking to marketing managers is like talking to New Labour spin-doctors. It's hard to get them to stop chanting the mantra of the day long enough to answer a direct question. Deepak Jolly, Pepsi's salesman-in-chief, was no exception. Today's slogan was '*Ye hi hai right choice*' ('it's the only right choice') and during our interview Jolly hiccuped the refrain as if it were a chorus in a pop song. 'There is a phenomenal passion for cricket in India and Pepsi has the passion to win. That's why Pepsi is a favourite product with our youth. Pepsi means: be young, have fun. It means: be fizzy and bubbly, like our cricketers. It means be successful. You see, we have not always had the winner's mindset here, but now it is coming more and more with people like Kapil and Sachin. They are the new role models for Indian youth. And they are saying, *Ye hi hai right choice*!'

We met in Jolly's surprisingly modest office in Pepsi's Indian headquarters on Delhi's Tolstoy Marg. He is a round, bloated character with a shiny head and an apparently endless store of good-natured belly laughs. I had told him on the telephone how impressed and amused I was by Pepsi's 'Nothing official about it' campaign and he welcomed me with a big smile and a cold Pepsi, though it was just ten in the morning. I have to admit it; I like the taste of Pepsi and drained it in a few gulps. Jolly offered me another and I accepted gladly. 'The Indian consumer has undergone a metamorphosis,' he explained. 'He is now more aware of his right to choose. And choice is the name of the game today. Choice is democracy. Choice is the market. *Ye hi hai right choice*. And we have provided the right choice.'

Pepsi was spending a fortune on its World Cup promotions, but Jolly was confident it was worth every rupee. 'World Cup cricket is a value-for-money investment. Most people are watching the World Cup on television, and our "Nothing official about it" campaign will reach hundreds of millions through Doordarshan. The "official" drink is only important inside the stadium, and we have sewn up the action outside the stadium.' He claimed sales were up by 50 per cent over the same period in 1995. Like everyone else making a buck out of Indian cricket, Jolly was quick to assure me that the company had the interests of the game at heart. 'Our aim is to excite young people and interest them in cricket. We are promoting cricket at the grass roots.' I could feel it coming and, sure enough, Jolly soon uttered the great cliché, 'Cricket in India is the unifier. It is the symbol of national pride. Sachin and Azhar and Kambli and Kapil stand out as examples of determination and the winning attitude. That's what our young people need. That's what speaks to them. They want to be winners. They're not satisfied with second place. And neither is Pepsi. *Ye hi hai right choice*!'

Jolly had previously worked for Hindustan Lever and had probably shown as much enthusiasm for them as he now did for Pepsi. He was a hired gun, like an overseas player in English county cricket, but he seemed to enjoy his work. 'I took Azhar to Ahmedabad, where there have been many bad communal flare-ups,' he told me. 'Azhar is a Muslim, so this is important. We called it, "Azhar tamara gharna" (Azhar in your house) and we invited local people to write a slogan for Pepsi. Would you believe we had 40,000 entries! We took Azhar all around Gujarat, to Ahmedabad, Baroda and Surat, and he met all the winners. We'd say, please be at home at such and such a time for Azhar's visit and don't forget to offer him a Pepsi. At the first house we visited, 2500 people turned up to welcome him. Rose petals were strewn on every step of his path, right from the gate of the building to the door of the fourth-floor flat. The entire family came out to greet Azhar – grandma, grandpa, everyone – and, do you know, they had made a ten-pound cake with "Pepsi" on it. This was some photo opportunity! We got a shot of Azhar cutting the cake with a little girl. The next house we went to there were 4000 people waiting. They all had these little bats ready for autographing. In all we visited seventy homes in five days in the three cities. It was exhausting, I can tell you, but a wonderful experience.' And profitable? 'Oh yes. Pepsi had not been present in Gujarat for several years because of a factory problem. We only relaunched in the state last year and six months later, thanks to our Azhar campaign, we have a 52 per cent market share.'

Jolly explained to me that India lagged far behind world standards of soft drink consumption, quaffing only three per annum per capita, compared to 500 in Mexico. What's more, imbibing soft drinks was still an urban habit. 'In Delhi we now sell fifty bottles per head each year. But we have not reached the rural consumer. Our biggest problem is cooling infrastructure. But with our franchise and distribution network growing all the time, that will be solved. We are here to build a market which doubles or trebles in the next three years.' But surely rural people on limited incomes had other spending priorities than purchasing ice-cool soft-drinks? 'No no. It is not a luxury item, despite the excise tax. Precisely because there is lack of safe drinking water in many areas, soft drinks are preferred. They are always hygienic.'

What was Pepsi's response to Indian protests against the incursion of multinational corporations? 'We are a very different kind of multinational. From the CEO down there is not one expatriate working for us. All are Indians. Pepsico has even taken Indian managers to run operations in South Africa and south-east Asia. Pepsico understand that India is a great source of managerial talent, and it encourages that talent. *Ye hi hai right choice*!'

When I first visited India in the seventies there was no Pepsi and no Coke. You had to choose between import-substitutes like Campa Cola and Thums Up. Since then, Cadbury Schweppes had taken over Campa Cola and Coke had taken over Thums Up, but Pepsi had outstripped them all, gobbling up 40 per cent of the ever-expanding market in only five years. Now both Pepsi and Coke plan to wean Indian customers off glass bottles and on to cans and plastic containers, which will add to India's massive waste-disposal crisis. Pepsi is shipping thousands of tonnes of plastic bottles from the US to India for reprocessing, an industry which produces toxic waste and pays its mainly female employees less than Rs30 (60p) per day. In addition, one third of the waste sent from the US is unfit for reprocessing and must be burnt, releasing yet more toxins into the atmosphere. While Pepsi and Coke are keen to publicise the hundreds of crores of rupees they have invested in India, they are less keen to highlight the profits they repatriate each year and their adverse effect on India's balance of payments.

Just weeks before the World Cup, the first Kentucky Fried Chicken outlet in the sub-continent was ransacked by angry farmers in Bangalore. The farmers feared that KFC, a subsidiary of Pepsi, would introduce massive factory farming of chickens (native to India) and thereby disrupt the food chain, distort agricultural development and corrupt the Indian diet. Pepsi had secured entry into India in 1988 by promising to foster a second green revolution through investment in agricultural research and development. In particular, it boasted of ambitious plans to set up new horticultural projects in Punjab – 50,000 jobs would be created and the country would accrue much-needed foreign exchange. Farmers in Punjab welcomed Pepsi and some converted their land to tomato-growing in anticipation of Pepsi's promised tomato paste processing plant. But Pepsi failed to deliver – on the research and development, on the jobs, and on the tomato paste plant. Punjabi farmers felt they had been duped by the multinational and attacked the government's failure to enforce the terms of Pepsi's entry into the Indian market. Many claimed that officials had been bribed to ignore the broken promises. In 1994, Pepsi formally withdrew from the agricultural sector to concentrate on soft drinks and snack foods. *Ye hi hai right choice?*

In his *History of Indian Cricket*, published in 1990, Mihir Bose wrote, 'Modern Indian cricket derives its strength from the money of the industrialist allied to the power of the civil servant.' Six years later, that formula was reflected in the highly effective Bindra–Dalmiya axis. But in the interim, a third and vital ingredient had been added. With the opening of the sub-continental economy to multinational corporations, and the rapid growth of Murdoch's television empire, global forces had entered the equation.

Business World called the World Cup 'the biggest marketing extravaganza in India this decade' and reported that companies were spending a total of Rs250 crore (£50 million) on special World Cup-related promotions – twenty times the amount spent in 1987. The crucial difference was the expansion of satellite television, which made this World Cup a genuinely global spectacle and in the process transformed its commercial value. Through satellite TV, Pilcom aimed to project sub-continental cricket onto the global stage and export the game to new regions (west Asia, south-east Asia and North America). Sponsors and advertisers aimed to sell their products to a global market, not least the vast but hitherto protected Indian hinterland. As Coke, Pepsi, Fuji, Visa, Reebok, Mastercard, Shell, Oneida, Sony *et al* vied for space on the cricket bandwagon, the World Cup turned into a carnival of globalisation. Advertisers made the link between the global cricket competition and the global marketplace explicit. The National Aluminium Company asked, 'What is common between World Cup cricket and NALCO, the country's largest producer and exporter of alumina and aluminium? It is in the teamwork. It is in the tenacity of never giving up. It is in the strategies of storming the wickets. It is in the world-beating stamina.' Next to an image of a cricketer playing a sweep shot on one knee, Tissot, the Swiss watch company, reminded consumers that 'The world is growing smaller . . . Watch Tissot and watch the world.' There was a boundary board advertising a careers magazine emblazoned with three words which could have served as the true slogan of the World Cup: 'Globalisation of markets'.

For the ideologists of globalisation, the World Cup was a powerful symbol. Here the various nations of the world were to compete on 'a level playing field', the favourite metaphor of the neo-liberal architects of GATT, NAFTA and Maastricht. Of course, the metaphor is a lie. The aim of competition among capitalists is to eliminate the competitor, just as it is in warfare: that is how markets are conquered and monopolies built. In sport, if you eliminate the competitor, you put an end to the competition. And would any true sports fan respect a competition in which some teams were fully equipped and others played with broken bats and in bare feet, and in which the umpires were appointed by the well-equipped teams? Yet that is exactly how the global economy functions. Its playing field is anything but level. And that is why the process called globalisation (which really means global freedom of finance capital) tends to exacerbate tensions and inequalities between and within nations, as was vividly illustrated during the course of the World Cup.

Watching Indian television, you would think that the main preoccupation of the country was deciding which car or refrigerator to purchase. In fact, only 1 per cent of households own a car and only 6 per cent a refrigerator. The total number of minutes of international phone calls made from India has increased by 142 per cent since 1990, but only 4 per cent of households have telephones (many elite homes have three or four connections). Foreign direct investment has increased twenty-five fold since 1991, but the country's trade deficit and foreign debt are rising. The IMF regime demands orientation to export production but fuels import consumption. Multinationals, banks and Indian industries (many now linked to multinationals) used the World Cup not to promote the export of Indian manufactured goods but to expand their niches within the Indian market. The only things India seemed to be selling abroad were its cricket and its image.

The gradual liberalisation of India's economy has been accompanied by mounting caste and communal tensions. The nineties kicked off with the 'anti-reservation stir', a bitter and often violent upper-caste backlash against the increasing political clout of the lower castes, who had turned away from the Congress to establish their own political formations. In tone and rhetoric, it was amazingly similar to the white backlash against black advances in the United States. At the same time the BJP, the Shiv Sena, and the associated champions of Hindutva waged a fierce campaign to replace the ancient mosque at Ayodhya with a temple. In December 1992, their devotees demolished the mosque – a naked assault not only on the rights of the Muslim minority but on the secular basis of the Indian state. Among the instigators of that vandalism were leaders of the BJP, the official opposition in the Lok Sabha, poised, some thought, to win power at the general elections that would follow the World Cup. Integration into the global economy, in India as elsewhere, had made questions of national identity more acute and more contentious. There was no consensus about who belonged and who did not belong.

The growth of communal and caste prejudice has been especially intense among those who have most welcomed and most benefited from globalisation: the elite and their middle-class camp-followers. This 150-million-strong army of potential consumers may form only a modest minority of India's total population but in absolute terms they outnumber the combined populations of Britain, Australia, New Zealand and South Africa and have therefore become cricket's single most economically weighty constituency. For multinationals seeking access to the hearts and pockets of south Asian consumers, cricket is a godsend.

Pace the Oneida ads, the Indian middle classes have little time for the old-style public school cricket venerated by some of their counterparts in England. For them, the only cricket that matters is global cricket, played to win. The World Cup was seen as a platform for liberalising, go-getting, entrepreneurial India to show the world what it was capable of. Cricket is popular in India partly because it is a global game and moreover the only global game in which Indians excel, at least for the moment. In England the middle classes used to warn their offspring, 'Success overseas counts for nothing.' In India, the formula is reversed. Success overseas is the ultimate vindication, proof that Indians can hold their own on the global stage. It is as if the middle classes were trying to compensate for the failure of Indian institutions by the obsessive celebration of individual success. Sunil Gavaskar, who tamed the world's greatest bowling attacks not only on Indian wickets but around the world, was their great icon. Now Tendulkar has emerged as his successor. Commenting on the young Bombay batsman's multi-million dollar five-year contract with WorldTel, the *Asian Age* praised Tendulkar as 'a thoroughly middle-class Indian' and 'thriving capitalist', whose success was great news for the country.

In the early World Cup matches Tendulkar's bat was conspicuously bare. Where was the logo? Days before the match against Pakistan in Bangalore, he signed a Rs1.5 crore (£1.5 million) endorsement deal with tyre manufacturers MRF (he had pledged not to advertise tobacco or booze). But in the meantime the ICC had ordered Azhar to remove the Akai label from his trousers, because the electronics company was not a sports goods manufacturer. For the same reason, Tendulkar was told to remove the MRF label from his bat. The ICC's belated attempt to police cricket's global marketplace may have been welcome to those who object to the disfigurement of the game by advertising logos, but it was illogical and hypocritical. The authorities made no complaint about Indian players whose bats bore advertisements for Four Square (a cigarette) and East West (an airline), and of course the teams themselves were all bedecked with the brand names of tobacco, brewing and soft drink concerns. The ICC's battle with Azhar and Tendulkar was not over either the aesthetics or morality of advertising, but over control of the most prime of prime sites, cricketers' bodies. Notwithstanding the ever-present rhetoric of personal choice, globalisation seems to subsume individuals into corporate identities – commercial as well as national and communal.

Akai decided not to enforce the penalty clause in its contract with Azhar 'in the larger interest of not putting undue pressure on the players at a time when their performance on the field is of the utmost importance to the country'. Like the judges, they refrained from insisting on the adherence to legal norms, so that the game could proceed. Coke lodged a complaint with Pilcom that Pepsi was using the words 'World Cup' in promotions (offering free tee-shirts and match tickets on television). Bindra quickly reminded Pepsi that the name of the tournament was a registered trade mark which could be employed only by 'official sponsors'. Wasim asked Coke to withdraw shots of him from their '*Hum jeetain gae*' video, because he was under contract with Pepsi.

One of the objections to globalisation in the third world, and in particular to its institutionalisation in GATT and the World Trade Organization, is that it will enable multinational corporations to claim patent ownership of natural products used in traditional agriculture and medicine. In the new world order, even the gene pool, it seems, is to be privatised. The same phenomenon was observable during the World Cup. Cricket, a public service, whose sole purpose is the pleasure it can give players and spectators, was being parcelled out and auctioned off, like British Rail.

Though there may have been 'nothing official about it', there was certainly something artificial about the Pepsi appeal. Pepsi sponsors a variety of cricket matches, domestic and international, and in that respect is every bit as 'official' as Coke. The rivalry between the soft drink giants is, of course, entirely commercial; from the consumer's point of view, the two drinks taste more or less the same. Both are the flagship products of huge corporate empires driven solely by the quest for profit, impervious to national or cultural distinctions – or to the impact of their business on the health and environment of their consumers. Both sought to camouflage this reality by associating themselves with the game of cricket. If anything, Pepsi's camouflage was the more contrived. It sought identification not merely with cricket but with a popular conception of cricket and, above all, a popular rejection of the slowness and stuffiness of traditional cricket. Thus cricket populism was made to serve the interests of the elite. The élan and individualism of sub-continental cricket stars became the human mask for a faceless multinational.

Advertising is as much the official wing of popular culture as government-sponsored folk festivals, although it pretends otherwise. Indeed, the whole history of popular culture in modern societies is one in which official feeds off unofficial. Black American rhythm and blues was the inspiration for white rock and roll, which became a massive profit-earner for the entertainment industry. But that industry has been forced again and again to raid the ghettos for new matter: soul, funk, hip-hop, rap, or venture further afield to the Caribbean or to Africa in search of inspiration from the grass roots of musical production. Likewise, Coke's 'fan of the match' competition, in which spectators scrawled slogans on 'official' placards. 'When Indians drink Coke Aussies choke' was the winning slogan at Bombay, where spectators were prevented from bringing in their own placards and banners. Thus the sub-continental cricket crowd's love of slogan-writing – spontaneous, often irreverent, sometimes offensive – was appropriated by the multinational to serve its media agenda. The collective creativity that south Asian cricket crowds share with British football crowds is often unruly but is certainly to be preferred to the placid consumerism of sports crowds in the United States. Under the regime of global sports, the fan becomes the epitome of the passive, atomised consumer in the market, free to 'choose' but powerless in the extreme. Instead of the vibrancy and unpredictability that make a cricket match in south Asia worth all the hassles that invariably attend it, we will be left with the conservatism and kitsch of the opening ceremony, an all too apt specimen of official popular culture in the corporate age.

It is interesting to contrast the post-World Cup fortunes of Pepsi's Bombay boys, Sachin Tendulkar and Vinod Kambli. Kambli was recruited by Pepsi because of his good looks, trendy clothes and flamboyant batting style; other established Indian stars with superior records did not appeal to the multinational. Kambli was the brashness of youth personified, the ideal pin-up boy for Pepsi's 'new generation'. Sure he was a Dalit, which is still a mark against him for many middle-class Indians, but in the printed adverts Pepsi lightened his skin to make him the same colour as Tendulkar. Brahmin and Dalit dancing together to the latest beat from their personal stereos. Could anything be more modern?

Following the World Cup, Kambli was unceremoniously axed from the Indian squad, even though his record at the crease could stand comparison with a number of those retained. Officially, Indian cricket bosses refused to explain the decision; unofficially, they spread it about that Kambli had problems with alcohol and with his personal life. Kambli was by no means the first talented player to fall victim to the long-standing tradition of opacity and disingenuousness in Indian Test selection. It seems he paid a penalty for the very flamboyance and openness that made him attractive to Pepsi. Kambli shows his emotions. He wept openly as the bottles hailed down at Eden Gardens. For the official cricket culture, his periodic fallibility at the crease became symptomatic of a fatal character flaw. Others equally fallible were examined in a different light. It would seem that brashness is acceptable only to a point.

One after another, in all three World Cup host countries, multinationals vied with each other to boost rival nationalisms. Pepsi and Coke produced music videos, television adverts and huge spreads in the newspapers, declaring their support for the local side and trying to identify their product with the national aspirations embodied in the World Cup teams. Every time India played a match, Coke printed this message in the newspapers: 'Let's make it happen again India. We did it in 1983. We won the world. That time has come again. A time for hope. A time to win. A time for pride, for us Indians. Coca-Cola joins millions of cricket fans all over the country in wishing our team all the very best. This time, to bring home the Wills World Cup 1996. Go for it India! We're with you all the way. Go for it all you cricket fans. Roar out your cheers. Let's make it happen. Once again.' The company sponsored a giant 'Good Luck India' bat which toured the cities. And in Pakistan the same company sponsored another giant bat, this time inscribed 'Good Luck Pakistan'. Javed Miandad appeared at one of the promotional events to declare the bat a symbol of 'national solidarity, peace and brotherhood'.

The morning after the Solidarity match in Colombo, Pepsi, in an uncertain attempt to capture the national mood, took out a half-page newspaper advert headlined 'WE MAY NOT HAVE CAUGHT THE KANGAROOS BUT WE CAN STILL CATCH THE CUP': 'Okay, so the Aussies hopped away and the Windies blew out of our grasp. Let's face it, they've been pretty official about the whole issue. But what the heck, we can still catch the thrills of international cricket. Just open an ice cool (and very unofficial) Pepsi, turn on your TV and tune into the action on the field. Remember, although it's cricket, it doesn't mean we've got to act official about it!' Here was an appeal to the cricket fan as layabout, taking national disappointment in his world-weary stride. But just to ensure that no one would think they underestimated the popular anger over the boycott, Pepsi added a PS: 'Let's tell it like it is – We all know the official position regarding the matches that were to be played in Sri Lanka. Now let's get unofficial about it. Write in to us at "My unofficial comments", PO Box . . .'

When Kapil Dev took his 400th Test wicket, Pepsi ran television adverts felicitating the 'proud son of India'. Cadbury's Chocolate filled a double-page magazine spread with an advert headlined 'Cricket beyond boundaries'; the glossy photograph showed three young women with their faces painted orange, white and green, the colours of the Indian flag.

Obviously, given the political tensions over economic globalisation, multinational corporations are keen to acquire Indian or Pakistani or Sri Lankan identities. Investment in cricket, the national game, is a quick and relatively cheap means of doing so. But multinational sponsored nationalism – 'Coca-Cola nationalism' my Sri Lankan friends called it – is a more insidious phenomenon, and not only because the multinationals have no loyalty whatsoever to the nations they claim to sponsor. National aspirations for success in the World Cup were intertwined with aspirations, personal and national, for success in the globalised economy, for a place in the new world order. Thus globalisation helped to make a fetish of national victory. As a result, the 'official' nationalisms sponsored by Coke and Pepsi ended up in practice more rigidly uncompromising, more elitist and exclusive than the flexible, improvised and usually forgiving brand traditionally associated with south Asian cricket crowds.

Pepsi's onslaught forced Coke to play down its official tag, and there must now be doubts within the company about the value of its investment in World Cup sponsorship. But Pepsi did not have it all its own way. Midway through the World Cup Coke released its elegant and artful 'Passion has a Colour' montage, which touched cricket fans across the sub-continent on a much deeper level than Pepsi's brash self-promotion. Here was a poetic paean to people's cricket, not big cricket played under floodlights for the benefit of TV cameras but cricket played in the *gallis*, the *maidans* and the fields, not by rich super-stars in jeans but poor kids in salwar kameez. Accompanied by the ecstatic chanting of '*Mast, mast*' (an untranslatable exclamation of transcendence and joy) and the soaring *qawali* singing of Nusrat Fateh Ali Khan, the montage evoked the diversity of sub-continental culture – Muslim and Hindu, urban and rural – and the unifying role of cricket within it. In contrast to the up-to-the-minute frenzy of the Pepsi ads, the mood of the Coke montage was tranquil and timeless. In response to Pepsi's triumphalist post-modernity, Coke had come up with a tribute to modest but indigenous pre-modernity.

The Coke advert was a vast improvement over the soulless abstraction of their initial campaign and cricket lovers swooned over it. But marketing experts questioned its effectiveness. 'The montage was probably aimed towards the slightly older, more sophisticated age group with its music, visuals and location ad aesthetics,' commented one. 'But the fact remains that the bulk of soft drink consumption is by the younger age group. Therefore one is left wondering how effective was Coke's communication during the World Cup.'

Like Pepsi's claim to be unofficial, Coke's appeal to the grass roots of sub-continental cricket was paradoxical. The distinctive dress, architecture and even agriculture depicted in the advert would be obliterated in a global marketplace dominated by the likes of Coca-Cola. 'Passion has a colour' ('*Josh mein rang hai*') claimed the advert, and the colour in question, repeatedly contrasted with the muted tones of sub-continental dust and stone, was the red of sun-ripened chilli peppers and Rajasthani turbans. It was Coca-Cola red, cricket ball red. But there was a snag. The cricket balls used in the World Cup were white. And in the version shown in Pakistan, the image of the Taj was excised. Though built by a Muslim ruler, it was a symbol of India. Even in this hymn to unity and peace, this curious by-product of a global economy, national antagonisms were honoured and ultimately reinforced.

11

Make cricket not war

On the flight to Bangalore I sat near Steve Bucknor and David Shepherd, the two umpires appointed to stand in the quarter-final meeting between India and Pakistan, and Raman Subba Row, the match referee, who read my paper while the two umpires, both large men, one tall and the other broad, squirmed in their seats. When we landed, Bucknor uncoiled to his full height and was immediately spotted by cricket fans. 'One million for an lbw, Mr Bucknor,' shouted a passenger gleefully and we all laughed, including Bucknor. In the last few years he had officiated in every corner of the globe, and, like his colleague Shepherd, was a worthy beneficiary of the ICC's new system of 'neutral' umpires, a system introduced in the face of prolonged resistance from the TCCB.

Credit for this long-overdue innovation belongs to the Pakistanis, and in particular Imran, who knew it was the only way to resolve the squabbles surrounding Pakistani umpiring. Indeed, the world's first neutral umpires appeared in the Bombay Quadrangular in 1916. In a Europeans *v* Hindus match an English army major had disputed the decision of a Hindu umpire. The Hindu Gymkhana reminded the British officers that under the laws of cricket, the umpire's decision was final. However, to avoid future controversy, the Gymkhana proposed that Quadrangular umpires be drawn from those communities not contesting the match in question. Thus the compulsions of colonial and communal amity led to the abandonment of one of cricket's oldest traditions – the provision of umpires by the home side. Similarly, the peculiar exigencies of cricket played between India and Pakistan forced the two countries to engage neutral umpires for their contests long before it became ICC policy.

Every team sport has its traditional derbies, those memory-laden encounters with a familiar opponent which count for more with the fans than they're worth in league points or even advancement towards a cup final. Tottenham and Arsenal, Rangers and Celtic, Real Madrid and Barcelona, Lancashire and Yorkshire, the Yankees and the Red Sox. I would submit that none, however, is as fierce as the cricket rivalry between India and Pakistan. It was not always thus. At the time of Partition, many in the south Asian cricket world hoped it would be possible to continue as one Test-playing entity. The team that toured Australia in 1947–48 was still drawn from 'undivided India'. But the communal slaughter that accompanied the birth of the two nations made a split inevitable. In May 1949 the Board of Control for Cricket in Pakistan was formed, and a few months later the Indian Board proposed that Pakistan be admitted to the Imperial Cricket Conference, the forerunner of today's ICC. Initially, the MCC resisted the addition of the new member (just as the TCCB was later to resist the entrance of Sri Lanka and Zimbabwe), but the Indians persisted. They ensured that visiting teams played unofficial matches in Pakistan, thus maintaining the standard of cricket there, and renewed their proposal every year until 1952, when the country became the seventh member of the exclusive Test-playing club.

Pakistan played its first Test series in India later that year. India visited Pakistan for the first time in 1954–55, when all five Tests were drawn. This tour marked the inauguration of an often exasperating tradition of defensive tussles between the two countries. On both sides of the border, however, the visiting teams were well received. There were plans for a regular exchange of tours and even proposals to integrate domestic competition. But cricket relations were ruptured in 1956, as the Cold War shaped the geopolitics of the sub-continent. Pakistan, under military rule, became an unswerving US subordinate; India, as a leader of the Non-Aligned Movement, retained friendly relations with the USSR. Contact was resumed when Pakistan visited India in 1960–61. The previous year had witnessed the triumph of the Oxford-educated Indian Muslim, Abbas Ali Baig, who had electrified Bombay with his half-century against the Australians. It was customary to garland batting champions; in this case Baig was rewarded with a kiss from a Hindu girl who ran onto the field (the symbolic significance of this event is explored in *The Moor's Last Sigh*). But against the Pakistanis, Baig failed. Suddenly he was not an India hero but a Muslim of dubious national allegiance; he received bags of hate mail and was dropped from the Test side for five years.

India and Pakistan did not play again for eighteen years. During this time, India was for several years captained by a Muslim aristocrat, Mansur Ali Khan, nawab of Pataudi. He never had to face the test which his lower-middle-class Muslim successor, Azharuddin, would undergo at Bangalore. In 1965, when the two countries went to war for the second time, Pataudi and the Pakistan captain, Hanif Mohammed, were both playing for a Rest of the World side against England at Scarborough. They sent a joint telegram to their respective governments: WE WISH TO EXPRESS DEEP REGRETS AT THE WAR BETWEEN INDIA AND PAKISTAN. WE FIND UNITY ON THE CRICKET FIELD BY REACHING FOR A COMMON OBJECTIVE. WE FERVENTLY HOPE BOTH COUNTRIES CAN MEET AND FIND AN AMICABLE SOLUTION. It is a measure of how much the climate in both countries has deteriorated since then that it is hard to imagine today's Indian or Pakistani cricketers issuing a similar appeal in time of war.

Contact was resumed in 1978, when an Indian squad captained by Bishen Bedi was decisively defeated in Pakistan. A superb batting line-up – including Zaheer Abbas, Majid Khan and Asif Iqbal – brutally exposed the waning powers of the great spin quartet. In this series Kapil Dev made his international debut. Kapil's parents had moved from Sahiwal, now in Pakistan, at the time of Partition. He took advantage of the opportunity to make contact with family members who had remained behind. 'It was a touching evening,' he recalled, 'but the next day it was back to "war" ', by which he meant, back to the Test series.

The Indians exacted revenge when Pakistan visited the following year. Thanks largely to Gavaskar and Kapil, they won the series – the second and to date the last time they have done so against Pakistan. Imran Khan remembered the tour: 'From the moment we arrived it seemed as though the entire country had become a huge spotlight, trained solely on us. The relentless publicity, the huge partisan crowds in the jam-packed stadiums, the expectations of our own public – all this was too much for some of our players.' The tour ended bitterly, with even the circumspect Asif Iqbal losing his temper. At home, the players were assailed in the press. 'No Pakistani team has ever had to face such humiliation, collectively or individually,' insisted Imran (this was several years before the 1996 World Cup). 'Our failure was attributed to non-stop partying and a thoroughly irresponsible way of life. Apparently we had all indulged in wining, dining and womanising.'

Pakistan won the next series, played three years later on home soil. The young Mohammed Azharuddin was omitted from the Indian touring party. Years later, Raj Singh Dungapur, the chairman of selectors, admitted the decision was made because they 'felt it might be a handicap for him to make his debut in a country where the culture so matched his own'. The fear of losing continued to paralyse both sides. A sequence of eleven draws came to an end with the Test at Bangalore in 1987. Thanks to what is euphemistically called an 'under-prepared' pitch, the deadlock was broken, and Imran led his side to victory – their first series win in India and only the second time either side had won a Test against the other away from home. General Zia wanted to use the tour as an example of cricket diplomacy, but it turned out to be a rancorous affair. At one point a day's play was lost when Imran protested over sawdust sprinkled on the pitch. The aggressive Pakistani appeals set off hoots of derision in the crowd. In Bangalore, as in Ahmedabad earlier in the tour, there were flurries of missile-throwing when Pakistan were in the field.

Between 1978 and 1990 India and Pakistan met in twenty-nine Tests, twenty-one of which ended as draws. But even as the Test duel became ever more defensive and inconclusive, the increasing importance of the one-day game was reshaping cricket relations between the two countries. Here the safety net of the draw was removed; there was no middle ground between victory and defeat. The world's first Test rivalry was forged by England and Australia. The first one-day rivalry with equal (indeed greater) resonance was forged by India and Pakistan, and it was a rivalry shaped not on the home soil of either but off-shore, in Sharjah, where the teams met nearly every year throughout the eighties. Javed Miandad's match-winning six off the last ball in the final of the Austral–Asia Cup in April 1986 became legend on both sides of the border. In Pakistan, it was, in the words of Saleem Lodhi's pop song 'Sharjah ka chhekka kargaye hukka-pukka' (Six in Sharjah devastated the world), the shot that established Pakistani supremacy in one-day cricket. In India, it was an act of impudence that left a festering wound. Since that day in Sharjah, ten years ago, Pakistan had beaten India in twenty-one of their twenty-six one-day encounters.

Miandad became the Indians' nemesis, the incarnation of the chip-on-the-shoulder Pakistani impudence which irritated Indians and English alike. Indians resented the fact that the Pakistanis seemed to reserve their best cricket for India and despaired that their team always seemed at its worst against

Pakistan. Again and again at Sharjah, the Indians buckled under pressure, and many Indian fans came to believe that their cricketers lacked the fervour motivating the Pakistanis. In keeping with the stereotypes promoted by the advocates of Hindutva, they perceived the Pakistanis as aggressive and unashamedly nationalistic, in contrast to the docile and apologetic Indians. Some even claimed that Pakistan's religious identity gave them an advantage on the cricket field. To match the enemy, India would have to emulate them; it would have to rediscover itself as a Hindu nation. One of the major themes of Hindutva has been the need for Hindu aggression to compensate for centuries of insult and injury at the hands of Muslims. In rallying the embattled majority against its imagined enemy, the BJP and Shiv Sena found it easy to play upon Indian discomfiture over Pakistan's cricketing supremacy.

With the rise of the Hindutva menace in India, and the sharpening of the conflict in Kashmir, cricket relations were again suspended. Pakistan's 1990–91 tour of India was called off after Shiv Sena activists spoiled the Wankhede pitch. Three years later, a scheduled appearance in the Hero Cup was aborted at the last minute, and the tour planned for later in the year cancelled. Between 1991 and 1994, India boycotted Sharjah in protest at alleged anti-Indian bias among (Muslim) officials.

The quarter-final at Bangalore's Chinnaswamy Stadium would be the first meeting between the two countries in either India or Pakistan for seven years. Their only previous meeting in the World Cup had been in Sydney in 1992, in the league round. India had the better of Pakistan that day but the Pakistanis had gone on to win the tournament. The two sides had last met at Sharjah, in April 1995, when India were defeated by what was described as a 'second-string' Pakistan team captained by wicket keeper Moin Khan. The country was still dogged by the Pakistan jinx. Bizarrely, the Indians had acquired an inferiority complex in relation to the Pakistanis in cricket, just as the Pakistanis had in relation to Indians in other spheres.

Thanks to the grandiose threats issued over the years by Bal Thackeray, the Shiv Sena found itself in an embarrassing position in the days before the Bangalore tie. In Bombay, it might have been able to carry out its threats; in Bangalore, it lacked the muscle power. What's more, the public wanted to see this match, they wanted the old rivalry resumed on home ground, and anyone who attempted to block it would suffer at the polls. Manohar Joshi kept insisting the decision was up to Thackeray, who was out of action, recovering from heart surgery in hospital. In Bangalore police took into custody eight top officials of the local Shiv Sena. The party announced that it would 'allow' the match to proceed, because it was 'an international event'. But it warned that 'any attempt to insult the national flag or national image during the match would not be tolerated'. It even had the cheek to claim that 'more than 80 per cent of tickets have been siphoned off by communal elements', i.e., Muslims, always suspected of failing the Thackeray test. In the Karnataka legislative assembly, the Sena's BJP allies worked themselves into a fit of indignation over reports that the Indian tricolour would be banned at the stadium. The Speaker assured them that the reports were not true.

The BJP had also been bleating about the Karnataka State Cricket Association's handling of ticket allocations for the quarter-final. Thousands had queued overnight outside the stadium only to be told within minutes of the counters opening that all tickets were sold out. When they protested, they were dispersed by a lathi charge. The KSCA had informed the state government that Chinnaswamy Stadium had a capacity of 50,000. They planned to issue 10,000 passes and 40,000 tickets, half of which were to be allocated to KSCA members, affiliated clubs and sponsors. Therefore 20,000 would be placed on sale to the public. However, only some four thousand appear to have been available at the ticket counters. It was alleged that the rest were held back, in case the India–Pakistan meeting materialised, when the black-market value of the tickets would multiply.

Erapalli Prasanna, the master off spinner of the seventies, now a BJP member, dedicated an entire newspaper column to bemoaning the KSCA's failure to provide him with more than one ticket. BJP members of the legislative assembly alleged that tickets for two stands in Chinnaswamy had been reserved for Gavaskar and Shastri for sale against foreign exchange, and that ministers and senior officials were hoarding tickets to sell on the black market. One Janata Dal minister fervently denied receiving any tickets. His stand was compromised when another tried to placate an aggrieved member of the opposition by offering his own ticket to the match. The state government announced an inquiry into the whole affair.

When I asked a KSCA official about the ticket imbroglio, he raised his palms in despair. 'What can we do? If we don't give tickets to the electricity board, the water authority, the police, we may find we have no electricity, water or police on the day of the match. These MLAs and ministers complain, but they demand hundreds of tickets each to hand out to their supporters. If we withhold tickets, the politicians and the bureaucrats will not co-operate.' On the eve of the match, touts peddled tickets in all price categories outside the stadium. A few token arrests were made, but for the most part police turned a blind eye. The mark-up was said to be 1000 per cent. Obviously, if you knew the right people and had enough money, there were plenty of tickets available.

The Pakistan government asked the Indian government to provide protection for the Pakistani players because of Thackeray's threats. The Taj Western hotel where the players were ensconced looked like a fortress. An Indian army officer claimed that he had seen tighter security only in Somalia. Units of the Central Reserve Police Force, the Rapid Action Force, the Border Security Force were deployed with local police not only around the stadium and the hotel but in 'communally sensitive areas'. Though there had been no visible communal tension so far, police assured the public that preparations were exhaustive.

Newspapers in both countries spared no hyperbole in building up the game. It was the 'match of the decade', 'the real final', 'a high-voltage contest', 'battle royal', 'an epic war around the corner', 'the mother of all cricket battles'. In other words, the match was being sold as war minus the shooting. The total amounts wagered were estimated at US$80 million. Bookies expected betting in Bangalore alone to reach nearly US$3 million. If India won, they stood to lose heavily but, according to press reports, even they had caught the patriotic fever. 'We don't mind losing as long as India is winning,' said one. Achin's maxim about betting on your fears seemed to have unexpected adherents.

In India, the papers took a positive approach to the renewal of Pakistan–Indian cricket ties and urged fans to welcome the visitors. There was nothing to compare with the jingoist abuse the English tabloids heaped on the Germans during the Euro 96 football cup. On the morning of the match, they were full of stories about players from the two countries mixing freely. At the WorldTel celebrity party the night before, a galaxy of politicians, movie stars, cricketers and corporate bosses was outshone by Imran Khan, welcomed in Bangalore as a prince in exile. Intikhab spoke out, as he always has, for more cricket contacts between the two countries: 'It is good for the cricketers and good for the two countries also.' Azhar also favoured resumption of regular play between the two. 'Caste, creed, and religion are personal things. It should not harm the human beings as such. If cricket can bring peace and unity between nations, I will be the happiest and the proudest.' For the Indian press, the Bangalore match was a special occasion, a time for 'Hindustani–Pakistani bhai bhai' (brotherhood). Many of the same papers which in their news coverage and editorial comment struck anti-Pakistani poses, backed nuclear weapons and high defence spending, and took a tough line on 'Pakistani terrorism' and Kashmir, now urged readers to celebrate the India–Pakistan contest in a friendly, if decidedly partisan, spirit. They did not challenge the underpinning logic of Indo–Pakistan hostility. Ironically, the few brave souls dedicated to promoting and popularising India–Pakistan amity, routinely denounced as traitors in the press, did not want the match at all.

In Pakistan confidence was high, the defeat by South Africa and Wasim's muscle-pull notwithstanding. Tendulkar was the only Indian they feared. For many, Miandad's presence in any match against India was like a talisman. But there were fears about the Indian crowd. *Dawn* warned readers that the Pakistan players would be up against 'a political dimension'. Most of the players had no experience of an Indian crowd and might be shaken by the 'acrimonious atmosphere'. After all, they hailed from 'a country where teams are backed or run down because of their performance, sympathy for the national side notwithstanding'. The match at Bangalore would be a 'test of courage, guts, commitment, nerves and pride'.

It was reported that a cardiologist at the Federal Government Services Hospital in Lahore had warned heart patients to stay away from TV sets showing the Bangalore match. 'The tension-filled final overs might drag them into another heart trouble as sudden surge in blood pressure is extremely dangerous.'

Both sets of fans perceived themselves as underdogs, for different reasons. Thanks to years of military dictatorship (with two military defeats) and decades of political demagoguery, many Pakistanis see India as a menacing giant, and the Indian team becomes the embodiment of all the advantages enjoyed by the national enemy. Now, their cricketers would have to venture into that enemy's territory, to fight for national honour against 50,000 screaming Indian fans. As for the Indians, a decade of humiliation at Pakistani hands made them feel that victory was against the odds. They perceived the Pakistanis as aggressive, uncompromising cricketers, and were not sure that their own players shared the same 'killer instinct'. Nor were either fans or cricketers convinced of the benefit of playing at home. 'We have certain disadvantages because we are on home ground,' Azhar confessed. 'We will be under tremendous pressure.' This was an amazing reversal of a century of international cricket experience. The globalisation of television and the intensification of cricket nationalism had turned the ancient law of home advantage upside down.

In the build-up to the match there was another striking symmetry in both countries. In India, Hero Honda filled a whole newspaper page with a simple message, '11 Heroes. 900 million people. One wish'. In Pakistan, the universally familiar orange Shell logo appeared with a new caption, 'The Shell Standard – flying for Pakistan'.

In Jakarta, Benazir Bhutto told a meeting of south-east Asian businessmen: 'The last decade represents a surge of internationalism, a breakdown of geographic boundaries, and an explosion of information technology. In the coming era trade and business will replace politics and warfare and markets will replace missiles as a measure of might.' People used to say the same about cricket, and some still do. And in the meantime these two nations rapidly integrating into Bhutto's brave new world were conducting a war with shooting two thousand miles from Bangalore. The night before the match one soldier was killed and nine injured in an exchange of fire along the Kashmir border. Despite the Conservative government's crass attempt to whip up a 'beef war' just before the Euro 96 football tournament, war between Britain and Germany remained laughably improbable. The same could not be said about India and Pakistan. On the morning of the match, the *Times of India* ran two headline stories, 'PAKISTAN IS PREPARING NUKE TEST' and 'A CONTEST FOR THE CRICKET GODS'. One of the disturbing aspects of this war minus the shooting was that the shooting, and the threat of shooting, went on regardless.

Bangalore has long enjoyed a reputation as a civilised city, and when I first visited it in 1984 (I watched Vishwanath wantonly dispense his square cuts in a Ranji Trophy match watched by five hundred spectators), I was enchanted, as many others had been, by its magnificent parks, broad tree-lined avenues and uncluttered skyline. Since then the city has become the high-tech capital of India, its streets are choked with cars and its offices, hotels, pubs and airport swarm with the minions of multinational corporations. In recent years the BJP has made gains here, not least among professionals and technicians, the vanguard of modernity in this self-consciously modern city – just as the Christian Coalition has among middle-class software programmers in Aspen, Colorado. In Bangalore, the BJP's promise of national strength, its proud assertion of rule by the religious majority, its rhetoric of discipline and order, appeal to the fragile sense of superiority of the new elite. But its bedrock remains communal suspicion. In October of 1994, there were attacks on Muslim districts following the state government's approval of the launch of a daily news broadcast in Urdu. The BJP had claimed that the 'pseudo-secular' Janata Dal administration was pandering to a minority, and that as a result the status of the Kannada language was under threat. The army had to stage a 'flag march' through the disrupted areas to calm the city.

In Bangalore I stayed with Ramachandra Guha and his family. Ram is the author of *Wickets in the East* and *Spin and Other Turns*, my two favourite books about Indian cricket. He played cricket for St Stephen's College, but turned to Marxism and gave away his cricket library. Later he fell out with the Marxists, moved on to radical ecology and returned to cricket. He likes to say that he has reversed the pilgrimage made by H.M. Hyndman, founder of Britain's first Marxist party, the Social Democratic Federation, who turned to socialism after being passed over for a Cambridge blue. He writes about cricket not as a journalist but as a fan, a cultured fan, and scrutinises its history with a critical fascination. And as a true fan – the only amateurs left in this game – he sees the plot of his life intertwined with cricket. In his tributes to the heroes of his youth – the great spin quartet, Gavaskar and Vishwanath, Engineer and Kirmani – he has chronicled what he calls 'Indian cricket's coming of age'. Ram became a Karnataka fan at the age of eight, and had watched with pride as Prasanna, Chandrashekhar, Vishwanath and Kirmani became national heroes and, incidentally, put an end to Bombay's long domination of the Ranji Trophy, assisting the vital process which Ram calls the 'decentring of Indian cricket'. Today there would be three local boys in the Indian side: Srinath, Kumble and Prasad. Like everyone else I spoke to, Ram was relieved that the tie was being played in Bangalore: 'Can you imagine how they would behave in Delhi or Kanpur?'

Ram is romantic, even patriotic about Indian cricket, has celebrated its geniuses, analysed its traditions and argued its claims; but he is no cricket nationalist and has grown increasingly impatient with the bellicose chauvinism surrounding the game. That morning I asked him which side he would support today. He found it difficult to answer. Normally, against other teams, he happily supported India. 'I suppose part of me does want India to win, but part of me can't stand the thought of what the Pakistanis would have to face at home if they lose.'

It had always seemed to me that the World Cup would have been incomplete without this match. Despite all the anxieties, I had wanted it to take place and I had wanted to be there. Now the encounter was at hand, I wasn't at all sure. For the first time in the tournament, I couldn't make up my mind whom to support. In this contest, I didn't want to choose sides.

I arrived early at the stadium. Outside the crowd was gathering and thorough frisking delayed everyone's entrance. Bottles, placards, firecrackers were all confiscated. Later, I learned, the Border Security Force staged a brief lathi charge to push fans back from the gates.

In the resplendent sunlight, the ground looked as beautiful as I remembered it. Extensive renovations had been carried out: there was a new press box and a state-of-the-art electronic scoreboard. The northern stand had become the IMG's hospitality village. The new eastern stand remained unfinished and exposed to the sun. The high floodlights towered over all. Their installation had proved a costly business for the KSCA. 'Loadshedding' had been averaging four hours per day in Bangalore. A black-out during the World Cup quarter-final could not be risked. The Karnataka Electricity Board offered to guarantee uninterrupted power if KSCA paid for the laying of a new cable from power station to stadium. The KSCA demurred and chose instead to invest in a 'captive power generator' (at a cost of £400,000). Every tier of the ground, finished or not, was bedecked in corporate banners. Sand Balm. Vimal. Vikram Premium Cement. Sansung. PunCom. SBI. Ajmal Estates and Properties. Rajashree Cement. A sign painted on a steel stanchion next to me in the press box read 'KISCO – High Grade Pig Iron and Ductile Iron Spun Pipes'. Did Bangalore cricket correspondents work as plumbing sub-contractors in their spare time?

An hour before the game, most of the stands were full. The Indian cricketers were greeted by the inevitable thunderous roar as they trotted on to the field to warm up. I was waiting for the response to the Pakistanis, almost with bated breath. They emerged diffidently and huddled together in a corner of the ground, clearly apprehensive. Then they set off on a warm-up lap around the boundary, and as they circled the ground most spectators rose to them, applauding and waving their flags as if to say welcome. Only a few miscreants booed and gave the thumbs-down sign. Relieved, local journalists reminded me that this match could only have been played in the south; Bangalore has a good crowd, a fair crowd.

Imran strode on to the field in salwar kameez. Persona non grata at the matches staged in Pakistan, here, in a foreign land, he could repossess his domain. Chatting to officials, inspecting the pitch, greeting the players, he seemed to be saying, 'This stage belongs to me.' He was cheered by the crowd. In contrast, Sohail was booed when he walked out for the toss. Wasim, it appeared, would not be playing. He had kept his decision secret from everyone, including his team-mates, until ten minutes before the match.

In the press box, we caught up with the action in Faisalabad, where England had scored 235 in fifty overs, thanks mainly to a raw and angry 67 by Defreitas, elevated up the order at last. It was the only counter-attacking innings played by an England batsman in the World Cup. Kaluwitherana was out early, but Jayasuriya was on the rampage, and had already equalled the World Cup record for the fastest fifty.

The first Mexican wave of the day rolled round Chinnaswamy, even before a ball had been bowled. Fans in orange 'I love India' tee-shirts dominated the new, expensive VIP section at the far end of the ground. There was a brief flurry of 'Pakistan hai-hai' but it was confined to a small group and quickly died out. Most spectators were excited just to find themselves in the stadium, present in the flesh at 'the mother of all cricket battles'.

Azhar had won the toss and decided to bat. The crowd welcomed the first good news of the day with applause. As the match got underway, towns and cities across India and Pakistan wore a deserted look. The streets of Colaba in downtown Bombay, usually choked with pedestrians, were left to the tourists, as was the beachfront in Madras. Chandigarh's humming Sector 17 was silent, and in Patna the members of the state legislative assembly gathered in front of the closed-circuit television set. Those without television followed on radio or through word of mouth. And, thanks to cable and satellite technology, they were joined by expatriates from both countries in London and Birmingham and Bradford, New York and Toronto, Dubai and Singapore and Durban.

It was Sohail's first match as captain of his country. But there were five ex-captains in the side. In the early overs, he seemed nervous, constantly fiddling with the field, as if to impress his authority on the game. Sohail is one of the few Pakistani cricketers of whom the word 'unbribeable' is used. Whether it is his upper-middle-class background or his dour temper, he is not a favourite with his team-mates. From the first, presumably following orders from Intikhab and Wasim, he employed containing tactics, looking to stop boundaries rather than take wickets. The early overs were a tense affair, with both sides intent on giving nothing away. Waqar beat Sidhu's outside edge three times in the first over, but thereafter the duel between them was a draw. Tendulkar's timing seemed awry. Constricted by the Pakistani pace bowler's full length, and perhaps the overwhelming weight of national expectations resting on his thick square shoulders, he refrained from stroke-making. Waqar's first four overs went for only ten runs. In Wasim's absence, it was clear Sohail would ration Waqar's overs as if they were drops of precious elixir which must be made to last a long journey. The wicket was slow. Bowlers had to pitch the ball up and batsmen had to guard against playing too early. After ten overs India had crawled to 37. Bizarrely, Sidhu had scored 21 off 33 balls and Tendulkar only 11 off 30.

The crowd was patient. I scanned the stands, looking for clues to the meaning of this long-awaited encounter. 'THIS IS THE WORLD CUP FINAL' was probably the least contentious of the scores of banners. 'YOUNG GENIUS SACHIN WITH A MAGIC STICK – OLD MAN JAVED WITH WALKING STICK' and 'MENU OF THE DAY – PAKISTANI GRILLED CHICKEN' expressed cheerfully partisan contempt. Strung across the tall rusty girders sprouting like tendrils out of the incomplete new stand, the biggest banner, 'PAK ENDS IN BANGALORE – INDIA IN LAHORE', had overtones of territorial conquest, and 'WAQAR = SCUD – SACHIN = PATRIOT' invoked the Gulf War in an obscure anti-Muslim jibe. Most disturbing was a banner on which the bold, ragged letters 'PAK' were being speared by a *trishul* – Shiva's traditional tridentlike accessory. The three prongs were labelled Venki, Srinath, Kumble (the three Karnataka players) and its handle daubed with INDIA. The message was clear. Hindutva would defeat Pakistan. India's embattled majority had been projected onto the playing field to vanquish the enemy who was simultaneously within and without. But I was cheered up by other banners, 'WORLD CUP FOR SECULARISM' and 'CRICKET FOR PEACE – NOT VIOLENCE'. 'THANKS

PRABHAKAR FOR HELPING INDIA PLAY AT BANGALORE' and 'WHERE'S DRAVID' (Karnataka batsman Rahul Dravid, left out of the World Cup squad) added a touch of parochialism to the international event.

Salim trotted in from the outfield to complain about an object thrown from the crowd. Neither the umpires nor his team-mates seemed to take it seriously and the mood in the ground remained calm. After twenty overs India had reached 83 for 0. Sidhu, gaining in confidence and sternly punching holes in Sohail's ring of fielders, reached his 50 off 72 balls. Stymied at the other end, Tendulkar dragged a ball from Ata-ur-Rehman on to his stumps, trying to angle it down to third man. Uncharacteristically, he had taken 59 balls to score his 31 runs. Manjrekar came in and for the first time at Chinnaswamy Stadium the floodlights came on. The Indian boat could well have capsized with the departure of Tendulkar, but Sidhu kept it afloat, despite a pulled leg muscle that necessitated a runner. The slow bowlers – Mushtaq, Sohail and Salim – bowled a monotonous off stump line and the field was packed accordingly. Salim's donkey drops begged to be hit to the boundary, but the Indian batsmen treated him warily, possibly because of his record of wicket-taking against them in Sharjah. Between the twentieth and thirtieth overs, India scored only 46 runs. Though it might have seemed dour and defensive, it was gripping. Here the one-day game had an advantage over the classical form: by limiting overs and eliminating the draw, it added inexorable forward momentum to what might otherwise have been a static encounter. Certainly the crowd enjoyed it and the Pakistani fielding, sharper than at any time during the tournament, drew applause. After a painfully meandering innings of 20 off 43 balls, Manjrekar skied Sohail to deep mid wicket where he was well caught by Miandad running around from long on. Sohail had consigned the old master to the boundary (cricket's equivalent of Siberia) from the outset, and never once consulted him.

The crowd were uncertain whether the Indian innings was

well judged or becalmed. They cheered when Sidhu finally blasted Sohail through mid wicket. Azhar, who had just joined him at the crease, congratulated him, but Sidhu looked through his captain as if he wasn't there. Their long-running feud was to explode in England four months later, when Sidhu, dropped once again from the side, abandoned the tour party and returned to Punjab muttering about the indignities he had suffered at Azhar's hands. For the introverted Sidhu, forever nursing his grievances, the innings at Bangalore was vindication. Dropped and recalled more times than any Indian since Mohinder Amarnath, he scored 93 off 115 balls with 11 hard-won boundaries before he swung across the line and was bowled by Mushtaq's googly. In the thirty-seventh over India were 168 for 3. Azhar and Kambli tried to pick up the pace, but could still only manage three boundaries between them. In the forty-second over, Azhar tried to play a lifting ball from Waqar through gully. Wicket keeper Rashid Latif's right arm seemed to extend beyond its physical limits, like ET's neck, as he plucked a breath-taking catch, probably the single most spectacular piece of wicket keeping of the tournament. At 200 for 4 Jadeja arrived at the crease in the forty-second over. Waqar rapped him on the pads with an inswinger, and finished the over with figures of 7–1–24–1.

In the press box, the Indian journalists were dispirited. The total would be inadequate. On an easy pitch, the Pakistanis had played percentage out-cricket and the Indians, over-wrought as usual in the face of their near neighbours and arch-rivals, had failed to take the offensive. A brief flurry of 'Pakistan hai-hai' swelled up from somewhere in the crowd, but quickly subsided. In the forty-sixth over, Kambli, advancing down the wicket to Mushtaq, missed a well-flighted ball and was bowled leg stump. It was the end of an edgy, unconvincing but useful innings of 24 off 26 balls. Soon after, Mongia was run out. At 226 for 5 in the forty-sixth over, Waqar returned. Running in faster than at any time in the World Cup, he seemed determined to end the Indian innings by sheer willpower.

Here was pride before a fall. Kumble, the first of the home-town Karnataka boys to make an appearance, lofted him straight and then turned him square off his legs for two boundaries, before relinquishing the strike to Jadeja with a quick single. Jadeja slapped Waqar through extra cover, then lifted him high over mid wicket for six. The crowd was ecstatic. 'Ind–ia! Ind–ia!' A few missiles fell near the Pakistani deep fielders. Umpire Bucknor ordered Jadeja to put a stop to the disruption and when he appeared reluctant pushed him towards the offending section of the stands – the cheap seats (i.e., the Rs100 seats sold for a mere Rs1000). More at ease facing Waqar than his supporters, Jadeja signalled nervously to the crowd and the brief episode of missile-throwing came to an end. Kumble was caught in the deep by Miandad, and replaced by Srinath, home-town boy number two, who kept up the slog. Until these final overs, Pakistan had stuck to their game plan, a conservative but effective one. Suddenly the placements seemed ragged and gaping holes appeared in the field. In the last over, Jadeja struck Waqar over long off for one of the grandest sixes of the tournament. When he was caught by Sohail trying to repeat the stroke, he had made 45 off 26 balls with 4 fours and 2 sixes. He had changed the complexion of the innings and given India what proved to be a decisive advantage. The firecrackers that were supposed to have been excluded from the stadium began to explode.

Jadeja's wicket was Waqar's two-hundredth in one-day internationals, but the fast bowler took little joy from it. His last two overs went for forty runs: the trademark thunderbolt yorkers had been dispatched to the farthest reaches of the ground. Waqar had played his trump card too predictably and Jadeja was prepared for it. It was brainless bowling. Afterwards, there was much speculation about how Wasim would have handled the crisis. Would he have tried to dissuade his fast bowling partner, one-time best friend and later bitter rival, from relying on brute force? Would Waqar have listened? Had Wasim been there, would he have been able to come up with a more effective strategy –

and to implement it? The Indians had put on 62 runs in the last five overs to finish on 287, their highest-ever one-day score against Pakistan.

The Indian press cheered up and the crowd enjoyed the interval. News came in from Faisalabad. Jayasuriya had surpassed even his Delhi performance, scoring 82 runs from 44 balls. Mahanama and Tillekeratne had steered the team to port sedately, passing the English total with 9.2 overs and 5 wickets to spare. The English had been comprehensively outclassed by the Sri Lankans, against whom they had condescended to play only five Tests in thirteen years (in the same period they had played eighteen Tests against New Zealand). No team contributed less to the competition, won fewer friends or made more enemies.

I was reminded of a joke Achin had told me about a public meeting in London during the Falklands crisis. The speaker stands up and declares, 'We will fight them on the land like Englishmen; we will fight them on the sea like Englishmen; we will fight them in the air like Englishmen; and if necessary we will die like Englishmen.' At which point a bemused Sardar (Punjabi) shouts from the back of the hall, 'Why are your ambitions so modest?'

Birds maddened by the floodlights swirled and fluttered above the playing field. The crowd was cheerful and optimistic, cooled by a welcome breeze on a humid night. Floodlight technology will extend the south Indian cricket season, and the KSCA has ambitious plans to stage one-off domestic and international contests. They will have to, if they are to pay off the debts incurred in installing the lights.

Jayasuriya and Kaluwitherana had stolen the limelight for much of the tournament, but at Bangalore Sohail and Saeed Anwar, the Pakistani openers, proved themselves an equally dynamic pair. The first five overs went for 41 runs. Prasad was punished by Anwar on both sides of the wicket. Sohail slashed Srinath through point and pulled him past mid wicket. In a bid to check the runs, Azhar brought on Kumble but the crowd's excited chant of 'Kumble! Kumble!' died as the Bangalore boy, the spitting image of the modern Indian middle-class high-technocrat, was struck for 26 runs in a three-over spell. In the press box, the grumbling started. Azhar had set the field too deep. At this stage he should be trying to take wickets, not merely contain. Meanwhile, the two Pakistani left-handers, lying back and waiting for the ball, belted it with panache all over the ground. Standing at backward square, Azhar seemed struck dumb. Mongia and Jadeja kept running up to him, apparently making suggestions, but the Indian captain seemed unable to respond. In ten overs, the score raced to 84 for no wicket. In the crowd, in the press box, and I suspect on the field, there was one thought: were we about to witness a reprise of the massacre of Feroz Shah Kotla? Surely Azhar would not let history repeat itself?

It is difficult to watch a game of cricket whose result means so much to so many, and not be able to decide which side you want to win. Throughout the day, I was constantly and uncomfortably aware that one team's fortune was the other's misfortune. All cricket contests carry a burden of meanings imposed by events outside the field of play, but this one carried more than its fair share. Watching the figures scampering about under the floodlights, I tried to strip all the meanings away. I tried to see this activity from a distance and see it plain. For a moment, it came into focus: the toylike stumps and bails, the primitive leather ball, the little men expending a lot of energy doing nothing very important. Then the roar of the crowd brought me back to Chinnaswamy and war minus the shooting.

History did not repeat itself at Bangalore, but Azhar had little to do with it. Anwar took a thoughtless swipe at Srinath and was caught by Kumble running back to deep mid on. 'INDIA ZINDABAD!' the crowd erupted. And the home-town wicket taker got his due as Chinnaswamy stadium echoed with his name, 'Srinath! Srinath!'

Anwar's innings was remarkable – 48 off 32 balls – but his

sudden and unnecessary dismissal revitalised India in the field. As the players conferred in the middle, it seemed that Tendulkar was doing most of the talking. Sohail reached his fifty (off 41 balls) by driving Raju flat through the air for a six backward of point. It was greeted by only mild applause. The Indian crowd was rapidly running out of generosity.

But it was now time for the third home-town boy, Venkatesh Prasad, to make his mark on the World Cup. He had been hammered in his opening spell, and despite the local favouritism, not a few in the crowd must have worried that his return might smooth the path for the Pakistani juggernaut. Now a stalwart of the Indian pace attack, and already a veteran of twenty one-day internationals, he had yet to play a single Test match. His loping run up and high action seemed to promise much, but on the low, slow Indian wickets he rarely looked more than medium pace.

Whatever else Prasad learned at Dennis Lillee's feet while studying at the MRF Pace Academy in Madras, he had perfected the fast bowler's glare; he turned it now on Aamir Sohail. With a flash of the bat, Sohail drove him square for four and then pointed aggressively to the boundary, as if to say he would deposit the next one there as well. The next ball was full and straight. Sohail heaved once too often across the line and was clean bowled. Prasad's boyishly grave features writhed in triumph and he sent Sohail on his way with an extravagant sweep of the arm. The crowd in the expensive seats above the players' entrance booed the left-hander every step of the way as he walked off. Sohail was pilloried in Pakistan for allowing Prasad to provoke him into such a cavalier shot. It was clear the pressure was beginning to tell on Pakistani nerves, but when Sohail left the score was 113 for 2 in the fifteenth over. The asking rate was a reasonable five runs an over. Sohail and Anwar had laid the foundation for victory, just as the Sri Lankan openers had. The difference was in what came next. Where the Lankan middle-order batsmen had paced themselves to perfection, the Pakistani counterparts, despite their vast collective experience, failed.

Reawakened in the field, the Indians sprinted and tumbled, while Jadeja, the squad cheerleader, clapped his hands and pumped up his team-mates. Frustrated by Prasad's line, Ijaz went for a big hit – the third daft stroke of the Pakistani innings – only to be caught at deep mid off by Srinath. Then Inzamam, playing away from his body, edged Prasad off his glove, and was caught behind for 12 off 20 balls. After his heroics of 1992, Inzamam had endured an anti-climactic World Cup and the Indian fans rubbed it in. His ever-expanding girth made the 'Multan fatso' an easy target, and the Bangalore crowd spared him none of the usual barbs.

In seventeen deliveries, Prasad had removed Sohail, Ijaz and Inzamam. From 113 for 1 they had plunged to 132 for 4. And the asking rate was now 5.6 per over. Spectators stood in their places, waving with arms extended. Miandad joined Salim. The stage was set for something exceptional from the two veterans, with more than fifty World Cup appearances between them. Everyone in the ground knew that this could be Miandad's final moment of glory. They were also only too well aware how many times he had turned the tables on them. Kumble returned to the attack and bowled a maiden, accompanied by ceaseless rhythmic banging, clapping and chanting. Malik and Miandad played a crafty, safety-first game, turning their noses up even at quick singles (perhaps because they couldn't run them). Jadeja and Tendulkar maintained the pressure, taking the pace off the ball and cutting it off the pitch, forcing the batsmen to take risks if they were to stroke it off the square. In the thirty-sixth over, Kumble had Malik lbw swinging across the line. With Miandad he had put on 52 runs in fifteen overs. The asking rate was now 7.85.

How had Pakistan fallen so far behind? Were Miandad and Malik being canny or complacent? Were they too experienced and therefore too cautious? Would younger, less wary players have been more effective? The crowd roared and leaped and swayed. In the field, the Indians started showboating, shying at the stumps at the slightest excuse. Azhar flicked the ball behind his back. Jagmohan Dalmiya entered the press box with a satisfied smile. Many were eager to shake his hand, as if he were the author of this famous victory. In the meantime, Miandad had crept to 23 off 52 balls without a single boundary. Bereft of speed of reaction, power of wrist or even the keenness of eye which had buoyed him up throughout his career, he was playing on instinct. There was no lack of determination, but in Bangalore determination wasn't enough. It was a sad spectacle, but the Indian crowd relished it.

With Rashid Latif at the crease, however, celebrations were premature. He took 22 runs off two overs from Kumble, including two soaring sixes. As Ian Chappell observed, 'This was brilliant cricket, attack and counter-attack.' The crowd went quiet. 'No, not again,' you could almost hear them thinking as Latif completed yet another clean, powerful stroke, 'They're not going to steal another victory from us at the death, not another Sharjah, please.' Could Latif repeat Jadeja's performance? For many in the crowd, it was a fearful symmetry.

Their last apprehensions vanished when Raju had Latif stumped in the forty-third over. Then Kumble removed Mushtaq first ball, diving, stretching and managing to hold the catch even as his heavy frame hit the ground. At the other end, Miandad was hopelessly stalled. In Kumble's final over, he was given run out by the third umpire. Jadeja's throw had reached Mongia long before Miandad was within reach of the crease, and there was never any doubt about the decision (Miandad himself had already started to walk), but umpire Shepherd wisely decided to ensure there was no controversy surrounding Miandad's final fling.

I will always remember the look on Miandad's face as he walked off the field. Anguished, frustrated, fighting back tears. In this moment of truth, he had failed. In ninety-one minutes at the crease, he had faced 64 balls, scored 38 runs and hit a measly two boundaries. But he still found it hard to come to terms with his decaying powers. Within days he was blaming the team's loss on the decision to send him in at number six and arguing that he and not Sohail should have been named as Wasim's stand-in. If he had come in at number three, he insisted, he could have guided the team to victory. The truth was that the Pakistan Board had done Miandad no favours by picking him for this tournament, and exposing his frailties to the harsh floodlights of Bangalore.

For the Indian crowd, Miandad's dismissal was the sweetest moment of the night. The flags waved as never before. At last, the man who hit the six heard round the world had got his comeuppance, and they offered no applause (some even booed) as one of the greats of modern batsmanship exited the international stage. Many of the same people who had cheered the Pakistanis on to the field early in the afternoon were now consumed with vindictive glee at the fall of an ancient enemy. Nationalism had drowned out sentiment. In the clubhouse, Ram rose, alone, to cheer him. 'What are you clapping for?' the man in the seat next to him demanded. 'You should applaud him too,' Ram answered, 'he is a truly great player and none of us shall ever see him again.' The reply was terse and put an end to the conversation: 'Thank God I shall never see the bastard again.' The Solidarity match in Colombo seemed to belong to another world.

The stadium shook with huge, cannonlike explosions as one firecracker followed another; paper torches burned and smoke drifted across the battlefield. The crowd danced as Waqar twitched awkwardly at the wicket, unable to lay bat on ball. The final overs were a formality. The Indian players, electrified with anticipated victory, moved sleekly and efficiently in the field. They had done it – they had broken the Pakistan jinx. During the last over every spectator in the ground was standing, waiting for the final moment of victory to cast off any remaining inhibitions. As the last ball was bowled, the new scoreboard flashed CONGRATULATIONS TO INDIA. Waqar, a picture of depression, shook hands with Azhar and Tendulkar. Soldiers in olive green and paratroopers in blue helmets deployed across the field.

Ian Chappell presented Azhar with the £5000 winners' cheque, but on this night the prize seemed even more insignificant than usual. Sidhu received the man of the match award from the chief minister of Karnataka, Deve Gowde, who within three months would be sworn in as India's prime minister at the head of a centre-left coalition. The Indian journalists were glowing. 'This is the biggest morale boost for Indian cricket in years,' I was told. And one friendly hack, noted for his acerbic criticism of the India team management, conceded, 'Now even I believe we can go on to win the Cup. India has reversed the pattern. For once we did not crack under pressure. They were aggressive but we fought back. And we prevailed.'

It was a fair description of an excellent match. But I felt ambivalent. In the morning I had been unable to choose sides. Now that there was a winner and a loser I felt nothing but sorrow for the loser. And I couldn't help but wonder, how would the crowd have reacted if India had lost?

Meeting the press afterwards, Sohail was quiet and distracted, but had the presence of mind to say that he hoped India would now go on to win the Cup. An unusually communicative Azhar beamed and bubbled, and even admitted merrily that he had wanted to bat second but had been dissuaded by wiser heads. He praised Sidhu but said that Jadeja should have been the man of the match. In a separate corner Sidhu declared, 'The love and affection of the Indian people enabled me to do this. This knock was for the people of India. I owe it all to them.' The implication was clear. The hero of the hour owed everything to the people – nothing to selectors, managers or team-mates, least of all his captain. Cricketers frozen out of their team's inner caucus, like politicians marginalised in their parties, have two choices: keep your thoughts to yourself and wait for better days, or appeal over the heads of the leadership to a broader constituency. After

Bangalore, Sidhu felt confident enough to pursue the latter course.

I met Ram outside, where the streets were thronged with celebrants. 'Have you ever seen such a vulgar display of chauvinism?' he asked, and waved a despairing hand at the youths racing up and down MG Road on motorbikes screaming 'Bharat Mata ki jai' and 'Mera Bharat Barra Hai'. The pubs had all shut early, fearing violence if India lost, but the pavements were packed with banner-waving, slogan-shouting citizens. Cars hooted and traffic stalled as middle-class teenage boys demanded that passers-by join in their chanting – not only 'Bharat Mata ki jai' but 'Pakistan hai! hai!' The next day the Indian newspapers depicted it as a friendly mob, but I wasn't so sure. A quarter-final victory over any other team would have been welcomed as a stepping-stone to the final and greeted with quiet satisfaction, not this eager jubilation, this dance of revenge. What was being celebrated was not merely victory but victory over Pakistan, the political, military, social and economic inferior who had so frequently upstaged India on the cricket field. Ram was disgusted. 'I am going to write a new book,' he said, 'and call it "Anyone But India".' He took delight – the only real pleasure of the night for him – in the performances of the Karnataka players, but was despondent at the reaction of the crowd, who had betrayed the heritage of the Chinnaswamy Stadium. 'The mentality of the Indian cricket fan has changed beyond belief,' he said. 'Our chauvinism is now as vulgar and complete as the English, Pakistanis or Australians.'

Later we learned that Imran Khan's windscreen had been smashed as he returned to his hotel, and that drunks had fought with the police in Cavalry Road. Muslim areas were placed under curfew. In Shivajinagar, a small group of Hindutva fanatics raised the tricolour in an attempt to provoke a communal incident. 'The tension was palpable,' said police, but no violence ensued. Sometime overnight, there was another exchange of fire along the Kashmir border. Casualties went unreported.

The next day the *Indian Express* ran a front-page report of the victory celebrations in Delhi's Jama Masjid area, which has a large Muslim population. The paper self-consciously referred to 'women in burqas' joining the street parties and everyone it quoted praising the Indian team had a Muslim name. Whatever the intention, the article served mainly to illustrate how precarious Muslim inclusion in the Indian nation had become. The newspaper was saying: you see, they do pass the Thackeray test. But the real question was, Why should they have been tested at all? Later a university teacher in Delhi, a secular Muslim, told me how his teenage niece had been approached by her friends in the street after the Indian victory. 'How do *you* feel about the match?' they had asked. She was startled that people who knew her well would suddenly look at her differently and question her national identity – just because of a game of cricket.

I had worried so much about the impact of defeat on the losers that I had hardly considered the consequences of victory for the winners. Because India won, the worst prognostications of communal backlash were not put to the test. But having observed the raucous belligerence in the streets of Bangalore, and the fall-out from the match over the following days, I am no longer sure which brings out the worst in cricket nationalism: victory or defeat. The scenes in Bangalore were repeated in Bombay, Delhi, Calcutta and Madras. Sweets were distributed and crackers and drums thundered late into the night. Youths blew conch shells and danced on top of their Marutis. The trade at liquor shops, licit and illicit, was brisk and in the elite clubs the bubbly flowed to honour what the papers dubbed India's 'champagne performance'. The next day's headlines were triumphalist. 'INDIA OUST PAK IN BATTLE OF NERVES – NATION ERUPTS IN JOY' shouted the *Indian Express*. 'INDIA SHUT OUT PAKISTAN FROM CONTEST – MIRTHQUAKE ALL NIGHT LONG' echoed the *Times*.

The press reported 'strangers embracing' in the streets and even the hard-hearted bookies, who had taken a beating because of the odds favouring Pakistan, were quoted declaring: 'We are all winners – let the party go on till March seventeenth.' The KSCA thanked the public for its co-operation. 'It was fortunate that the match was held in Bangalore where there is a knowledgeable crowd who put the game above everything else,' said the *Hindu*, 'surely the Indian spectator has come of age.'

Although the ever-diplomatic Intikhab called the crowd 'sporting', Pakistani newspapers denounced it. They had seen the offensive banners on television and were sensitive to every bottle thrown and even the faintest 'Pakistan hai! hai!'. Omar Kureishi, who had so yearned for this meeting, was bitterly disappointed by the 'shamelessly partisan, utterly graceless crowd':

> A kind of primitive behaviour had taken over, raw emotions had been unleashed, people as if possessed went into a trance, their eyes glazed. These were not people going to a cricket match. These were people going into battle. I have covered cricket for nearly forty years and this has included many tours of India. I was in Bangalore in 1987 when Pakistan had won a test match and the series. But it was different this time. The same city, the same people, but a whole new ball game.

Both sides were right and both were wrong. Watching the crowd in Bangalore, I had found reasons to be cheerful and reasons to despair. It was true that a north Indian crowd would have been far more obnoxious, and possibly violent. It was also true that the Bangalore crowd had displayed a mean-minded vindictiveness in victory. The most important battle at Chinnaswamy that day was fought not between India and Pakistan on the field but between nationalism and cricket within the hearts of spectators. And the result was inconclusive.

Rao was quick to congratulate the team, followed in quick succession by Scindia and the usual gaggle of party politicians. BJP leader L.K. Advani inaugurated his Suraj Rath Yatra (an abortive attempt to re-ignite the Hindutva cause by staging a nationwide march for 'good government') by comparing the cricket triumph to the coming BJP victory at the polls. In

Bangalore BJP legislators attacked Deve Gowde for failing to attend a dinner in honour of the Indian team. Gowde's spokespersons were quick to assure the public that the chief minister had been unavoidably detained and intended no disrespect.

As for the cricket, R. Mohan described the events at Chinnaswamy as 'India's greatest night out in a long time'. Reporters heaped praise on all the Indian players and the belly-aching over Indian team selection and management was forgotten. At last, the Indians had matched the Pakistanis in fighting character. The self-restraint notable in the run-up to the tie dissolved in a wave of ebullient national pride.

Lahore had fallen silent at 2 p.m. Eight hours later the peace was rent by cries of anguish and rage. Immediately after the match, PTV played slow mournful sitar tunes, as if a great leader had died. The defeat was mentioned only briefly towards the end of the newscast that followed. Aggrieved fans, chanting anti-Wasim slogans, gathered outside newspaper offices. Youngsters disrupted traffic by parking motorbikes across main roads. Posters of Wasim and Sohail were smeared with mud. PTV, government and newspapers were flooded with angry calls. One demanded that the author of 'Hum jeetain gae' ('we will win') be punished for duping the people.

'A WAVE OF GRIEF HAS SWEPT THE COUNTRY. WE HAVE LOST OUR GLOBAL HONOUR' was the headline in *Al-Akhbar*, an Urdu-language daily. 'The humiliating defeat dashed all the hopes of the nation,' reported *The Nation*, under the headline 'PAKISTANIS COMMIT HARA-KIRI'. The front-page cartoon in the *Frontier Post* showed freshly dug graves with a sign sardonically quoting Zardari's promise, 'A plot for each player'. Defeat, said the *News*, 'left the whole nation in despair and disappointment'. The PPP Women's Wing general secretary, wealthy socialite Imbesat Yousuf, who had sponsored the overly official Basant Mela, issued a statement: 'We lost the match for no reason. I am so depressed that I cannot comment.' A crowd with banners and rotten eggs gathered at the airport to meet the returning cricketers; forewarned, they landed in Karachi. The frustrated demonstrators then marched to Wasim's house in Model Town and pelted it with the eggs. The World Cup videos were whipped off the air and, in shop after shop, the cassettes consigned to the dustbin.

In the assembly the opposition blamed the defeat on the government. 'Countries without a leader and teams without a captain never succeed,' declared one politician. The PPP was accused of spreading obscenity through PTV during the World Cup. Allah had punished Pakistan because the government had insulted Islam. 'Hum jeetain gae' should have been 'hum jeetain gae, inshallah' ('we will win, God willing'). 'Any nation which made a woman its ruler never prospered,' declared a right-wing mullah, ignoring the fact that Sri Lanka was currently ruled by a woman, as was India when it had won the World Cup in 1983. Donkeys were labelled with the names of the Pakistani cricketers and led in procession through the heart of Lahore.

Initially, Bhutto tried to soothe the country's nerves. 'A game is a game and we should accept the results with grace.' But having sought to exploit the Cup to her government's advantage, and having stoked the fires of national expectation as much as anyone, she was in no position to detach herself from defeat. An irate letter in the *News* made it clear why she would not be let off the hook: 'Madam prime minister, can we as a nation be proud of excelling in any other thing, e.g. good governance, education, health care, welfare, justice? The answer, regrettably, is no. Therefore, please do not trivialise this débâcle. It should be thoroughly investigated so that corrective action is taken to regain the pride of the nation.'

Bhutto's husband Zardari resigned as chairman of the World Cup Committee, and soon joined the chorus of those demanding an inquiry. For the factions in both politics and cricket the defeat was a chance to settle scores. Hasib Ahsan, a deposed chairman of the selection committee, asked, 'How many chances will these ignorant officials give Intikhab Alam who has been unable to extract the best from the most talented side in the world?' PCB president Syed Bokhari, who had kept his antagonism to Abassi under wraps in the months preceding the World Cup, now saw a window of opportunity. He announced, 'An inquiry is necessary to put cricket affairs on the right path to avoid such defeats in the future.' Sarfraz Nawaz held a press conference whose sole purpose was to attack Imran, whom he held responsible for the corruption of the Pakistan side.

Bizarrely, some citizens sought redress through the courts. A neighbour served a writ on Wasim accusing him of 'criminal negligence' in the defeat. The Lahore High Court accepted the writ for hearing, the judge noting sternly that 'corruption has destroyed cricket in Pakistan'. An advocate petitioned the court to establish a commission headed by the chief justice of Pakistan to probe the allegation that the team had been bribed to lose. He also petitioned for a permanent ban on the playing of cricket on the grounds that the game promoted gambling, squandered resources and wasted time.

In the liberal *Friday Times*, a commentator observed, 'Losing at Bangalore was all the more unbearable because, with the exception of Tendulkar, the Pakistanis are, man to man, better players than the Indians. The problem is that we don't have a team.' Omar Kureishi insisted, 'I still maintain that Pakistan was the best balanced team in the tournament but it was the least prepared.' There was some truth in these assertions, and they were more useful contributions to the debate than anything the politicians had to offer. But there was a reluctance to accept that it had been a closely fought cricket match and that the result could easily (and would easily on another day) be reversed, and that maybe the Indians were a better side than Pakistanis were willing to concede.

In accounting for victory or defeat in cricket, the cock-up is generally to be preferred to the conspiracy theory. But in the context of the long build-up to the World Cup, and the grandiose claims and national sentiments that accompanied it, people were driven by a need to explain defeat, to assign it a moral or political meaning. It could be argued that no World Cup championship ever meant more, or had more political ramifications, than Pakistan's win under Imran in 1992. Their four years as World Cup title holders had been tumultuous, but through it all the Pakistani fans had believed their team could and should win the title again, and this time at home. Many therefore concluded that Pakistan cricket had been undone by enemies within and without.

It was claimed that RSS and Shiv Sena activists had telephoned the Pakistan dressing room during the match and threatened to kill the players if they beat India. Terrified, the twelfth man had carried instructions to Sohail to throw his wicket away. Others suggested that in the interval the Pakistan players were given drugged snacks. The drugs took effect slowly, hence the falling away after the brisk start. 'Indians proved their jealousy and hate by showing pin drop silence at the time of a hit for four by our batsmen,' said a letter writer. 'Our cricketers looked like orphans because no prominent personality from the camps of government, opposition or other areas except Imran Khan was seen. Nobody was there to tap their shoulders at a good shot. In all these circumstances we cannot expect our cricket heroes to win.'

Wasim took the brunt of the anger. 'If Wasim Akram was fifty per cent fit, he should have preferred to die on the pitch rather than sit on his haunches in the pavilion,' wrote an angry fan in *The Nation*. 'I have been receiving death threats on my life,' Wasim told the press. 'My home at Lahore has been stoned. My family members are harassed and intimidated. If this situation continues I have to reconsider my position as a player and captain of the national team.' Newspapers quoted cricket fans who claimed to have seen Wasim dancing at the Oasis discotheque in Bangalore the evening before the match. 'He can dance with girls but when he plays for Pakistan his back hurts.' Some journalists seemed to be suffering from short-term memory failure. 'Till the morning of the match, no one had any clue about Wasim's mysterious injury,' reported one. 'The gambler's grapevine gives a sum of Rs20 million as the price the bookies were prepared to pay for duping the public into believing that Wasim Akram would be playing in the quarter-finals.' Offended, Wasim offered to swear on the Koran that the gambling allegations were false. But the cynics insisted, 'Everyone knows a non-starter favourite is the biggest boon a bookmaker can wish for.'

Intikhab came to his players' defence. Surely, given Zardari's promises, any Pakistan player would be better off winning the World Cup than losing the quarter-final. 'Ah, but it is easier to lose than to win,' said the cynics. And in any case, Zardari's promises were themselves a symptom of the corruption of Pakistani cricket.

When I returned to Lahore a week after the defeat at Bangalore, the arguments were still raging in the newspapers. But most of the fans I spoke to were ashamed of the spectacle the country had made of itself. Again and again I was told, 'It's only a game'. They readily acknowledged that what hurt was losing to India, and that was why people had over-reacted. Very few however were prepared to rule out the possibility that gambling interests had been involved. There was no concrete evidence to support this belief, but given past controversies, it was not surprising that the conviction that money changed hands was so widespread. Only days before the match, Qasim Omar, a former Test player, revealed that he had accepted payment to throw away his wicket in a match against Australia in 1984. Ultimately, the lingering doubt about the probity of the Pakistani players reflected a much wider loss of confidence in the integrity of anyone in public life.

Fareshteh Gati, one of Pakistan's small but intrepid corps of young women cricket journalists, discerned a morality tale in Pakistan's World Cup fate: 'As a people we did not cherish this event. We, every single man, woman and child involved with the World Cup, was [sic] more on the look-out for a short-cut to the million dollar mark than taking pride in hosting the most prestigious event in world cricket. We paid for that shortcoming with the loss to India.'

In portraying the country in the grip of hysteria, Pakistani, Indian and English journalists simplified the reality. There was a debate in Pakistan, as there had been in the crowd in Bangalore, a debate conducted between and within individuals. You could follow it in the papers in the days after the match. It was not merely a colloquy between reason and unreason; it was an anguished dispute over the meaning of cricket and its place in the life of a modern nation-state. 'Like all the poor nations of the third world, both India and Pakistan find the field of sports a cover-up for their backwardness in all other modern fields,' wrote a columnist in the *News*. 'Did Pakistan "rule the world" after winning the last Cup title? Not even in cricket.' Another observed,

> No matter how many times Pakistan beats India and vice versa, in cricket, hockey, fencing, kabaddi or Graeco-Roman wrestling, it is irrelevant to the greater issues underlying the relationship between the two countries. However, it is paradoxical and worth pondering why young men who have lost a mere sporting contest are being so reviled, while those who lost much more serious struggles with India, on the battlefield and in the global marketplace, remain unpunished and in some case allowed to rest on pedestals of civic honour.

In *Dawn* a writer found that the best way to understand this 'war minus the shooting' was to compare it to the shooting war Pakistan had lost to India thirty years previously. 'For months the nation was fed on a steady diet of jingoistic propaganda constructed around the premise that one Pakistani (Muslim) soldier was equal to ten Indian (Hindu) soldiers. Just as we sought scapegoats in 1965, we are trying desperately to blame somebody, anybody, for our defeat last Saturday.' The Bangalore match was advertised as 'War Minus the Shooting' and welcomed on the basis that this was better than war with the shooting. But what happened in the end showed that you cannot promote cricket in this fashion without unleashing the emotions and follies of war, the over-valuation of victory, the obsession with betrayal.

Across the border, the Indians shook their heads at the tumult in Pakistan. Chandra Mitra, editor of *Pioneer*, cited the Pakistan over-reaction to defeat as evidence of 'the inherent superficiality of the Pakistani "nation" '. Painting a bleak picture of a country 'sinking into adolescence or worse', he ended his article with the sardonic hope that 'Maybe in a few years from now Pakistan will be mature enough to play cricket for its own sake instead of demanding that its players use the bat and ball as a substitute for its nuclear arsenal.' The smug voice of Indian superiority spoke too soon.

From Bangalore I flew to Madras for the quarter-final between New Zealand and Australia. Discussing the tie with Ravi Shastri on television, Ian Chappell contrasted it with the confrontation in Bangalore: 'We're near neighbours too but we tend to fight wars together not against each other.' The remark seemed bizarrely jovial, but it contained an uncomfortable nugget of truth. Shastri could find no reply. In Madras, I caught up with Graham, a friend from London and long-time Labour Party drone who coupled a die-hard commitment to socialism with unshakeable allegiance to Essex County Cricket Club. He was making his first visit to the sub-continent and was enchanted, despite a punishing bout of diarrhoea. 'I've got the soul of an internationalist,' he moaned, 'but the stomach of an Englishman.'

The mood at the Chepauk Stadium was relaxed. It was as if, having withstood the trauma of Bangalore, fans, officials, journalists could once again breathe freely, despite the viscous air that envelops this city of humidity. Night cricket had come none too soon to Madras. Rs5 crore (£1 million) had been spent equipping Chepauk's tall, snug circular ground with floodlights. The open-air press box and modest players' facilities were berated, but ticketing was fairer and the treatment of fans more courteous than elsewhere. Even the police presence was relatively discreet.

Fifteen thousand spectators turned up one and a half hours before the match to cheer the warm-up routines. The Madras crowd is proud of its reputation as one of the most knowledgeable and appreciative in India. Today the fans were here to enjoy good cricket without worrying much about the result. They came to worship Warne, Waugh and the Australian super-stars, but in the ends their hearts were given to New Zealand's Chris Harris, whose efforts ensured they had a match to watch.

After an early batting collapse, Harris joined his captain, Lee Germon, in a sustained display of aggressive hitting. They took 13 off one over from Warne, his most expensive yet in the World Cup. Harris set his sights on the boundaries and hoisted McGrath, Fleming and Warne for sixes. The tall, fair-haired, bland-looking bits-and-pieces cricketer seemed an unlikely person to play a rampaging heroic innings, and the crowd loved it all the more because it was so unexpected. 'WE WANT SIXER!' they shouted as he took strike, and his every scoring shot was cheered. When Germon was out for 89 (including ten boundaries) in the thirty-sixth over, the score stood at 212 for 4 and New Zealand seemed set for a large total. But the lower-middle order – Twose, Cairns, Parore – failed to build on the foundation. As wickets fell at one end, Harris struggled with cramp at the other. (On this same ground eighteen months before I had watched a sweat-drained Brian Lara nearly pass out at the crease.) Though looking increasingly lame, Harris kept swatting at the ball and running for every available single. In the forty-ninth over, he played a last, exhausted pull shot off Warne and was caught at deep mid wicket. He had struck 130 off 124 balls, with 4 sixes and 12 fours. As he hobbled back to the dressing room the crowd rewarded him with a standing ovation.

New Zealand's final total of 286 forced the Australians to work for a victory that everyone had assumed would be achieved with ease. Tight bowling and vigorous fielding kept the Australian batsmen at bay in the early overs. The Chepauk crowd undulated as the Mexican wave rippled round the ground time after time, an impressive display of spontaneous collective co-ordination. A banner declared, 'WE LOVE YOU CAMERA-*PERSONS*; SEE – NO GENDER BIAS!' Graham was delighted with his first taste of cricket in south Asia, and munched happily on the vegetarian snacks provided to the denizens of the press box, despite his tender bowels.

With a high quick action, Harris bowled a straight line and a full length, but Cairns, the prima donna of the New Zealand side (and a favourite with Indian crowds) was no more successful with ball than with bat. Ponting and Mark Waugh both drove him contemptuously to the boundary off the front foot. He was replaced by Thompson, whose accuracy restricted the run flow. Suffering untold aches and pains, Harris limped bravely back to his mark after each ball, then turned and darted in quickly, never flinching or favouring any part of his body. When Ponting was out for 31, Taylor promoted Warne up the order. It was an unexpected manoeuvre whose logic soon became apparent. The leg spinner smacked Harris for six over cover point, then pulled Thompson over mid wicket and again over square leg for two more. The crowd loved it. Here was yet another side of the ever-surprising Warne, the clinical slogger approaching his batting duties with earnest, unsmiling aggression. He was soon out lbw to Astle but his 24 off 14 balls gave Australia a vital push out of the shallows, into the open seas. Mark Waugh, hitherto cautious, now accelerated smoothly and the New Zealanders, scattered deep in the field, lost heart. His second 50 came off only 34 balls and featured three fours and two sixes. When he was out in the fortieth over for 110 off 114 balls, he was greeted with the applause due a masterful display tailored to suit the needs of his team yet never less than pleasing to the eye. Sixty-nine runs were required off the last ten overs, but such was the ease of the pitch and the limitations of the New Zealand bowling, Steve Waugh and Stuart Law were able to slash their way to victory with two overs to spare.

Earlier that day, the West Indies had upset South Africa in

Karachi. The ever-innovative Woolmer had dropped one of the fastest bowlers on earth, Alan Donald, in favour of playing two spinners. It was bold and creative and perhaps a gimmick too far. Even the best organised fielding side in the world had no answer to Brian Lara (dropped by Rhodes), whose 111 was his best innings of the World Cup. He was out in the thirtieth over with the score 180 for 2, but once again the West Indies middle order buckled, and their total of 264 seemed vulnerable when South Africa reached 198 for 3 with ten overs in hand. Then in the space of 4 overs, Adams removed Cronje, who had threatened to overhaul the West Indies total single-handedly, and Harper despatched McMillan, Palframan, Rhodes and Pollock. In the final over, South Africa were all out 22 runs short of their target.

The four 1992 semi-finalists – South Africa, New Zealand, Pakistan and England – had all been eliminated in the 1996 quarter-finals; the four teams contesting the semi-finals – West Indies, Australia, India and Sri Lanka – had all qualified from Group A. Those who had argued that the early World Cup matches were meaningless were now confronted with semi-final pairings that rematched competitors from two of the most dramatic encounters of the first round. As it turned out, the experiences of the group ties left scars which affected the outcome of both semi-finals.

12

The nation shamed?

I arrived in Calcutta to find the city preoccupied with the semi-final rematch against Sri Lanka. 'INDIANS MAY JUST HOLD THE EDGE' claimed the banner headline in the *Telegraph*. Command Mobile Phone Service bought half a page to remind the Indian cricketers of their national duty: 'Today 110,000 Calcuttans take command of the stands. They want their team to take command on the field.' Rotomac Ballpens told the players, 'You carry the hopes of 900 million Indians . . . Set Eden Gardens on fire with a performance that will do every Indian proud.' Hallmark, the greeting cards giant, kept its message fittingly epigrammatic: 'Jayasuriya stumbles . . . Lankans K'r'umble . . .' Asian Paints filled a page with a picture of a pale blue Indian World Cup strip with the caption, 'Hamara wala blue! (We are the blues) Never before has a single colour meant so much to so many.' The Calcutta Municipal Corporation tried to strike a more balanced note: 'Calcutta has the spirit of internationalism – cricket for friendship.' Chief Minister Jyoti Basu, multinational capital's favourite communist, told the press, 'I wanted to attend a rally in north Bengal but my party colleagues told me that at present people were more interested in cricket than politics.'

The bookies made India marginal favourites and the Reserve

Bank of India issued a clearance for the sale of tickets to the final at Lahore. Azhar reminded fans that Eden Gardens was his lucky ground (I had seen him score a century against England on his Test debut there in 1984–85). In the last few years the stadium had witnessed a series of Indian one-day triumphs, always accompanied by spectacular celebrations. Hero Honda invoked one of the fondest of recent memories by urging 'Azhar's Heroes' to 'Recreate the Hero Cup Magic', a reference to victory over the West Indies in 1993. It was assumed that India's home advantage would be magnified at Eden Gardens, where Sri Lankan nerves would be tested by 110,000 vociferously partisan spectators. What's more, the boundaries at Eden Gardens were too big for sixes. If Jayasuriya and Kaluwitherana took the aerial route, they would be caught in the deep.

The cracker shops in Burrabazar had virtually sold out. '*Anars* are selling the most,' a newspaper reported. 'People plan to light them in between the rows of bonfires while savouring the moments of victory.' Whistles, brightly coloured hats, heaps of red, green and yellow *gulal* (powder) were also selling briskly, as were crates of beer for those planning to savour the contest on television.

A record number of security personnel had been deployed in the city. Senior intelligence officers had been flown in from Delhi to advise on possible LTTE terrorist attacks, and a team of commandos protected the Sri Lankans round the clock. Photo identity cards were issued to staff at the Taj Bengal, where the players and officials were camped, and a bomb disposal squad combed the stadium. Under pressure, the Public Works Department had issued the CAB with a last-minute 'provisional structural certificate' for the newly built tier of seats. Twenty-five people had been arrested for black marketing tickets: 'Club officials are trying to raise funds by selling tickets at a premium,' said police. But since the bulk of this unofficial trade was conducted over the telephone, it escaped detection, even though the going rates were published in local newspapers. The much sought after clubhouse passes, marked at Rs1500 (£30), were selling for up to Rs12,000 (£240).

Graham had preceded me to Calcutta by a day. When his plane landed, over-eager passengers leaped up to remove belongings from the overhead compartments while the aircraft was still moving, only to be reproved by the pilot: 'You are cricket fans. I do not expect you to behave in this manner.' Offended, the passengers threatened to *gherao* (blockade) the pilot, and only after protracted negotiations were they permitted to disembark. Graham spent the next twelve hours searching for a ticket to the match. When he had first applied to the CAB last October, he had been told that tickets for the semi-final would go on sale on the first of January, but when the new year came around, his repeated letters, faxes and phone calls went unanswered. Eventually he was told by a minion that the tickets were sold out. It became apparent in Calcutta, however, that many had been withheld by officials who knew their value would increase exponentially should the Indian team appear in the match. After fruitless forays to Eden Gardens and phone calls to the British consulate, he contacted a young businessman whom he had met on the flight and who was able to secure him a ticket (at a price) through his employers, a multinational corporation.

I had assumed I would be spared these hassles because of my press pass, but on arriving at Eden Gardens on the morning of the match, I was refused admission to the clubhouse because I lacked the additional, local pass issued by the CAB itself. Outside the gates, several hundred would-be spectators jostled each other in increasingly desperate attempts to convince the security guards to grant them admission. But their entreaties seemed no more successful than mine, and even attempts to invoke high ranking contacts – 'Mr Dalmiya has put tickets aside for me', 'Tell Azhar so-and-so is here', 'I am a cousin of the minister' – were met with impassive glares.

'Where do I get the extra pass?' I asked.

'You go to Taj Bengal,' I was told, before being shoved out of the way, with other suitors, so that Clive Lloyd, the match referee, could squeeze through the narrow opening in the gate. I took a taxi to the Taj Bengal, heavily guarded by paratroopers in blue camouflage uniforms. Fans stood on the driveway outside, waiting patiently for a glimpse of their heroes. I walked through the crowd, past the paratroopers and into the hotel lobby without once being asked to identify myself. But white skin privilege did me no good when I finally tracked down the CAB press liaison officer, who was having a bad day. 'I have no passes here,' he told me impatiently. 'They are being distributed by the Sports Journalists Federation.'

'But I was told to come here.'

'Derek Pringle knew where to go!'

Ah, so it was all my fault. I hurried from the Taj back to Eden Gardens and was presented with my CAB pass by the highly efficient Sports Journalists Federation in their marquee opposite the ground. The sun was out and the ticket holders filed towards the gates in orderly queues. By the time I had taken my place in the press box, most of the crowd were in their seats, though the match was not scheduled to start for another half hour. They were in buoyant mood, expecting a high festive day of cricket and national triumph.

The press box was suspended at a vertiginous height at the very top of the clubhouse, so elevated you felt you were hovering in a spaceship above the ground. The figures on the field looked minuscule, as they did from almost any vantage point in this vast wondrous arena. From our eyrie, we enjoyed a view of the Hooghly and the new suspension bridge that crosses it. Dwarfed by the scale of the stadium, sponsors' hoardings and boundary boards seemed less egregious than elsewhere, and the Wills banners suspended from the top tier added a pleasant splash of colour to the acres of freshly whitewashed concrete. Half the ground has no cover, and spectators there, already burning in the unremitting sunshine, fanned themselves with pieces of cardboard or newspapers, creating a flickering effect, as if across a giant television screen.

I was glad to see Abdul Rehman, the legendary scorekeeper of the Eden Gardens press box, already at his post, surrounded by record books, coloured pencils and vast, desk-filling scoresheets. Rehman is a railway clerk who for two decades has been given time off for his scorekeeping duties. He is a cricket pedant par excellence, gushing statistics ceaselessly (and always at the top of his voice). Nervous and peremptory, he treats the journalists like unruly schoolchildren, and in return they tease him mercilessly.

Below, Percy Abeysekere was already parading his Sri Lankan flag back and forth behind the twelve-foot wire fence that separated the crowd from the field. It was Percy's first visit to Eden Gardens, and his fare had been paid by his employers, a Sri Lankan cable company. According to the morning papers, he had been worried that security personnel would confiscate his flag, but apparently they had decided it would be churlish to stop this lone specimen of Sri Lankan support. After all, today it would be 110,000 to one. In the press box we chewed over the latest rumours. Patil and Wadekar were feuding. The Indians had offered the Pakistanis US$6 million to shift the final to Calcutta. Abassi wanted to switch the venue from Lahore to Karachi. If Sri Lanka won today, the match would be transferred to Colombo. The Australians or West Indians would have to play or forfeit! My favourite pre-match comment came from Duleep Mendis. Neatly reversing decades of patronising appreciation, he told journalists, 'We're not going to take India lightly.'

White-limbed technicians were out in the middle furiously repairing the damage to their stump camera wires, which had been nibbled by rats. It was a classic example of what Marxists call 'combined and uneven development'. The wicket had been damaged during the opening ceremony, and had been quickly relaid. Expert opinion in the morning papers had been nearly unanimous: given the doubts about the wicket, and the recent history of Eden Gardens, where sides batting second had been defeated in a series of one-sided fifty-over matches, Azhar must bat first if he won the toss. On the front page of that morning's *Telegraph*, Ian Chappell had asked, 'Does Azhar play to his strength or invite Sri Lanka to bat first?' His answer was unequivocal: 'He should play to his strength.'

Azhar won the toss. And decided to bat second. The groundsman had already declared that the wicket would turn, but memories of the defeat in Delhi were fresh, and the Indian brains trust feared a repeat. They left Raju out and brought in the off spinner Kapoor to inhibit the Sri Lankan left-handers. Within ten minutes of the start of play, Azhar's gamble seemed to have paid off. Kaluwitherana sliced his first ball from Srinath high and deep to backward point where Manjrekar, running around, took a good catch. Jayasuriya, who had crossed to the striker's end, played the next ball and was out, caught by Prasad, in mirror-image fashion. The right- and left-handers had both swung wantonly at off stump balls, as if they had come to believe in their invincibility in the early overs. Perhaps they had read too many awe-struck accounts in the newspapers. Or perhaps, as predicted, the law of averages had caught up with them. Suddenly, they looked foolish instead of bold.

Jayasuriya was the man India had wanted to get, and the crowd celebrated his dismissal with a thunderous cheer. They had won the match in the first over! When Gurusinha followed in the seventh, trying to pull a short ball from Srinath, the Indian flags fluttered again, but the reaction was tepid. Although the wicket had brought India that much closer to a decisive victory, the spectators had paid a lot of money to get in here and they wanted to see a match of some kind. Besides, the Sri Lankans had played so well until now, it would be a pity if they let themselves down badly on the great stage. Ted Corbett, who over the years had covered innumerable football as well as cricket cup competitions, reminded us that semi-finals often proved anti-climactic. 'We'll be home early,' was the view in the press box, where there was plenty of support for Sri Lanka, even among the Indian journalists. Suddenly Azhar was a tactical genius. India's early success owed everything, in fact, to Srinath, who opened with a magnificent spell of seven overs for 34 runs and 3 wickets. It was to be his last in the World Cup. Throughout the tournament, he had demonstrated superb control and sustained hostility. During the past eighteen months, he had emerged from Kapil's shadow and was now hailed everywhere as a world-class seam bowler.

At 35 for 3 a respectable Sri Lankan total seemed out of the question. De Silva, however, had already made 31 off the 12 balls he had faced (Gurusinha had managed only 1 off the same number), and seemed unperturbed by the loss of early wickets. When Prasad erred microscopically on the leg side, De Silva flicked him to fine leg. Prasad adjusted. Like all the Indian bowlers, he knew De Silva's strength on the on side. But it made no difference. De Silva drove him through the covers with his elbow high. The next ball he stroked through point. Azhar put another fielder on the off side, close in at cover point. De Silva pulled through square leg, just vacated. Despite the fielding restriction in the first fifteen overs, De Silva refrained from lofting the ball. Instead, he played his shots along the ground, bisecting fielders with breathtaking precision. It was Test-match batting at an accelerated pace. Everything was correct and controlled, but the scoring was relentless. The strokes were out of the text book, executed with a perfect timing that sent the ball speeding across the turf. There was no hope of cutting off these boundaries; the fielders moved only to retrieve the ball from the fence.

'Thirty-six fifties in his career,' Rehman shouted as De Silva reached his half century. 'You please write down! Third fifty in World Cup in 17 innings in World Cup in 19 matches in World Cup. Write down. No argument!'

This was an innings for aficionados, and it is the World Cup innings I would most like to watch on video. Every one of De Silva's 14 boundaries was a gem, and every one was warmly applauded by the crowd and greeted with oohs and aahs from the connoisseurs in the press box. De Silva boxed the compass, stroking the ball through off side and on, forward and square and behind. His innings was an exhibition of applied trigonometry, and probably the most aesthetically scintillating display of the World Cup. Cricket writers sometimes talk of the game as if it were a fine art whose norms have nothing to do with victory or defeat, but even an innings like De Silva's is judged in the end by its relation to the game as a whole. And by these standards it was, if anything, even more outstanding. His quick scoring compensated for the early wickets and took pressure off those who followed him. He was out in the fifteenth over, bowled by Kumble, with the score on 85 (of which he had made 66 off 47 balls). De Silva had been looking to push to the off side for a single, but played down the wrong line. Ironically, it was a one-day shot that cost him his wicket. The rest of his innings was played in classical style.

De Silva's dismissal left Mahanama, hardly noticed until then, on 14. Until this match, he had batted only once in the World Cup, and made nought not out. Now Ranatunga joined him, and together they set about the long hot work of accumulating a respectable total. Ranatunga played in his customary dismissive style, letting the bat fall on the ball at the last moment. Watching him you would never know he was playing in front of 110,000 Indian fans willing him to fail. He transcended the pressure by ignoring it; Mahanama, calm and straight, did so by channelling it. Kapoor came on and turned the ball from the beginning. Somehow Mahanama and his captain managed to score 5 an over, mainly by gliding the ball behind square or pushing it gently into the covers for singles.

Meanwhile the crowd sweltered in the heat. Already, the vendors had run out of Coke and there was no drinking water available except in the clubhouse and the VIP enclosures. Nothing could more clearly confirm the deep love of cricket in the subcontinent than the willingness of fans to endure all kinds of indignities and discomforts to watch it. Even as the late afternoon sun bore down on them, the crowd seemed patient and attentive.

In the middle, Mahanama began to limp and soon it was obvious he was suffering from cramp, brought on by dehydration. After a friendly chat with Ranatunga, Azhar agreed to allow him a runner.

While Kapoor struggled to control the turn, Tendulkar produced his best spell of the tournament. Mixing off spin, leg breaks, seamers, donkey drops and cutters (in the press box, Ayaz Menon of Bombay's *Mid-Day* dubbed his style 'right arm over everything'), he kept the wary batsmen guessing. It was junk bowling perfectly suited to the wicket. When Azhar seemed to run out of ideas, Tendulkar took command, setting the field and at one point grabbing the ball impatiently out of his captain's hands. A leg break trapped Ranatunga lbw for 35 in the thirty-third over. Five overs later, the exhausted Mahanama was carried from the field in distress. He had contributed an almost unnoticed but ultimately invaluable 58 not out, spread over 130 sun-blasted minutes.

The floodlights came on and the sun began to set behind the thick-leaved trees of the tropical gardens. In the distance, the Hooghly looked slick and silvery. The crowd was bathed in the glow of twilight and the heat began to ease. After Mahanama retired, the Sri Lankan innings spluttered. Tillekeratne laboured against Tendulkar and Kapoor for a slow 32. Despite Vaas's 23 off 16 balls, the slog at the end was half-hearted, with the Sri Lankans managing only four boundaries off the last ten overs. From such a disastrous start, 251 for 8 after fifty overs wasn't bad, but most observers agreed that the Sri Lankans had left themselves 20 runs short of a defensible total. As the dark closed in, the crowd broke into a Mexican wave. Under the floodlights, the playing field looked burnished and bright – more like television than reality.

'SHRI RAM V RAVAN' read one banner, a reference to the Ramayana story in which the Prince of Ayodhya makes war against the Demon King of Lanka. 'RAMA' read another, simply and insistently. These were the telltale signs of the long campaign waged by the forces of Hindutva to replace the mosque at Ayodhya with a temple to Ram, who had been promoted in recent years as not merely a Hindu god but an Indian national hero. Such sectarian invocations were relatively new to Indian cricket, despite the long history of the communal competition in Bombay, and they brought a touch of menace to the relaxed atmosphere. For some in the stands, this was a contest not simply between two cricket teams or even two modern nation-states, but between two ancient civilisations, a grudge carried forward from pre-history. 'KUMBLE BRING BACK THE MAGIC OF THE HERO CUP' at least had some relevance to both the cricket and to Calcutta.

Dalmiya appeared in the press box and was roasted for the poor facilities, notably the paltry allocation of three fax machines to serve over fifty reporters. It appeared the local telecommunications body was punishing the CAB for a shortfall in its quota of complimentary tickets. The members of the press were exhausted by now, and some slumped over their desks unconscious. Weeks of travel, of hotels, of copy deadlines, of struggles with new technology had taken their toll.

Vaas opened the bowling for Sri Lanka and had Sidhu, the hero of Bangalore, caught by a diving Jayasuriya for 3 in the third over. Manjrekar entered, embarking on a twenty-over partnership with Tendulkar. Tendulkar was in fighting mood, but so were the Sri Lankans, who let nothing slip, and were applauded by the crowd for their efforts. Muralitharan turned the ball at right angles, and with Dharmasena bowling accurately at the other end, scoring was difficult. Tendulkar, aware that the result was still in the balance, opted for judicious attack. Manjrekar was the sheet-anchor.

Sometime early in the Indian innings I realised how committed to the Sri Lankan cause I had become, so much so that I could not take pleasure in Indian successes, even though they were the work of players whose talents had given me much delight in the past. The crackle of Tendulkar's driving, both square and straight, left me ambivalent. Yet I knew that if India won today,

I would be backing them to the hilt in the final. As Tendulkar reached another 50 (his fifth of the tournament) in 67 balls with 7 fours, firecrackers boomed across the stadium. Slow and steady, the partnership advanced towards the target. After twenty overs, the Indians had reached 83 for 1, and the game seemed to be drifting away from Sri Lanka. The crowd was confident and relaxed. Tendulkar and Manjrekar needed to do no more than keep their present course.

The Sri Lankans had a conference in the centre, and Jayasuriya was brought on to replace Murali. The slow left-armer bowled into the rough outside the right-hander's leg stump, a stratagem he had learned from Shane Warne. In this manner, those who naturally turned the ball away from the right-hander could contain scoring and frustrate stroke-makers. In the twenty-third over, Tendulkar, tied down and looking for runs, lurched out of his crease, was brushed on the pad by a leg-stump ball and set off for a leg bye, unaware that Kaluwitherana had collected the ball. Even as the wicket keeper swung his arms across to remove the bails, the batsman realised his error, braked, turned and tried to scramble back to his crease – too late. Tendulkar was out for 65. Was he stumped or run out? The question was academic, one of cricket's eternal conundrums. Kaluwitherana and Jayasuriya had failed with the bat, but they had combined to remove the Indian danger man with the score 98 for 2.

Azhar came in and was out for a duck. Dharmasena held back the ball, Azhar groped for it, and the rebound off bat and pad fell into the bowler's hands. It was only one of many poor, impatient shots played by the Indian captain over the last year, but he was to pay a greater penalty for it than for all the others combined. Saddest of all, the usually elegant Azhar looked ungainly. As he trudged back to the dressing room, his eyes were blank, as if he could not bring himself to contemplate what horrors might now be in store for him. A rumour began to make its way around Eden Gardens' sprawling terraces. Azhar, perhaps others, had been bribed to throw the game. The bookies were making another killing.

The Sri Lankans were now hurling themselves around the field and appealing for everything. Curiously, though India had never lost to Pakistan in a World Cup tie, they had never beaten Sri Lanka. I started to wonder if the Indians had been wrong about their 'jinx side'. Kambli, once again in Ninja turtle guise, joined the becalmed Manjrekar. Having crept to 25 off 48 balls, he tried to sweep Jayasuriya and was bowled off the back of his thigh.

Srinath was promoted up the order, presumably to emulate Shane Warne and smash the spinners off their defensive line. The ploy was never tested. Srinath was run out by Murali's excellent throw from the deep to the non-striker's end, where it was gathered cleanly by Jayasuriya, stealing the show like a ham actor. The television replay verdict seemed to take an inordinate time, and grumbling spectators noted caustically that the third umpire was Mehboob Shah, a Pakistani. When he finally gave Srinath out, someone muttered, 'Crackers must be bursting in Karachi.'

As the wickets tumbled the crowd sank into sullen dismay; this was not what they had expected. Only moments before they had been preparing to celebrate a national triumph, to send their team off to Lahore with a barrage of firecrackers and a galaxy of burning tapers. Suddenly it was 110 for 5 in the twenty-ninth over and the required run rate was 6.6. Stunned and silent, they watched Jadeja try to sweep Jayasuriya only to have his leg stump knocked out. Another front-line batsman gone for a duck. This was becoming a rout. Some in the crowd started to make for the exits. Even the voluble scorekeeper Rehman, unable to keep up with the fall of wickets, was speechless. Mongia, having learned nothing from others' mistakes, tried to sweep De Silva's off break, only to sky the ball to mid wicket where Jayasuriya plucked it out of the air and danced joyously. More spectators headed for the exits. Kapoor entered and soon faced Murali. Astonishingly he too played the sweep, sending the ball high and backward of square, where De Silva, running in from the boundary, made yet another difficult catch look easy. Kambli was bent double in despair – 120 for 8 in 34.1 overs.

Bottles started to rain down from the stands. Clive Lloyd strode on to the pitch and brought the players off. The distraught Kambli, who had struggled to make 10 runs in an eventful hour, pleaded with the West Indian for a last chance. Did he think he could score at 8 runs an over with 2 wickets standing? Unreal it may have been, but I warmed to the man. He wanted a chance to go down with all guns blazing.

A fan held up a hastily scrawled placard for the television cameras. 'WE ARE SORRY. CONGRATS SRI LANKA.' Afterwards, commentators often referred to this incident as a lone example of civilised behaviour in a stadium seething with barbarism. But reality was more complex. My friend Graham had been sitting happily in the stands all afternoon and evening, cheering Sri Lanka and India impartially. 'All day the mood had been buoyant,' he recalled; 'people thought India were winning. When Tendulkar and Manjrekar were batting, it seemed easy, possibly because it was hard to tell how much the ball was turning, at least from where we were sitting. When the wickets fell in a heap like that, it was a complete shock. People started to leave, and suddenly there were bottles being thrown on the pitch. It was as if disbelief had turned to anger. But I never felt threatened. There was nothing xenophobic or anti-Sri Lankan. It was a kind of rage of disappointment, and for most people it was expressed simply by going home in silent disgust.'

Police were deployed in the stands but with no apparent plan or purpose. Most of the bottles thrown on to the pitch were plastic mineral water bottles (half full for ballast) and some of the spectators displayed amazing 'long arms', hurling these less than aerodynamic containers forty metres through the air. Lloyd appeared on television: 'I'm very disappointed in the crowd's behaviour. I'd like to finish the game. I've asked the ground staff to clear the ground of glass and the police to get the crowd to desist. After all, India won the toss.' Lloyd gave what was left of the crowd a chance to cool down and the police a chance to restore order, but there were no public announcements. Even the press box had no idea what was going on. The rostrum for the post-match presentations was rolled onto the field, then hastily removed. After a twenty-minute hiatus, Lloyd tried to restart the game, this time with a flustered and sweating Dalmiya in tow. Small fires flickered in the stands, three quarters of which were now empty. Most of the spectators who remained applauded the return of the players, but those now bent on disruption had gathered in pockets near the fences, where they were able to hurl more bottles on to the field. Suddenly, the police, present in such impressive numbers outside the ground, seemed scarce, and the few who wandered aimlessly in the stands were unwilling or unable to interfere. No one appeared to be in command and there was no evidence of any strategy for dealing with crowd disorder. After a glass bottle nearly struck Sri Lankan twelfth man Uppal Chandana, stationed on the boundary, Lloyd ordered the players off the pitch. 'I had no choice but to abandon the game and award it to Sri Lanka,' he explained.

The crowd – even the bottle-throwers – clapped and cheered the Lankans off the field but booed the Indians and especially Azhar. Kambli wept. Placards in Bengali appeared making insulting references to Azhar's sex life with Sangeeta Bijlani. The authorities decided to proceed with the presentation as if nothing had happened. Azhar's appearance was greeted with cries of 'Chor! Chor!' (thief) and 'Azhar – hai! hai!' by the few remaining spectators. Jyoti Basu, who had remained impassive in his VIP seat throughout the disturbance, presented the man of the match award to De Silva, then left the stadium and was unavailable for comment for the next twenty-four hours. Ranatunga, gracious as ever, was the only one to try to offer Azhar succour. 'It was a good toss to lose,' he said, 'we saw the cracks in the wicket when we were batting and we knew we had a chance.' Not once during the day's play had I heard the dreaded 'Pakistan – hai! hai!', but now as the players filed into the clubhouse, the last, tattered remnants of the crowd – no more than a few hundred still venting their spleen – cried out: 'India team – hai! hai!'

In the clubhouse, a drained Azhar with vacant eyes confronted Indian reporters, his mumbling even more inaudible than usual. 'The batsmen let us down . . . the bowlers bowled badly . . . we knew it would turn but we had to stick to our plan . . .' He wasn't even there. Anticipating the calumny about to be unleashed upon him, he had retreated deep into himself. Standing at the back of the scrum, I lost the thread as the captain's voice sank ever lower, and asked an Indian colleague next to me what he had said. 'He is talking out of his arsehole, as usual,' was the reply. What did the press expect? Defeat cannot always be explained. The only point of any significance Azhar could make was the one that he did make, insistently, over the next few days. Inserting the Sri Lankans after winning the toss had been 'a collective decision'.

A smartly dressed, middle-aged man holding his young daughter by the hand calmly edged his way into the crowd of reporters. He smiled at me and I assumed he merely wanted a closer glimpse of the famous cricketer. He then screamed at the top of his voice (terrifying his little girl in the process) 'Divorce cricket – no good!' and with a self-satisfied grin led his shaken daughter away from the mêlée. Just what standards of morality did he think he was upholding by this performance?

Wadekar remained dignified. This match marked the end of his four-year stint as India's cricket manager and he rightly saw no reason to hang his head in shame. 'I am very proud that we made it to the semi-final of the World Cup. That is an achievement.' But what about the loss to Sri Lanka? 'It's a game of cricket and such things can happen.' He wished the Sri Lankans the best of luck in the final. 'I will be backing them now. I think we all should back them now. We want to keep the Cup in south Asia.'

In the Sri Lankan dressing room, Ranatunga spoke up for

Azhar. 'I don't think it is fair for the crowd to treat their players like this. The players sacrifice so much for the team – their families, wives and personal freedom. They should not be given this in return. India has played so well in this tournament and just one bad day does not mean that the players should get this treatment from people.' He promised his team would do their best as 'the only Asian representative left'.

Outside the B.C. Roy Clubhouse, a small group of young men surrounded the Indian team coach and subjected the exiting players to taunts and slogans. 'Money has bought the Indian team,' one told me. 'Our team built up our hopes, only to let us down. It would have been better if we got eliminated in the preliminary rounds,' said another. 'It's natural we will react like this if they let us down so miserably,' a third argued, 'losing is no disgrace but this was abject capitulation.' 'I think our block threw the most bottles!' boasted a boy who could not have been more than fourteen. I asked him where he had been sitting. 'In the Rs1500 enclosure,' he said with nonchalance – the most expensive seats in the house.

Azhar was the main target of their ire, and though I could not understand the Bengali abuse, it was hard to miss the references to his religion and his love life. 'The Indian team is good at chasing girls but not runs,' I was told. One boy in a baseball hat screamed boldly, 'Azhar ke kelabo. Dekhbi aai.' (I'll bash Azhar. Come and watch.) The flak-jacketed Special Protection Group, armed with assault rifles, ignored him. The coach drove away, back to the safety and relative serenity of the Taj Bengal, and the youths dispersed. The next day the papers claimed the team bus had been stoned as it left the stadium, and the stone-throwing youths of Eden Gardens became part of the mythology of the night. But I saw no stone-throwing, and I had been present throughout. 'Heavy stone throwing' was also reported in 'sensitive' areas (as Muslim neighbourhoods are coyly referred to in the Indian press) in Bombay and Ahmedabad. This I believed, not least because such incidents are usually played down by the police. As in the past, India's Muslim citizenry were made scapegoats for India's national frustrations.

At the time, it seemed that the 1996 World Cup would be remembered mainly for the riot at Eden Gardens, yet it was a strange kind of riot. There was no fighting among spectators or between spectators and police. Not one arrest was made and not one injury reported. Graham, a West Ham supporter, found it all quite mild. Compared to the violent display put on by the British National Party at the England *v* Ireland match in Dublin in 1995, it was a tea party. And even by cricket's standards, it was not as disorderly as the NatWest semi-final tie at Headingley in 1995, when drunken fans engaged in random punch-ups and subjected Anil Kumble to racial abuse. Eden Gardens has witnessed worse. In the 1967 Test against West Indies, a full day's play was lost when police lathi charged and tear-gassed fans who had spilled on to the ground because the authorities had sold more tickets than there were seats. Two years later, a stampede outside the ground, where 20,000 fans were queueing for 7000 tickets, left six dead.

Much was made of the bonfires in the stands. Surely spectators who would incinerate their own ground, like ghetto-dwellers who burn down their own neighbourhoods, had taken leave of their senses. The fires became symbols of the collective madness of Indian cricket fans. But the problem with this interpretation of events was that Eden Gardens spectators customarily light fires to celebrate victory. Certainly, there was far more smoke in the air when India beat the West Indies at the ground in the finals of the Hero Cup in 1993 and the Wills Cup in 1994. For different reasons, it suited the English, Pakistani and Indian media to blow the events in Calcutta out of proportion. For the English, the Eden Gardens 'riot' confirmed what they had always believed: the sub-continent was no place to stage a World Cup. Its denizens had been derided as volatile fanatics since the days of Empire and their inability to cope with defeat proved that they were still beyond the pale of civilisation (and its English epitome, the game of cricket). In Pakistan, India's demise in Calcutta was compensation for defeat at Bangalore and cause for celebration. Lahori youths climbed on motorbikes and crammed into open-topped jeeps to roar around the city in raptures, shouting pro-Sri Lankan and anti-Indian slogans. In the posh Gulberg precinct, the middle classes danced, burst crackers and lit fires.

But what mattered even more to some than India's defeat on the cricket field was its embarrassment at the behaviour of the fans. PTV, which had downplayed the Bangalore result, made the Calcutta riot its lead news item. 'India may forget its defeat,' the newscaster told the nation, 'but it will take a long time to repair the damage done to its reputation.' An editorial in the *News* warned that 'the next time there is a game in India, the visiting team will have to guarantee that it will not win, otherwise it will not be allowed to play'. Bhutto's foreign minister declared, 'India is out to plague even sports in its craze to manifest itself as a regional power.' The Urdu press featured banner headlines denouncing the barbarism of 'the Hindus'. Nor was the communal perspective confined to the vernacular press. In a front-page column in the *News*, associate editor Z.A. Suleri denounced the behaviour in Calcutta as a prime example of what he called 'the Hindu mentality':

> Thanks to the international television coverage, billions of people the world over saw with their own eyes the true character of the human species called Hindus . . . This is a blessing in disguise. India is not only known as a sporting country but made much of in the west as the largest democracy on earth. And morally too it is put on a high plane and for his non-violence creed Gandhi was almost regarded as Jesus Christ. This myth has now been exploded. The Indians have been seen for what they are. As for us in Pakistan, we have known them all along.

Suleri had been a crony of General Zia and a supporter of martial law. When I asked friends in Lahore about him, one commented wearily, 'You would not think so much malice and stupidity could be packed into one sack of flesh and bone.'

It was not surprising that India-bashers in England and Pakistan seized on events at Eden Gardens and gave them their own twist. More perplexing, at first sight, was the relish with which the Indian media joined the fray. 'CALCUTTA SHOWS ITS UGLY FACE AS INDIA CRASHES TO DEFEAT' ran the huge headline in the *Telegraph*. 'CALCUTTA CROWD SHAMES THE NATION' declared the *Times of India*. *India Today* denounced the 'pathological jingoistic hysteria'. All the patronising disapproval of the 'over-reaction' in Pakistan was turned on its head. The *Indian Express*, in a front-page editorial headlined 'SHAME IN CALCUTTA', lectured the nation:

> It is impossible today to be an Indian and not be ashamed . . . The embarrassment will not be confined to Calcutta. It will shame the entire sub-continent as it follows the disgraceful way the Pakistanis behaved after their defeat. This was a World Cup that the sub-continent snatched out of England's hands on the strength of the crowd support that the game enjoyed here. It will now be a long time before the world's most cricket-crazed region wins another vote at the ICC . . .

All the papers raked over the bottle-throwing in lurid detail. Eden Gardens was depicted as a hotbed of bloodthirsty fanaticism. Self-laceration was the predominant note, and there was little patience with measured analysis. The national mood had swung from elation to despair in a matter of days. For Delhiwallas, there was pleasure in seeing the smug Calcuttans get their comeuppance. The Bengalis had claimed to be the most cultured and intellectually sophisticated of Indians, and indeed West Bengal and Calcutta had often remained calm when the rest of the nation was in turmoil (conversely, there had been periods when West Bengal alone was afflicted with extreme political violence). The day after the bottle-throwing, film-maker Mrinal Sen observed, 'We were all proud of Calcutta and thought our city was the least parochial but that pride is destroyed now.'

Yet the Eden Gardens crowd had always been considered, in the words of Richard Cashman, 'the most rowdy, passionate and volatile assembly of India, disturbing to some cricketers and exciting to others'. Many regarded the rowdiness as a spill-over from football, always Calcutta's principal sporting pastime. Throwing objects, mainly fruit, at the players on the field became commonplace in the 1960s, but it was never a partisan activity (ask Polly Umrigar and Dilip Sardesai, both targets of Eden Gardens projectiles) and did not reflect a diminished love of the game. The crowd that had fought police during the West Indies Test of 1967 returned the next day to resume watching the cricket in perfect order. In 1977, 80,000 turned up for the final day of the Test against England, even though India were bound to lose and play was unlikely to last more than an hour.

In the last decade the atmosphere at Eden Gardens had changed. After Gavaskar was abused by an angry crowd in 1987, he vowed never to play there again. Rudrangshu Mukherjee, journalist, Gandhian scholar and lifelong member of the CAB, was present at the famous Hero Cup victory in 1993. 'The crowd reduced the game to simulated warfare complete with missiles and bombs,' he wrote in the *Telegraph*, and analysed the social changes behind the unpleasant transformation:

> The knowledgeable and keen spectator who came to Eden Gardens every winter had been replaced by ignorant and irresponsible hooligans . . . Only two decades ago crowd behaviour was less frenzied. This is not to say that the spectators of the 60s and 70s were not partisan. They desperately hoped and prayed that India would do well . . . but knowledge and enjoyment of the game were never sacrificed to vulgar displays of jingoism . . . The Bengali gentry no longer form the elite of the city. The corporate world once dominated by the English was taken over by a non-Bengali business class. The scions of this class in their quest for respectability now come to sit in the clubhouse. They have the money and the connections to buy the high-priced tickets which allow them to sit in what in cricketing terms are the best seats in the stadium. Unfortunately this group goes to Eden Gardens more out of a desire to be seen at the right place at the right time than out of a genuine affection for the game.

Like the mess in Delhi, the disruption at Eden Gardens was the result of what some commentators have called the lumpenisation of the Indian middle class. This was not a riot of the dispossessed but a self-indulgent demonstration by a small and relatively privileged minority. It was not an attempt – either spontaneous or pre-meditated – to halt the match and save India from defeat; it was not an outburst of anger at the inoffensive Sri Lankans. It was a protest against India's defeat and elimination from the World Cup, aimed at the Indian team. It was, of course, stupid, rude and dangerous. Above all, it was futile, as all such protests must be. But it was a perversely logical response to the nationalist hype which preceded the match.

In the midst of the Indian batting collapse, an angry Indian fan had asked Graham how much he had paid for his Rs500 seat. Rs2000 was the reply. 'You're lucky,' said the Indian. 'I paid Rs5000 for this rubbish.' In other words, at that price he expected nothing less than an Indian victory. What was anticipated was not a cricket contest but a national triumph. The celebration of 'the spirit of winning' had obscured the fact that a game that has a winner must also have a loser. Enchanted and enthralled by the great myth of liberalisation – that once we are all free to compete in the marketplace we can all be winners – many Indian middle-class spectators had no way of assimilating defeat. Impatient with and sometimes disgusted by many of the realities of Indian life – corruption, poverty, inefficiency – they still desire to assert themselves as Indians, and cricket has allowed them to do this. But defeat exposed the hollowness of this compensatory cricket nationalism.

In what sense then was 'the nation' shamed? Why should blame fall on the majority who did not throw bottles, who may have been disappointed by India's defeat but understood that in the end this was a cricket match and nothing more? All the newsprint moralising and earnest self-laceration served little purpose because the culprits remained so vast and amorphous: the modern world, the younger generation, the national malaise.

I had seen a similar response in Britain to the nation's footballing embarrassments. Whenever hooliganism struck, politicians and commentators seemed to revel in the national shame. As they vied with each other in attributing the latest outbreak of anti-social behaviour to ever deeper but more intangible causes, the blame spread so far and wide that no one was ever held to account.

In fact, the scenes outside the ground during the Delhi match were much more disturbing than anything that went on in Calcutta. The difference was that they took place off camera. In India, the 'shame' of Eden Gardens seemed to stem from the fact that the events there were globally televised. The World Cup, which was to project India as a modern, competent nation doing big trade in the world marketplace, had ended up displaying the country at its most 'barbaric' – unable to accept the rules which ostensibly govern global competition. In other words, the pundits were angry because 'India' had lost, which was exactly what had upset the bottle-throwers.

The over-reaction in both Pakistan and India to elimination from the World Cup revealed not only the depth of feeling the game engenders in the sub-continent but the forces that threaten to disfigure it there. The Indian mood swing, from elation in Bangalore to enraged despair in Calcutta, would be categorised by psychoanalysts as a symptom of paranoid schizophrenia. And the virulent manner in which the erstwhile gods of Pakistani cricket were turned upon by their devotees displayed the same syndrome. Both Azhar and Wasim came under heavy fire from their home supporters and both were accused of selling the World Cup to gambling interests. The accusations were groundless, but, in the era of hawala, it was not surprising to find cricket fans in both India and Pakistan ready, almost eager, to believe that their heroes would sell their country for a fistful of rupees. For their own reasons the media, the sponsors and the advertisers had turned these fallible human beings into super-heroes who, unlike the rest of us, could never commit blunders or experience failure. No wonder the backlash was so intense.

Pundits attributed the failure of their respective national sides to whatever they happened to think was wrong with the country as a whole. Those who believed the youth of today were decadent, spoiled and Westernised harped on about Wasim's ear-ring and Azhar's divorce. Those who saw money as the root of all evil muttered about commercialisation and gambling. Those who saw the nation's principal problem as a foreign enemy claimed the players lacked national loyalty. A vituperative letter to the *Times of India* summed up the feelings of some super-nationalists: 'Sri Lanka never won at Eden Gardens; our boys just handed it to them on a platter because they were mortally frightened of playing at Lahore, even if not against Pakistan. Put each member of the team under a lie detector test and I will be proved right. I hold the Calcutta crowd (indeed the whole of India) were rightly incensed. My all important question is, was the BCCI involved in what happened? If so, it was a greater debauchery on the people than the hawala scam.'

In one sense the events at Eden Gardens did 'shame the nation'. The very idea of nationhood as projected in the World Cup had proved psychologically and politically untenable. Add together Bangalore and Calcutta, and the reactions and counter-reactions in India and Pakistan, and you have a demonstration of the weirdly sado-masochistic character which nationalism in both countries has taken on in recent years. As globalisation strides forward, the search for national identity becomes ever more desperate and ever more dominated by hostility to perceived national enemies, both within and without the country's borders. Thus the carnival of globalisation turned into an orgy of nationalism. Those who sought its roots in some sub-continental sub-consciousness, who saw ancient prejudice spilling through the cracks in the modern veneer, missed the essence of the World Cup. The nationalism that disfigured the tournament was of the up-to-the-minute, satellite television-age variety, more the child of globalisation than its antithesis. It was a nationalism manufactured by politicians, multinational corporations and media moguls, and not everyone bought it.

Two suicides were reported as a result of World Cup defeats, one in Pakistan and one in India. The symmetry was neat – perhaps too neat. Even if these incidents did occur (attempts to confirm the reports were not successful), their link with the World Cup seemed mainly circumstantial. In countries of this size there are a number of suicides every day. In the west, the suicide stories were seized on as evidence of the deep irrationality of the sub-continent. And in India and Pakistan they were presented as salutary lessons about what happens when cricket is taken too seriously. But I doubt if they represented anything more than journalistic myth-making. Yes, some fans in south Asia do take cricket too seriously. More to the point, they take cricket as an embodiment of the national destiny too seriously. Nonetheless, for the vast majority in both countries life went on after defeat just as it had before. Speaking with ordinary cricket fans at the grounds, in offices and restaurants and in the streets, I found that they did not share the madness to which much of the media had succumbed. In both India and Pakistan, disappointment was sharp but tempered by a broader awareness that this was, after all, only a game.

So why then did India lose the match at Eden Gardens? Was it just one of those accidents of the game and nothing more? Not quite. India failed to take its opportunities to bowl Sri Lanka out or to occupy the crease. The decision to insert the Sri Lankans first on a pitch that was bound to turn was indeed as daft as the commentators said – possibly the single greatest tactical miscalculation in the history of the World Cup – but it had its roots in the traumatic defeat at the Kotla, which in turn was partly the product of juggling the side (and dropping the spinners) in a silly over-reaction to the defeat at Bombay. The panic and scapegoating reflected the huge pressure the Indian team management was under from the media, but it was also characteristic of an old, inward-looking streak of insecurity in Indian cricket, still far too anxious to establish its global stature after all these years.

In contrast, the Sri Lankans were never discomfited. From the beginning, they felt they had the measure of their opponents. Eden Gardens held no terrors for them. In Colombo the streets were deserted during playing hours and every Indian wicket was greeted with firecrackers, but the major celebrations were left until after the final. The goal for Ranatunga and his men was to win the World Cup, not to beat their neighbours.

In the *Indian Express*, Roy Dias pleaded, 'My Indian friends, do not be disappointed. Please join this very special moment of our short history. At last we have found a voice on the international stage. We have waited long enough for our moment under the sun and for God's sake do join us in this splendid moment. India, we are looking at you. Hopefully, you would not disappoint us.'

The re-emergence of sub-continental solidarity was long overdue.

Graham and I flew to Delhi from Calcutta and took a taxi from the airport to Achin's and Pam's. Our driver was full of cynical jokes about the Indian squad. Despite the fact that he was one of a group of drivers who had collected Rs30,000 for a World Cup victory party, only to find the effort wasted, he remained cheerful, and was able to chatter in detail about the foibles of the Indian side and the strengths of the Sri Lankans. With Anish and Samar we watched the opening overs of the second semi-final in Chandigarh, the only truly fast pitch of the tournament. We were all West Indies fans and were cock-a-hoop when Ambrose and Bishop, bowling with the old venom, removed Taylor, the Waugh brothers and Ponting with only 15 runs on the board. Graham and I left for the airport and our flight to Lahore eagerly anticipating a West Indies–Sri Lanka World Cup final.

13

Betting on your hopes

Thanks to our third party passports (neither Indian nor Pakistani), Graham and I moved swiftly through immigration and customs at Lahore airport, grabbed a cab, checked into our hotel, and switched on the television just in time to watch the tightest finish of the World Cup. A 138-run stand by Law and Bevan enabled the Australians to recover from their disastrous start and complete their fifty overs for 207 runs. For the West Indies this target should have presented few problems, and while Lara was adding 45 runs off 45 balls it seemed as if the Australian total would be overhauled with overs to spare. Even after his departure, Chanderpaul and Richardson seemed in control. Together they took the score to 165 before Chanderpaul was out. At this stage West Indies needed 47 runs and had 7 wickets and ten overs in hand. Then McGrath removed Harper and Warne bamboozled Gibson and Adams. Fleming had Arthurton caught behind for another duck. It was a display of abject panic: 14 runs were needed off the last two overs. Richardson was still at the crease, but in what was to be his last international match it became sadly apparent that timing and power had deserted him for good. The boundary eluded him. Like Miandad, he found at his moment of crisis that acumen and grit were not enough.

Warne, in his last over, pinned Bishop to the crease with the flipper for a plumb lbw. He finished with figures of nine overs for 36 runs and 4 wickets, merely a dim reflection of his persistent aggression and inventiveness. At the crease Ambrose seethed. He was a great bowler betrayed once too often by his batsmen. The West Indies needed 9 runs off the final over, which Taylor assigned to Fleming. With an angry fling of the bat, Richardson finally connected, pulling the first ball to the boundary through mid wicket. Five to go. Richardson glided the next ball behind the wicket, but Ambrose wasn't fast enough to run two and was given out by the third umpire. Walsh, the last man in, was promptly clean bowled by Fleming. The Australians had come from behind, with the bat and in the field, to snatch victory from the bewildered West Indians. Having seen their collapse in Pune, I was less shocked than some by their ineptitude in losing 8 wickets for 37 runs in 51 balls. A despondent Michael Holding declared the West Indies cricketers had 'no one but themselves to blame', which was true, but the Australian achievement was nevertheless astonishing. Sensing the unease gnawing at the West Indians, Taylor kept turning up the pressure, and unleashed Warne, who sniffed the frightened prey and pounced. Had the West Indies managed to scrape victory in that last over in Chandigarh, an injustice would have been done. Caribbean cricketers have been a source of inspiration to many over the years, but this team did not deserve to contest a World Cup final. In contrast, the Australians had displayed a cunning resilience time after time in the tournament – an achievement I recalled uneasily as I waited for the Sri Lankans to begin their assault on the Australian total of 241 in the final at Gaddafi Stadium.

'Cricket should be banned in all countries of the sub-continent,' Tehseen told me on my return to Lahore. He was not in the least surprised, though thoroughly disheartened, by the reactions in India and Pakistan to events in Bangalore and Calcutta. 'They should not be allowed to play international matches against each other, or anyone else for that matter.' The night before the World Cup final he took me to a food and handicrafts *mela* at Racecourse Park. There were no cops, no politicians, no corporate sponsors, not a foreigner in sight. It was a delightful and instructive antidote to the VIP-blighted Basant Mela I had witnessed on my earlier visit to Lahore.

The crowd of lower- and middle-class Lahoris included many women, young and old, families and groups of teenagers; everyone laughed easily and mingled freely. The trees were festooned with coloured lights, and a band played Punjabi pop music, blending folk tunes, Bollywood and rap. Young people clapped and danced. 'Under martial law, this would have been impossible,' Tehseen said. 'It has taken a long time for people to come out of their shells. For so long the country was frozen with suspicion and distrust.' Under the Zia regime, Tehseen had once been arrested for laughing in a public place. Such evil days seemed far away amid the merry throng at Racecourse Park. There were jewellery and leather and woodwork stalls and a potter selling plates with pictures of Imran and Jemima and even one with Princess Diana. Young women from Punjab University art department drew charcoal portraits of sheepish-looking young men. Someone asked me if I was Gary Kirsten. We sat on the ground and ate hot *bhattura* and beef *nihari* and drank Pepsi. The mela was a living rebuttal of Pakistan's cult of official nationalism – a cult which declared Urdu, the preferred tongue of a minority, the 'national' language and a particular brand of Islam the 'national' religion, which demanded that Punjabi, Sindhi, Mohajir, Baluchi, Pathan, Shi'ite, Ahmadi, Christian and atheist subordinate their identities to an official national and religious identity. Tehseen looked around at the gaily coloured hubbub with a mixture of wonder and recognition. 'You know I am thinking this really is a secular society.' Then he confessed that he was taking his daughter to the final, having secured tickets to one of the enclosures from a friend of a friend of a friend.

The next morning, three Indian friends dashed to the ground from the border – a mere twenty kilometres. They had been lucky enough to secure tickets through an acquaintance who worked for a multinational in Bangkok, but had spent three days holed up at the Wagah crossing, waiting for permission to enter Pakistan. It is not difficult for businessmen to fly from Karachi to Bombay, and smugglers seem to penetrate the border with ease, but for ordinary people seeking to visit family (or attend a cricket match) passing from India to Pakistan, or vice versa, can be a prolonged trauma.

One of the friends was Mushirul Hasan, an eminent historian whose championship of tolerance and secularism has earned him the enmity of both Hindu nationalists and Muslim fundamentalists. 'The scene at Wagah was one of the saddest things I have ever witnessed,' he told me later. 'Every evening crowds gather on both sides to watch the military ceremony as the flags come down. And they wave at each other across the border.' In the eighties it was possible to move freely through Wagah, but Mushirul and his friends were the first Indians to cross in four years. 'Wagah is a symbol of the deterioration of relations between India and Pakistan.' They dashed to Gaddafi, tired and hungry and without a Pakistani rupee in their pockets, but were offered food and drink by Pakistanis sitting in adjacent seats. Mushirul, who hails from a Muslim family in Uttar Pradesh in north India, spoke to them in Urdu, the official language of Pakistan and widely understood, though in Lahore the language of daily use is Punjabi. The only problem he encountered all day came not from anyone who took umbrage at his being Indian but from a local youth who had occupied his seat and was reluctant to move. When Mushirul reproved him, the youth said bitterly, 'Uncle, this is Lahore, not Karachi.' In other words, he assumed that the Urdu-speaking gentleman must be a Mohajir, a descendant of Muslims who had migrated to Pakistan after Partition. Mushirul's experience confirmed one of the lessons of the World Cup

– the key to the divisions between nations is usually the divisions within them.

The floodlights flickered and for a moment between innings some feared that 'loadshedding' (power cuts), the bane of the sub-continent, would plunge the World Cup final in darkness, but the authorities were simply taking advantage of the break for a precautionary change of fuses. Within minutes the floodlights returned to their full brilliance, bathing the Gaddafi Stadium crowd in an unearthly electric aura. Through my binoculars, I studied a banner in the patrons' enclosure. It was a riposte to the trishul banner at Bangalore: a brahmin with shaved head and top knot was labelled 'India' and was depicted grovelling before a trishul labelled 'Sri Lanka' – with Jayasuriya, Ranatunga and Mahanama named on the prongs. Reversing the communal connotations of its progenitor in Bangalore, the banner was a triumph for globalised communications: spreading tit-for-tat ethnic hatred. Out in the middle, the World Cup trophy was on display. The organisers were proud of the ornate piece of antique silverware they had purchased in London, so proud that the winners of the Cup were to receive only a replica. The original would remain in the possession of the World Cup title sponsor, ITC.

The Australians took the field to a mix of cheers and boos. In the second over, Jayasuriya tipped the ball to third man, took a single, then set off on a second run. The television replay showed that McGrath's throw from the deep had beaten him by a millisecond. The Australian bowlers ran in at full tilt, seeking quick wickets, and Kalu looked nervous. In the sixth over he pulled Fleming to Bevan at square leg. For the second successive match, the feared Sri Lankan openers had destroyed themselves in a wanton fit. It was 23 for 2 and I was despondent. Surely no team could stage a miraculous recovery from early disaster twice in succession: 241 suddenly seemed a formidable total. When an edgy De Silva nearly ran himself out backing up too far I wondered if the Sri Lankans were finally going to crack.

McGrath's line and length were unerring during his first spell, and Gurusinha and De Silva contented themselves with playing their shots off the less consistent Fleming. In Australia, De Silva, frustrated by the umpires and upset at the allegations, had fared poorly with the bat. He had averaged more than 50 in the World Cup so far but now he faced, for the first time in the competition, a well-rounded attack and an aggressive captain. Taylor brought Warne on and the field in for the eleventh over. The aerial route and the short boundaries beckoned, but De Silva kept the ball along the ground. He cut Warne late with a full swing of the bat, then opened the blade to stroke the next ball backward of point. The last ball of the over was a googly. It took the inside edge of De Silva's bat, barely missed the stumps and somehow evaded Healey's grasp. My heart skipped a beat. A furrow appeared between Warne's bleached eyebrows.

In Calcutta, De Silva mastered the Indian attack and the ball was his to do with as he willed. In Lahore, conditions (and the opposition) were more awkward. The dew on the field was heavy and scoring required luck and perseverance. In an attempt to step up the run rate, Gurusinha and De Silva embarked on quick singles, but the tactic seemed to put more pressure on the batsmen than the fielders, who pounced eagerly to cut off the drives and flicks. Warne, mixing googlies and leg breaks, tied down Gurusinha. De Silva cut and drove through the narrow gaps. His 360-degree field awareness seemed uncanny. After fifteen overs, Sri Lanka had reached 71 for 2, level with the asking rate. Gurusinha lofted Mark Waugh over mid off, where Fleming skidded past the ball, which ran to the boundary – the second difficult chance the Australians had missed.

A huge roar erupted from the bank of seats to our right. Javed Miandad had been spotted. After a moment, he rose to acknowledge the cheers. He clearly loved the adoration and would miss it desperately. The crowd's love was his bulwark against all the demeaning insults he had suffered, both abroad and at home. The evening was mild and a gentle breeze ruffled thousands of Sri Lankan flags. It would take a painter to capture the scene:

the parti-coloured crowd dense and delighted, clapping and whistling, revelling in the sheer joy of big cricket under the floodlights.

Gurusinha finally got hold of Warne in the twenty-first over. He belted a short ball through mid on to take Sri Lanka past their 100, then struck a steepling straight six with a cross-batted tennis-style forearm. This laconic bear of a batsman exudes lazy strength. Warne, flustered, bowled a no-ball, flat and wide. Two overs later, the two batsmen reached their fifties. Shortly after, Gurusinha lifted Bevan against the spin high to deep mid wicket, where Law cupped his hands in front of his face, waited patiently for the descending ball – and dropped it. Was he too casual or too nervous? Delighted with the error, the spectators hooted and waved their Sri Lankan flags. They were beginning to believe in a Sri Lankan victory. But a voice inside me warned, 'Remember Chandigarh, remember Calcutta.' In the thirty-first over, Reiffel spotted Gurusinha charging down the wicket and knocked his off stump out of the ground with a full-length ball. The Nalanda Old Boy had scored a measured and invaluable 65 runs off 99 pressure-primed balls.

When Ranatunga came in the game was still to be lost or won. The Sri Lankans needed 95 runs off nineteen overs, with 7 wickets in hand. Ranatunga was off the mark gliding Reiffel behind for a single. Taylor brought Warne back into the attack, to a chorus of boos and whistles, and stationed himself menacingly at slip. Watching Ranatunga, Warne and umpire David Shepherd standing together at the non-strikers' end, I reflected that despite modern training regimes this could still be a game for rotund men. Warne's over yielded only one run. As in the Australian innings, the boundaries, though temptingly close at hand, remained frustratingly out of reach. Warne's second spell of three overs went for only 7 runs. The Australians were fighting back, covering the outfield and blocking scoring shots, but De Silva and Ranatunga, who between them had appeared in more than 300 one-day internationals, retained their poise. Both sides still believed they could win the match.

The two Sri Lankan veterans ran more singles that night in Lahore than they had in the whole of the rest of the tournament. De Silva, who had begun imperiously, retrenched in the middle overs. At this point, I confess I seemed to be the only person in the press box who thought Sri Lanka could lose. The Australian pressure was relentless and the batsmen seemed adrift, huffing and puffing up and down the pitch. I could not bring myself to believe that what I had so much wished to see was happening in front of my eyes. But the wisdom of the Sri Lankan captain and vice-captain became apparent in the fortieth over, when they ran four singles and struck two boundaries off Mark Waugh, unsettled by the left-hand–right-hand combination. That left 50 needed off ten overs. Ranatunga and De Silva had calculated their assault to the decimal point.

Taylor brought back Warne for his final spell in the forty-first over. A couple of quick wickets now and the Sri Lankans could still be in trouble. De Silva chose this moment to assume command. He deftly cut the leg spinner behind for two, drove an off-stump ball cleanly to the deep for two more, before swinging to leg for a single. In the next over, elbow high and head still, he caressed Reiffel through the covers. Then he leaned forward and turned his wrists to despatch a ball on middle stump crisply through mid wicket. A Mexican wave circled the ground.

Warne's final over, the forty-third of the Sri Lankan innings, was the Australians' last chance. Enveloped by a deafening cacophony of derisive whistles, the leg spinner wheeled in for the last time in the 1996 World Cup. De Silva pushed him gently for a single. Then Ranatunga, as if to prove his claim that Warne was an 'over-rated media hype', danced down the pitch to drive the ball fiercely though the air. It flew through the bowler's clammy hands and bounced into the sightscreen. Annoyed, Warne unleashed a full toss, which Ranatunga, in a rare display of muscularity, pulled for six. The next ball the Sri Lankan captain slashed high towards long on for two more runs. Warne seemed unable to fathom what had happened to him: 12 runs had come off the over. The dew on the grass made the ball wet, but I suspect that was only one reason for the Australian's loss of control. Had Ranatunga's gamesmanship struck home? Had the Sri Lankan captain intuited that the bulky, brazen Australian was thin-skinned? Suddenly Sri Lanka needed only 17 to win with overs and wickets in hand. I began to relax.

Both Ranatunga and De Silva clipped the hitherto dominant McGrath for fours in the next over. De Silva reached his 100 with a leg glance to the boundary and raised his arms aloft. He was embraced by Ranatunga. After years of being patronised by the big cricket powers and persecuted by their home board, these two savoured their joint moment of triumph. After all the hoopla about Lara, Tendulkar and Mark Waugh, it was Aravinda De Silva who turned out to be the batsman of the tournament. De Silva's century in Lahore was less domineering but more demanding than his effort in Calcutta; eschewing pyrotechnics, moving with dainty but decisive footsteps, he had proved himself a master of the one-day art. Now he cover drove Reiffel to level the scores. The crowd clapped in rhythm, building in crescendo as McGrath ran in to bowl. Ranatunga ended the match by repeating the stroke with which he had got off the mark, gliding the ball with minimum effort to third man for four, a reminder of the relaxed hedonism of Sri Lankan cricket at its best. Clearly, Ranatunga remained a man who believed there was no reason to run when you could walk.

The Sri Lankan players dashed to the middle and engulfed the two batsmen. Even Gurusinha smiled, at last. The cricketers were followed by a mob of spectators, politicians, cameramen and journalists. Where were the 7000 policemen said to be on duty? Where were the heavy-handed security officers who had kept the denizens of the general stand out of the ground till halfway through the Australian innings? As so often in this World Cup, the police were absent when they were most needed. As the floodlights burned through the thickening mist, the military band struck up a victory march. Keeping their ranks tidy, they presented the only element of order in a scene of chaos. The Sri Lankan players tried to regroup for the presentation ceremony; Benazir Bhutto, bereft of protection, made her way through the crowd to the podium. Percy ran in manic circles with his giant Sri Lankan flag. The crowd was on its feet, raining prolonged, heartfelt applause on the winners, and chanting 'Allah illah Allah illah' (an Islamic invocation which had recently become popular at Pakistani cricket grounds). The Muslim League loyalists packed into one of the patrons' enclosures booed the prime minister as she presented the trophy to Ranatunga and the outsize man of the match cheque to De Silva. The mist turned to rain and quickly soaked everyone on the field but did not hinder the impromptu dancing in the middle. In the mayhem several Sri Lankan players were knocked down and the World Cup winners' cheque was picked from Ranatunga's pocket. Later it was cancelled and replaced by Pilcom, who topped up the pot with an additional US$100,000; the disparity between the millions they were raking in and the relatively derisory prize money had become too embarrassing.

The 97-run match-winning stand shared by De Silva and Ranatunga was a masterpiece of cricket nous. Together they had outwitted Taylor, nullified Warne, and made the 7-wicket victory look easier than it was. In this low-scoring battle of nerves it was those notoriously hard competitors, the Australians, who had cracked first, while the Sri Lankans just kept playing cricket. Ignoring the sledging that had distracted them in the past, the Lankan middle-order batsmen kept their minds on the target. They made errors. There were alarms. But after every mishap they picked themselves up, brushed themselves off and got on with their accustomed game.

At the post-match press conference, Mark Taylor was asked whether he had any regrets about boycotting Colombo. 'People tell us when we're here that we have to understand other people's cultures and we try very hard to do that. But I'd like people to look at things from both sides. Put yourselves in our shoes and look at the way we live in Australia compared to the way other people live in the sub-continent.' A month later, a deranged gunman took thirty-five lives in Tasmania. Four months later, a bomb exploded at the Atlanta Olympics. Taylor's remarks were patently sincere and his intention was, as always, constructive, but what a cosmos of misunderstanding was revealed by his comments. Underlying his appeal to multicultural tolerance was the assumption that mutilation and sudden death were intrinsic to south Asian culture and alien to Western culture. The carnival of globalisation had concluded with an assertion of the unbridgeable gulf between first and third world peoples.

When his turn came to face the press, Ranatunga performed his own variations on the multicultural theme: 'We don't keep any grudges. That is the culture we have been brought up in.' Asked about sledging by the Australians, he conceded mildly that there were a 'few incidents' which he attributed to 'frustration when a team is not doing well'. Some English and Australian journalists tried to lure him into a war of words with Taylor over the chucking and ball-tampering allegations. Casually defusing their verbal grenades, Ranatunga was a picture of mellow bliss. He thanked the Pakistani public: 'They gave us a lot of support. It felt like playing at home.' And in his hour of triumph he remembered to pay tribute to Azhar and Wasim 'for coming to Colombo when we were in trouble'. Later he reflected, 'We had suffered a lot from the administrators back home. They were wrong. They treated us badly. We had grown up and maybe people didn't want to notice it. Most wanted to put us down.' He was saddened that the bats he had sent into the Australian dressing room to be autographed after the final were returned minus the signatures of Shane Warne and the Waugh brothers.

'Do not be afraid of losing,' had been Dav Whatmore's advice to his team. 'Stay relaxed.' Throughout the tournament the Sri Lankans played fearless but never macho cricket. In Lahore, in front of a friendly but forgiving crowd, they had the best of both worlds. India's and Pakistan's elimination had left the sub-continent free to unite behind the Sri Lankans, whose victory offended no one. The result was good for cricket, good for the sub-continent, and a fillip for small nations everywhere. In the age of globalisation it was heartening to find that not all the spoils belonged to the superpowers and that victors need not be lean, mean monomaniacs dedicated to winning at all costs. The new world order often seems nothing more than the old Social Darwinism writ large, but in the end the World Cup turned out to be a case of the survival of the fattest.

I had been rewarded for betting on my hopes. But the reward was not quite what I had expected. The element of personal vindication was dwarfed by an almost physical sense of sharing the satisfaction the Sri Lankan victory had given to so many people in so many places for so many reasons. As Graham and I indulged in a celebratory sundae in one of Lahore's excellent ice-cream parlours, I studied the beaming faces of the city's trendy, well-heeled youth. All of us, here and across the sub-continent, had supped from this World Cup. Internationalism is sometimes dismissed as an abstract, unreal creed, but I knew from experience, not least my experience during the World Cup, that it could be as intimate, profound and sustaining as any national identity. And it has this advantage: it places no restrictions on your growth. It has no limits. Later, I went to bed in a kind of post-coital buzz. My romance with sub-continental cricket had been consummated.

Critics in England derided the 1996 World Cup as inefficiently organised, excessively commercial, corrupted by politicians and besmirched by the bad behaviour of overly nationalistic host country fans. All of this, they argued, was symptomatic of south Asian society, a place quite unfit to host an event of this kind. Within months, however, the same features disfigured the Atlanta Olympics. Clearly, whatever was wrong with the World Cup was wrong with global sport in general. As for me, I loved the World Cup. In spite of self-serving officials, vulgar profiteering, and ugly zealotry, the tournament had proved a success – a giant, sub-continental festival of cricket whose impact could be seen in roadside *dhabas*, college hostels, bazaars, buses, trains, *maidans* and all the other locales where the 'unofficial' culture of cricket is forged. I felt privileged to have enjoyed such a wide-angle view of this epic saga. Players and journalists complained about having to travel to far-flung venues, but the sheer scale of the Cup was part of its fascination. Travelling from city to city, constantly crossing not only the borders of states but those of language, religion, culture, I was afforded countless glimpses of my fellow human beings in all their variety, as well as a ripening insight into our essential oneness. This was the deceptively modest grail at the end of my quest: that cricket can be unifier or divider, symbol of solidarity or 'war minus the shooting'. It's up to us.

It doesn't happen often in sport, and even less often in real life. But in the World Cup final, justice prevailed and the underdog triumphed. It was the kind of rounded conclusion more commonly found in fiction than in the unsentimental battlefield of international sports. But events that followed the World Cup proved less tidy.

On the West Indies' glum flight home, an inebriated Brian Lara delivered his parting shot of the World Cup. 'I got rid of Richardson and Roberts,' he shouted at Dennis Waights, the team trainer, 'and I'll get rid of you.' Global celebrity had turned the modest genius into an egomaniacal monster. A bitter Manoj Prabhakar retired from cricket. 'I have no motivation left to continue after the treatment I have received from some of the esteemed men who run cricket in this country.' Two days after the final, the dates for the Indian general elections were announced. Prabhakar declared that he would stand for the South Delhi constituency on the ticket led by Congress rebel Arjun Singh, who told the cricketer, 'We want you to bowl a googly for us' – which showed how little he knew about both the game and his party's candidate. 'I need some platform to raise my voice against the injustice being done to me,' Prabhakar explained, and it often seemed that his campaign was aimed at securing a place in the Indian cricket team rather than a seat in parliament. Kapil Dev toured the streets with his old bowling partner, but made it clear that he had nothing against either the Congress or the BJP. Prabhakar insisted 'the people are with me' but he went down to humiliating defeat, massively out-polled by both major parties. In contrast the hawala-tainted Madhavrao Scindia, spurned by the Congress, swept to victory as an independent in Gwalior.

Although the BJP's share of the popular vote remained the same as in the previous election (about 21 per cent), they emerged as the single largest party, thanks to the collapse of the Congress and the first-part-the-post system India inherited from Britain. A thirteen-day interregnum of BJP rule ensued, but the Hindutva combine was effectively quarantined by the other parties and was unable to command a majority in parliament. The stock markets and financial institutions backed the short-lived BJP regime, but an analysis of the popular vote made it plain that they had no mandate from the people, who had cast their ballots decisively against communal forces and in favour of social justice. Eventually the coalition of left-wing and lower-caste 'third force' parties, together with the various rebel Congress factions, formed a government under former Karnataka chief minister Deve Gowde. Like Tony Blair, Gowde was quick to meet with and pay homage to Rupert Murdoch. Although he owed his election to a popular backlash against the Congress's economic reforms, his government persisted with the neo-liberal policies of its predecessor. Meanwhile, Star TV announced a change of policy. Instead of trying to build a single, all-embracing Asian market, it would in future tailor its programming to the separate cultures that made up the region. Cricket, it seemed, was just about all they had in common. New Pepsi banners went up around Indian cities: 'CHEER UP! IT'S NOT THE END OF THE WORLD. THERE'S ALWAYS SHARJAH . . .'

In Pakistan, Imran Khan announced the formation of a new movement for radical change. Within days his cancer hospital was bombed, and six patients were killed. No one claimed responsibility. It was the first of a series of mysterious explosions in Lahore, Islamabad and Karachi. Meanwhile, Bhutto travelled the world, preaching the virtues of the free market, and her husband purchased a multi-million pound home in Surrey. At the postponed AGM of the Pakistan Cricket Board, Arif Abassi was replaced by Majid Khan, and Intikhab Alam was dropped as team manager.

The Pilcom books were audited and a net profit of some £21 million declared. Meanwhile, the Calcutta Municipal Corporation, the customs authorities and the West Bengal government were all demanding payment of various duties owed by the Cricket Association of Bengal. A police commissioner's report lambasted the CAB's handling of the semi-final in Calcutta. Income tax authorities mounted investigations into Pilcom and WorldTel. Pilcom had deposited a portion of its revenue in a London account, and argued that because the profits derived from a global activity not all of them could be taxed by the Indian government.

In July, the ICC met at Lord's to elect a new chairman. Jagmohan Dalmiya was the front-runner, but his candidacy was virulently opposed by the English cricket establishment. The Calcutta tycoon was painted in the British press as a menacing figure, bent on replacing the ritual of Test cricket with an endless circus of one-day internationals. 'Let's stop this Indian takeaway!' bellowed the *Mirror*. In contrast, the record of Dalmiya's chief opponent, Australian Malcolm Gray, whose intransigence over the boycott of Colombo had nearly wrecked the World Cup, went unscrutinised. On the second ballot, Dalmiya defeated Gray by 25 votes to 13. He was backed by India, Pakistan, Sri Lanka and Zimbabwe as well as three quarters of the associate members. But outgoing chairman Clyde Walcott ruled that the winning candidate must command a two thirds majority of Test-playing nations. Thus a (mainly white) minority was awarded a veto over the democratic choice of the rest of the cricket world.

Did the Sri Lankan victory 'unite the nation' as so many claimed?

At Lahore and later at the reception in Colombo, Sri Lankan government ministers vied for a share of reflected glory, and found themselves pilloried in the press for trying to upstage the national heroes. The morning after the great victory, Union Assurance, Ranatunga's employer, declared in a half-page newspaper advert, 'Every Sri Lankan wherever in the world he lives is roaring like a lion', then, acknowledging the inevitable consequences of collective celebration, it added, 'If we take longer to answer the phone today, please forgive us.' President Kumaratunga, however, downplayed the victory, refusing to declare a holiday. Her predecessors – Jayawardene and Premadasa – would have exploited it shamelessly. In fact, on my return to Colombo one week after the final, I was struck by the absence of posters, banners or hoardings celebrating the greatest sporting achievement in the island's history. Had India or Pakistan won the World Cup, the visitor would have been reminded of it at every street corner. I was told that on the night of the victory the parties went on into the early hours and that the reception in Colombo the following day was enormous. But the high tide of excitement had quickly receded. At Liberty Plaza, Colombo's temple to consumerism, there were no tee-shirts, caps or other World Cup memorabilia on sale. Although Ranatunga suddenly found himself 'the most popular man in Sri Lanka', he made it clear he would not emulate his father (who was an SLFP minister) and would shun a political career. 'We have enough and more politicians here.' He acknowledged that winning the World Cup was a mixed blessing for Sri Lanka: 'It's the best and the worst thing that could have happened to our cricket. Now we will be expected to win every match.'

Sri Lanka seemed to have taken the unexpected victory in its stride. On the surface, at least, it appeared a saner society than its sub-continental co-hosts. Yet, on closer inspection, it was in some ways more deeply sociopathic. After all, this is a country with one of the highest suicide rates in the world.

I was watching the first all-Sri Lanka 'Ladies Club Cricket Final' at the venerable Colombo Colts ground when startling news came from the Cricket Board's annual general meeting. Ana Punchihewa had failed to secure a second term as president. In a bitter contest in which money was said to have changed hands, he had been defeated by Upali Dharmadasa, the businessman who had distributed the Sri Lankan flags at Lahore (and provided eighty bottles of champagne to cricketers, officials, journalists and hangers-on travelling on the Air Lanka flight back to Colombo). Dharmadasa's father was a timber merchant who had amassed a fortune under the post-1977 UNP governments, of which he was a staunch supporter. The contest was close: 63 votes to 58. Dharmadasa owed his margin of victory to the surprising support he received from Punchihewa's former power base – the provincial 'outstation' associations. I was astonished when I heard the news; less than a fortnight after presiding over the World Cup triumph, and in spite of the universally positive publicity he had received in the foreign media, Punchihewa, the very model of the modern corporate manager, had fallen victim to the old political chicanery. Apparently, it was business as usual at the Sinhalese Sports Club.

I should not have been taken by surprise. Winning the World Cup had enhanced the commercial and political value of Sri Lankan cricket many times over. The competition for the spoils was bound to become more intense. A human rights activist I spoke to believed that Sri Lankan cricket would now lose its last shreds of innocence. 'We are a society that apes others,' she said. 'First, we aped the English gentry. Now we will start aping the Indian *nouveaux riches*.'

In an article in *Pravada* entitled 'Cricket mania, men and politics', Janaka Biyanwila observed that 'The Buddhist clergy were liberally displayed on television and newspapers throughout the tournament, dispensing cosmic favours on the local cricket team. All members of the team participated in Buddhist rituals on their return, despite other religious or atheist preferences.'

Indeed, in the week following their return, Ranatunga and his men toured the south and west of the country with the (replica) World Cup trophy, receiving benedictions from the *bhikkus* (Buddhist monks) who had engineered the most violent anti-Tamil flare-ups in the recent past, and who even today were at the forefront of the clamour to discard the devolution package and fight the LTTE to the bloody finish. The players did not take the trophy to Jaffna or indeed anywhere in the war-torn north or east of the island.

Many of those I spoke to in Colombo feared that the nation whose triumph was being celebrated was the Sinhala nation, not the multi-ethnic, devolved nation-state which they sought to build. 'It's as if we had won a war,' commented a friend, 'but what happens now if we lose?' In his *Pravada* article Biyanwila castigated the World Cup as 'a sporting event debased to reflect the extent of ethnocentric masculine neurosis in the subcontinent' and concluded that in the future cricket in the region was bound to be more closely linked to 'commercialism, nationalism, patriarchy and violence'.

Mulling over the curious paradox of Sri Lanka's response to World Cup success, my Marxist acquaintance said, 'Sri Lanka is a wounded nation. The Sinhalese feel they are losing battle after battle, that their status in the world is low, that they are always being asked to make concessions to others. The euphoria is a response to the restoration of pride. But it will not last for ever. They will wake up one morning soon and have to face the same intractable dilemmas.'

Within weeks, the country was gripped by a power-workers' strike. Kumaratunga responded with mass arrests. The LTTE guerrillas struck back in Mullaitivu in the north-east, inflicting what was described as 'the biggest ever débâcle suffered by the Sri Lankan forces in the history of the conflict'. Shortly afterwards, a commuter train in the capital was bombed. The devolution package languished, and there was no end in sight either to the war or to the ethnic hatred that had begotten it.

In Madras for the Ranji Trophy final, I sweltered in the humidity. The M.A. Chidambaram Stadium (named after an agro- and petro-chemical magnate) is one of my favourite cricket venues, but it does suffer from a crushing design flaw. The high tiers and circular outer walls block off the sea breezes that were once a feature of cricket in Chepauk, and turn the arena into a steam bath. The sub-aqueous sensation was reinforced by the cricket: Tamil Nadu were playing Karnataka and the game crept forward at a pace that the Pepsi adverts would describe as leisurely.

Batting first, Karnataka passed 200 for the loss of 2 wickets in the 105th over, mid way through the first session of the second day. Twenty years ago, a major Ranji fixture in Madras might attract 20,000 spectators; today, there were fewer than one thousand. The rivalry between Tamil Nadu and Karnataka was not only an old one – continuing as it does the colonial-era clash between Madras presidency and the Mysore princely state – it is also overlaid with political significance. For decades the two regions have been locked in a fierce dispute over distribution of the Cauvery river waters. Yet the city seemed largely unaware that it was hosting the premier match of the country's domestic season. After weeks on the World Cup trail, watching cricket played with a red ball by men in white flannel before a derisory audience felt like returning from orbit. The pitch was dead, the bowling accurate and the batting so cautious it was in danger of being diagnosed as catatonic. Sometime in the afternoon, Rahul Dravid reached his century after 6 hours and 24 minutes at the crease. Originally, the Ranji Trophy was 'timeless', i.e. matches were played to the finish, no matter how long it took. As that was no longer practical, most Ranji matches were these days decided on first innings lead. Classical two-innings cricket it may have been, but it was every bit as contrived as the one-day stuff. Humidity-addled, heat-hypnotised, cricket-mesmerised, I felt reduced to a vacuum, a pure watcher, anticipating nothing.

The cricket was timeless but it was also doomed. Just before the final, I had attended a press conference at the Taj Palace hotel in Chanakyapuri, Delhi's diplomatic enclave. There, flanked by Bindra and Abassi, Mark McCormack, the American founder, president, chairman and chief executive of the International Management Group, announced the inauguration of a new international cricket competition: the Friendship Cup, a series of five one-day internationals between India and Pakistan, was to be staged annually in Canada. The matches would be sanctioned by the ICC (though interestingly neither IMG nor the two Boards had bothered to seek prior approval from the sport's governing body) but would be directly managed and marketed by McCormack's outfit.

The enterprise was a logical extension of the World Cup rhetoric of globalisation. For Abassi and Bindra, it was a case of taking cricket boldly where no cricket has gone before. Their obsession with North America amused me. It was as if they believed that cricket would not rise above the second rank in the global hierarchy of sport until the Yanks adopted it. 'This should be the job of the ICC,' Bindra noted, 'but for historical reasons it has failed in its duty. Somebody has to fill the vacuum. North America is the world's largest market for sports – and it's a virgin market for cricket. The sky is the limit there.' Abassi made the warning to the ICC explicit: 'If the authorities fail to develop the game to its full potential, private forces will fill the gap.'

McCormack prophesied that 'cricket will have a great place in the hearts of North American people'. All the revenues would be ploughed back into the grass roots of the game. 'We in IMG believe in cricket. We want to serve the game. After all, we're all cricket fans.' At this point, having spent ten weeks following the World Cup and its aftermath, I thought that if I heard one more businessman, bureaucrat or politician announce that he was only in it for 'the love of the game', I would puke. After the press conference, an IMG official conceded to me, 'We're doing this as a service to our clients. The real market is here in south Asia. And it has only begun to be tapped.' The plain reality behind the Friendship Cup is that when it is 9:30 a.m. in Toronto it is

6 p.m. in south Asia – prime time. Whether or not a single soul in the North American continent shows any interest in the series, it will generate huge profits for the two Boards in the form of television rights and spin-offs.

Over the years, the IMG empire has acquired a daunting span. It has graduated from managing individual players to organising and running whole sports, notably tennis and golf. In the past, it specialised in elite, capital-intensive recreations (where endorsements can be auctioned for huge sums), but in recent years, mindful of the impact of satellite television and the growth of the Asian marketplace, it has moved in on Chinese football and Malaysian badminton. As in politics, so in sport. Those who control the interface between the game and the public will become its unaccountable governors. IMG's designs on sub-continental cricket confirmed my worst apprehensions about the future of the game.

The driving force behind the Friendship Cup is not the globalisation of cricket, but the exploitation of globalised (and privatised) communications. As the communications revolution proceeds apace, Murdoch and his ilk will be ever hungrier for 'cricket, CRICKET, *AND MORE CRICKET*'. But what kind of cricket will we be offered on our multi-channel digital receivers? Ironically, the Masters tournament for the over-35s held at Sharjah prior to the World Cup gave us a glimpse of the future. Competing for a cash jackpot twice the size of the prize money on offer in the World Cup itself were Gooch and Gatting, Richards and Greenidge, Gavaskar and Srikkanth, Zaheer and Sadiq Mohammad. Spectators were notable by their absence, but television addicts could revel in the familiar figures reprising their past glories. This was virtual cricket, pastiche cricket, in which authentic competition was repackaged like a convenience food. With the appearance of IMG on the scene, cricket's greatest rivalry could now undergo a similar transformation. Since live spectators are no longer of any financial consequence, India may as well play Pakistan in the Antarctic, as long as satellite television can beam the images back to the sub-continent. The principal irony of the Friendship Cup is that it cannot be held in either India or Pakistan. So what kind of friendship is being celebrated here? This is war minus the shooting adapted for the entertainment industry of the twenty-first century.

The experience of Sharjah shows that the sublimation of the India–Pakistan rivalry off-shore intensifies it on-shore. Globalisation creates not a global culture of sport but a televised substitute for it in which national identities are commercial playthings. For all the pains and perils of playing on home soil, in front of unruly and partisan spectators, the only hope of reclaiming cricket in the sub-continent from bigots and demagogues lies with the crowds themselves. Only in the democratic domain, where cricket and its meanings are shared and shaped by multitudes, can there arise a force strong enough to override the manipulations of the elite. As Wole Soyinka, reflecting on the tragedy of Nigeria, has observed: 'A nation is a collective enterprise – outside of that it is a gambling hall for the opportunism and adventurism of power.'

Pete Davies

I LOST MY HEART TO THE BELLES

Pete Davies spends a season with the Doncaster Belles and finds a unique group of people with an abundance of talent and a vividly earthy humour. They play hard in the pit villages and nightclubs of South Yorkshire, they play hard on the tatty pitches in run-down suburbs and industrial estates – but they play for love too, and to a standard that could convert the most blinkered chauvanist.

'Superb'
Independent

'A true labour of love'
GQ

'Davies paints a picture of a world in which sport is every bit as important to young women as it is to young men, as a way of breaking out of the cycle of poverty and spirit-numbing boredom of British working-class life'
Sunday Times

'Witty, warm, wise and inspiring . . . This is that rarest of sports books a cracking good read that will appeal to the reader without the slightest interest in sport'
Yorkshire Post

Bill Buford

AMONG THE THUGS

A book about the experience, and the attractions, of crowd violence.

'Buford gatecrashes a social world that most of us have spent some portion of our lives avoiding and brings it to life on the page with a ferocious relish that only someone who was a foreigner to soccer could manage, or stomach'
Jonathan Raban

'Compelling, intelligent and fully engaged'
Martin Amis, *Independent on Sunday*

'The excellence of Buford's descriptive writing takes the reader to the centre of the mob . . . His words have the fragmented accuracy of a hand-held televison camera in a war zone'
John Stalker, *Sunday Times*

'Superbly written . . . darkly exhilarating, a sort of roller coaster chamber of horrors'
Guardian